The

HOUND
OF
HEAVEN

The HOUND OF HEAVEN

Glover Wright

ARBOR HOUSE / New York

First published by Arbor House in 1986.

Manufactured in the United States of America

10 9 8 7 6 5 4 3 2 1

Library of Congress Cataloging in Publication Data

Wright, Glover.
  The hound of heaven.

  I. Title.
PR6073.R488H68   1986   823'.914   85-15797
ISBN: 0-87795-767-3

To Carmela, with love

I fled him down the nights and down the days;
I fled him down the arches of the years;
I fled him down the labyrinthine ways
Of my own mind; and in the midst of tears
I hid from him, and under running laughter.

FRANCIS THOMPSON, *THE HOUND OF HEAVEN*

Contents

PART ONE

The Soldier

Vietnam 1967

They killed slowly, mercilessly, at intervals. When they killed, the act was performed languorously; more disposal than killing. First the raising of the slim, honed blade, then the downward-sweeping silver arc slicing through both monsoon rain and the pale braced necks.

The torrential rain dispersed the blood quickly while the mud absorbed its colour, leaving only the white upturned faces, eyes and mouths wide with shock, as evidence of the deed.

They slouched away, sandals slopping mud onto the severed heads of the nuns.

'Three,' Cardin breathed beneath his binoculars, then shifted his attention once more to the man nailed to the tree.

'Five to go,' said Rent, the sometime marine. 'You think they're going to make it with 'em one more time?'

'Asshole,' Gaillard the coffee-skinned Creole murmured, keeping his soft dark eyes on the clearing ahead.

Rent smile unpleasantly. 'That's pussy out there. Without the robes that's just pussy! So what're you looking at, nigger?'

Gaillard let his eyes slide to Rent's flat, freckled face and the vacant eyes between the smudged stripes of jungle paint. He turned away, settling the wide conical straw hat lower over his own. 'Asshole,' he repeated.

'Cut it,' Cardin ordered.

Gaillard breathed out.

Rent smirked and Cardin sensed it but did not turn around. 'You enjoy your work, Rent?' Cardin asked quietly, still looking forward. 'This? You enjoy watching this?'

Rent ran the wet sleeve of his black Viet Cong uniform

13

across his streaming nose, leaving a trail of mucus on the poor material. He frowned at it, then watched the rain dissolve the stain.

'Is that why you need the dope?' Cardin asked, though his question might have been put to the crucified man – so intense was his concentration on the brutalized figure.

Die, Cardin urged silently. Die. Give it up!

'I don't need anything,' Rent said.

'You need *us* baby,' Gaillard growled. 'There's a million slopes out there and we're in the middle.'

'Plus one,' San Li corrected between mouthfuls of rice.

'You planning to go out there and get your share?' Rent asked the South Vietnamese.

San Li chuckled and swallowed more rice. 'Not this year,' he answered, his accent entirely American. 'When you dipshits leave with your Coca-Cola machines and your PX then I'll switch sides. Right now I'm a reactionary – later I'll join the revolution. That's how you survive in Indo-China.'

A piercing scream rose up from the clearing.

'Four?' asked Rent, urgently.

Gaillard shook his head. 'They're not through with her yet.'

Rent chewed his lips, watching intently. 'Why're they doing it like that?' he demanded of San Li.

'You Caucasians got bad breath. Face to face is impossible.'

Rent mouthed an obscenity, then tugged at Gaillard's binoculars. 'Share it then!' he hissed.

The Creole slipped the neck strap and sat up, cursing the incessant rain. Rent jammed the glasses to his eyes, his tongue flicking restlessly between his lips.

Cardin shifted his own binoculars reluctantly from the crucified man and fixed on the huddled group of naked nuns, their white habits tossed out of reach like sodden, fallen washing. A little way away sat the children from the mission school, wide-eyed with terror. Like Cardin and his three companions, they too had been forced to watch the humiliation, abuse and death of the nuns.

The guerrillas pushed the nun they had raped to the tree

14

and Cardin tracked them with his glasses. The nun wailed, knowing the pattern by now. For Cardin the roar of the monsoon rain hammering onto the green roof of the jungle faded to a distant hiss through which he could hear his own breathing. The nun shrieked as her head was forced over, then the crucified man's lips moved with words which seemed to calm her – to give her strength.

Cardin wished he could hear them.

The man's eyes were kept prised open with sharpened slivers of bamboo and yet, although the pain inflicted upon him was terrible, they were without pain, without anger. Peaceful eyes, startlingly blue and filled with compassion.

I am in another place, another time, Cardin thought irrationally. Centuries ago. The Centurion at the foot of that other cross bound by the orders I must follow. I cannot stop this. His feeling of unreality was growing now and he wondered if the fever strains which tainted his blood had taken over completely. Why have *I* been placed here? he demanded. I don't believe. Not in God. Not in love. Not in peace. I'm a paid killer with a loaded gun and when I die I'll die screaming. I don't want to watch a man being killed by inches, with compassion in his eyes for his butchers.

The sword flashed and a guerrilla swooped for the nun's bloodied crucifix in the mud. Laughing, he twisted it cruelly around the genitals of the hanging figure. The strange blue eyes forgave, so the guerrilla lashed at the impaled feet with his rifle butt. There was no sound, no cry, no protest.

Die! Cardin pleaded inside. Just die and let me get away from here.

But there was no escape and he knew it. Not until the crucified man was dead and, before him, all of the nuns. No escape.

Only twenty-four hours before, he had been dry, cautiously drunk and very sure of who and what he was. Saigon, he remembered. Whore city and dubious paradise for any man who existed on self-deception – and most of us feed our souls on that!

He remembered, because it was the only escape possible.

* * *

Michael Cardin was dark, with searching eyes that had seen too much and had discarded all illusion. He used the girl beneath him ruthlessly, for his own fulfilment. Her eyes shone with pleasure and something which might have been love. Valued, thought Cardin, at fifty dollars US in anybody's money.

The knock on the door was harsh; the voice the same. 'Lieutenant? Lieutenant Cardin?'

Cardin pushed the whore away and sat up on the bed, closing his eyes to steady the room. The girl pulled a thin, patterned silk shift over her small hard breasts and neat shaven pubis. She had a virgin's body, which made her expensive, and a woman's technique, which trebled her fee.

The knocking now was insistent.

Cardin placed money on a fragile lacquered table, then looked at the girl and nodded at the bills, saying nothing.

'You come back next time,' chirruped the girl. 'I give you extra hour, OK? Maybe I show you something different?' She was proud of her sexual technique. 'You ask for me – not other girl, OK?'

'Lieutenant? They said now!'

'ID,' Cardin called. 'Under the door.'

The plastic card spun on the floor after it was pushed through fast. Cardin put his bare foot on it, picked it up, glanced at it and tossed it onto the rumpled bedclothes, his hand already going for the taped butt of the holstered magnum revolver on the solitary chair. He opened the door quickly, standing aside. The whore smiled at the military policeman, unafraid. Uniforms held no terrors for her. Uniforms meant love and love meant money.

'Inside,' said Cardin. 'How did you find me?'

'Cruised the bars – then the cat-houses, sir.'

'What's the word?' Cardin demanded.

'The word is Hailstone, sir.'

Cardin holstered the weapon and began dressing swiftly. 'Transport?' he inquired.

'Outside, blocking the sidewalk. They said to take you to –'

Cardin drove four rigid fingers into the MP's gut,

16

doubling him over onto his knees. 'The whore's paid for but she's not bought! She's the enemy. They're all the enemy! When are you people going to realize that? Get up.'

The MP pulled himself up on Cardin's offered arm, his lungs dragging breath back in. Cardin strapped on the shoulder holster, then tugged a cotton windcheater over the weapon. 'Let's go,' he said.

Still clutching his stomach, the MP led the way down to the US military jeep jammed up on the pavement creating a bottleneck in the turmoil of the narrow street. The driver sat nervously behind the wheel, eyeing the crowds. He stuck out his arm to keep begging children away from the vehicle. When they persisted, he did the same with his high laced-up boot. 'What's up?' he asked, studying his partner.

'Just drive,' Cardin ordered.

The driver turned the ignition and forced the jeep into the teeming crowds.

'What?' Cardin snapped over the noise of the horn and the Saigon backstreet babble.

The MP clutched his stomach, retching drily, head down between the gleaming toecaps of his boots. 'Never saw it,' he gasped. 'Didn't see you move!'

Cardin turned away, settling lower into the seat, his hand within the windcheater, fingers resting on the taped butt.

Thirty kilometres outside the city, an Oldsmobile sedan was parked by the roadside, well away from the trees. The driver of the jeep jerked to a halt beside it, cursing as rain fell in a sudden sheet without warning, filling the footwells in seconds.

Cardin was already inside the long sedan. 'Hailstone,' he said.

'Crap,' said a man with iron-grey hair lolling against the cushions. 'Goddamn country! Either drowning or burning. Both! Goddamn country.'

'Where?' Cardin asked as the car began moving, the driver silent.

17

'Highlands. Some sonofabitch headman wants to give us a few dink heads.'

'Terminate or talk?'

The iron-grey head lifted, revealing a grandee moustache and trimmed beard on a deeply lined face. The skin on the face was patchy, brown and white, from being too hot or too wet for too long. 'Talk. Leave them in place for now but get the names. This time we've got a chance at a couple of fully trained commissars and what they know is going to save us a lot of grief. We'll snatch them later.' He passed over a thick package in waterproof wrapping. 'Pay our man – and watch out for Charlie in the hamlet: he's there.'

'Everywhere,' Cardin stated, flatly.

'Sure.'

'How dirty is the trail?' Cardin asked, using the jargon for communist presence.

'What do you think I've got! An agent in Hanoi? It's dirty. You want it clean, transfer out.'

'Anyone we'll have to take out to cover the mission?'

The lips under the moustache twisted. 'Right word. Mission. Catholic school and hospital. Small. Run by one priest and maybe eight nuns. They're giving God to the dink kids who'll believe all that crap – then the commies will tell them that God is a slant-eye whose real name is Uncle Ho and heaven is a city called Hanoi.'

'So what's the directive?'

'The directive is you go around it. You do not let them know you're there. They've got medical aid in that mission – but you get hit, any one of you, and you don't use it. You keep moving.'

'We won't need their help. What's the problem?'

'The problem is the guy who wears skirts and lives it up in Rome. They're not involved. No sir! Not involved. Like the goddamn Limeys and all those other closet queens who're supposed to be our allies.'

'We'll go around.'

'Damn right. You get dropped before first light – while the slopes are still coming to from the night-before's smoke. Read this. Headman's name and map reference. Gone in?'

Cardin nodded. The rain drummed like massed tympani

18

on the steel roof as the Oldsmobile slithered to a halt in the mud.

The jeep had the canopy and sidescreens up; the two MPs crouched miserably inside, smoking. Cardin clambered in behind them.

'Go,' he ordered.

The Fairchild AC-119G Shadow sat inelegantly on the runway. Cardin could see it in the distance, its body black and sluglike, fixed between twin tailbooms and straight wings. Between himself and the aircraft was his own reflection: gaunt, dark eyes sunken deep in a pale face. His black hair was cropped close to the skull to defeat the lice – thick enough to allow nothing of his scalp to show through. It's not the face I remember, he thought. Not even a face I know. The tanned, chiselled features with more than a hint of his French ancestry had long since gone – along with the overlong black hair which had been the subject of derisory comment throughout his shining college days. The war has done it, they might have said back home if he took leave – which he did not. Not the war, he thought. My war. The way I have chosen to conduct it. I've lost the face I came here with – in the jungle – stripped away by the foliage, the sun, the rain and the sweat. Stomped into the mud, decayed and forgotten like the bodies we leave behind after we have drained them of all they know. There must have been one particular time, one mission, when he stopped feeling – or caring . . .

The Bloody Mary at his elbow was ice-cold and stung the exposed flesh of his lean but hard-muscled arm. He welcomed the piercing sensation; it confirmed reality, and above all things Michael Cardin was a realist.

'You entitled to be in here?' a grating voice snapped. An air-force colonel stood over Cardin, surveying with distaste the windcheater rolled into a bundle on the table and his creased shirt and jeans. 'This is officer country.'

Cardin pulled a black leather case from his back pocket, flipped it open on the table, then drank from the tall, frosted glass.

19

The colonel touched the open case with one hard finger as though it might be contaminated, then turned it towards him. Glancing at the ID card, he pushed it back. 'You people give this war a bad name. Goddamn freaks.'

Cardin lit a cigarette.

'You need to get shaved before you come in here,' the colonel grumbled, and stalked back to the bar. There, he jerked a thumb back at Cardin and made an obscene comment to a group of fellow officers.

Feared by the enemy and hated by our own, Cardin thought savagely. And probably the reverse. Anyone who volunteered for Special Operations, especially an officer, was automatically considered beyond the pale as far as the military establishment was concerned. A half-breed, holding a military rank yet controlled by civilian government agencies, not trusted, not accepted. The only time we're accepted, Cardin thought as he finished his drink and arose, is when they ship us back in the body bags – and right then, who gives a damn anyway? He retrieved the windcheater and the holstered magnum it contained and made for the exit of the officers' club and the humid heat beyond.

'Goddamn freaks!' Cardin heard again, quite clearly, as the glass double doors swished closed behind him forbidding the entry of untreated air.

He shook his head as he walked, anger and frustration long since blunted by impotence. They sit, coolly, in air-conditioned sanitized comfort, viewing the peasants through tinted sound-proofed glass, believing that theirs is the way to win. Victory does not come out of the snapped-open lid of a Coca-Cola can – it comes, as Mao said, out of the blazing barrel of a gun. And there are enough peasants out here who know they will never attain the American Dream and are willing to curl their fingers around a trigger.

The 'hutch' was a long walk away, the farthest side of the sprawling base – separate and detached both for security purposes and to limit the spread of its disease. Inside, Rent, Gaillard and San Li waited like passengers in transit, reconciled yet impatient. The clothes of their enemy which

20

they were to wear themselves, later, lay in a cardboard carton on a steel table, the weapons they favoured beside it: Soviet-made Kalashnikov automatic carbines, because their enemy used them and the enemy knew what suited the jungle best; cut-down shotguns to blast away the foliage and the hidden men beneath; grenades, flash-bombs and ammunition. Next to these were the true weapons of their profession: the black-bladed knives, the silenced pistols, the wire garottes. Cardin, Rent, Gaillard and San Li, experts in political conversion by the simplest of means: intimidation by fear. And, masters of silent killing.

'Get some sleep,' Cardin said as he entered the hutch. 'Anyone need anything?'

Rent rolled another joint while Gaillard shook his curly head slowly. San Li grinned.

'You didn't leave a forwarding address,' said Rent, curled into an upright foetal position on a battered armchair. 'Those meatheads been screaming for hours.'

Cardin ignored him.

'Where?' Gaillard asked.

'Highlands,' answered Cardin.

'What?'

'Talk, that's all.'

'Maybe,' said Gaillard.

San Li pulled the ring on a can of beer. 'Who's the source – one of ours, or Charlie's?'

Cardin shrugged.

'Charlie,' muttered Rent. 'Nothing happens 'cept it's Charlie. Charlie shits and we get latrine duty.'

'We're qualified,' said Gaillard.

'Amen,' Cardin murmured.

They sat in silence while Cardin stripped down the magnum, retaped the butt and rubbed Vaseline into the inside of the leather holster. 'I'll sleep,' he said finally and made for one of the small cubicles.

The air-conditioners whispered and groaned intermittently, like secret lovers: the only sound in the low concrete bunker.

Cardin heard Gaillard say, 'You know what I'm afraid of? I'm afraid of not being afraid any more.'

21

Silence.

Rent snorted.

Lying on the bunk, Cardin thought: Take any decent civilized human being, give the devil in him free rein and the end product is us. He smiled, then slept. It was all that was left to do.

The Fairchild AC-119G Shadow was a gunship. Some named it Spooky, others Puff the Magic Dragon. Neither name was suitable. The Shadow and the Douglas AC-47 were pure killing machines which laid down a withering hail of fire from their banks of electronically controlled mini-guns. Anything caught in their firestorm was reduced to nothing. Trees to sawdust, people to pulp.

'We'll drop you!' yelled the pilot. 'Turn and put down some fire! We have enough night-illumination equipment to blind the dinks. You'll be outside the light halo.'

The noise of the engines, because of the open gunports, was deafening, so Cardin simply nodded.

'Great hat!' the pilot screamed, dipping his helmet at the coolie's hat strapped to Cardin's chest. Cardin turned away and made his way back in the darkness, gripping the safety rails hard. He squatted beside the others between the banks of guns. San Li grinned at him, his white teeth shining in the glow of the pin-lights from the systems controls of the mini-guns.

One of the 'gunners' – there only to reload and clear blockages, as all aiming and firing of the robot-controlled weapons was done by the pilot – slapped Cardin's shoulder and tilted the dome of his helmet at the open port.

They exited in a stick, opening their black parachutes as late as possible to avoid detection from the ground, and landed hard but without injury. As they grouped together, part of the sky to the south became a circle of white light, and the tearing sound of the mini-guns was already reaching their ears. They moved off into the darkness, killers, perfectly trained and at one with their environment. Soon, the sun would rise.

* * *

The rain had not started for the day when they heard the first scream. It seared the dank morning air like tracer, leaving its anguished imprint on their minds. They dropped instantly, their reactions honed almost to the speed of thought. 'Child?' Cardin asked.

'Woman,' Gaillard said.

'One of yours,' San Li murmured.

'How d'you know that?' Rent demanded.

San Li's face was inscrutable. 'There's a difference.'

'Nun,' Cardin said. 'There's a Catholic mission ahead of us.'

'Was,' smiled Rent.

'We keep away,' Cardin said. 'That's the directive.'

'It's in front of us,' Gaillard stated.

'We detour around it.'

'Not a chance,' San Li interrupted. 'If Charlie's moved into the mission, he'll have every hill around this basin covered.'

'So we go through his lines or we wait,' said Cardin.

'How tight is our schedule?' asked Gaillard.

Cardin shrugged. 'As tight as the tongues in the target hamlet. If they're loose, the headman's dead and the names he's got are gone. We're paid for results – we have to move fast.'

'And survive,' said Gaillard.

Cardin turned to the South Vietnamese. 'What are our chances of getting through Charlie's lines?'

San Li shook his head.

The flat crackle of automatic fire reached them, the sound blunted by the wet jungle.

'AK,' said Rent. 'Charlie's there.'

'Here,' San Li corrected. 'All around us.'

A hopeless howl drifted up the hillside to them, followed by thin shrieks in profusion like scattering, frightened birds. Then, more gunfire.

'That's the kids taken care of,' said Rent.

San Li shook his head. 'The Cong save children for indoctrination. They're eliminating any locals who've been helping in the mission. Nothing changes; it was the same when the French were the masters.'

'What clown would keep a mission station going up here!' exclaimed Rent.

'A dedicated one,' said San Li. He tilted his head down the hill. 'You want me to go on down and assess their strength?'

'Negative,' Cardin replied. 'We stick together. What's Charlie's weakest point in this sort of operation?'

The South Vietnamese unsheathed his knife and drew a circle in the sodden, steaming earth, then plunged the blade into its dead centre. 'Charlie isn't afraid of anything really close to him – simply because he doesn't believe that anything can get that close. Usually he's right and that's why we're losing the war. Hit and run, that's how he works best. No matter how many troops we send after him, they never even begin to get close. He's gone, leaving your conventionally trained army spinning round its own ass in the jungle. Then he begins to pick you off one by one.' Li smacked the blade in deeper. 'That's where we've got to be, in the centre, under heavy cover, and wait him out. We continue to sit up here, and the patrols he's got working down from the ridges of the basin will flush us out for sure. He's not searching for us – if there was a tip-off, he'd have hit us at the drop zone to make sure; he's searching for anyone from the hill tribes who shows an interest in what's happening down there in the mission. It's his way of sorting out the believers. We're just unlucky – we landed in the right place at the wrong time.'

'The right time – for Charlie,' Gaillard observed drily.

'So?' Cardin asked, his eyes still on San Li.

'So we move in as close as possible to the mission, now, ahead of the patrols, and go to ground.'

Cardin frowned. 'We could be trapped down there for days. There's no way we can know how long he'll take to do his business.'

San Li looked away and down the hill. 'He'll never risk being exposed for too long. One day. One long day for those sisters down there. The longest of their lives.'

'And their last,' Gaillard murmured.

San Li smiled but without humour. 'They'll be glad it is at the end.'

'We don't get involved,' Cardin warned, looking at each of them. 'No matter what happens we stay out of it. Our business is on the other side of these hills.'

Gaillard shrugged.

'Fucking right!' exclaimed Rent.

San Li surveyed their faces. 'Any of you ever see the Cong work – I mean, close up? When it's actually happening?'

'We've all seen the results,' Cardin answered.

Li breathed out heavily and sheathed his knife. 'Like I said, it's going to be a long day.'

Cardin pushed himself up. 'Let's start it then.'

They moved silently down the hill toward the mission.

The Viet Cong had no questions to ask. It was purely an exercise in terror. Terror was their most effective weapon in their unequal fight against the advanced technology of the American superpower and they used it ruthlessly. To boost the effects of psychological terror in the minds of the people, they perpetrated, at periodic intervals, acts of horror. Terror and horror: each feeding off each other and spewing out fear.

The Cong began first on the priest because he was the strongest. He stood tall and straight when they approached him, yet without arrogance in his bearing. He knew their purpose, yet his vivid blue eyes held no trace of fear. His face, so close to Cardin's own through the lenses of the binoculars, seemed strangely unlined, though he was not a young man. Cardin could not estimate his age, but his extraordinary eyes seemed wise beyond however many years he had behind him, and forgiving, even as the first rough hands were laid on him. The butchery of the Vietnamese Catholics and the rape of the nuns somehow seemed secondary to the violation of the priest's body as the long rain-rusted nails were driven through to the tree.

Cardin and his men watched without speaking; the courage of the priest was beyond their experience and, because of this, it appalled them.

Beside the crucifixion tree one of the guerrillas sharpened

bamboo stakes to needle points, then dropped his black trousers, squatted and excreted. He smeared the points in his exreta, then pushed them in the earth below the nailed feet so that the soles rested on them. This done, he reversed his carbine and brought the wooden stock down hard on each bared shoulder, then swung a careless blow to the top of the priest's head. Blood seeped steadily from his scalp, clotting in the fair hair.

The mission was wrecked systematically, particular attention being given to religious objects; only medical supplies were spared. Then, as the patrols came in with more unfortunates caught in the hills, the Cong amused themselves with cruel games which they always won and which all resulted in death.

The rains came at midday, darkening the basin and the surrounding hills as if it were already night, so they sheltered in the mission taking the nuns for their amusement. Cries, like those of wounded animals, came from the mission through the falling torrent of water.

The priest's body began to die, dragging downward on the nails, but his eyes, jammed open with sharp slivers, remained fixed ahead, alive and forgiving.

Somewhere inside Michael Cardin, so deep that it remained untouched by his own brutalization, he cried out, though his face remained cold and set, with only proxy tears formed by the rain betraying the devastation he felt yet could not understand.

At mid-afternoon, ignoring the rain, the Viet Cong guerrillas filed out of the mission and began executing the nuns at the feet of the man they had crucified.

'Four,' said Rent, and Cardin's mind was returned brutally to the reality of the present. He turned away from the scene, forcing down the irrational urge to act that was growing uncontrollably inside him.

San Li's eyes met his and he could feel Gaillard's fixed on him also.

'*C'est impossible*,' said the South Vietnamese softly in

26

French, a common language between Cardin, the Creole Gaillard and Li.

'He'll die anyway,' Gaillard said, using the same language. 'Even if we got to him.'

Cardin studied Gaillard's face. 'You feel it too?'

'I feel it.'

Rent lowered the binoculars and faced them. 'What's going on?' he demanded, his quick eyes searching their faces suspiciously, unable to understand their soft words.

The rain stopped, creating an unnerving silence broken only by the hushed ticking of wet leaves. Even the wails from the clearing had ceased momentarily.

Drops of water gathered slowly, then dropped to the earth from the wide rim of Rent's coolie hat. 'No!' he whispered, but it could have been a roar of anger. 'Not a chance!'

'I have to try,' Cardin said softly. He could hardly believe he had spoken the words.

Rent snapped back in fury. 'No matter what we stay out of it! That's the directive – right? Your words, right!'

'I,' Cardin repeated. 'I have to try.'

'With Charlie all around us? Fuck you!'

'I must.'

Rent lifted his AK-47 and edged backward on his knees, rainwater trapped in the foliage cascading around him as he backed up.

'You fire that and we're dead,' said Gaillard.

'If he goes down there we're dead! You guys gone *crazy?*'

Gaillard seemed to consider this, then nodded. 'You're right.' He moved beside Rent. Rent gasped, still kneeling, the gun loose in his hands. Gaillard took it from him, then eased the body face-down into the mud, the haft of his knife protruding from below Rent's left armpit. He withdrew it and cleaned the blade with leaves. There was very little blood.

Gaillard said, 'He turned his gun on us.'

'Killed in action,' said San Li.

Madness! thought Cardin. Finally it's got us. 'You can both work your way out to the south ridge,' he told them. 'The target hamlet is around twenty clicks on. See the man

27

and get the names. Use the downed-aircrew frequency – they'll get you out.'

'Always works,' agreed San Li.

'Use it now,' Gaillard said.

Cardin stared at them. 'Why?'

Gaillard squatted on his haunches propped against Rent's gun, his eyes fixed on the clearing. 'When I was a kid my mother used to kick my ass if I didn't make it to mass. One day I asked her, "If Jesus was so special that he has to mess up my every Sunday, then how come those guys who nailed him up didn't know it?" She said, "They did. They were just plain afraid to show it. They knew. They just figured there was nothing they could do to stop it." ' He strapped his knife back onto his calf. 'Some things don't have a reason. You just know.'

San Li dropped his eyes to Rent's body. 'Some don't.'

'He didn't have his ass kicked to mass on Sunday,' Gaillard grinned. 'Call in the air force.'

They came in force, openly, like conquering heroes, which they were destined never to be.

The first sign of their presence was the deep drone of a multiple piston-engined aircraft at high altitude. Cardin knew it would be a Lockheed EC-21 codenamed Warning Star acting as a radar picket, monitoring enemy surface-to-air Soviet-supplied SA-2 missiles. Then came a twin-boomed OV-10 Bronco, the vanguard of the rescue force and its Forward Air Control. Behind this came the helicopters and their escort of six piston-engined Douglas Skyraiders.

The attack jets screamed out of nowhere.

The jungle erupted as though the trees and vegetation were trying to heave themselves free from the tortured earth. The hills surrounding the basin were capped with fire which ran down their sides like searing rivers, consuming everything in their path. Occasionally something would leap from one of these rivers of flame and plunge, shrieking, down the hillside, forming its own firestream before life was extinguished.

In the centre of it all, at the clearing in the heart of the basin, it might have been the pit of hell.

San Li broke through first, his oriental appearance giving him a fractional advantage and the edge they needed. He cut down the perimeter guards as they ran for the frail safety of the mission walls. Cardin and Gaillard circled left and right, killing as they moved with disregard for their targets. Everything in their way died: the cardinal rule of behind-the-line counter-terror groups. Everyone was the enemy. The innocent-looking child with a grenade in its pocket, the young girl with the incendiary device strapped between her breasts, were equally deadly as a trained guerrilla. Killers all, as Gaillard might have said. Us and them. The bullets and the shrapnel and the fire don't kill; hesitation kills you first – the dying comes later.

Cardin crashed into San Li as he reached the surviving nuns, the noise of the air attack distorting their screams so that their voices, the squeal of bombs and the shriek of rockets were mixed together like music created by the insane. The nuns were knocked flat but their backs were arched so that, in their nakedness, they seemed to be offering themselves obscenely for further penetration. There was blood on their thighs but most of that had already dried – internal wounds from torn tissue which might in time have healed. But the gaping wounds in their backs from which their entrails protruded would never heal – nor would the blue-black entry holes in their white abdomens.

One of the guerrillas sat duck-squatted in the mud, his hands on his head, fingers tightly interlocked, his weapon tossed aside, its banana-shaped magazine in San Li's hand. Cardin could see the flattened, scored heads of the rounds. He looked once at the crucified figure, then quickly shot each of the nuns in the head, his fist bucking high with the recoil of the magnum. The white limbs flailed in spasm, then stilled, the agony over, the gift of death accepted.

San Li bent over the squatting guerrilla, then stood back to avoid the fountain of arterial blood which spurted from the severed jugular. The man spun in circles, trying hopelessly to stem the flow. Cardin began his run for the tree.

Gaillard was already there, down on the ground, propped against the trunk at the feet of the crucified priest, sitting, long legs stretched out in a pool of his own blood. The wound was in his groin, where the pain was the worst. His coffee-coloured skin had turned grey where it was not splashed with crimson.

'Morphine?' Cardin asked as he turned, crouching, watching for a breakout from inside the mission.

'Get him down,' Gaillard said.

Cardin turned to the hanging figure, looking at the impaled feet. He could not face the purity of the staring blue eyes. 'I can't do it alone,' he said.

'You have to!' Gaillard snapped through his terrible pain.

The concussion of a double explosion made Cardin turn. He saw San Li throw a third grenade then swing around, ready to run. The South Vietnamese staggered, legs flying, as if he had tripped over an invisible wire, then flopped into the mud, jerked once, then died.

'Get him down!' Gaillard ordered through his teeth.

Cardin pulled out the long rusted nails with the trigger guard of his AK-47, using the length of the assault rifle as a lever. He could not begin to imagine the agony he was inflicting on the hanging figure, yet not a sound of protest was offered. As last the shattered body fell into his arms as he freed the impaled hands.

'Oh, dear God,' Cardin whispered and then, with the bleeding head so close to his own face, the strange blue eyes locked with his. The torn lips moved. 'Save the children,' the priest said.

The heavy beat of a big Sikorsky transport helicopter obliterated Cardin's reply. He screamed again, 'I can't! There's no time! I can't do it!'

Again, softly, but quite clear despite the thunderous clatter from above, came the words: 'Save the children.'

Cardin felt the tears on his face and was shaken. He could not remember when he had last wept. The broken body seemed now to have no life left whatsoever as it hung in his arms. Cardin stood interlocked with it, holding the fractured head aginst his face, his tears mingling with the blood. He felt Gaillard grip his ankle fiercely.

'Take it!' the Creole yelled, holding up the chained crucifix which had fallen loose from the priest's genitals. 'Put it on him! Now!'

Cardin grasped it but slipped it over his own head. 'His skull's smashed! I'm not touching his head.' The wind almost toppled him and he fought to stay upright as the blast from the helicopter's rotor ripped through the clearing. He heard the sound of a heavy machine-gun and screams of pain from the direction of the mission building. Gaillard was on his feet and Cardin could only guess how much the effort had cost him.

'Let's go,' Gaillard gasped, his voice barely a rattle now, and Cardin knew that he was already dead and only the power of his will was driving him on.

'I'll take him' Gaillard said.

'You can't!'

Gaillard's grey face was almost touching Cardin's. 'I'll take him. We'll go together. You cover us as we move.'

'Gaillard!'

'Now!'

They moved out into the open, the three of them, the priest's body hanging over Gaillard's shoulder while Cardin raked the surrounding area with a continuous blast of fire from their two assault rifles. Ten feet from the helicopter, Gaillard fell to his knees, the body slipping down into the mud but still held by the Creole's arms, as his strength finally ran out. He looked down at the ashen face, his almost bloodless lips twisted in a smile distorted by agony. Cardin crouched beside them, his black pyjamas whipped by the downdraft of the whirling blades, the wet mud flying like pulpy insects at his face, his ears buffeted by the roar of the engine.

Gaillard lowered his head. 'Remember me,' he said.

The priest raised his bleeding eyelids, the wounds freshly opened where Cardin had removed the needle-sharp bamboo slivers. Despite his weakness, despite the noise of the machines and the fire-fight, his reply was utterly clear. 'You will be with me for ever.'

31

Gaillard died, the smile still on his lips, on his knees, holding the cruelly broken body.

Cardin could hear, as if in the distance, a voice shouting over and over. He turned to the helicopter. A helmeted figure was screaming insanely at him as the spinning barrel of the machine-gun beside him blasted flame.

'Come on, you crazy bastard! They're gone! Leave them!'

Michael Cardin lifted the priest's limp form and carried it the last few feet to the aircraft. He felt the machine lift slightly as the pilot freed it from the sucking mud. 'Damn you, wait!' he bawled and turned back for Gaillard's body. He saw the rapid twinkling from inside the mission but did not hear the sound of the weapon. The last things he remembered as he crashed down was the petroleum smell of napalm, Gaillard's still-kneeling dead figure and those strange, forgiving blue eyes.

Michael Cardin drifted toward consciousness. With his eyes still closed in a twilight sleep, his mind scanned the entire area of his body, searching out the injuries: passing signals to nerve endings and testing the responses; checking if all the limbs were still intact; gauging the extent of the injuries by the degree of pain and the level of drugs introduced into the complex organism.

The body had been wounded before and the mind knew from experience precisely what kind of damage could be done by concussion, by explosives, by fire, and by the ripping effect of bullets or shrapnel.

The skin tingled – but it felt no worse than severe sunburn; so no major burns, just exposure to extreme temperatures. The tender tissue inside the nostrils felt raw, with an uncomfortable prickling when air was drawn through the cavities. So: naked flame. There was an odour too, blunted by the passage of time but traces still remained. Gasoline. Napalm!

His eyelids snapped open, total recall coming instantly like a door kicked open. He saw hell inside his memory. He remembered the inner peace which had shone through

32

all the agony from the priest's eyes. He felt that same peace flow through him now, as it had done across the clearing in the jungle, offering him comfort; a faint gossamer touch of paradise. He felt no pain.

'You caught a full burst,' said the man with the grandee moustache who used the name North when dealing with Cardin's team. For others he used another. 'You'll live – but you'll wish you hadn't.'

Cardin tilted his head on the crisp white pillow. 'The priest?'

'Didn't have your luck. Last seen dying. You blew everything for a corpse.'

'Last seen? Is he dead?'

'Sure. By now. What did you expect? You saw his injuries. They flew what was left of him out.'

'They? Who?'

'His people. Some Catholic order. Monks.'

'But he was dead?'

'His heart stopped as they were transferring him from the ambulance to the aircraft. He hadn't regained consciousness from the time you brought him out – that was over a week ago. One of his brothers was trying to thump his heart back to life as the plane was taxiing for takeoff; the other was giving him the last rites. Maybe they figured that God couldn't make up his mind?'

Cardin turned his face away, silent.

'No one survives injuries like that,' said North. 'When the chopper got him here, the medicos called his people right away. They were told to see to his soul; there was nothing that could be done to save the body.' North stood up. 'You're the one who's got the problems now. Think about that! The air force is going to crucify you, and no one's crazy enough to try and cut you down.' North tilted his head at the locked door. 'Outside that you've got two armed MPs, and down the corridor, pulling at their chains, a couple of air-force brass-hats just itching to nail you up. Maybe I should do it for them, you've wasted the best team I had. Take it easy, Mike, and forget the priest – he's caused enough grief already.' North rapped on the door.

33

'He's conscious,' he said to the MP who unlocked it. North left; he did not turn around.

An army doctor came in with a nurse in attendance. They carried out a series of tests while, in dead silence, an air-force colonel and a major clutching a briefcase waited by the door.

'I'd prefer you to wait outside,' objected the doctor, but neither man moved. The doctor exhaled briefly in resignation and continued with his task. Finally, he stood back and faced the officers. 'I'll stand no harassment of this patient. His condition is still poor. It will be weeks before his strength returns fully. He's certainly in no shape for lengthy interrogation. His wounds and general condition –'

'He's not worth healing,' the colonel cut in. 'We're going to take him apart anyway.' The youthful-looking major shifted his feet and clutched his briefcase tighter to his chest.

'This man is under my care!' the doctor retorted in anger. 'Your rank means nothing in this hospital, so don't try and intimidate me, colonel!'

'If you want to patch him up, that's your good time wasted. I'm going to break him.'

'Colonel! I warn you –'

'Let it go,' Cardin said. 'They've made up their minds already. Maybe they're right.'

'Damn right!' snapped the colonel.

'You've got five minutes. Five!' the doctor snapped back.

'That's all we'll need to read the preliminary charges,' said the major soothingly. 'This officer will not be questioned at this stage. Just the charges.' He placed a chair by the side of the bed; the colonel remained standing, menacingly, at the foot.

The major unzipped his case, withdrew papers and began: 'Lieutenant Michael Alain Cardin, I have to advise you that, through your misuse of an emergency-distress radio frequency, reserved specifically for aircrews of the United States Air Force and Army Air Force brought down by enemy action behind their lines, a total of five United States aircraft and their crews have been lost. As your mission was in enemy-occupied territory, it is certain that any surviving aircrew members are now in enemy hands. I must further advise you that your action will be the subject of a military court-martial hearing during which every effort shall be made to prove that you committed this act wittingly and with foreknowledge of the cost in American lives and aircraft. You will, of course, be able to speak in your own defence and you will be supplied with the services of an officer to advise you on all legal matters.'

The colonel's eyes were blazing as he counted out on his fingers. 'One EC-121 radar picket shot down by North Vietnamese fighters over the DMZ. Exploded in mid-air. No survivors. Crew eight. One OV-10 Forward Air control hit by an SA-2 missile. Crew two. No survivors. One HH53C helicopter knocked down by small-arms fire. Crew four. Captured or dead. Two Skyraider escorts, hit by anti-aircraft fire. One pilot baled out. Captured. The second didn't make it.'

'And three members of a Special Operations unit under your command,' put in the major. 'In total, nineteen lives either lost or captured.'

'One hell of a price to pay for a dead foreign civilian,' the colonel said icily.

'Also you failed to carry out your mission,' added the major. 'Which will undoubtedly cost us more lives in the long term. This will be the subject of a separate charge. That is: disobedience of a direct order and dereliction of duty in the field.'

The colonel leaned forward over the bed. 'We don't execute our own men in this war, Cardin, so you're lucky. But I can promise you that by the time we're through with you you're going to wish that you'd left that priest nailed to that tree in the jungle.'

Cardin propped himself up on his elbows with difficulty, pain searing through his body. 'You weren't there – how can you expect to understand?'

'Leave the bastard,' said the colonel.

'You'll never get clearance for a court martial, major,' Cardin said, his face almost white with pain. 'My mission was classified. It didn't happen. *I* don't exist officially.

Don't you realize that! You charge me, and you'll be raising the stone on things no one will admit responsibility for. Whatever I've done – and I accept the responsibility – they will never allow you to do that.'

'We'll get a ruling to have the case heard *in camera*,' the major replied, standing.

'They won't even allow you that.'

The colonel stood by the open door. 'We'll fix you, Cardin. One way or another, we'll fix you. Whatever it takes. You won't get any protection from your own people, I guarantee you that. You're one of the bugs that crawled out from under the stone and they're turning the other way. You've got no place to hide. Be seeing you.'

The doctor pushed both officers out of his way and made straight for the bed. 'Get out!' he snarled, bending over Cardin. 'Nurse!' quickly he prepared a syringe and injected the needle into Cardin's arm. 'Easy,' he said. 'Just take it easy.'

Cardin lifted his eyes but the lids were already too heavy. 'Wake me when it's over,' he said.

'I wish to hell I could,' the doctor answered, but Cardin could not hear him.

London 1970

He sat on the park bench gazing up at the huge bronze eagle, the symbol of American power, grateful that he had survived its vengeance. It had ripped his life apart then released him, but was there ready to hunt him down if he approached its territory. He stretched out his legs and shifted his position, for the pain was always with him, a reminder of his costly act of disobedience.

From the wide steps of the embassy the noise of anti-war protesters grew in volume, their frustration and anger cutting a swathe through their idealism. He looked at them across the gardens.

'*Out! Out! Out!* America *out!*' The chant was building again, whipped up by the ringleaders, whose motive was more political than idealistic. These would be picked out and their faces recorded on film by silent, serious men at the windows of the great concrete building. Their names, their faces, would be filed and later – perhaps even after they had outgrown their commitment – they would find life a little more difficult. Michael Cardin knew what the silent men could do.

'*Ho! Ho! Ho-Chi-Minh!*'

Closer, in the gardens, a small more inventive group were singing a protest song, and the strummed notes of a guitar drifted over to him. He shook his head. It was all pointless. He could not understand why they bothered. They had their victory already but were too blind to see it. America had lost the war before it had joined it. The administration had adopted a 'no-win' policy right from the start and that, in real terms, meant 'lose'.

He stood up and walked away, not looking back at the massive building. He stepped out of the gardens and passed the American Library, picturing, as he did so, the guarded

37

rooms behind it with their electronic bafflers against eavesdropping. The time he had spent in them seemed to belong in some other life.

He travelled on the underground to West Kensington, where he had basement rooms, cool in summer but undoubtedly cold and damp in winter. He did not plan on finding out. He never stayed in one place for very long.

His needs were simple, even frugal: four walls and a bed, somewhere to clean up, a regular supply of dope from a cautious dealer across the street when he felt like smoking, and the occasional bottle of whatever he felt like drinking. He usually managed to stay in one place for six months but then, inevitably, they would track him down and life became a hassle again. A break-in, just to disrupt his temporary liberation from their attentions – usually purely destructive, but sometimes they stole money if they found any. A mugging, when they realized he kept his valuables on him – but that had only happened once and they learned not to attempt it again. Drug-squad tip-offs which were laughable, because they knew he was a master of concealment. Framed charges, which usually entailed his spending a series of uncomfortable nights in unsavoury prisons – always when he travelled abroad; he supposed they considered British prisons too luxurious – but always minor and without sufficient substantiation. Harassment at foreign borders by immigration officials after malicious tip-offs regarding either his character or the legitimacy of his documents. All these and more – yet he learned to shrug off their efforts and continued existing as best he could. He knew they intended to break him, but was determined that they should not. He was tired and he was empty. Nothing, after what he had experienced in the jungle, meant anything any more. He moved on, not only because they pressured him, but also because he was searching for his reason for being. To glimpse, once again, what a tortured, dying man nailed to a tree had shown him: a vision, as fast as a blink of his eye, but retained for ever, of paradise.

His hair was long now, almost touching his shoulders, and he had grown a drooping moustache because it gave him a sense of anonymity in an area where just about every

38

male looked exactly as he did. They were a new breed, these children of that time, hopeful and loving, believing they had found a new philosophy. He knew that they were deceiving themselves and that their reliance on drugs was simply an escape from their self-deception. It would all turn around, he knew, some day soon, when the flowers they use as their weapons wither and die and the love they so openly express is rejected that one time too often. When that happens, they will fall into step with the rest and, sadly, it might all have been a dream. Nothing more. They might even laugh at the absurdity of it.

But for now, he thought, as he descended his basement steps, they believe in their dream.

The steps were of grey stone and worn at their centres. At the bottom he saw the note pinned to his door: 'Party! Flat four. Bring a bottle! OK?'

Then he heard the blare of the heavy-rock music from above and supposed it had been going on all the while. He let himself in, rolled a joint, then smoked it carefully. He felt better.

The music was reaching him now; the deep notes of an electric bass reverberating through the foundations of the old building. Purple, he thought; great heavy purple balls bouncing down each stairwell until they reached his hide-away. I am hiding, he admitted to himself. But from what? Shame? The lives I sacrificed? I am not ashamed of what I did. Guilt? He stood up, found a bottle in a cupboard, drank from it, then cleared up the makings of the joint and stowed the dope away safely. He remembered he had not eaten but baulked at the idea of preparing food. There would be food at the party. He picked up the bottle.

The door to flat four was open and they greeted him like a well-loved friend, though he had never exchanged more than a passing greeting with them. This was their way; part of their philosophy. Instant brotherhood.

They sat in groups, on the floor or on cushions, having no need nor desire for furniture. Their dress was uniform – though they would deny this vehemently: kaftans, jeans, beads, headbands. Their hair too followed a pattern: long

39

and lank, or full and frizzy. From behind he could not differentiate between the sexes.

He spotted a space against a wall, away from the massive stereo speakers, stepped over the bodies and sat down. Someone offered him food, so he took it, but refused a drooping joint. Beside him, on a cushion, sat a girl with bandaged eyes. The bandage had been painted with abstract shapes in bright poster-paint. He put the bottle in her hand.

'What is it?' she asked, grasping his hand and pulling herself towards him, her accent New England.

'Bourbon,' he answered.

'American?'

'Me or the bourbon?'

'Bourbon *is* American, no doubt about it! You.'

'Right,' he said. She tilted her head towards him, as if listening – or waiting. 'Your headband's slipped,' he said.

She laughed, her teeth made too white by the glow of an ultra-violet bulb screwed into a sidelight.

'Wait,' he said, got up and unscrewed the bulb.

'Hey, man?' someone objected, so he pointed at the girl's bandaged eyes.

'Yeah, OK. Good thinking, man.'

He sat beside the girl again.

'What did you do?' she asked.

He gave her the warm bulb. 'Black light. Ultra-violet. Damages the eyes. You've already got problems.'

She laughed again, and this time he could hear the strain. She touched the bandage. 'I couldn't see through this anyway.'

He reached for the bottle and drank from it; there seemed to be no glasses anywhere.

'How did it happen?' he asked, then waited. She fumbled for the bottle and swallowed deeply. 'Maybe you don't want to talk about it?' he said.

'It's temporary. Flash damage. A magnesium flare exploded. I was too near when it ignited. Typical me, always getting burned.' She laughed once more but he could see the fear around her mouth as she remembered. Her lips and the skin around her jaw and cheeks were flaking still. She had been lucky; he'd seen flare burns down to the bone.

'Nam,' she said, when he didn't ask for an explanation. 'In a chopper. I went out as a photo-journalist. I wanted to,' she insisted, as though he might object.

'So why London?' he inquired.

'There's this great eye hospital. Moorfields. It's the best.' She moved closer and touched his face, feeling the contours. 'You're avoiding the draft,' she said but without accusation.

He did not answer, so she assumed she had been correct. 'Good! It's terrible. If I were a man, I'd refuse to go.'

'You went.'

'To show what it's really like!'

'And?'

'I can't describe it.'

'But you must have done?'

She turned away and rocked to the music for a while. 'Do you smoke?' she asked, finally.

'I smoke where it's safe.'

'Where's safe?'

He pointed downwards, then remembered her blindness. 'Basement. I live here.'

'I need a smoke. The stuff here is junk.'

'I know, I can smell it. Now?'

She nodded.

He took her hand and pulled her upright. She swayed momentarily, laughing. 'Balance,' she said. 'I'm still not used to it. There's no point of reference.'

'I'll guide you.'

'My own guide dog!' she exclaimed too wildly, then gripped his arm with both hands as he picked their way through the prone bodies. 'You're hard!' she exclaimed again, squeezing with her fingers. 'Your *arm*! The muscles are really *hard*!'

They were outside the flat now, moving down the stairs. 'What do you do – break rocks?' she whispered, holding onto him. 'You're an escaped convict, shot your way out after five years in the pen.'

'So why am I in England?' he asked, playing her game.

41

'America's not safe, stupid.'

He smiled. 'Of course.' He wondered what colour her eyes were and if the part of her face hidden by the bandage lived up to the promise of her mouth and fine jawline. Her blond hair seemed natural and could have been beautiful – if she had bothered to care for it.

'So come on,' she began again, shaking him. 'Seriously now. What do you do for bread? Are you independently wealthy?' She had a deep matronly English voice for the last question. 'You're a dealer!' she exclaimed. 'You keep the best dope in the world in the basement!'

'Sorry,' he said.

She pouted, then shrugged. 'Blown out again, Catherine W.,' she cried.

'What's the initial for?'

'My father's good name – or what's left of it. Weston, a good old WASP name. Do you plan on sleeping with me? I'd better know your name if you do.'

They had reached the basement now. He let her in, turned on the light and sat her down.

'What are you doing?' she demanded as she tried to follow his movements with her ears.

'Fixing you a smoke.'

'Good and faithful guide dog.' She hesitated. 'Well, do you?'

'Plan on sleeping with you?'

'Yes.'

'Do you? Even if you can't see what I look like?'

'Lean,' she said. 'Hungry. Too hungry. High cheekbones. I'm crazy about high cheekbones.'

'You must have fingers with twenty-twenty vision.'

'A joke! He made a joke! I was beginning to think you thought laughter was a federal offence. Where's that goddamn joint?'

He put it between her lips, then waited while she drew on it and held the smoke in. At last she exhaled and smiled.

'Good?' he asked.

'Wonderful. Take me to your dealer.'

He smiled and sat down close to her.

She snapped her fingers. 'Name?' she demanded.

42

'Michael.'

'Michael who?'

'That's right.'

She gave a thin smile. 'OK, so you don't trust me. Press and all that. I'm out of that sewer anyhow. Thank God.'

'More bourbon?'

'I never mix highs. Maybe later.'

He poured a large measure into a glass and drank it.

'Whatever you're running away from, if you drink that hard you'll be dead before it catches up.'

Cardin took the joint from her, inhaled, then placed it back between her parted lips.

'You don't talk much, Michael Who.'

'I was looking at you.'

'Slipped headband and all?'

'Yes.'

She smiled and he knew she was beautiful.

'It's chill in here,' she said.

'It'll be worse in winter.'

'I wasn't planning to stay, but thanks for the put-off.'

He smiled and, with that extraordinary sense the blind have, she knew it.

'You just smiled. The room lit up.'

'It's the dope.'

He took the joint from her lips, the paper sticking slightly.

'Hey! Just watch the skin, friend – it's delicate.'

'How long,' he asked. 'Since . . .'

'A while.'

He gave her back the joint. 'OK.'

'Too long,' she said, drawing deeply and not releasing the smoke.

'You have to breathe some time,' he said, grinning.

She exhaled. 'Wow! You really do have a great dealer. I'd like a sip of that bourbon now.'

He poured two measures and put one glass in her hand.

'Is it dark outside?' she asked, turning her head to where she sensed a window might be.

'It's evening.'

'And in here?'

'The drapes are drawn. There's one light.'

'What is it like?'

'Here? Cold, small. Sufficient.'

'Describe it.'

'A table, three chairs, usual kitchen hardware. Bathroom behind me, bed to your left.'

'Was there anyone else you preferred at the party?' she asked unexpectedly.

'I didn't look.'

'Why not?'

'I'm not looking for anyone.'

'But you found me.'

'You needed a smoke.'

The joint was finished. He took it from her, broke up the remains, then washed them down the sink, letting the water run.

'You're very careful,' she said, listening to his movements.

He sat opposite her again.

'Would you turn out the light if I asked you?' Her head angled with the question.

'Now?'

'Now.'

He arose and flicked the light switch off, then moved back to his chair.

'You're very sure of your way in the dark.'

'It's a trick ... you close your eyes for a couple of seconds before you turn off the light. Do you feel on equal terms now?'

'Perhaps. Where did you learn your trick?'

'I've forgotten. You ask too many questions.'

'I'm a journalist.' She reached forward and found him, then pushed her hand under his shirt and felt the naked skin of his back. Her fingers skimmed over the hardened ridge of a scar. She stiffened. 'What happened?'

'It's just a scar. Would you like another drink?'

'Can you find it in the dark?'

'I remember where I put the bottle.'

'Another trick?'

'You're crazy, has anyone ever told you that?'

44

'They say nothin' else, my friend.'

'I can believe it.'

She put both her arms around his waist and rested her head against him. 'You know what I think, Michael Who? I think you're too old to be a draft dodger. I think you've been out there – I can sense the deadness in you. I think you were out there and decided you'd had enough.'

'Deserted?'

'You had enough, dropped out, split. That's why you're hiding.'

'Am I?'

'For sure.'

'Is that what you want to believe, Catherine? Because you're against the war? Or is it the journalist probing?'

She held him tighter. 'That's the first time you've said my name. I like it. I won't give you away. Listen! I understand. Really. Sometimes it takes more courage to run away from something than to stay and see it through.'

He reached for the bottle, poured a large measure and placed the glass by her face. She found it with her lips and drank. 'Firewater heap good for squaw,' she murmured.

He finished what she had left.

'Can two fit into your bed?' she asked, rocking against him gently.

'With difficulty.'

He pressed her head against his body and could feel her trembling, knowing it was not caused by the evening chill of the basement.

'I want you to hold me,' she told him. 'For a long time. I'm afraid because the light's gone out and it won't come back on again. I want to be held.'

'I know,' he said. He lifted her and took her to the bed, moving carefully through the darkness. She sat up and reached for him.

'Let me,' she said. Then, carefully, feeling her way with light fingers, she undressed him. He lay on the bed listening to her movements as she took off her own clothes.

She came to him slowly, her lips finding his then moving away as her breasts touched his mouth. She was warm and soft as he found her, and he longed for the peace which eluded him. He held her tightly and sensed that she was weeping, though her tears could not penetrate the dressings over her eyes.

The irony struck him cruelly. He was a man haunted, awake or asleep, by the eyes of a dead man, and now he was seeking peace and giving of his own strength to a blinded girl.

'You will see again,' he murmured to her. 'One day you will see again. I promise you.'

She gasped above him as he found release, then, joined him.

She returned two days later, in a taxi.

Michael heard the noisy rattle of the diesel engine from the street above as he sat at his table drinking. He saw the blurred heavy shape of a man through the frosted glass of the door and put down his glass. He studied the man from his window, then opened the door.

The taxi driver stood on the doorstep, a suitcase in one hand and a bulging carpet-bag in the other; under his arm he gripped a small portable typewriter; around his neck, on straps, were three cameras in cases.

Catherine stood at the top of the basement steps, both hands fixed tight to the iron railings. 'I'm lost!' she called looking straight ahead, half laughing. 'Keep bumping into things. My wonderful coachman told me he knew where this totally marvellous guide dog lived. Coincidence!'

Michael saw the white stick hanging from her wrist by a leather loop.

The cabbie coughed. 'I picked her up outside Moorfields Hospital – the eye place. You know?' He dropped the luggage but kept hold of the typewriter. 'Sitting on the pavement . . . on the suitcase.'

She had put her long thigh-length suede boot up on the low wall between rusting railings and swung gently, from side to side. 'Don't you go making up stories, mister coachman,' she called airily, 'let him make up his own mind.' Her head dropped between her outstretched arms and Michael could hear her muted sobbing.

'She's upset,' the cabbie said, uselessly.

'Put her stuff inside,' Michael said, then eased past him.

'We drove around,' the cabbie said, stopping him. 'Then I got this address out of her. Took some doing, mate. Couldn't drive around for ever.'

'It's all right, I'll see to her.'

'She a lovely girl.'

Michael nodded and climbed the stairs. He touched her hair. 'What's happened?'

'Oh hell!' she swore.

'What did they tell you?'

She raised the arm with the white stick. 'Standard issue.' Her head was still down, her words choked.

'Permanent?' he asked, gently.

'Of course not! The stick's for beating up on old ladies.'

'I'll take you down.' She did not move. 'Catherine?'

'Do you want the responsibility? Do you need the hassle?'

'Come on down.'

'Tell me!'

'We'll take it one day at a time.' He eased her down the steps and through the door.

'What does she owe you?' Michael asked the cabbie.

'He's been paid!' she snapped. The man nodded.

'Thanks,' Michael said.

'Any time,' the cabbie replied. 'She'll be all right with you, then?'

'She'll be all right.'

'I'll be off, then. You take care, miss.'

Cardin put her on the bed and sat beside her. 'Are they sure?'

'They'll try again in six months. Six months! Jesus!'

'Then they haven't given up?'

'I have.'

'For the moment. It's shock. You'll get through it.'

'Easy to say, Michael Who. You try it. Just for one day!'

He held her to him. 'Catherine, I can't take it from you. I can help, but I can't take it from you.'

She released herself and lay down on her side, her long legs drawn up to her breasts. 'You don't want me around.

47

You've got your own life. Your own problems, your own way to go.'

'Right now I've got nowhere to go, so we may as well sit it out together.'

'You're sure? Six months? What about at the end . . . if . . . ?'

'I'm sure. We can worry about later – later.'

She found his legs and clung to them hard.

'Do you want a drink?' he asked.

'Not yet.'

'Is there anyone you need to contact? Parents, friends?'

She shook her head.

'Do your parents know?'

'Perhaps. I dropped out of college. They said go to hell. I did. I went to Vietnam.'

'Your magazine would have notified them. The military must have done.'

'They did. I got a phone call from home. I told them to go to hell!'

'They didn't come anyway?'

'Perhaps they did. By then I'd split. Had a Reuters stringer lead me all the way to London. He wanted paying in kind. I put out. Shocked?'

'You needed someone.'

'You're an easy-going sonofabitch!'

'Good, get angry. It shows you're fighting.'

She broke completely, hanging onto him as if her life depended on the strength of her hold.

He waited until finally the sobbing diminished and she fell silent. 'Does anyone know where you are?' he asked.

'Only you,' she answered wearily.

'I won't give you away,' he said. 'If that's the way you want it.'

She raised herself up, searching blindly for his lips. He kissed her for a long while, then released her.

'Nor I you,' she whispered, her face almost touching his.

'Cardin,' he said. 'It's Michael Cardin.'

He saw her mouth tighten and she moved away from him a little. 'Yes,' she said after some time. 'I remember. They tried hard to keep the inquiry secret. A lot of us dug

48

around till we came up with a name – there were plenty of air-force guys who were only too pleased to leak it. Cardin. Michael we didn't get. Just Cardin.' She fell silent and Michael watched her. She continued: 'There were wild rumours about some operation being blown by an officer. One of *those* officers; a "funny". An official, unofficial operation. Lots of planes went down, men too. He called in the cavalry to save a priest. Went crazy, they said. The story died a couple of months later when Calley wasted Mai Lai.' She snorted. 'If it really was Calley.' She sat facing him, her face set. 'Why didn't they put you on trial? No, don't tell me. You didn't exist, so how could they?'

'A court martial would have found me guilty. No question. I'd be free to appeal. They couldn't hold an appeal *in camera*. They'd never have kept the wraps on it. They convened an inquiry instead. Closed, no outsiders. They couldn't sentence me so they kicked me out and told me to keep moving. Anywhere as long as it wasn't toward the United States of America. That's exactly what I did – have been doing, since.'

'There's no service record of you. People looked.'

'They wiped it – if it ever existed at all. The operations we carried out were illegal – as far as the conventional rules of war are concerned. We did a job which no one wanted to do but everyone wanted done. We found the enemy where no one else could find him – at home. That's where we stopped him.'

'Dead. Stopped him dead! At home. With his family. Kids!'

'Those too. We were there to hurt. We hurt him. He understood our kind of war – it was the war he waged himself. We'd have beaten him.'

'Jesus!'

'It's over now.'

'For you! Aren't there others like you still out there. Now?'

'I doubt it. Not after Mai Lai.'

He could sense her anger without looking at her set jaw and the high colour of the skin at her neck and cheeks. Like all the rest, he thought, she sees me as a pariah.

49

Coldblooded and probably a psychopath. Then, inescapably, came the prodding questions which were never far from his mind. Had he killed because no one else would do the job? The women, the children? Or had he some basic defect in his character which had blinded him to compassion and pity? Had the ruthlessness always been there, and the conditioning, the grinding months of training, merely been a physical expression of it? Finally, the last devastating question: had he saved the priest as an act of contrition? He would never know, for so much of his past was now blurred, and that, he realized, was probably his mind's condemnation of his actions. Yet the memory of the priest was clear. Pristine. Three-dimensional and vivid. He could close his eyes and see that face and those eyes now, yesterday, tomorrow and for ever. No escape. He would search for ever, hopelessly, for that stark, but exquisite moment of truth.

'I'll take that drink now,' Catherine said.

He touched her cheek but she was still cold and far away from him. He found the bourbon and gave her a small amount in a glass.

She sipped. 'Prohibition been declared? The first time – upstairs – you gave me the whole damn bottle.'

'You don't need it.'

'Says who?'

'You. You know you won't take that route.'

She sighed. 'So you're an out-of-work killer and I'm an invalided-out journalist who'll have to learn to read Braille.'

'You won't go that route either – self-pity.'

'What the hell do you know, Michael Cardin!'

'Not your style.'

She drank the bourbon in one swallow and held out the glass. 'Try me.'

He refilled it.

'More,' she demanded.

He added another measure.

'All right,' she said. 'Why? Why after all the things you must have done – and spare me the details – did you blow

50

everything on a man you had probably never seen before in your life?'

'Why do you want to know?'

'Why? Because I need to know just what I'm into here! I've come to you and I want to stay. I want to. I need you. I want you, past and all, but I need to know who you are now; and why, because there's no way you could have done what you did and still remain the same man you were before. Right?'

Michael took the glass from her, drank from it, and placed it back in her hand.

'Rationing me?' she asked, and smiled, the warmth returning in her. 'Start,' she ordered.

'Where?'

'Where it matters the most.'

He studied her for a moment, then said, 'The priest.'

'Just like that,' she interrupted. 'Straight to him. He mattered that much to you.'

'He still does.'

'He's dead.'

'What he gave me – what he let me see isn't. It never could be.'

She reached out for him and moved closer, her body warm against his as the day darkened outside, giving way, reluctantly, to evening.

'Tell me about him,' she whispered, her face against his legs.

'They crucified him,' he began, touching her hair and letting his fingers work their way through the tangles. 'Torture first and a savage beating. Then, crucifixion. Not a cross, a tree. They'd planned it, they'd brought the nails with them.' He related the whole incident, leaving nothing out, so that the horror of it lay heavily on the darkened room when he had done, like dank smoke from a fire, doused but not extinguished.

They sat in silence, both in their own darkness. Finally she said, 'You've told me how – but not why.'

'If I knew why, I would have my own answer. I might be content. As it is, now it seems somehow . . . unfinished.'

'You're still searching?'

'Always.'

'Why do you say unfinished?'

She felt him stir restlessly beside her, as though he might pull away, so she held him tighter. 'Tell me!'

'I thought about it constantly over the last three years. The frightening thing, looking back, was the inevitability of it all. That whole day seemed to be out of control. Out of *my* control. I did what I did – I tried to save him – yet my actions and those of two of my men seemed out of our control. We could not stop ourselves – even though we all knew it was utter madness, even suicide. I know, now, that that day could have had no other end.'

'The priest had this power?' she asked, incredulous, but trying to understand – wanting to understand. 'The power to control you and your men?'

He hesitated, unsure now of himself; it was the first time he had discussed the incident and his motivation so openly. At the inquiry in Saigon he had given nothing away of his feelings – just the facts; any mention of the rest would have convinced them that he was completely insane. Strain, they would have decided, nervous collapse, what can you expect? Hospitalization in a psychiatric ward with no recommendation for release: that would have been their solution and one they would have relished. So he told them nothing beyond the basic facts.

'Yes,' he said at last, then stopped himself. 'No.' He shook his head. 'Of course he couldn't have had that power over us. But there was something that gripped that clearing. I can't describe it but it was there. I swear it was there.'

'But the priest had some power over you? He must have!'

'Yes, he had power.' Michael's voice had fallen so low that she shook him as if he were sleeping.

'Tell me! Describe it!'

'You would never believe me.'

'I believe in you, so tell me. What was his power?'

'Forgiveness,' he answered, in an odd detached way, as if he were still in the clearing. In a way, she was there too, with him, comforting him through the memory of it, but her hearing was in the present and his voice seemed, uncannily, to have come through the years to her. She shivered and was afraid because, for a moment in time, she had stepped beyond her frail, limited, human understanding. The warmth of his body was a blanket she hugged around herself, like a child in winter, cold, in impenetrable darkness. The room was like ice, as though evil had concentrated all its forces in that one place at that one time. Nothing, she thought pitifully, could be worse than dying now. Then, as he spoke again, warmth returned and in her blindness it seemed like sunlight.

'He had the power to forgive. He saw his enemies, his torturers, the butchers of his people, and he forgave them. And they *were* forgiven. I swear it. He had the power of forgiveness!'

She was silent, still clinging to him.

'Catherine?'

'Go on,' she answered and he could barely hear her.

He pulled her face up, the new bandage with which they had dressed her eyes glowing stark white in some reflected light from the street above. His hands grasped her face tighter and pulled it closer to his own. 'I'm as blind as you are. I don't understand. The meaning of it all – if it has any meaning – is beyond me. But I know it's not over yet. Don't ask for explanations because I have none. All I know is that what happened then was not an end. It was a beginning. I feel, even now, that I am waiting! And sometimes the impatience inside me is so great I feel that I want to tear myself apart.'

'Michael, I'm frightened. Frightened for you.'

He released her face and held her body to him, giving her his strength because he knew that her fears for herself would return when this moment was gone.

'Will you love me, Michael? Not now, not bed. I mean love me?'

'I'll try. I want to. I could love you easily, Catherine.'

'*He's* stopping you.' The priest. He's pushing everything else aside.'

Michael could feel hot tears pressing at his closed eyelids and waited until he knew he could speak. 'I know. And I want to understand why. I have to find a way to understand. I don't think I can live without knowing.'

'Michael,' she said. 'I'm blind. Please don't push me aside.'

He lay down beside her, comforting her as she wept, loving her more with each passing moment and each hopeless tear – yet, still, part of him was elsewhere, waiting and, also, crying for guidance.

'Are you a Catholic, Michael?' she asked some five months later, on a Sunday, as they walked along the embankment by the Thames, the traffic meagre both on the streets and on the grey river. Even the occasional hoot from passing pleasure-ferries seemed muted.

She tugged at his arm as they strolled, her steps more confident now. 'Well?' she demanded, putting on her false angry voice. 'Talk to me, dammit!'

'If you feel like going to church, I'll come with you.'

'I asked if you were a Catholic.'

'Lapsed.'

He squeezed the arm she had locked through his own. Barges passed in line, linked together, about ten of them, like a meaningless message in morse with the dots missing. He stopped. 'The crucifix?' he asked, turning her gently.

She nodded. 'You never take it off. Whenever I touch you, you're wearing it.'

He shifted his gaze to the twin towers of the bridge, watching them open to allow a vessel clear passage.

'It belonged to him.' she said. It was a statement. She waited. She knew his silences now; even understood them. They were like moments of reverence. Acts of remembrance.

'It wasn't his,' he answered finally as the bridge closed. 'They tied it to him. It was an insult. Degrading his faith.'

'And you kept it.'

He screwed up his face and looked hard down the length of the river. 'I put it on – then. They'd tied it – you can guess where – Gaillard wanted it taken off. He was crazy with pain but he couldn't stand to see it there. It wasn't anything to do with faith, I just put it on.'

'Gaillard?'

'One of my men. He died.'

She squeezed him. 'I'm glad *you* didn't.'

He might not have heard her. 'I woke and found it by the bed – in hospital. They must have assumed it was mine.'

The sound of a tug drew her face towards the river. 'If you threw it away – now – took it off and threw it into the river, would it release you? Release you from him?'

'No!' he said sharply. 'When I find the truth – the meaning of it all – even the beginning of the truth – *then* I won't have need of it.'

'And if you never find . . . your truth?'

He turned her around to face him. She wore glasses now, over smaller dressings, mirrored lenses which cast his own reflection back at him. A thin, haunted face, clawed by the agony of his quest. Journeys back, through entire sleepless nights. 'I shall,' he told her.

'And then? Will you leave me then?'

He touched her face, his fingers tracing the fading scar tissue; her skin now was almost unblemished, even around her eyes. 'I can't answer that until I'm faced with it.'

She tilted her head and a sudden, quick breeze whipped at her blond hair, brushing strands over her face. She did not move them. 'So tell me about *now*. Forget *then*. What do you feel now? For me?'

'What do you want me to say?'

'Don't evade it! Say what you *feel!*'

'I need you.'

'Need? Need how? You need my body? You need me around? *How?*'

'I need you here – now.'

'Only *now?*'

He lifted her easily, though she fought him angrily, and sat her on the grey embankment wall, keeping hold of her because of the drop and the river below. 'If *now* was before it happened,' he said, 'or even if it had never happened – I would be in love with you. Perhaps I am now but it's clouded, don't you see? I can't make that commitment. Not until I can see the truth.'

'We're a real pair, aren't we? You not able to see and me blind!'

He grimaced. 'That was thoughtless, I'm sorry.'

'Don't be. It was what you meant. I'd rather you say what you mean, whatever your choice of words. Don't ever feel that each sentence is a minefield. Listen!' she exclaimed without warning. 'Can you hear them?'

'Hear what?'

'Bells! God, my hearing is getting more acute every day.'

'It *is* Sunday,' he said, but she was no longer listening to anything except the bells, which were, to her, clear and impossibly *visual* images of sound. All he heard was a faint melodic underlay beneath the sounds of the traffic and the river.

'It's like a little miracle,' she said, coming back to him. 'I can almost *see* through sounds. I'm coming to terms with being blind.'

He lifted her down onto the pavement. 'Well, don't get too used to it. You've only got a few weeks to go – and this time the specialist seems more than hopeful.'

He could see the stillness settle over her, like shock after bad news.

'Catherine? They mean it! I talked with them. They were confident.'

She reached out for him and gripped him. 'If they make me see again – if I'm no longer blind – you'll leave me. There'll be nothing left to keep you.'

'I don't care for you because you're *blind!*' he exclaimed, appalled by her judgement of him.

'No, but you're tied to me because I am. I can't help you find what you're searching for – but you have to help me find *everything*! When you don't need to do that any longer, you'll go. I know you will.'

'Let's go home,' Michael said.

'You see! You can't even admit it to yourself.'

'You don't see anything,' he retorted.

'Boom!' she cried, then laughed. 'You just stepped on a mine.'

* * *

'You're not to visit me,' she stated, a month later. She had packed for the hospital, her carpet-bag filled. Above, on street level, the taxi was waiting, engine thudding, the driver – her coachman, now a favourite and well used to the trip to Moorfields – smoking contentedly in the cab. 'When it's all over,' she continued, 'I'll come back. Either way. Whatever the result.'

'This is stupid,' he said.

'It's how I want it.'

'You'll need someone there!'

'I'll always need you, Michael. But you have to decide whether staying with me is going forward or going back – or maybe not going anywhere at all.'

He sighed, realizing argument was futile. 'Everything will be fine. I know it will.'

'Probably. This time they seem . . . almost sure. But if – when – they make me see again and I'm a complete person, things are going to be different. They're bound to be. We will both be *changed*. I won't be reliant on you and you will no longer feel responsible for me. We'll try to hide the changes but they'll still be there – and they're going to be pretty drastic.'

'What are you saying?'

'What I want is to walk through the door and for you to see me as a new person – just as I will see you – for the very first time.'

'That's impossible.'

'Or,' she continued, finding his face with her hand. 'Or not see you at all.'

'Do you believe I'd desert you if you were still blind?'

'No. No, I don't. But that isn't what I meant. I'm giving you the choice, Michael. Be there . . . or don't be there. It will be up to you.'

They rode in silence in the cab, each aware that, whatever the result of her operation, a period of their lives had ended.

The cabbie knocked on the partition.

'We're here,' Michael said.

'I know. I can smell it. *Listen!* I have to warn you – if

57

you're still home when I return, blind or sighted, I'll never give you the chance to leave again.'

He opened the door and stepped out onto the pavement. 'I'll take you in,' he said.

She leaned forward and found the glass partition behind the driver. 'Wait please, mister coachman,' she said, as the cabbie slid the glass open. 'Don't go without him. Hear me?'

'I'll be here. Hope it's all right, miss. You just call when you're ready to leave. No blocking the pavement this time.'

'A week,' she answered. 'I'll call.'

Michael took her hand, and with the carpet-bag in the other led her into the hospital reception area.

'Now go,' she ordered. 'Get the hell out. Wait! Kiss me first.'

He kissed her, then turned and walked away quickly.

Outside he paid off the cabbie. 'I want to walk a little,' he explained.

'She'll be all right,' said the cabbie, reassuringly.

'Yes.'

'In a week then,' the cabbie said, changing the meter flag.

Michael nodded. 'A week.' He watched the taxi swing hard into a gap in the traffic, then began walking, no particular direction nor destination in his mind.

After more than two hours had passed, he stopped at a small, near-empty cafe and bought himself coffee. He missed her badly. He sat by the window smoking and drinking as people hurried past in the gloom of evening, watching the buildings spill out their workers, each rushing to familiar destinations, minds intent only on arriving, journeys inconsequential; shuttered minds in sealed capsules opening, somewhere, on freedom.

It began raining heavily, the water outside the plate-glass window seeming to blend with the condensation inside. He put his hand on the glass and wiped away a square of the streaming moisture.

The church opposite was built of grey stone, dulled black by pollution and set grimly behind iron railings. The notice read 'St Thomas's' and, although it also proclaimed its denomination and its services, it seemed to Michael to be too poor, too shabby in its upkeep, to be in use. Then he saw the priest, skirts trailing wetly through the puddles, black umbrella thrust at an angle into the gusting rain. He stopped at the iron gate, fighting both his umbrella and the rusted catch before mounting the steps and entering the church.

The priest was not elderly – judging by his brisk strides and movements – yet he conveyed to Michael the defeated air of the aged; as though he and the church shared the same neglect, the same fruitless passage of time and opportunities. Lights glowed dully through the grimy stained-glass windows, at first steady and then flickering. Michael could picture the figure inside putting flame to candles, then moving about his business in the certain knowledge that God existed and that he was tending His House – however decrepit. He wondered if the priest saw the church as he could see it now, filthy and blackened like old buildings backing onto a railyard, or if he saw it as a part of God, wondrous in aspect, golden, gleaming – or however God was supposed to look.

The rain swept him back suddenly to the jungle and in a brief, startling moment of revelation he saw the real wonder of God in a pair of amazing blue eyes. He stood up, experiencing a strange drawing forward. Irresistible yet gentle – but growing, crushing his will. He put money on the table and stepped into the blinding rain. Across the street the filthy, arched windows cast trembling colours through the sheets of water.

Michael turned away once, squinting hard through the rain, but he saw nothing. Nothing. He stepped down onto the black, shining road.

'You had better wait,' Catherine told the cabbie.

He opened his door. 'I'll give you a hand down, miss.'

'No! I can do it on my own. I want you to wait up here.'

He closed his door and watched her as she descended the steps to the basement. She was pale but with a high flush to her cheeks, reminding him of a painted porcelain doll he had once bought his daughter. She still wore the mirrored glasses so he had seen her eyes only briefly, as she patted her anxious face with something taken from the carpet-bag. He had imagined them to be blue, because of her golden hair, but they were light brown and bright, like amber. He had not seen any scars on her face in his driving mirror but he knew that, even scarred, she could still be nothing else but beautiful.

He envied the lean, hard-looking young man she loved so obviously, but thought him strange, and even, in some indefinable way, dangerous. There was something in his dark, piercing gaze which made you look away. Also, he was too quiet. Too still. Like he was waiting for something to happen but afraid to move. Pleasant enough, polite, but not right. Somehow not kosher. The cabbie lit a cigarette, switched off the engine and waited.

Catherine inserted her key into the lock and opened the door.

She knew he had gone.

The note was on the table where they had first sat after the party, propped against a bottle of bourbon. Beside it lay the crucifix. She saw the crucifix first and her heart plummeted. The note was a formality, though she read it anyway; the unwritten message of the discarded crucifix was completely final, without reasons.

She read, 'I know you are able to read this because I checked with the hospital. What more can I say except that I am so very glad. Catherine, there is a time and a place for everything – especially love. I've run out of time and my place is no longer with you. It isn't that I don't love you enough to stay; it's simply that I have seen that there is a greater form of love and I must find my way to it, Michael.'

She did not know how long she stood there, his note and the crucifix dangling on its heavy chain in her hand. She did not move when the driver rapped hard – for the umpteenth time – on the open door. Finally she turned to him, keeping her tears for later.

'You going somewhere, love?' he inquired with surprise,

looking first at her packed luggage then around the deserted room.

'Home,' she said. 'Mister coachman, home.'

PART TWO

The Risen Saint

1

The South Atlantic. Tomorrow

The sleek silver executive jet cleaved the slate-grey sky over
the South Atlantic Ocean, racing away from the ominous
black horizon and the towering thunderheads of the storm-
front as fast as its four tail-mounted jets could propel it.

On the flight deck, the co-pilot looked anxiously at the
fuel reading, the deep creases around his tired eyes giving
away both his fatigue and his anxiety. The chartered
aircraft had been refuelled at intervals on the flight but on
each occasion they had been on the ground only long
enough for the fuel to fill the tanks to capacity. What little
sleep he had snatched in-flight had been nervous, his body
and mind strung with tension and unable to rest because
of the secrecy of their mission and the eminence of their
passenger. Now, on the final leg of their gruelling journey,
both the co-pilot and the fuel tanks were almost drained.
He wiped sweat from his face and found his skin was
clammy, despite the heating; it had been that way from the
moment their passenger had boarded at the small company
airstrip outside Rome, bundled to the ears in a heavy
overcoat, scarf and Homburg – or, more precisely, when
the outer garments and hat had been stripped off, revealing
the stocky figure's true identity.

In the left-hand seat, the captain rubbed his temples
wearily, then focused his bloodshot eyes on the radar
screen. For a fractional moment his exhaustion still pinned
him, leaden-bodied, to the seat, then he reacted, faster than
he had ever done in his life. He snapped in Italian, 'Aircraft
to port! Fifteen miles – closing. Three of them.' Two more

blips appeared on the screen, gaining rapidly on the first three. '*Height! Quickly!*'

The co-pilot pulled the control column back immediately, as the captain reached forward, boosting power.

Behind, in the main cabin, the dozing figure in the luxurious reclined seat was awoken by the distinct and instantaneous change in engine note. Beneath his slippered feet the carpeted floor inclined upward steeply, causing a set of white robes, draped carefully over the high back of a seat in readiness for their owner to don them before landing, to fall crumpled on the thick pile.

Further down the slim-bodied aircraft, the cabin's sole other occupant saw the robes slip and pulled himself up from his seat, fighting the angle of climb as he heaved his way forward along the aisle. Gripping a seat for support, he knelt to retrieve the fallen robes, but they slid away as the plane, still in its steep climb, tipped over in a hard bank to the right. Turning now, with concern, towards the reclining figure, he saw an expression of pain pass over the strong, intelligent face, giving way almost immediately to a transcendent smile of joy.

'Holy Father?' cried the kneeling priest, clinging hard to the seat for support as the plane tilted further.

The Pope, still smiling, raised his right hand and placed his lips to his heavy solid-gold ring, fashioned into the shape of a crude cross. With a firm, clear voice he began speaking in Latin, the thundering shriek of the engines obliterating his words.

The pilot of the leading Fuerza Aerea Argentina Mirage 111A jet-fighter watched his radar screen, seeing the two blips which he knew would be Royal Air Force Phantoms scrambled from the new airstrip on Fortress Falklands. His orders had been explicit: make the British get their fighters into the air, then run for the edge of the exclusion zone, and safety. Harass the enemy but do not engage him. This, for the moment, was the official policy. But the pilot knew that very soon – perhaps in a matter of days only – the running-away would be over. Revenge and victory would be theirs and the Malvinas Islands would belong, rightly, to Argentina.

Sharply, he snapped an order to his two wingmen and the three Mirages blasted forward as their afterburners ignited. But, in his frustration at having, once again, to turn tail and run, the leader's concentration strayed momentarily. His mind failed to register another, larger, blip on his radar screen ten miles on and dead ahead. At Mach Two it was no more than a double heartbeat away.

The aircrews of the RAF Phantoms saw the flash simultaneously, then the growing orange ball against the backdrop of black storm-laden clouds. Then came the shockwave. Heavy grey rain began falling to the angry ocean as the storm broke, heralding its fury with a deep, agonized, rolling groan of thunder before the heavens exploded.

The two surviving Mirages raced into the heart of the storm, the Phantoms for the safety of the islands.

Jerusalem

The room was stark and white, like the gaunt features of the figure laid out in death on the simple metal bed. One small window, set high in the cool colourless wall, admitted a shaft of afternoon sunlight which came to rest as a square on the scrupulously cleaned floor. This light and the slow-burning steady flame of the long candles fixed in tall wooden candelabra at the four corners of the bed were the only illumination in the hushed, darkened room.

Beside the plain bed a young monk dressed in a habit of coarse wool, the colour of oatmeal, knelt in prayer. His prayer was fervent and his grief barely concealed beneath the cowl which hid his head and face. Even in death, the very presence of the man for whose soul he offered his prayers seemed to engulf his entire being. The monk lifted his bowed head and opened his tear-filled eyes to gaze at the dead face before him. He felt a tremor of wonder course through his body as he faced the realization that he was touching, *actually touching*, the mortal remains of a true saint.

Unable to contain himself, he reached forward to the marble-cold flesh of the wondrous face; his fingers, trembling over the sunken cheeks and cheekbones, touched the hard ridge of the straight nose and wide forehead above the closed eyelids. The fair hair had been allowed to grow long and framed the classical features, bequeathing softness to the hard face of death.

So awed was the young monk by the wonder of that moment of physical contact that he did not see the crimson stain spreading beneath the folded hands of the body. It was the warmth that made him glance down. More than warmth. A growing heat! He gasped and emitted a strangled cry of horror, leaping from his knees and backing away from the corpse until the cold wall slammed into his back.

Blood flowed from four points on the body, and as his mind registered these he wailed aloud as if struck by madness. His face draining of all colour, he crashed to the stone floor, narrowly missing the banks of switched-off life-support units by the bed.

Outside, the urgent sound of sandalled feet running hard on stone echoed along the arched corridor like blows on naked flesh, halting abruptly at the door to the white room.

The figure on the bed arose slowly; his startling blue eyes opened wide, unfocused, displaying the blank innocence of the newly-born. He left the bed and its crimson-stained shroud and walked to the window. There, gazing out over Jerusalem, he murmured three words.

Behind him, monks fell to their knees, each of their faces transformed by the same beatific expression. They believed, beyond all earthly doubt, that they were gazing upon the face of glory.

The man turned from the window and smiled at them, and they wept.

'Heaven is here,' he repeated.

Rome

From the air, Rome seemed like a vast antique gold brooch, its monuments and buildings displaying the art and craftsmanship of centuries fixed in a setting of glittering highways, while overall hung that aura of timelessness which makes it the Eternal City. To the west lay the Vatican, Rome's finest jewel, a hard priceless stone washed red by the human blood spilt for the faith it personified.

For each of the sombrely clad men who had been summoned there that night, Rome held a unique significance. It ruled their lives. It was the rock upon which their very existence depended. Its strength built their stamina; its weakness caused their trembling.

Over the centuries since its foundation, the Holy Roman Catholic Church had suffered periods of weakness, even of evil, but the rock stood firm and unshakable – even, some held, immortal. The men who had been summoned believed that it could never be destroyed – but, if destruction seemed imminent, they would be expected to save the Church and the Faith with all means at their command.

That night, and in the days yet to come, they would be put to the ultimate test.

Because they had travelled by different routes and from points of departure around the globe, their times of arrival had been staggered, yet each was met at Fiumicino airport exactly on time by plain-suited men at the normal arrival gates – for the travellers had been ordered to proceed to Rome immediately, without formal announcement, in plain business clothes, avoiding VIP lounges and first-class tickets despite their exalted positions in the ecclesiastic world. So well managed was their unannounced arrival that only the sharpest and most well-informed observer might have realized that several princes of the Roman Catholic Church had arrived in the Italian capital.

From Fiumicino airport, anonymous saloon cars drove each man along the same route towards Vatican City, through the Arch of the Bells, around the back of St Peter's Basilica, through the Cortile della Sentilla and onwards to the Cortile San Damoso. Here the passengers alighted from the cars and hurried towards the lift which would take them to the Vatican's Secretariat of State; each, without exception – despite their weariness after hours of travelling and their advanced age – displayed the alertness and urgency of men summoned by the highest authority. Yet none knew the purpose behind their summoning and this accounted for the wary look in their tired eyes, for the Vatican is not excepted from political manoeuvring or power struggle. The unexpected message they had all received personally held no hint whatsoever as to the reason for this powerful gathering. Simply the order: Come at once, without delay, but discreetly, to Rome. And they had obeyed.

The Secretariat of State is situated on the third floor of the Apostolic Palace. At its head stands the Cardinal Secretary of State himself, then, below him, his deputy or *Sostituto*, the chief organizing executive of the Secretariat. Next in line is the Sostituto's assistant or *Assessore* and a staff of around one hundred, including a dozen diplomatic personnel and twenty members of religious orders. Because the Secretariat works so closely with the Pope himself, and also because of its immensely strong constitutional position, the Cardinal Secretary of State wields enormous influence within the Vatican. In the event of a tragedy, he is ready to grasp the slipped reins of power.

The current holder of that post, Cardinal Giorgio Cinalli, a Sicilian and a Jesuit – a formidable combination – had never been more aware of the responsibility placed upon him than on that evening as he welcomed each of his cautiously chosen brothers in Christ through the doors of his private apartments. Inside, seeing to the needs of each cardinal as he arrived, was Cinalli's Sostituto, Monsignor Benito Marco, a dark Roman aristocrat, small and precise, again a Jesuit, who had risen fast within the Vatican hierarchy. Some said, and not without good reason, too fast. However, as far as Cinalli was concerned, Benito Marco was the perfect Sostituto: a deputy of supreme, perhaps overly ruthless, efficiency – but undeniably courageous in his handling of other princes of the Holy Roman Church, who often sought to waste a Secretary of State's time with requests or petitions of a personal or unwelcome political nature. Cardinal Secretary Giorgio Cinalli had long since decided that, if anyone at all in the Vatican were indispensable, it had to be his Sostituto, Benito Marco. Above all else he was loyal, and loyalty in that byzantine court where intrigue and power play were the daily norm was as priceless as the papal triple crown. Cinalli knew the crown could be his, and that Marco would do all in his power within the jungle of the political lobby – where his weapons of charm, cajolement and subtle threat made him a master – to place that crown upon his head. At the time of the Watergate scandal in the United States, a cruel but humorous story spread through the corridors of the Vatican that Monsignor Benito Marco had supplied Richard Nixon with the idea of bugging the opposition. The question was then asked: Why did Nixon get caught? The answer: In case Giorgio Cinalli wanted to run for the Presidency! The joke caused great mirth, but the laughter was always tempered with caution, for it was accepted that human ears are as capable of listening and recording as hidden microphones, and Benito Marco held control over many such ears.

Cardinal Cinalli moved around the growing gathering, occasionally asking an inconsequential question but in general remaining silent, allowing the others to talk while refreshing his memories of these foreign power-brokers of the Catholic Church, gauging them as he did so, in readiness for what he had to reveal.

Finally the last arrived, jet-lagged from his journey from the far side of the Atlantic Ocean. Cinalli gave him no time to recover, nodded to Marco to place a stiff drink in the American's hand, then ushered them all through to an inner chamber furnished with a large circular table and chairs. He waited for Marco to close the doors, giving his Sostituto a small warning glance to remain outside in readiness for the end of the meeting, then began:

'You have all been called here because we are faced with both a catastrophe and a dilemma,' he began brutally, discarding niceties or protocol. 'Only we can deal with both. Our position demands it and gives us the power to

71

make immediate decisions.' The word 'power' caused an uneasy shuffling around the table, as though the Secretary of State had committed a social *faux pas*, but the mention of 'immediate decisions' stopped this dead.

Cinalli continued: 'First I must inform you, with a heavy heart, that the Holy Father is almost certainly dead.' He allowed the shocked response to stretch into a long silence, although he was obviously impatient for this to end. Some of the men who watched him were puzzled by his seeming lack of pain and reverence.

'*When!*' one of the cardinals exclaimed, breaking the silence. '*How?*'

Cinalli raised his hands. 'He had a mission which he considered worth the loss of his life.' The faces around him remained perplexed. 'We are all aware of the threats to world peace. Everywhere small conflicts have grown into minor wars, minor wars which threaten to escalate into global involvement, and confrontation between the super-powers. Central America, the Middle East. But more immediate is the certainty of another war over the Falkland Islands. Democracy has one again collapsed in Argentina and the new junta is even more repressive than that led by Galtieri.'

The impatience around the table was close to explosion. Cinalli sensed it but still held the cardinals in check. 'You must hear it all, every detail,' he insisted. 'The Holy Father made the decision to inform the British that a new better-equipped invasion of the Falklands by Argentina was imminent. They were unimpressed; their own intelligence had also given them adequate warning of this intention by the new junta. However, the British Foreign Office advised caution in any military response or alert status. Trade, banking and diplomatic relations with Argentina have improved and they did not wish this state of affairs to be endangered or reversed by premature military action. With these facts in mind, and certain in his mind that the junta were preparing for a massive assault on the Falklands, the Holy Father then made the fatal decision – against my counselling – to undertake the journey, by air, and in total secrecy, to the islands. Upon his arrival there, his intention

72

was to announce his presence by radio to both the British government and Argentina. He was certain, absolutely certain, that no attack would be made while he remained on the islands. He hoped that the time bought by his intervention – physically – would allow reason to prevail. Sadly, his mission was never accomplished. The chartered aircraft is reported missing, and, as the Milan businessman to whose corporation the jet belonged was listed as the passenger, no news of the fact that the Holy Father was aboard has broken. I have since spoken with the businessman – he is one of us, a member of Opus Dei and a Knight of St Columbus. Understandably, he is distraught, but is holding himself in readiness for our decision.'

The faces around the table cast quick glances at each other. But behind the bewildered looks as they faced the Secretary of State a hint of wariness was apparent.

Cinalli nodded briefly, as if acknowledging this. 'So. Apart from this gathering, the businessman in question and my own Sostituto, no other person is aware that the Holy Father is no longer within the walls of the Vatican. To the world, he is alive and conducting the business of Holy Mother Church.' Cinalli's heavy face gave warning that he would accept no question, no interruptions, until he had completely finished.

'Given the area in which the aircraft was lost the grave question is raised as to whether it crashed through some mechanical malfunction or whether it was shot down, either by accident or intent. According to our information there appears, at the time of the plane's disappearance, to have been some aerial activity involving both British and Argentine warplanes in the same sector.'

Even Cinalli's stern face could not stifle the clamour that arose from the table. He slapped his palm on the polished wood a number of times before order returned. Then he waited for complete silence.

'That is the catastrophe, and it is terrible enough – yet I doubt if it is more terrible, in terms of the future of the Catholic Church, than the dilemma we face at this moment.' He placed both hands flat on the table and pushed himself up from the chair, moving to the fireplace,

73

where he stoked the coals with a heavy brass poker. Raising his bulky body once more, he leaned against the marble and spread his palms wide:

'We can elect another Pope – indeed we must, if it is not the Lord's will that the Papa be returned to us safely – but what we cannot do, must not do, is allow the destruction of that most Holy Office and, perhaps, the faith itself.' Cinalli gave a grim smile and locked his hands behind his back. 'I see that you feel I speak in riddles? Very well, I shall be plain.

'It is virtually certain that the Papa is dead. There is little hope of survival – even if the pilot landed the aircraft on the sea in one piece – in an open lift-raft on the South Atlantic Ocean. At this stage, we are in possession of few facts. They may or may not come out later, but sadly we must assume the aircraft and all those aboard are lost. But this is not a time when the Church can be seen to be without its spiritual head. At this precise moment we need to be seen at our strongest. Not felled by this cruel blow; not divided by the politics of election; not – and this most importantly – shut away from the world in conclave.

'My dear friends, my brothers in Christ, the Holy Roman Catholic Church – and perhaps all of Christianity – is facing its most deadly threat since the foundation of the faith. The Bible warns us that this epoch in which we live will be the most crucial for mankind and that it is also the time when Lucifer, the fallen angel, will be free and at his strongest to wreak havoc on the world. I believe that he has worked his evil in the most perfidious way. Pierre Labesse has returned from the dead.'

There was no response from the seated men, except on their faces. Disbelief. Cinalli nodded. 'Some things are beyond us but, even in our mortal blindness, we must face them. We above all. We are the only ones who can. We are responsible! Pierre Labesse was a man of courage, a meek yet strong man when it came to his work in God's name. He suffered as much, if not more, than any of the greatest martyrs in the name of Christianity. No one knew this more than the Papa himself, who came to love that lifeless form, sleeping in a parody of death for over a

74

decade, more than any other man. Yet the vexed question as to the wisdom of the Holy Father's decision to begin the beatification of Pierre Labesse while he still lived – albeit only with the aid of the machines of modern scientific medicine – has raged for many years within our most secret councils. Even his right to make that decision was questioned. Nevertheless, the process of beatification was begun, in secret.'

Cinalli moved to the table, sipped water from a crystal goblet, then sat down. The atmosphere seemed charged, as if a powerful current flowed from the man who was now effectively in control of the Vatican and the Catholic faith.

Cinalli continued, dabbing his full lips: 'The Holy Father decreed that a date and a time should be set when the machines should be switched off, thereby allowing the body of Labesse to die naturally. Expert opinion, given by our own finest doctors, predicted that death would occur within minutes.' Cinalli checked his gold watch. 'The date set for the machines to be shut down was today. The time almost twenty-one hours ago. In fact – and make of this what you will – almost to the minute when the aircraft which carried the Papa went missing. Please bear with me,' he urged. 'You must hear everything before you pass judgement. At the decreed time, the brothers of Labesse's order, who had tended him for so long, switched off the life-support machines and Labesse died. Within minutes, Labesse died. His brainwaves have shown no activity for many years but now his heart stopped beating, his breathing ended. Life was extinguished and the death certificate issued.' Cinalli rubbed his palms together in a gesture signifying finality.

'Nine hours later, the wounds of crucifixion suffered by Labesse all those years ago began to bleed. I am sure you can imagine the pandemonium which took place in the monastery. His brothers knew, you understand. They *knew* that a papal decree had been made directing that upon his death Pierre Labesse was to be canonized. Labesse had died. For nine hours he was dead. Now, he was alive.' Cinalli hesitated. 'If it has not struck you already, let me point out the significance of those nine hours and its effect on the brothers. You will all recall that history records the

75

period of time Our Lord suffered on the cross. Nine hours. Coincidence? The brothers did not see it as such. What they had witnessed was a miracle. What they had *before them* was a miracle. A miracle of immeasurable dimension.'

'Perhaps the doctors made a mistake?' a voice said carefully. 'It has happened before.'

Cinalli shook his head. 'There was no mistake.'

'Then it *is* a miracle!' cried another.

The American leaned forward on the table, gazing shrewdly at Cinalli. 'There's more,' he said. 'I think we'd better hear it all.'

Cinalli lowered his head gravely.

'Much more,' he said. 'Labesse opened his eyes, arose from the bed and walked unaided to the window. *Unaided!* A man whose body was wasted and weak from a coma lasting more than ten years. He gazed out of the window, down the Mount of Olives and upon Jerusalem. He spoke three words. He said, "Heaven is here." '

The silence in the room was absolute. Around the table a few of the cardinals crossed themselves.

Cinalli flicked his eyes toward them, shook his head slowly and smiled. 'Do not deceive yourselves. This "miracle" is not of God's making.'

One of those who had crossed himself, a Spaniard, spoke up: 'But this could be a true miracle! These words uttered by Father Labesse might be a revelation from God!'

Cinalli nodded sombrely. 'I understand what you are feeling. In these troubled times it would be a great comfort for all who believe to have such a miracle occur. The temptation to seek the true word of God in this simple – yet ambiguous – statement made by Labesse is very strong. But we must not be deceived. These words are evil, coined by the great deceiver himself to confound us – even to divide us!'

'So what does Labesse mean by "Heaven is here"?' the American cardinal asked. 'Does he understand them himself?'

'Has he said more?' demanded another.

Cinalli withdrew papers from scarlet-trimmed black cassock. 'The brothers themselves begged him to reveal the

76

meaning of his words. You shall hear now the true extent of this evil – the utter blasphemy of his statement. These are Labesse's own words, taken down and telephoned to us by one of his brothers: "I have been with God. I have been in His presence and have heard His wisdom. *Heaven is here!* We, mankind, are the creators of our own paradise ... and our own hell. I have seen the future and it is perfect. We are dragging ourselves from the flames of hell toward the perfection of heaven. Heaven here on earth. God's role is that of architect and overseer but our road is our own. Mankind will struggle forward on this road and all signs will seem to be leading him towards destruction. But he shall overcome. He will see the truth. He shall reach a state of perfection here on this good earth." '

'Heresy!' came one cry.

'Blasphemy!' shouted another.

A calmer, English voice cut through the sudden anger. 'What of the soul? He speaks of "the future". A perfect earthly future. Yet an earthly future can only contain the souls of those who exist at that time! Our Lord promised all mankind a place in paradise if they lived by His word. Every generation since time began would be given the chance of everlasting peace.'

Cinalli sighed. 'This too, Labesse has an answer for. He says, "The soul of man passes from generation to generation, not reincarnated but *transferred* within the chemistry of our human bodies. Future scientific medicine will discover amazing and revealing secrets in the hereditary cells of man. Each generation passes on God's imprint, taking mankind one step further toward perfection. The image of God is within us and we are moving forward toward its revelation. Christ was just such a revelation." '

The uproar now was uncontrollable.

Cinalli stood again, leaning forward onto the table. 'Our anger will achieve nothing! Understand our dilemma. One man is offering to this confused world exactly what Satan tempted Our Lord with: the world itself! Labesse does not say when this "perfect future" will come. This so-called "state of perfection". He will not say. It could be tomorrow. In this generation – or the next. Imagine how destructive this will be – and how tempting. Christians, if they choose to believe him, will be set on a road to the destruction of their very souls! They will no longer seek a spiritual heaven, they will no longer seek a spiritual union with God. They will trade these for the shallow promise of eternal life on earth.'

'Labesse must be silenced! His evil gospel must not be allowed to spread! He must be held in seclusion – never, never allowed a platform from which to speak!' All these solutions and many others besides were thrown at Cinalli from around the table, but he shook his head slowly, like a teacher who could not make his students understand.

'Still!' he barked. 'Still you don't see. We have beatified a man for the goodness of his deeds, for his sacrifice to God. We have nurtured his body, then allowed him to die, and upon his death we have canonized him. Pierre Labesse may be the deadliest enemy of Christianity but he is also *a risen saint*!'

The cardinals stared at each other across the table, devout, highly intelligent men perplexed by this supreme irony. For that moment at least the fate of the Pope was temporarily forgotten. They understood, now, the Secretary of State's apparent disregard of the tragedy.

The Englishman spoke, his tone negative. 'We can do *something*, surely? We can take some action?'

Cinalli nodded. 'Of course we can. What the Holy Father created we must destroy – in the name of God. We must fight with all our strength because this is a battle we dare not lose. We will use our power and influence discreetly to trivialize, even dismiss, Labesse's pronouncements – but we must not expect to defeat him conclusively because he will be given every platform, every opportunity, to spread his gospel of lies. This is not a devil we can keep chained for ever. Even now, rumours are spreading beyond the walls of the monastery that Labesse died and now lives. The doctor who was brought in to witness his death and issue the death certificate has had to be recalled. His tongue will not remain still. We must assume that a legend is growing as we speak. It cannot be contained. The media, as we know, have ways of finding out everything in this modern society of ours; soon they will have the story. Perhaps they have already. A risen saint! Such a man is more than just news – he is a phenomenon! It will not take long before the entire world will be hearing his story. And his words. So, if our initial efforts fail to silence him, then, however distasteful it may seem, we must resort to other means. He must be discredited – or he might destroy the foundations of the faith.'

'Discredited?' the Englishman queried. 'Discredited how?'

Cinalli stared at his large beringed hands. 'Discredited as a man. There are secrets in every man's life. No man goes through this life unblemished. Once, twice, maybe more times, he stumbles. At some time in his life, Pierre Labesse must have stumbled. Somewhere there must be a secret he hides.'

The deep voice of the American rumbled from the farthest end of the table. 'In America that might be termed blackmail.'

'In Italy also,' replied Cinalli. 'I have already warned that other methods we may have to use could prove distasteful to us.' He waited for further reaction. None came. He began again: 'Time is our enemy. How long are we able to keep the death of the Holy Father from the media and the people? If we act in concert and none of us breaks silence on the matter, we should be able to conceal the fact for a reasonable amount of time. Enough perhaps for our needs. First, a story must be fabricated as to why the Papa will not be keeping his scheduled appointments. We can thank God that he had no tours planned for the next few months.'

The Spaniard broke in. 'The aircraft? Surely someone saw him go aboard? Workers at the airport? Customs officials? The crew might have talked to colleagues? It is very dangerous to assume . . .' His voice trailed off and he sat hunched forward, deeply perturbed.

'No,' Cinalli stated. 'On this matter we are covered. The Papa went aboard the aircraft in plain business clothes, his head and face well concealed. Also, the aircraft took off at a private airstrip owned by the corporation to whom the plane belonged. He was accompanied to the airstrip by my Sostituto, who himself remained concealed in an ordinary saloon car without Vatican numberplates. Monsignor Marco assures me that the airstrip was deserted – the hour was late – and all customs formalities had been completed earlier by the crew. There is no need for concern regarding this.'

The Spaniard nodded and permitted himself a small smile of relief, which immediately vanished upon Cinalli's next words.

'We must act immediately against Labesse because once suspicions regarding the Holy Father begin mounting – which they surely will do if he is continually unavailable – Labesse's words may take on an even greater urgency and a timeliness which might prove difficult to counteract.'

The American cut in suddenly. 'You realize that, if the news of the Pope's death breaks and it becomes known that we were responsible for a cover-up, our attacks on Pierre Labesse will become weapons to be used against us? We will be accused of trying to silence him. It might easily be construed by our action that we were unprepared in our fight against his words. We would be seen to be weak. Worse! We would be made wrong and Labesse right. I move that we forget any attempt at hiding this tragedy – no cover-up; the Catholic Church is strong enough to withstand the words of any one man, whatever his status. The faith has been attacked before. Martin Luther tried it, but he didn't bring down the temple!'

Murmurs of agreement began around the table.

'Martin Luther,' said Cinalli heavily, 'caused the Reformation. And he was not a saint!' Anger was evident now on the Secretary of State's face; his frustration at the procrastination causing his temper to rise. 'Luther was not crucified! Nor martyred! Martin Luther was not personally chosen by a Pope for canonization! Martin Luther was a monk, a plain monk with a doctorate in theology who disagreed with Rome – and he virtually split the Church

80

in half!' Cinalli was on his feet now. 'Martin Luther,' he said harshly, 'was not a risen saint!'

The American and the Sicilian glared at each other across the table, neither one prepared to damp down the volcano of emotion which had exploded so unexpectedly.

The English cardinal frowned in disapproval, then said reasonably, 'Let us be realistic. There have been many cases of people apparently dying then returning to life. The human body is a complex organism, and with present-day advances we are constantly pushing the true measure of death to its outer limits.'

Cinalli slumped down in his chair, shaking his large head wearily. 'If you wish to risk the stability of the Church, I cannot stop you.'

'*Non!*' came the simple but sharply spoken negative from Cinalli's left. The Secretary of State raised his eyebrows at the small Frenchman in steel-rimmed spectacles.

The Frenchman, too, was a Jesuit and was renowned for the authoritarian manner in which he fulfilled his duties on Rome's behalf in France. He scowled and shook his head sharply, his hard close-set eyes fixed first on Cinalli; then he selected the American cardinal as the target for his attack. 'The Holy Catholic Church teaches that it is the "Church of Christ" or the "Church of the New Testament". This means that the Catholic Church is the visible society of the faithful living according to the New Testament. A fine description. What does it mean? I shall tell you – not to teach, you comprehend, but to make clear how dangerous this situation is for us. The basis of our faith is taken from the words of one man – a man whose words are now believed implicitly by millions, Jesus Christ Our Lord. Of course, now, we recognize Him as being the Son of God but, when He first trod this earth, to the people He was nothing more than a simple carpenter with a message of hope. Why did the people listen to Christ? And listened in thousands! Not because they believed He was the Son Of God – not in the beginning. They listened because He had *charisma*. You know the meaning of this word? Of course. It means a spiritual power.' He adjusted his spectacles, then looked up again, thoughtful. 'Pierre

Labesse has spiritual power. He too has *charisma*. I know, I have met him and have felt that pull. If the Holy Father has called him saint, then, believe me, the people will call him saint also. We have all met priests like Labesse at one time in our lives. Meek men who can strike fear into you with one glance. They never rise in the Church – we will not let them. They are dangerous because they are different from us – and they might even be better than us. This position we are placed in is also dangerous. I have said it already, and I believe it. We dare not risk being locked away in conclave at this time, in enforced silence, while he has every opportunity to spread his word. Cinalli is right! We fight him with the entire body of the Church, not with our voices silenced by the prison of the conclave. *Non!* The Papa is alive and here in the Vatican. He is exhausted perhaps and in seclusion, but he is alive!'

'And how will he answer the words of Labesse?' asked the English cardinal archly. 'He must do that.'

Cinalli spoke. 'We are his voice. We shall answer. But only from the platforms from which he chooses to speak. To answer him directly from Rome is to give his words greater credence in the eyes of the people. But wherever he speaks – press, television, radio, public gatherings – our presence will be felt, unofficially. I have a list of those suitable for this task compiled already. No time has been wasted.

'Also, I have drafted a statement for your approval – to be issued under the papal seal as if from the Holy Father himself – which will declare that, although Labesse has been canonized, he is nevertheless an ordinary mortal and therefore subject to human failings. Like many devout men before him, he has misinterpreted what he believes to be the word of God. Also, his statement regarding his supposed presence with God will be disputed – in the kindest way. The Papa will point out that the injuries he suffered by crucifixion and the subsequent years of coma might have caused damage to his mind. Such an assumption is not unreasonable, I think. But we only issue this statement if absolutely necessary.'

'Damn right!' snapped the American. 'It will be proof of our duplicity!'

Cinalli ignored the outburst and looked inquiringly around the table.

'I suppose we have to do whatever is expedient,' muttered the Englishman unhappily.

'Everything that is necessary!' snapped the Frenchman. 'Yes,' he affirmed.

The others nodded their agreement.

Cinalli glanced at the American, who leaned back into his chair resignedly, then shrugged, accepting defeat. 'I have no choice but to go along with you,' he stated. 'I think I've made my doubts clear enough. However, if we must carry out this deception regarding the Pope, let's made sure it's done efficiently. You've taken care of the wider issues, but what about the nuts and bolts? His personal staff? The nuns who look after him? His private secretary?'

'His private secretary was on the plane also,' Cinalli interrupted.

Momentarily there was silence. The American groaned. 'This gets worse by the minute,' he said.

'Not necessarily,' said Cinalli. 'The nuns believe the Papa is travelling somewhere on the Church's business but they know nothing else. Knowing the way they chatter amongst themselves, they have probably already concluded his mission is secret. He even packed his own clothes, so rumours must have begun immediately. For the moment we let them believe what they will, but if we have to put out a cover story or our prepared statement, I will act according to the situation. They will obey whatever orders they are given.'

The Frenchman cut in. 'The nuns are of no consequence, but the private secretary will be missed immediately. He handles all appointments – including personages too important to pass off with excuses. I have a suggestion to solve this.'

'Yes?' Cinalli inquired.

'With the Holy Father . . . indisposed . . . the day-to-day operation of the Church falls on you, Cardinal Secretary.

83

Indeed, if the truth of the matter were known, you would be in supreme control until the next Pope is chosen by conclave. My suggestion is that your own Sostituto handles all inquiries; he is a very able man in this field – as we have all found out at one time or another.'

Cinalli watched the nods from the assembled cardinals. 'Agreed,' he said. 'So, are we also in agreement over everything discussed here tonight? Very well. Now you must all return immediately from where you came. If there are any leaks regarding your combined presence in Rome tonight, we shall link it with the story of the Holy Father's decision to rest in seclusion for a period of time. He wished to see you all together to avoid disrupting rumours being spread.' Cinalli stood up.

'One final point,' said the Englishman apologetically. 'And forgive me for going over what we have discussed, but I see this as vital.'

'Yes?' said Cinalli, concealing his impatience.

The Englishman coughed and studied the figures around him, some already rising from their chairs. 'We are all agreed that Father Labesse was . . . is . . . an exceptional, if not extraordinary, man. A man, as has been revealed, of great personal charisma. A man, in fact, who, had it not been for his prolonged comatose state, might well have become . . . one of us. We have seen that a man of such deep spirituality and charisma can attain the triple crown. The Holy Father himself is . . . was . . . such a man. He too suffered in the Lord's name. He too had the power of *reaching* the people.'

The cardinals were stilled, each held in their positions, waiting.

'Go on?' Cinalli said.

'What will happen if Labesse does confound our efforts to dismiss his words? If medical opinion proves he is unaffected physically or mentally by his experience? If our . . . inquisitors find nothing for us to use against him – his personal life must have been checked thoroughly by the Holy Father himself before his decision to canonize was made? If, subsequently, too many choose to believe him? What if all we can do is simply not enough?'

Cinalli dipped his head slowly, folding his hands. 'We place our trust in God,' he answered quietly.

As the cardinals moved slowly from the chamber, speaking in muted tones amongst themselves, the Frenchman held back, waiting for all to leave.

He approached Cinalli, standing again by the handsome marble fireplace.

'God has entrusted His Church into *our* hands,' he said in a lowered but severe voice. 'We are its guardians.'

Cinalli looked down on the smaller man, his reply chilling: 'The Holy Bible, the very word of God, warns us of the appearance of many Anti-Christs. We have one now. Perhaps the most powerful of all – and he is of us! Satan has awakened his Hound of Hell – we must find our Hound of Heaven.'

After the French cardinal had left, Sostituto Benito Marco slipped into the inner chamber. He poured cognac from a crystal decanter into two goblets and handed one to his superior.

'Time is our enemy,' Cinalli said, troubled. 'We cannot afford to waste it.' He drained the goblet and placed it on the mantelpiece. 'Do this,' he said decisively. 'Choose a man you can trust with the life of the Church from within the Secretariat. He must speak French fluently – preferably, he should be a French national. Swear him to secrecy, then give him the task of dissecting the entire life of Pierre Labesse. Everything! We must know everything Labesse ever did, every movement he ever made. Where he lived, how he lived, before he came into the Church. His background, friends, enemies if any. Labesse is a ticking bomb placed at the heart of the Catholic Church, and if I am to defuse that bomb I have to know every millimetre of its mechanism.'

Marco swirled the cognac in the goblet between his hands. 'Eminence, I already know of such a man – he is not of the Secretariat, but he is perfect for this task and is also completely secure.'

85

Cinalli smiled wryly. 'You knew I would not wait. Who is he?'

'Father Phillipe Recamier.'

'I know of him. He works for Vatican Radio.'

Marco nodded. 'As a producer of our foreign broadcasts. Recamier is French. He is also clever and can be cunning. Somehow he managed to establish contacts in Poland during the Solidarity crisis and kept the links going throughout the most difficult – and most dangerous – phase of the crisis. Once Recamier has decided he will go after something, he does not let go. He worries at it until he is successful. Whatever the means.'

'And you are confident he can perform this task, loyally – and in secret?'

'Better than any other. He is a trained and skilful investigative journalist with numerous contacts. He can move freely and ask the right question. If there are any secrets to be uncovered in Labesse's life, Phillipe Recamier will search them out.'

'Very well. Set him the task.'

'How much am I to tell him?'

'Can he be trusted with the truth?'

'I believe so. But to be realistic, Eminence, can we trust him with less than the truth? The entire truth.'

'Make your point,' Cinalli said, warily.

'Both Recamier and Labesse are Frenchmen. From different parts of France, perhaps, Labesse from Brittany, Recamier from Corsica, but both still Frenchmen. Unless the real reason for this inquiry and the urgency of it are given to him, he might be tempted to omit, shall we say, minor incidents in Labesse's life which may, to Recamier, seem merely the product of youthful excess – but to us could be built into something far greater and potentially damaging.'

Cinalli held out his glass for another drink and Marco refilled it.

'I agree,' Cinalli said, savouring the golden liquid this time. His Sostituto's presence always raised his confidence. 'Give him the entire truth but swear him to total secrecy.

86

Swear him to a holy vow and warn him of the consequences of breaking that vow.'

'If you wish it, Eminence. However it may not prove necessary. Recamier, too, has secrets in his early life which he believes are well hidden. But his loyalty to the faith may prove enough.'

Cinalli studied Marco steadily. 'I believe I would rather put my hand into a nest of vipers than place my past in your hands. But a mind like yours is exactly what is needed at this moment.'

The Sostituto inclined his head, then said, 'Recamier will have to be in constant contact with the Secretariat –'

'No!' Cinalli interjected sharply. 'Not with the Secretariat. With you. Your private apartment is outside the Vatican. Have him report directly to you. And he is to be careful – extremely careful – as to how he words his reports. I suppose the use of the telephone is unavoidable because of the time factor, but telephones are dangerous. Give him some name with which he should identify himself to you – a false name – and he is never to mention the Vatican, any offices or persons within it, nor the name Pierre Labesse on any occasion he calls you. I don't want any link to be made with us. See to it.' Cinalli turned his back in dismissal as he stoked at the fire once more.

'Time,' he murmured to the fire, as his Sostituto moved towards the door. Then aloud: 'The work of centuries could be destroyed in a matter of days. Tell Recamier that! Tell him we have very little time.'

Marco slipped away silently, as he had come.

The Cardinal Secretary of State stared deep into the flames, his lips moving in soft prayer: 'Lord, if my path strays now or in the days to come from Your way, forgive me, for I am a man alone with the burden of Your Church on my shoulders. If I must sin to save it and my soul is cast into eternal damnation, then so be it! I accept your judgement.'

Fiercely, he thrust the glowing poker into the red-hot coals.

2

Catherine Weston drove the long nose of her new sports coupé forward to within an inch of the wall. She revved the powerful engine loudly, thrilled by the deep roar from the exhausts in the enclosed space. She gave a sly, self-satisfied grin of pleasure, then swung her long legs out of the low car, taking care with the door on the side wall. Giving the gleaming red coupé one final glance of pride, she walked, shoulder-bag swinging, toward the underground-garage checkout.

'Nice one!' whistled the lad manning the glass booth. 'What'd you do to get it?'

'Got promoted,' she answered, tossing the keys at him. 'No bumps, OK?'

'All right for some!' yelled the lad, his voice ringing hollowly up the tunnel after her as she stepped into the crisp morning air. Normally she would take the soft route through the park but today, with a new desk awaiting her, the crowded pavement won out over the beauty of nature.

The London offices of *Fact* magazine were halfway along Park Lane, sandwiched between a luxury-car showroom and a gentlemen's club of some standing. On a good day she could reach the offices within three and a half minutes. Today she was flying and she made it in just under three.

Her new desk and job as features editor were waiting on the third floor and so was the magazine's editor-in-chief, Saul Luman. In his hand was a Reuters printout.

'Pick up the new wheels yet?' Luman asked, smiling widely.

'Someone gave you a good night,' Catherine remarked, noting Luman's smile, which was not an expression he wore lightly. 'This morning. It's fantastic. Told them to bury the old one at sea.'

Luman's smile had faded. 'You're going to have to moth-ball it for a while.'

'What do you mean?'

Luman grabbed her easily by the waist and propelled her along the corridor to his own office. 'Sit,' he ordered. 'Pull all that hair away from your ears and listen good. You want coffee?' Luman enjoyed his reputation as a no-nonsense New Yorker.

'No, I don't want your damn coffee! I want to get at my new desk, OK? I know how you work, Luman, you're setting me up for something. Well, forget it, I'm sick of airports, sick of being sick in airplanes and lonely in bad hotels. From today I'm deskbound, right? I've settled down, got married to routine.'

'Finished? All right, hear me out, then we'll see if you want to jump straight behind that desk. Don't start yelling! The job's still yours. Just hear me out.'

'What's in that damn Reuters sheet you're waving about?'

Luman leaned back in his executive chair, swinging slightly to his right and jabbing his second cigar of the day at the window. 'Great day,' he said.

'Come on, Luman,' she moaned.

'Catherine, this magazine has done well since its first publication five years ago. Very well. And you've been a part of its success. You're the best investigative journalist I've ever worked with.'

'Are you sure I've still got that job?'

'Sure you've still got it.'

'Then cut the crap and let me get on with it. You don't have to tell me how good I am. I'm good and I know it. But now you've got a replacement and I'm truly happy about that.'

'Do you remember, oh, maybe three years ago . . . a couple of years after you joined us anyway, give or take a few months . . . we went out for an early evening drink which ended up with dinner? Just you and I, remember?'

'I remember. You'd just divorced Luman number one and hadn't landed Luman number two. The drinks were dry, you were hot and I ended up fighting World War

Three with your hands all through dinner. Sure I remember.'

'I was out of line.' Luman grinned ruefully.

'You were out of luck.'

'You told me this story – probably to get me off you – about some guy you'd met. You were back from Vietnam. Flash-blinded. Temporary. Have I got it right so far?'

Catherine stared at him, saying nothing.

'If I'm opening old wounds, I'm sorry, but this is important. This guy you knew had also been in Vietnam, just like you, only he was playing other kinds of games. Games we Americans don't like to admit we were involved in? My memory still good?'

She nodded.

'He'd blown everything to get this other guy out from behind VC lines: his unit, a rescue operation, his career – if that's how he saw his work – anyway, the whole sackful of dreams. Right?'

'I hope to hell, Luman, that this has some relevance, because if you're playing games . . .'

'No game, Cathy. A story. *Numero uno*. The big one.'

'Go on.'

'He blew it all for a crucified priest. Everyone else got wasted but your friend got out – with the priest.'

'The priest died in Saigon.'

Luman did not comment.

'So what the hell?' she retorted.

'Your friend was really hooked on this crucified priest, right? Must have been, considering his actions! Used to moon around, worrying at it, afterwards – when you two were together. When you got your sight back, he split.'

'I must have been smashed to have told you all this.'

'Not so much. Maudlin. You wanted to get it out. That's all. OK, forget your friend, he's not important.'

'So who is?'

Luman raised a hand. 'Wait. You told me you'd like to write up the story. But you felt it didn't have an ending. No last punch. It just faded.'

'And you pointed out that certain spheres of military

90

operations in south-east Asia were still classified and we couldn't print it anyway.'

Luman handed her the Reuters release. 'There's your ending. I think we just might be able to persuade our backers that this could be the right moment to risk the wrath of the US government and spill something about covert operations.'

Catherine read the release:

JERUSALEM. 'Father Pierre Labesse, Roman Catholic monk, in coma since 1967, died at two minutes past midnight local time yesterday, Sunday, after life-support units had been switched off on direct order from Vatican. Death was certified by Israeli authorities. At 9.00 a.m. local time life returned to "corpse" and Labesse reportedly arose from deathbed and walked unaided. News of "rising" only released by monastery, where Labesse has lain during period of coma, at 1.00 a.m. local time today. Delay presumably on Vatican instructions though no explanation available. Monastery claim that Labesse had been beatified while in comatose state and subsequently canonized upon carrying-out of Vatican directive to switch off life-support units has neither been confirmed nor denied by Rome. Vatican Radio has not covered this event in their broadcasts. In Jerusalem, brothers of Labesse's order are visibly shaken by what has happened and in many cases are declaring his "rising" to be "divine intervention" even, a "miracle'. Further bizarre aspect to story is that Labesse had lapsed into coma after crucifixion by communist guerrillas in 1967. Word of this event has already spread and crowds of "pilgrims" are beginning to gather outside monastery walls awaiting appearance of this "risen saint", many anglicizing his name and dubbing Labesse the "new St Peter". Notably, two prominent local Jewish rabbis have visited the scene because of, quote: "The historical importance of the site to the Jewish Faith." The monastery is built on the upper slopes of the Mount of Olives, the prophesied biblical site for the appearance of the Jewish Messiah.'

Catherine re-read the release carefully, then placed it on Luman's desk. She glanced at him. 'It isn't necessarily him,' she said softly, visibly shaken. 'You're assuming –'

'Assuming!' Luman retorted. 'Work it out yourself. What was the year you met your friend?'

'Late summer, 1970. That makes a three-year gap.'

'In which your friend did what?'

She turned away toward the window. 'Drifted. He travelled around, that's what he told me.'

'You've heard nothing from him since?'

'Nothing.'

'So there's no way we can get him to identify this Labesse as the same guy he pulled out of the fire.'

'Off a tree,' she corrected.

Luman grunted, thoughtfully.

'Are they absolutely certain that Labesse was dead? There are stringent tests to prove that. Were they carried out?'

'Read the release again. The Israelis themselves issued the death certificate. I've run a check – an Israeli doctor was called in when the monks pulled the plug. He certified that life was extinct. Nine hours? I mean . . . Jeesus!'

'And the Vatican's reaction? Why was there nothing on the news? I'd have thought they'd be playing this up for all it's worth. A risen saint! It ought to pull all their strays back into church like –'

'Exactly!' Luman snapped. 'Don't tell me you can't smell a story?'

'Doesn't make sense,' she agreed. Despite herself, she felt her curiosity beginning to itch – and an odd excitement building. 'Obviously the answer lies with Labesse himself. Has anyone got in to see him yet?'

Luman shook his head. 'The latest word we've had is that the Father Superior has locked the gates. Waiting for Rome to do something, I suppose.'

Catherine shrugged. 'Then that's what we'll have to do.'

'Cath! Go to Israel. You've already got half the story. You'll be way ahead of the others!'

'By the time I get there, the place will have wall-to-wall reporters and TV crews.'

'Doesn't matter. Let them do straight news coverage; you've got an eye-witness account – no dammit, a participant's account – of *how* Labesse got to be in a coma. You can do a complete in-depth story on the man.' Luman slapped his desk hard. '*Jesus!* Is he still a man? What the hell is a saint who comes back to life?'

'Someone special,' Catherine murmured.

'Come on, Cath, this guy who got him out. Can't we run a trace ... We've got sources? Maybe it's worth a shot –'

She shook her head firmly. 'Sorry, Luman. I'm not going through that again, not for you, not for *Fact*, not for anyone. It's over. Dead.'

'So was Labesse.'

Catherine stood up.

'All right! We'll forget him – but get the story, Cath. You can't throw away the lead you've got on this.' Luman studied her face. 'OK, bad memories. I can see that.' He hesitated, then, in a gentler tone, said, 'You told me, that night, that you would have given anything to have met the man who could change people's lives just by the look in his eyes.'

'You don't forget a thing, do you?'

'Do you still feel that way? Wouldn't you like to know why your man couldn't stay with you? The reason's out there, locked away in a monastery on the Mount of Olives. Take the job, Cath, go there, find the key to unlock the gates on Labesse. Make a heavy donation.'

She glanced down at Luman, a fleeting look of contempt touching her face. 'If Labesse is who you think he is, money won't buy his time. You never really quite understood the story I told you, Luman. It didn't contain anything that even hinted at ... our values. It was above those. So far above that even human lives were worth sacrificing. That is where the real story lies. What could make ... Michael's actions worth the cost in human life.'

'Not what,' said Luman. 'Who. And you know damn well who.'

'There is a way Labesse might see me,' she said after a moment. 'But I won't go for you, Luman. If I go I'll go for me.'

'Just go! So how?'

'My business.'

Luman relit his cigar. 'OK.'

'What about a visa?'

He opened a drawer in his desk and withdrew her passport, which he normally kept in his wall-safe along with those of his other journalists for just such an occasion. He held it out.

'You were sure of yourself!' she said, frostily. 'It's Monday morning. What did you do, seduce the Israeli ambassador's secretary?'

Luman grimaced. 'She looks like Golda Meir did – on a bad day. Hell no. But what religion do you think our backers practise?'

She took the passport, placed it in her shoulder-bag, then held her hand out. 'Ticket?'

'First-class, just to show my appreciation. Pick it up at the El Al desk at Heathrow.' He pushed his chair back and stood up, steering her to the door. 'Park your new baby at the airport – we'll pick up the tab – that'll give you a chance to open her up a little. But don't get arrested, OK?' He tugged at his sleeve. 'You've got just over three hours to pack a bag and make the flight. Enjoy the ride, Cath – and get the story!'

'Perhaps Labesse is not the same man. Michael never discovered his name before he –'

Luman turned her towards him, grinned wolfishly and kissed her full on the mouth for too long. She let him because it crushed her clamouring memories for that brief moment.

'I guess I'll never know what I missed out on that night,' Luman said ruefully, releasing her.

She gave a small shake of her head.

'Too bad.'

Luman walked her to the lift, his arm linked tightly with hers. He pressed the call-button and when the lift arrived kissed her again – this time lightly.

'I still want my job,' she warned, entering the lift.

'It'll be waiting. On your way. And watch out for Arabs in the departure lounge. They'll do anything for a blond lay!'

Catherine raised one finger to him but the lift door shut him from her. She leaned back against the panelling. Damn you, Michael Cardin, she said inside, then repeated it aloud.

Outside, the pavement was spotted with rain and she ran through the drops for her car. I thought I was all cried-out, she thought, furious with herself. All through. A dried-up woman, pushing thirty, with a taste for things material. And love, when I can be bothered with it, is a three-letter word that ends with X; and washes away in the bath afterwards.

In her car she turned the ignition key and jabbed the accelerator fiercely, trying hopelessly to obliterate the sound of a voice in her head which she had loved so deeply that she would have relinquished the gift of her return-ed sight to hear it now. As she drove, she wept for the body and the face she had felt so close, so tenderly, yet had never once seen. 'Oh shit, Michael! Why do you always make me cry?' she yelled aloud, and drove even faster.

Vatican Radio's transmission centre is situated at Santa Maria di Galeria near Rome, covering an area of more than one thousand acres – roughly ten times the size of Vatican City itself. Here, a winged statue of the Angel Gabriel, the patron saint of communications, stands guard, watchfully, over twenty-nine sky-scraping towers; a giant, skeletal steel cross bearing four dome-shaped receiving aerials beamed in on St Peter's Basilica; and a 175-ton twin-pylon rotating aerial which is the largest of its kind in the world, capable of transmitting a radio signal to any point on earth.

Father Phillipe Recamier sat in the front passenger seat of Sostituto Benito Marco's green Alfa Romeo saloon and studied the wires of the massive aerial, shining like a steel curtain between their twin supporting towers, as if nothing of the conspiracy had been explained to him.

Recamier was a hard, dour man, a tall, wiry Jesuit with a sharp brain, an eye for detail and a sensitive ear for information of a clandestine nature. His hatchet face bore scars which he never discussed and few asked about, for, like many other men of God, he had found his salvation late and by a circuitous route. He might, if he had not taken vows, easily have become a dangerous and successful espionage agent.

It was Recamier who, during the explosive Gdansk workers' riots in Poland, infiltrated that country and, by means he would not disclose, got information back to Rome which was transmitted to the Polish workers informing them of events they might otherwise never have known. It was he, also, who smuggled out and broadcast the actual text of Charter Seventy-Seven, the Czech dissidents' plea for human rights, thereby incurring the wrath of the Kremlin.

There was no doubt whatsoever in the mind of Benito Marco that Phillipe Recamier was the ideal man for the task of discovering any secrets or indiscretions in the life of Pierre Labesse.

'You understand the urgency of this matter?' Marco questioned.

Recamier lowered his head sombrely.

'Where will you start?'

'At the beginning, Monsignor. Father Labesse was born and raised in the corsair town of St Malo in France. I shall begin there, naturally.'

'Why waste time? What we're looking for will not be found in his childhood.'

'The key to any man's life lies in his childhood,' Recamier stated flatly, watching two crows tumble in a flurry of black feathers from the aerial wires. Close to the ground they broke from each other and soared away to the right-hand supporting tower. There, the conflict rested.

Marco placed a slim manicured hand on the folder he had placed on the Alfa's dashboard. 'Everything about his life is in there. It is very comprehensive, fully documented. The Holy Father had personally seen to the preparation of this history for the purposes of Labesse's beatification. Of course, for the early part of Labesse's life, we have had to rely on Labesse's own statements and those of the sisters who cared for him. Oddly, there is a period between his late teens and mid-twenties which is sketchy – there's a record of army service, of course, but little or no record of regular employment. He travelled on foot a great deal, this he mentions in the record for that time; a bit like an American hobo, from the sound of it. Perhaps he was searching for God? He came to us not long after this period.'

'Reminiscent of Our Lord Jesus,' Recamier said.

Marco looked at him sharply. 'What?'

'The period where the history is unclear. It is reminiscent of Jesus's life.'

Marco glowered, then shifted his attention back to the folder. 'Everything is in there,' he reaffirmed. 'Everything we know.'

Recamier turned to face the Sostituto. 'What is in there is what Labesse wanted us to know – that part of his life before he came to the Church, I mean. And there isn't a man born who tells the entire truth of his life. Some parts he omits because he has genuinely forgotten. Others he has fabricated, then believes in his fabrication for so long that the lie is the only truth he knows. Then, of course, there is the genuine lie – but that is both the most difficult and the most easy to discover. Difficult because, if it is an important lie, he will have covered it very well indeed – and in experience men only go to great lengths in covering lies if they are, to them, important. And easy, Monsignor, because to cover a lie one must spin a web of lies and all one needs to destroy a web is to grasp one weak thread. Do you know which men are the most dangerous of liars, Monsignor? I shall tell you. Those whose lives hold secrets which they then reveal in such a way that others will believe them to be lies. That way, they are completely safe.'

Recamier's eyes had drifted away from the Sostituto's face as he had spoken but now they came back, dark and hard. 'You wish to leave now Monsignor, but before you do, you believe it is necessary to warn me that you hold certain information on me which would destroy my life?'

Marco opened his mouth but Recamier closed it with his next statement.

'You have discovered that I killed a girl – my lover – and that I did not report this fact to the French authorities. Instead, I did what many men in that situation do. I joined the Legion – from which, later, I escaped. Which makes a double count against me in the outside world. You know this because, after I found God, my conscience forced me to make confession of my mortal sin. It does not matter who informed you, because I understand that every priest has a conscience and sometimes this is greater than the confidence of the confessional.' Recamier smiled. 'Or perhaps, Monsignor, you were your own informant? Perhaps it was your ear I poured out my troubled spirit to?'

Marco said, 'You were truly repentant and God forgives sinners who repent. It is finished.'

Recamier's shrewd eyes fixed on the Sostituto. 'God might forgive me, but you still have that information.'

'All I ask is that you say nothing regarding this inquiry to anyone. Do this and I will continue to say nothing.'

Recamier lifted the folder from the dashboard and opened the car door. 'I'll do your work for you, Monsignor, but not because you have the means to destroy me. The Holy Catholic Church is my life and my saviour. For you, I believe that it is a vehicle for your ambition. Your background ordained that you should rise to a position of power, whether it be in the Church or the state. You were born to it. I had no such privilege. Yet, I will do anything – anything – to stop the destruction of my faith. I shall contact you daily, Monsignor. Goodbye.'

Benito Marco watched the tall, slightly stooped figure lope away. He started the Alfa's engine and drove past him, raising a hand in farewell. Recamier did not return the gesture.

Recamier flew direct from Rome to Paris, arriving in good time to make the connecting link to the French capital, then had to wait for a little less than an hour for the train to St Malo.

He barely noticed the journey for, apart from an occasional distraction caused by rowdy students, his mind was firmly locked in concentration on the file which Benito Marco had given him. From this it became plain that

Labesse certainly had a habit of disappearing. He disappeared during the period Marco had mentioned but also later, after he had come to the Catholic Church. There were two distinct vanishing-points: the first China and the second South-east Asia. Of course the Church knew in which country he had landed, but, after he travelled into the interior – usually with a number of nursing nuns purloined from the central Catholic missions – his whereabouts were unknown for months on end. The matter of the nuns had caused a minor furore at least twice, for bitter complaints had been forwarded to Rome regarding Labesse's 'uncaring' and 'arrogant' attitude to the ageing priests who administered these central missions. In fact, Labesse had answered these charges at a later date by pointing out that the particular missions in question were overstaffed and his need – and those of 'his poor' – were greater. He had been exonerated of any blame, and the two administrators in question had subsequently had their staff quota reviewed. It appeared that Labesse, for all his lowly standing, could exert influence at the top.

Recamier noted these incidents but placed little importance on them, for he knew that, by reputation, Pierre Labesse was a man who invited the jealousy of others. His powerful, though reserved, personality virtually guaranteed this. But the business of the nuns deserved closer attention. Recamier accepted the fact that it was not unheard of for nuns – of various ages – to devote themselves to one single priest and treat his words and deeds as if they were the Holy Scripture itself; and this failing, though relatively rare, seemed only natural in women who had disavowed their basic nature. Yet, in the case of Labesse, it should not be ignored. Beneath the surface of all the deeds of men, there are often two reasons for performing them, Recamier mused, repeating one of his favourite beliefs: one clear and enlightened, the other blurred and dark – and usually unrecognized.

He read on:

Labesse had been raised as an orphan at a Catholic orphanage and school outside St Malo, cared for and tutored there by the nuns. He was not an exceptional student – although one of his reports noted that he had ability which he seemed wilfully to suppress – but it seemed he had an inner calmness which made him popular, even sought after, by both children and nuns alike.

The young Labesse also had a natural bent toward healing – not of the *spiritual* kind, one sister had written pedantically – regularly treating cuts and bruises suffered by school-fellows in the rough and tumble of orphanage life where games equipment was ramshackle and old. Pierre always seem to be on hand in the event of some minor accident with a soothing ointment, a spotlessly clean white bandage and comforting words spoken in his gentle accent-less French. Strangely, though, his patients' wounds healed surprisingly quickly.

The sisters thought he might have had a vocation for the priesthood, even at that early stage of his life, but as he developed into his teens he showed little interest in the discipline of the Church. Then, inevitably, the army claimed him for the statutory period of conscription into national service but, after this period and his induction into the priesthood some seven years later, the file was sparse and without verifiable facts. Only Labesse's own explanation was set down on record and that, at best, was – as Benito Marco had accurately described it – sketchy.

So what *did* the mature young man do, Recamier pondered, for nigh on five years? He discounted the extra two because those would have been taken up by both his actual preparation for priesthood and, before that, as Recamier knew himself from personal experience, long months of thought and consideration. And soul-searching.

Now go slowly, Recamier told himself sternly. Be steady and thorough. Go back a little. The army. Labesse's military record gave away immediately what was later to become fact. The sisters had not been so wrong after all for here, in black and white, was the first real sign that Labesse was listening to the Lord's insistent, but probably unclear, voice. He had immediately rejected any military role – claiming objections of a religious nature – but had accepted training as a medic. He had seen action in Indo-China but had no citations for bravery under fire, or so

100

the record stated. Recamier sniffed here. In *that* war the wounded were usually hacked to bits before a medic could get to them. Nobody was going to be a hero for a dismembered corpse!

So, finally, Labesse completed his duty to his country and was demobbed.

Recamier turned the page and once again was faced with too few details covering too long a period of time. Very well. He would concentrate on Labesse's period in the wilderness, as he termed it, using again – and he imagined Marco's disapproval – the parallel with the life of Christ.

Every man tends to return to his roots at moments of great decision – or disillusionment – so St Malo was definitely the right place to begin. Labesse's contemporaries or friends, if he had any (Recamier made this observation for, even on paper, Labesse had a singleness about him which seemed to preclude any deep relationship), might fill in the vacuum of the missing years.

The first place to visit, he decided as the train pulled into his destination, was the orphanage. Learn first about the boy, and the man would come to him, step by step.

As the Jesuit stepped down onto the low platform he felt a fierce chill pass through him though the sun was shining and the leaves of late summer still hung tenaciously from the trees. The sudden cold had stopped him dead. He fell to the ground as a blow struck him, the papers from the folder scattering.

'Watch where you're going!' Recamier shouted in anger at the student who had barged into him then ran on, unconcerned.

The student stopped abruptly, turned and sauntered back, standing over Recamier and not bothering to help the Jesuit to his feet.

Recamier gathered in the papers and drew himself upright, dusting down his black cassock. 'You should look where you're going!' he complained.

'You were in the way, *priest*,' the student said coldly. The others of his party had gathered around now, oddly menacing.

'Go away!' Recamier snapped. 'Get away with you!'

'What'll you do if we don't?' asked one of them, a pretty, dark girl. 'Condemn us to burn in hell? Shut us out of heaven?'

They burst into laughter suddenly, all at once, as if they had a secret joke he could not understand.

Recamier pushed forward, suitcase first, parting them, but they swaggered beside him, tauntingly. Then they were chanting and he could not understand their words until the same girl ran before him, backwards, holding up that evening's Paris paper. The same words as they chanted were printed in heavy black newsprint and, below them, a fuzzy, out-of-date photograph of a young fair-haired man who had uttered them.

'Heaven is *here*!' the students chanted as they quickened their step to match Recamier. Before the Jesuit knew it, he was running. '*Heaven is here! Heaven is here!*'

As he finally escaped them at the barrier, Recamier had one searing thought: the man he had come to find had found him!

3

Jonathan Barton strode swiftly into the huge newsroom of ITN's London studios in Wells Street, greeted by the feverish stutter of typewriters and tickertape machines.

Mary Edgington, the editor for the day, stopped him. 'There's still no reaction from the Vatican on the Labesse story. They're stalling. No doubt about it.'

'So how far do you want to go on it?' Barton queried, fending off the attentions of a make-up girl who had spotted the shine on his forehead.

'All the way! This could be as big a story as the assassination attempt of the Pope in '81.'

'Bigger,' Barton observed. 'Popes die all the time – but we've never had a saint raised from the dead!'

Mary Edgington frowned. 'Rome hasn't confirmed that he *was* canonized.'

'But we have the quote from the monastery in Jerusalem. That was firm enough. There's no way we'll be in trouble on that. Where's our theological expert?'

'Standing by. Nervous as hell!'

Barton grinned. 'Hell? Heaven is the place that's making him nervous.'

'I hope he makes all the right noises; we're ahead of the Beeb on this one.'

'Don't worry. I'll pressure him just enough to make him say something controversial.'

'Not *too* far, Jon, there's a lot of Catholics out there who're going to be pretty shaken up by this.'

'Not *just* Catholics, darling. If only half of what Labesse is supposed to have said is believed to be genuine, then ninety-nine point nine per cent of Christian dogma goes right out of the window.'

'Just be careful,' urged Mary.

'Don't worry. Is Bailey Boy here yet?'

'Arrived twenty minutes ago. Looked like he'd come through a rugger scrum backwards.'

'Who were in the opposing team?'

'Half the world's press, by the sound of it. Even the Russians flew a camera crew out to Jerusalem.'

'They would. It's good-news week for them, isn't it? "Heaven is here"? They're bound to interpret that as the true meaning of communism.'

'They have already. PRAVDA has put out a special edition using Marxist arguments as the basis for Labesse's statement.'

'Good! That'll make a good tailpiece. I'll work on something.' Barton glanced at his watch. 'Where's Sara?'

'In the studio, having the finishing touches done to her hair-do.'

'I'll go through and rehearse the "bongs" with her.'

'Remember to go easy, Jon,' Mary reminded.

'Everybody downstairs!' the senior director called, heading her team of floor managers and production assistants to the ground-floor studio-control.

In the studio itself, a floor manager brushed a few specks of dandruff from Barton's dark suit as he rehearsed the lead items between the chimes – or 'bongs' as they were known – of Big Ben.

In an adjoining studio the vision mixer sat before the huge console of switches and buttons, calmly studying the twenty-eight television screens which showed a mosaic of the items each film, camera and videotape would contribute to that evening's programme.

'Fifteen seconds. Stand by,' the senior director's voice murmured in Barton's earpiece. Everywhere the usual air of tension had built up to a new peak. The feeling that that evening's lead story could be, perhaps, the most bizarre ever transmitted had reached fever pitch.

The commercials faded and the chimes of Big Ben rang out.

Barton began, after the fifth chime, 'Risen saint speaks with God. Declares, "Heaven is here!" ' As the remaining 'bongs' rang out, Barton inserted the leads for the other news items, then, almost impatiently, despite his known coolness on camera, he returned to the main story. 'So, is heaven *here*? Will man reach a "state of perfection here on earth"? A so-called risen saint says – *yes*! Meanwhile the Vatican remains strangely silent. So where does Christianity go from here? We ask a leading theologian. Also an exclusive eye-witness account of how Father Pierre Labesse, the monk claimed by the Father Superior of his order to be a risen saint, died, then, after a nine-hour interval, returned to life.'

Barton paused, lowered his head to his papers, in momentary silence, then raised his head once more, his face set and eyes intense. It was a technique he used to build suspense and he performed it masterfully.

He spoke: 'In the Holy City of Jerusalem yesterday, an obscure Roman Catholic monk who has been in a state of coma for more than a decade was declared officially dead by an Israeli doctor – only to return to life nine hours later in the most dramatic circumstances. Here now, back from Jerusalem less than one hour ago, is our reporter Richard Bailey with a first-hand account of this extraordinary phenomenon of a man who rises from the dead to find himself canonized and then makes a statement which has shaken the Christian world to its foundations.'

Richard Bailey's face was drawn with fatigue, which even cosmetics could not disguise. His voice, too, showed his exhaustion, his normally clear and precisely enunciated delivery marred by a raw huskiness – the inevitable result of trying to make his own questions heard above the vocal barrage which had assaulted the dismayed monks outside their normally peaceful retreat on the Mount of Olives. This, and the furious dash to Israel and back in the dry, pressurized air of a jetliner.

Despite this severe handicap, he made his report with the urgency of a man who had been present at an historic event:

'Pierre Labesse, only twenty-four hours ago, was a name which few people outside the closed confines of the Roman

Catholic Church could have known. Today, that name is splashed across the front pages of virtually every newspaper in the Christian world – and reportedly in many of the countries of the non-Christian world as well. Even the Soviet Union has covered this extraordinary happening.

'Yet little is known of Pierre Labesse, for the one state which should be hailing this unknown monk with joy has remained silent. That state is the Vatican.

'So, what *is* known of Pierre Labesse? Labesse was a missionary who tended to the spiritual – and human – needs of the poor in many countries over many years. Apparently, and there is no confirmed date or location on this at the present time, he lapsed into a coma after suffering at the hands of guerrillas whilst in the Far East or South-east Asia. His suffering was caused by crucifixion.'

Bailey paused, allowing his last words their full effect.

'Details of his rescue from the guerrillas have not been made available and unless the Vatican decides to break its silence and release them it is probable that we shall never know. What is known, beyond doubt, is that Father Pierre Labesse died – and was certified dead – for a period of *nine* hours. The previous record set for a person who revived after his life had been declared extinct stood at three hours and thirty-two minutes. That record has been shattered.

'At one minute past midnight in the first hour of Sunday morning, the machines which made life possible for Labesse while in coma were withdrawn. His ventilator was switched off, the intravenous drips removed, the cardiac monitor and encephalograph consulted for the last time. Pierre Labesse, finally, was allowed to die. And die he certainly did. I spoke with the Israeli doctor who carried out the tests on his body which are designed to determine death and eliminate error in this highly technological age when the fine line between life and death becomes less and less distinct with each advance in modern scientific medicine.'

Bailey relaxed, off camera now, as the videotape took up the story.

'Dr Levin,' asked Bailey's voice of a small, tense, overweight man, seated in a high-backed leather chair.

'Can you be absolutely certain that Father Labesse *was* dead at the time of your examination?'

'Beyond all reasonable doubt,' stated the physician. 'After the ventilator was switched off, there was approximately fifteen seconds of ventricular contraction – a classic syndrome. After this, the cardiac monitor ceased to register any heartbeat whatsoever and the EEG – the device which monitors the brain pattern or waves displayed a flat trace. However, Father Labesse has shown no brain activity for years.'

'This "flat trace" would signify so-called "brain death"?'

'Not necessarily. It merely informs us that that there is no activity in the brain.'

'But the heart had definitely stopped beating?' Bailey questioned, forcefully.

'Definitely, yes.'

'And at this point you considered Labesse to be dead?'

Levin raised a stubby, dry finger. 'At this point I carried out standard tests which would determine – beyond any doubt whatsoever – that all life had ceased.'

'In simple terms these would be . . . ?'

'The pupillary test – that is testing reaction of the pupils to light; reflex reactions – sharp blows with a patella hammer; cold water poured into the ear canal. I even touched the cornea of each eye with cotton wool as a final test.'

'And after these tests, did you have any reason to believe that Labesse might not be dead?'

'None whatsoever. My instructions, from the Father Superior, were that I must be absolutely certain before I certified that Father Labesse was truly dead. I was.'

'Then he was concerned, even at that stage, that life might not be extinct?'

Levin shifted uncomfortably. 'I'd overhead something earlier between the Father Superior and a senior monk. It seemed that the Vatican had issued instructions that there should be no doubt at all. None. Labesse, upon indisputable confirmation of his death, was to be canonized – canonized, that is, at the moment of actual death.'

107

'Yet, despite all your rigorous tests, Dr Levin, Pierre Labesse still lived?'

'No!' Levin reacted loudly, causing distortion on the microphone. 'He returned to life. Father Labesse was dead. As dead as any mortal can be!' He spread his hands hopelessly. 'Don't ask me to explain it. I cannot. The man was dead. For nine hours, dead! Now he is alive. Don't ask me how. I cannot give you any answer.'

'Would you say that this might be termed a "miracle", Dr Levin?'

Levin smiled. 'I practise medicine. Miracles I leave to God!'

Live again, in the studio, Bailey leaned forward and picked up his report as the videotape ended:

'Men have woken from a state of coma before. Men have also been declared dead and have subsequently – and inexplicably – returned to life. But no man who has returned from an apparent state of death has, within known history, been beatifed during the period of his coma so that, upon his death, he may be immediately canonized. In simpler terms, there has never before been a "risen saint" – as Father Labesse has been dubbed by the press.

'The Vatican, up to the present time, is remaining totally silent on this issue, neither confirming nor denying the canonization report. Labesse himself is being kept in seclusion but is, apparently, in good health, though understandably weak. No one outside the monastery – which stands coincidentally on the slopes of the Mount of Olives, the place where another victim of crucifixion, Christ Himself, is prophesied to reappear on earth in all His glory – has actually seen or spoken to him yet. However, the Father Superior held a brief news conference and what he had to say does seem to confirm that the supposed canonization was ordered by Rome. Also, as you will hear now, he reveals some remarkable facts of the actual "rising" of Pierre Labesse.'

Bailey's eyes flicked sideways to a monitor screen, which began displaying a scene of complete pandemonium, with flashbulbs exploding incessantly while microphones and small cassette recorders were thrust into the face of an ageing and obviously overwrought figure clad in a long oatmeal-coloured habit.

'On Sunday morning, at nine a.m.,' announced the Father Superior, 'Father Pierre Labesse was returned to us from the grave. According to the dictates of the Holy Father himself, our brother Pierre was beatified during the long period of his coma, brought on by injuries and suffering inflicted upon him by those lost souls who have refused the light of the Lord. He had suffered a living death in the Lord's name until, finally, he was released from this world.' The Father Superior's face suddenly beamed, becoming almost incandescent in the bright floodlights. 'And the Lord has returned him to us! We have no doubt that we have witnessed a true miracle in this holy place – a miracle by God Himself, confirmed by the bleeding of the cruel wounds of crucifixion at the moment of Father Pierre's return to this world.'

Bailey's voice on the videotape cut through the confusion. 'Have you received word from Rome confirming Father Labesse's canonization?'

The monk's eyes shifted away from the camera momentarily, then he shook his head.

'Are you expecting confirmation?' another voice yelled.

'I have nothing further to say at this time.'

Bailey called quickly, 'The words Father Labesse is reported to have said – "Heaven is here?" Is it true that he claims they have divine origin?'

'I cannot answer for him. In time he will speak for himself.'

'When?' shouted a dozen voices.

'Soon,' the Father Superior replied, calmly. 'Very soon.'

'Is it true that he believes he has actually spoken with God?' Bailey jumped in.

The monk nodded. 'He believes it.'

'Do you belive him?' Bailey's voice again, shouting now.

'I believe,' said the monk simply, then turned away and re-entered the monastery gate.

The studio monitor faded and Bailey addressed the

camera once more. 'One fact seems clear from the Father Superior's words: there is a distinct lack of communication between the Vatican and the monastery. This could be construed in a different way. There may be a difference of opinion – or possibly a rift – between this small order and the governing body of the Roman Catholic Church in the matter of Labesse, and I have no doubt at all that the Father Superior and his monks have been ordered to remain silent on this issue, an order which they are obviously not prepared to obey. The mystery of the Vatican's own silence, however, is not difficult to understand, because they are undoubtedly faced with a great, if not their greatest ever, dilemma. That is: How can they deny a papal edict – and remember, the Pope is considered to be infallible on religious issues – that declared Father Labesse be canonized upon his death, without completely undermining the Pope's supreme authority? Yet do they dare confirm the existence of a risen saint whose first words, *as a saint*, appear to contradict the very basis of their doctrine? In other words, to declare Labesse truly a saint risen from the dead – thereby accepting his words as having divine authority – would be tantamount to declaring the Holy Gospel a lie. For, if "Heaven *is here*", where then is Jesus Christ's promised "Kingdom of God"?'

'Superb,' the director whispered in the control room. 'Go to, Jon.'

Barton was ready, a man seated either side of him. 'Questions which need answering,' he began. 'And in the studio tonight, two men who will attempt to answer them. First, Dr Harold Lovelace, Reader in Divinity at Cambridge University. Dr Lovelace, can you comment on the extent of the damage which might be done to the Christian faith if the reported words of Father Labesse – we won't call him St Pierre yet – are given any credence?'

Lovelace was a thin, grey figure wearing a costly herringbone three-piece suit and affecting a pale blue hankerchief tucked into his right sleeve.

'If Rome decides to confirm Labesse's canonization, then every word the man utters will be a brick knocked out of the Vatican's walls. I said man because, until Rome confirms canonization, aloud and with no reservations, that is exactly what he is. However, let us put this whole business into perspective. Quite obviously, Father Labesse has suffered considerable and probably irreparable brain damage during his coma which has since been compounded by this so-called period of "death". I'm astonished that the man can speak at all when you consider for how long oxygen was cut off from his brain.'

'But,' Barton said, 'he did speak. Brothers of his order have made clear statements as to his words and we all know what those were. So, your answer then is, he could damage Christian belief.'

'Faith!' Lovelace corrected. 'Christian faith. If Christians believe this preposterous idea that heaven is here, they will, quite simply, lose faith in everything written in the New Testament. Most of that in the Old, also. But we cannot make any judgement yet because we do not know exactly what Labesse means. Does he mean that God's coming is imminent? Or does he mean – as the media have assumed – that heaven is physically here? In other words, that this world we live in, this time we exist in, is our ultimate state? Until now he has not clarified his statement but personally I hope to God that people dismiss all he says because, whatever interpretation one places on his words, the end result will surely be chaos!'

'Do you believe – as the monks have claimed – that he has spoken with God during his period of death?'

Lovelace made an agitated, impatient gesture. 'The man is confused. And the media are making far too much of this event. I believe that nothing can be gained by giving this sort of circus credence by reporting it seriously.'

'Dr Harold Lovelace, thank you.' Barton swung around in his chair. 'Also with us in the studio tonight – and very much at the last moment – a Roman Catholic priest noted for his outspoken, even revolutionary views on his own Church. Father Timothy O'Hara. Father Timothy, thank you for taking the time to be with us at such short notice this evening.'

The dark Irishman dipped his head at the camera, his

tight curls a solid iron-grey. His complexion was sallow, almost jaundiced.

'Father, I understand that in your work as a Jesuit priest in South-east Asia, you actually met Pierre Labesse.'

'I did.' O'Hara's voice was extraordinarily deep, with the barest hint of his Irish homeland.

'Can you give us an idea of what the man is like? Was there any outward sign then that Labesse was someone out of the ordinary?'

O'Hara gave a wide smile which almost became laughter. 'Nothing was ordinary about Pierre Labesse!'

'So even then – some fifteen years ago is it? – he had something special about him?'

'He was always "special", if that is the correct word.'

'What is the correct word, Father, with which to describe him?'

'Apart,' O'Hara replied without hesitation. 'He was with us – yet he was not of us.'

'How, exactly? Can you give us an example?'

Again the priest's reply was immediate – yet not delivered rashly. It was spoken clearly and seemed preconsidered. Barton was rocked by it.

'In the same way that Jesus Christ was apart from man.'

'You would compare Pierre Labesse to Jesus Christ!' Barton exclaimed.

'In his singleness, yes. I worked with Father Labesse, yet I did not know him. No one knew him. Somehow he was – apart from us. Perhaps even above us: myself, the sisters who were devoted to him, the wretched poor and sick he tended.'

The studio had fallen silent. In the control room the director had her hands pressed hard to the console, willing Barton to break it. 'For God's sake say something!'

Barton fingered his earpiece as the frantic plea came through. He said, 'Father Timothy, could it be possible that Pierre Labesse might be speaking the *truth*? That he might *not* be suffering from brain damage and delusions, as Dr Lovelace has suggested?'

O'Hara eased himself lower in his chair, obviously relaxed and unaware of any pressure upon himself.

112

'Obviously Father Labesse suffered injuries. I was not there personally but I heard – and later saw – what state his body was in when he was rescued.'

'Who rescued him?' Barton asked quickly.

'Why, the Americans, naturally. Who else could have done?'

'Then this was in Vietnam?'

O'Hara nodded. 'The mission station was in the north. The communists butchered them all. Labesse had been crucified. This was the story I heard – much later. But I've no doubt it is the truth. Such things happened there.'

'How did the Americans get involved?'

'I'm not certain but the story was that an American aircraft crashed in the area and the crew had to be airlifted out. They crashed close to the mission presumably and radioed for help. Labesse was also rescued. When I passed through Saigon some months later, I inquired for more details, but everyone was too busy losing the war to bother with a curious visiting priest.'

'But you did find out that Labesse was alive?'

'I did not. I was told he was dead. Later, when I visited Jerusalem and the monastery of his order, I became aware of the truth. He was alive but in a deep coma. All this was many years ago of course.'

'Have you see him in the monastery since?' Barton urged.

'On one other occasion. I did not repeat it again. It was too distressing to see such a man in . . . that state. I am glad that the Holy Father decided to end his life.'

Barton leaned forward, towards the Irishman. 'But Labesse's life did not end, did it, Father? He died for nine hours and has risen again?'

O'Hara gave a twisted ironic smile. 'Nine hours, the number of hours Christ spent suffering on the cross.'

Barton leaned even further toward the priest. 'Father Timothy, let me get this absolutely correct. Are you implying that there is some . . . connection . . . some parallel between Jesus Christ, the Son of God, and a French missionary priest named Pierre Labesse?'

'We are all connected with Jesus,' O'Hara replied with another smile.

'That is not quite what I meant.'

'I know exactly what you meant, Mr Barton. What I believe is that we are witnessing the most important event in our understanding of God since the birth and ultimate crucifixion of our Lord Jesus Christ.'

'And Labesse's words: "Heaven is here"? What do you take them to mean?'

'Mr Barton, do we understand all that Christ said?'

'Father Timothy?' Barton exclaimed. 'Surely you are not saying that Pierre Labesse may be Christ returned?'

'He may be. It is time.'

'Then, if we go by what you have just expressed, we may have to believe in the words of this . . . obscure French missionary!'

'Mr Barton,' O'Hara said slowly. 'For centuries, we have believed implicitly in the words of an "obscure" Jewish carpenter!'

'The switchboard will be jammed in seconds,' the director breathed as Barton thanked the two men and moved on to that day's other stories. She turned to Mary Edgington, who was standing to her right. 'I rather think that Father O'Hara is due for instant excommunication.'

A male voice to the director's left muttered, 'He's taken the Vatican's finger out of the dyke, that's for certain. They'll have to say something now.'

Mary Edgington said nothing, her face troubled in the hushed gloom as she watched the flickering screens.

Barton continued on camera, 'The Ministry of Defence has announced that RAF Phantom jets pursued three Argentine Air Force Mirage fighters who had entered the exclusion zone yesterday. One of the Argentine jets exploded while still some distance from the RAF Phantoms and outside the zone. The new Argentine junta has accused Britain of shooting down their aircraft and killing the pilot, but this has been strenuously denied by Whitehall. The Ministry of Defence insist that the Argentine Mirage collided with an unidentified aircraft which appeared suddenly on radar, then disappeared after the explosion of

114

the fighter. At present no other aircraft has been reported missing, although an air and sea search is being carried out in the area of the explosion. A late report from the Falklands has stated that search vessels and aircraft are being harassed by the Argentinians themselves. The most likely explanation for the mid-air explosion is that the Argentinians had another aircraft approaching the zone, and because of the extremely high-speed pursuit in progress it was not identified as being on a collision course by the Mirage pilot. The RAF don't hold out much hope of finding any wreckage because of the ferocity of the explosion and present weather conditions.

'This latest incident in the protracted state of tension which continues between Britain and Argentina, since the military coup in that country has rekindled the Falklands issue, pushes any hope of a peaceful settlement further away than ever.

'Now, world news . . .'

The telephone by the director's elbow buzzed softly. 'Yes?' she inquired, lifting it. 'Thank you. I guessed as much.' She put the receiver down. 'Switchboard jammed,' she confirmed to Mary Edgington, then passed the message to Barton via his earpiece with an instruction to announce it over the air.

Barton received the message and, pausing between items, urged viewers not to telephone ITN. Then, he continued, 'In Moscow, Chairman Vaigauskas has launched yet another scathing attack on the Israeli government regarding Israel's military advance across Syria's border. He also said that the Soviet Union is prepared to stop – by military means if necessary – Israel's imperialist adventures against neighbouring Arab states. Libyan leader General Gaddafi has hailed Chairman Vaigauskas's words as being the "beginning of the end for the illegal state of Israel".

'Latest figures by the recently established Council for the Alleviation of World Poverty announced today indicate that almost two thirds of the world's population is nearing starvation level. The Council concludes that, unless immediate and drastic steps are taken, these latest figures are a recipe for economic disaster.

'A study conducted by the World Council of Churches into constantly rising levels of crime and immorality gives cause for great concern. The very fabric of civilization, the report says, is in danger of being ripped apart unless this trend is halted.

'Both America and the Soviet Union have announced substantial boosting of their nuclear arsenals. Present stocks held by both superpowers are – even at current levels – well above the number needed for the so-called Mutually Assured Destruction or MAD factor.

'One late item just in: His Holiness the Pope is suffering from exhaustion complicated by an influenza virus and will be confined to his private apartments, not seeing anyone other than his personal physician and staff for an undefined period. The Vatican has stated that there is no cause for concern regarding the Pontiff's health at this stage and the confinement is merely a precautionary measure. During his confinement the affairs of the Roman Catholic Church will be conducted by His Eminence Cardinal Secretary of State, Georgio Cinalli. No response to the strange case of Father Labesse, the so-called risen saint, has been made as yet.

'Finally *Pravda*, the official publication of the Soviet Communist Party, has hailed the words of Pierre Labesse – the controversial "Heaven is here" statement – as being a "true recognition of Marxist principles". Heaven, *Pravda* claims, is no more than the peaceful co-existence of the workers of the world after they have finally won the battle of oppression in the historical class struggle between the workers and their capitalist oppressors. This battle, *Pravda* states, is virtually over, the capitalist system is dying and the day of the workers' paradise is here.'

Barton smiled at the camera. 'Well, I suppose if ever there was a time for the return of Christ, it couldn't be more welcome than right now! Good night.'

The studio lighting faded as the *News at Ten* theme music began.

Barton said a quick farewell to Lovelace and Father O'Hara, who had both stayed to watch the rest of the

116

programme, then made his way to the ground-floor studio-control.

Mary Edgington was waiting for him. 'Well?' she asked.

'Well what?' queried Barton.

'O'Hara? Don't you think he went a bit over the top?'

'He's known for going over the top.'

'Jonty,' she said, calling him by the familiar name she only used when she was deadly serious about something. 'Tell me I've got a sneaky, devious mind, if you like, but I've got the feeling we've been set up.'

'Set up by who?'

'Rome.'

Barton grinned. 'You have got a sneaky, devious mind!'

'Listen to me. As a risen saint, Labesse is believable – weird but believable. The facts are there and they can't be denied. That doctor's tests, etc., OK?'

'OK. So? Where's the set-up?'

'People – believers – can accept Labesse as a risen saint; he's still human, all he did was die for a while then woke up again. All right, he's a phenomenon, I agree, but he's still one of us! But Jonty, if people are told he's Christ returned, he'll be treated as a nut. Nobody will believe a word he says.'

'Except other nuts.'

'Exactly! That's my point. Or rather, Rome's. They might want that. The way he is now he's just too damn hot to handle – but if they can relegate him into left-field somewhere, where only the lunatic fringe take him seriously, they have effectively defused the situation.'

'You're saying that O'Hara was a plant. He'd written his story beforehand?'

'Or it had been written for him.'

'What about Lovelace, then. Is he in on it?'

'I doubt it. Lovelace is a prim, slightly eccentric don whom most people in tele-land will think is an old queen who studies the Christian Church because it's a sure way of getting a regular supply of choirboys. He's not convincing – but O'Hara *is*. *Too* damn convincing!'

'Well, I admit I believed him. Not what he was saying, but I believed he meant it.'

Mary nodded. 'That's how he came over all right. A lot of people will have watched him and, right now, are making judgements. Maybe wrong judgements.'

Barton put an arm around her. 'You know something? You worry too much.'

Outside, in Wells Street, Timothy O'Hara stepped into a waiting car. The passenger beside him in the rear tapped the glass partition and the driver pulled away from the kerb.

'I saw it at my club,' said the passenger. 'Went very well, I thought. Just the right amount of sincerity but a hint of fanaticism, just enough to cast doubt. Excellent, well done. Heavens, that man Lovelace becomes more insufferable by the year. You'll hold yourself available, Father, for any further interviews we'd like you to attend?'

'Of course, Eminence.'

The English cardinal relaxed against the cushions. 'Must be pleasant putting up at a decent hotel after some of the squalor you've been used to in your work.'

Father O'Hara nodded his iron-grey head as the car sped through darkened London.

4

Father Phillipe Recamier sat across from the aged nun at the plain wooden table, listening attentively to her every word, committing everything to memory and nothing at all to paper.

The nun was as old as Recamier had imagined her to be, older, yet her mind had remained sharp, her recollection accurate.

Occasionally she would gesture with her leathery hands, knuckles swollen and deformed by the disease which had attacked her so cruelly in her later years, leaving her crooked and pain-wracked, so that even the act of kneeling in prayer needed all her courage.

But, most of all, the pain was evident in her eyes; green Irish eyes washed grey by time and fading sight. The spectacles she should have worn stayed on the table for, at that moment, she needed only to see inward – and there her vision was clarity itself.

'I loved him,' she stated, her French perfect. 'We all did. It was impossible not to, you understand. His gentleness was what did it of course. If he touched you – which he rarely did – it was as if the sun had touched your skin. More than touched. Deeper. A power.' She smiled brightly, as she had done constantly throughout the interview. But not for the benefit of Recamier. For herself and for her memory, which threw up pictures of a boy – startlingly clear images which surprised her with their absurd reality. A lean, fair boy who stood apart from the roughage heaved into the orphanage by so-called human beings who did not – could not – understand that, when they walked away into the security of their own grubby lives, they were leaving behind a life! A small, living person with little past of any worth and a future, at best, uncertain.

She and her sisters became surrogate mothers from that instant, doing their very best to show love, and usually, because of the damage already done to the little unfortunates, failing.

'Pierre was different,' she said, coming back.

'How?' Recamier inquired patiently, pushing the urgency of his quest – and its murky reason – far back into his mind. 'Different how?'

'He came to us as a baby. A baby left on our doorstep. A story such as one might read in the newspapers.'

'Except nobody came forward to reclaim him. No remorseful mother with too many mouths to fill? No young girl who had slipped?'

'The Boche,' she said. 'They were here then. There was a war then – how many remember any more?'

He inclined his thin face sympathetically. 'Indeed,' he murmured.

'The child could have been the bastard son of one of them,' she offered. 'Born of a local girl. The fair complexion, the hair, the blue eyes?' She raised her shoulder, wincing with the movement.

Recamier caught the shift in her eyes, declaring her detour from the truth. He fixed his stare on her. 'You have some other theory? A feeling, perhaps, regarding his parents? Something you discovered later?'

The old nun twisted her frail body and the curtain lifted off her pain, then dropped again. But something else fell with it – a thin veil of suspicion. 'In Rome, how do they view this child? This very special child – now a man? A very special man. The purpose of your mission is still unclear to me, Father.'

'I have explained already.'

'Please, explain once more; my mind is old and does not grasp things so easily.'

It grasps things well enough, Recamier thought. Too well, perhaps? He answered, 'Rome must know everything regarding Pierre Labesse. If he is to be called a saint, then no corner of his life may be secret.'

'If?' she reacted sharply. 'Is is not so already?' Do the

newspapers lie? Our brothers in Jerusalem? Do they lie also? No, he is already a saint!'

'Still, we must know.'

'We? The Holy Father? Who is the we in this case, please?'

'The Holy Catholic Church. It must know.'

'Ah! The councils of power. Father, sometimes even men of God can be far removed from Him. Perhaps the words Pierre has spoken are not welcome to such men – coming from the mouth of a . . .'

'Risen saint?' Recamier suggested. 'His words need understanding. Possibly there is some deeper meaning to them. He shall have every opportunity to explain himself.'

'An inquisition?' asked the nun, her eyes glittering now, and Recamier saw, past the pain, past the anger: fear.

'He has been crucified once,' she pleaded. 'Would you do it again?'

'Do not forget yourself!' Recamier snapped, harshly. 'I am sent from Rome! It is not for you to ask anything of me. It is I who have come to you for answers.'

The old nun fell silent, accepting the rebuke, but, Recamier sensed, building her defences also.

'Your theory please, Sister Theresa? This feeling you had regarding the child's parents?'

She looked straight at his eyes and knew he could defeat her. This was a man used to unlocking secrets, and both she and her secret were too old to withstand him. She pointed towards the window. 'Slaves,' she said, softly. 'The Boche brought them here from Germany. From every country they conquered. They used them over there – on the islands.'

'The Channel Islands.'

She nodded.

'And Labesse could have been the child of one of these? The son of a slave worker used by the Germans? A Jew? Labesse might have been born a Jew!'

'The son of a Jewess is born a Jew,' she stated.

'Why do you think this? There must be a reason?'

She did not answer.

Recamier placed both arms on the table, closing the

121

distance between them. 'Sister Theresa, I have asked a question and I demand the answer! The truth! Why do you believe he was a Jew!'

She remained silent but her tears were proof that she had broken.

Recamier let his voice become more gentle. 'There was something left with the child? A letter? Something you have kept hidden all these years? I can understand. You wished to keep the child – you loved it instantly. You wished there to be no problems about its being taken in? I charge you to speak the truth. If you lie, I shall know it.'

He watched her, waiting, willing her to break; knowing that a secret kept for so long would not be easily released.

Finally, and with her head held low to avoid his searing eyes, she found from somewhere in her clothing a tiny shining object wrapped in tissue. She placed it between them on the table. Recamier stared down at the small Star of David in gold.

'We baptized him into the Christian faith,' she wept. 'Only I knew the truth.'

'Did *he* know? Did you tell him? Sister, hear me, did you ever tell Labesse the truth regarding his origin?'

She shook her head, then wailed, 'He is a Christian! A priest of the Catholic Church! He made that choice himself!'

'Choice!' Recamier exclaimed. 'He had no choice! He was born into the Jewish faith, then abandoned. His mother had no choice. Was there a Jewish orphanage here? A synagogue? Under Nazi rule! She left him here because there was nowhere else. She left the Star of David to prove he was a Jew. She believed you would understand. Yet you betrayed her trust – and you betrayed him. You allowed him to be baptized as a Christian knowing he was a Jew. Hiding that fact. Lying before God! Did Pierre Labesse have a choice of faith? No! He had only what he knew.'

'There are Jewish Catholics, Father,' she cried.

Recamier slapped the table. 'Converts! Labesse was not converted; he was denied access to the faith of his people. He was tricked by you!'

'But he came to accept Christ. His work –'

122

'Accept!' Recamier blurted, his voice rising, both out of impatience with the old woman and a sense of triumph. 'What else could he accept? Christ was forced upon him. He knew no other way except that of Christ. If you had told him the truth, would he have still become a priest of the Catholic Church? Or would he have become, instead, a rabbi? Can you answer that question with all certainty?'

'He was a child of God. He is a child of God!'

'Sister,' Recamier said, rising. 'Pray that this is truly what he is.' He walked to the door of the room. 'You will await my return. There are other questions I must put to you. When that is done, you will return with me to Rome.' He closed the door on her weeping, his mind quickening, his step picking up the same urgency. He stopped once at the sombre office of the Mother Superior, gave his orders and left, releasing the reins on his sharp hunter's mind.

'Of course we have a record of him,' growled the Inspector of Gendarmes in St Malo. 'He had to register after the army demobbed him. First for his resident's permit then for his employment card.'

'Do you know where he lived and worked during this period?' Recamier inquired.

The inspector clicked his fingers at the gendarme waiting at the door grasping a folder not dissimilar to Recamier's own. 'Come on, give it to me!' he ordered, eager to show off his authority to his visitor from the Vatican – even if the fellow was only a radio producer with a dog collar instead of a tie. Still, good for public relations, and he would get his name mentioned on the air. He rifled through the pages, then stopped.

'Lived out of town on a small farm. Worked for his bed and keep. Night-time, he did bar work.' He peered over his heavy horn-rimmed spectacles and the file. 'Not what you might call a respectable establishment. For a man who was later to become a priest . . . and now . . .'

'You mean a bar with a bad reputation?' Recamier asked. 'Violence? Late drinking? Rowdy?'

The inspector coughed. 'Worse, I'm afraid. I don't think

you'd want to mention this in the programme you're planning. It was a . . . house of ill repute.'

'A bordello?'

'Well, yes. Precisely that.'

'Was he involved?'

'Involved? Um . . . perhaps not directly involved. But certainly he kept bad company. The girls . . . they liked him. They liked him very much indeed. He had a way with them.'

'Why do you say that?'

'They listened to him. He talked a lot. They spent hours listening to him.'

'That's all he did? Talked?' Recamier asked.

'Perhaps he helped them. Medically, I mean. He had the training from the army,' the inspector suggested.

'In what way? How could he help them medically? Why use an ex-army medic? I'm sure they could afford a qualified doctor.'

The inspector coloured, realizing too late he had been pushed into a corner. He did not like being at the wrong end of an interrogation. 'Father, this is a port. Many men come through here. It is easy for the girls to get . . . infected. You are a priest, Father, but I'm sure you follow me? Of course we have regular examinations for such things . . . but it happens. Also . . . things can go wrong for a girl in that business.'

'Inspector! Are you implying that Labesse performed abortions on those young women?'

'I cannot prove such a thing,' the inspector answered hurriedly. 'Who can prove anything with whores? They stick together. For those they love they will do anything. They would have protected him even if it meant jail for themselves.'

'So this is speculation only?'

'Naturally. But he worked there – that is a fact. He tended bar, cleaned up the mess and talked to the girls. Always talking.'

'What about?'

'Ask the whores yourself, Father. I never listened. My time was better spent.'

'Where is this establishment, Inspector?'

The policeman grinned. 'You wish to visit them? They'll have a fit!'

'I'll change my clothes. They won't know I'm a priest.'

Still the inspector's face remained doubtful.

'Inspector,' Recamier said impatiently. 'I live in Rome. In Rome we have more prostitutes than a street dog has fleas. I've heard confessions from whores!'

'That must have been interesting,'

Recamier allowed himself a smile, matching the policeman's smirk. 'The name of the bar, please?'

'The Bar Corsaire. But nobody calls it that here. Simone's place. Ask for Simone's and anyone will point the way.'

Recamier stood up and offered his hand. 'Thank you. I am grateful. I'll let you know in good time when we plan to broadcast the programme.'

'Father!' called the inspector when Recamier was already outside the door. 'Remember to change your clothes please!'

The Jesuit could still hear his bawdy laughter as he stepped onto the cobbled street.

Later, Recamier strolled along the pavement, the high rampart of the sea-facing defending wall towering gloomily to his left. It was early evening. The last straggling groups of tourists were in their hotels eating their meals; visiting yachtsmen were cooking in their cramped galleys; and the locals were relaxing in their homes, thankful that the tourist season was ending. Only hardened drinkers and the lonely ventured out at that hour.

Neon lights, bright and garish, illuminated him with their colours as he walked; jukeboxes thumped and shrieked, deafening him momentarily, when in their range, with music he could not comprehend. There is a certain madness in our world in this age, he thought, and the music is audible evidence of it. A warning of violence before the deed.

The Bar Corsaire was down a narrow side turning; a cobbled alley, wet with slops. Inside there was more music but this tuned low and very French. He might have stepped back in time. Behind the bar, on perches, were three large tropical birds – all alive, though from their lack of movement they might easily have been dead. He sat down on a bar stool and made noises at the nearest.

'They don't speak, m'sieur,' said a slim raven-haired woman behind the bar, farther down, where the lights were dimmest. 'It's the noise. They've given up. When it's busy you have to shout. It's like a war. Nautical people make a lot of noise when they reach land. They go mad from the silence out there.'

Close to, the woman was old. Painted and dyed to look twenty years younger. Her skin was like a canvas used too many times by different painters.

Recamier recognized the look of the prostitute: dried-out, body and soul both.

'Madame Simone?' he inquired.

'Mademoiselle. I am she. What is your pleasure?'

'Cognac – and perhaps some conversation?'

'Cognac you pay for, m'sieur – conversation is with the courtesy of the house. When it's this quiet, you get it anyway, even if you don't want it.' She poured his drink and the same for herself, studying him as she did this. 'Your clothes are Italian but your French is French? Have you come to St Malo to study birds?'

Recamier smiled, toasted the parrots, then sipped. 'Journalist. Freelance, based on Rome.'

'Freelance? That's hard. Do you make money at it?'

'Enough for my needs.'

'Then your needs must be limited, my friend – or you make much money.'

'I'm researching a story,' said Recamier. 'The life of a man.'

'Why bother? All men have the same story. Write your own, and call it his – no one will tell the difference.'

'This man is different.' Recamier flicked his eyes toward the soundless images on a small television set at the end of the bar. 'You might have heard his name on that. Perhaps you knew him? A man who died – but now lives.'

'Him?' Recamier saw her painted lips tighten, her over-made-up eyes lose their friendliness. 'Who sent you here?

126

The *flics?* That overeating clown of an inspector who likes my girls but not my prices?'

'No,' Recamier lied. 'I have a contact in Paris who knew Labesse at Dien Bien Phu in fifty-four. That's the story I'm after. Did something happen to Labesse in Indo-China which turned him towards the priesthood?'

Simone smiled pityingly. 'Listen, my friend from Rome. Pierre didn't suddenly decide that God was calling him. He always knew. It was simply a matter of when he made the jump.'

Recamier frowned, as if puzzled. 'But my contact gave me the impression that he was – well, not averse to more earthly pursuits? You are Simone, this is the well-known Simone's bar where he spent considerable time and – with respect – it is no temple of the Lord!'

For a second, anger flared in Simone's eyes, then was extinguished as if brought under control. 'You are the first,' she said coldly. 'But you won't be the last who will crawl down to the gutter looking for something to sensationalize about his life. I sell sex, m'sieur, and I admit it. I sell it openly, like fish on the slab – you and your kind sell it under the counter, hidden between fancy prose. Others like you will come here and they will all want to hear the same sordid story of how a saint came to spend time with whores. It is not unprecedented, you know, you're a journalist – read your Bible.' She studied Recamier again, swaying gently to the soft accordion music from a tape. One of the parrots shrieked and it seemed to bring her back to life. 'Very well! You shall know the truth. Perhaps you will believe it – perhaps not. But it is the truth and it should be printed as such.'

Recamier pushed his glass forward for another drink. 'I shall accept it as such.'

Simone refilled both glasses. This done, she told her story.

Later that evening, almost at midnight, Phillipe Recamier telephoned Benito Marco at his apartment in Rome. His words gave nothing away – certainly no details – but there was no doubt in Marco's mind by the end of the call that the Jesuit had succeeded in his quest. Recamier's insistence on returning to Rome was proof enough.

'When will you leave?' Marco asked.

'First thing in the morning. I'll be bringing someone with me. One of us. An old woman.' Recamier hesitated, sensing Marco's alarm. 'Her presence is vital. She guessed our purpose. She knew!'

The Sostituto fell silent, leaving Recamier with a crackling receiver by his ear for long seconds. Finally he spoke: 'Very well. Is the lady well enough to travel? Her advanced age?'

'She has no choice – nor do we. What she has to tell us must come from her lips alone.'

'It is in your hands,' replied Marco and hung up.

Recamier stared at the dead telephone, then replaced it on its stand. Again, the chill he had experienced at the station struck at him. But now it was stronger: a searing cold which near paralysed him. He was terrified. He fumbled with the doors of the cubicle, forcing them open, then stood breathing hard outside. Inside him was a realization which he pushed down so hard that his mind rejected it. He knew the source of the unearthly cold but he did not dare put a name to it. But he knew now his purpose was evil.

Back in his hotel he knelt beside the bed, praying as he had never done before. When he finally slept, he slept with his crucifix clutched in his hand so that, on the next morning, his palm was deeply scored with its imprint.

He faced the day, and its long journey, with trepidation, for his purpose – once so clear – had become obscure and seemed fraught with danger. He felt as he stepped out onto the street, turning his collar up against the steady drizzle, almost as if he were a soldier abandoned in enemy territory. He no longer felt that he was going home. Instead, Rome and the Vatican seemed like the heart of the enemy stronghold. Yet, like any loyal soldier, he marched forward because there was no other way to go. No retreat. He marched, and the chill moved with him.

5

From the summit of the Mount of Olives, overlooking old Jerusalem, Catherine Weston understood why the three great religions of the world, Christianity, Islam and Judaism, had all gravitated to this same ancient walled city. She experienced, as countless others had done, a near-mystical awareness of being nearer, here, to her creator, than at any other point on earth.

With dusk approaching, the walls leading down to the Dead Sea were dressed royally in shades of purple and it was easy to see why Christians believed that the Son of God ascended into heaven from where she stood, and why Hebrews believed that the Messiah would make his appearance there, coming down from the Mount to save the world.

'Well?' asked Ben Stein, the Reuters stringer who had attached himself to Catherine from the moment she had stepped onto Israeli soil.

'Not everything can be explained in words,' she said, then smiled. 'Even those of us who make a living using the damn things.'

Stein said, 'I come up here occasionally to put myself in my place – when I get to believing I influence the way people think. I always return from the Har Hazeytim a less self-opinionated fellow.'

'Har Hazeytim? Is that Mount of Olives in Hebrew?'

'Now. In olden times it was called Har Hameshiha – the Mount of Anointing. It was a place of worship long before Christ did his levitation bit up here. King David's time, in fact.'

'And do you believe that the Messiah will appear here first?'

Stein chuckled. 'If he's going to appear anywhere, he couldn't better the view from up here. Mind you, once he goes down into the real world he might just wish he hadn't bothered.'

Catherine laughed. 'What makes us such awful cynics? Our work?'

'Observation. We see it like it is. At ground-zero. Or lower. The drainage system. Some of the crap members of our profession produce makes me wonder sometimes if we're not the world's sphincter muscle.'

Catherine tossed the hair from her eyes. 'Only some,' she reminded. Her gaze shifted down the Mount to the monastery, settled, then moved back to Stein. 'The sewers? Is that the level we should see *him* from?'

'God?'

'Pierre Labesse.'

Stein shrugged. 'He's news. Capital N. I can't place him at any level. Wouldn't want to. Best to write him up from a distance. No personal views, they only cloud the issue.'

'You haven't seen him yet?'

'No one has. Only the brothers of his order and the doctor who issued the death certificate.'

'I'll see him,' she stated.

Stein grinned crookedly. 'You won't get past the gates. Nobody has yet.'

'I'll get in. And, what's more, he'll want to see me.'

Stein smiled again. 'Sure, you've got something the rest of the world's press hasn't.'

Catherine nodded, quite serious. 'That's right.'

Stein took her arm, half grinning, but curious. 'Tell me about it.'

'And give you my story? Like hell! Just watch.'

The monastery stood a little way before a mosque which had within its grounds the small circular Church of the Ascension. The crowd of reporters – most of whom seemed to be spending their time between the monastery itself and the bar of the Jerusalem Intercontinental Hotel on the summit of the Mount – had depleted after the earlier chaos, but the evidence of their continuing presence was still visible. Empty cigarette packets, used film packaging, gum wrappers and the like littered the ground around the strong, wooden, iron-studded gates.

Two persistent television crews, American and West German, played cards for the contents of a growing pot at their centre, bored by waiting but still ready to pounce at the merest hint of activity behind the monastery walls.

One reporter, crippled by drink and the sun, had persuaded a small boy to hire him his donkey, then fell off the beast repeatedly – to the wild hilarity of the crowd – and made no progress whatsoever towards his room at the hotel.

Israeli policemen stood silently by, occasionally making efforts to keep order, but mostly just watching. The earlier air of expectancy had been almost bludgeoned to death by inactivity.

The stonework of the monastery was rose-tinted by the light of dusk and the heavy dark gate seemed like an arched hole in the walls. By the gate, nailed to a dry, cracked, wooden beam some hours before by one of the monks, was a bulletin. Catherine stood with Stein in front of it.

'I told you,' Stein confirmed. 'No one gets to see Labesse. He'll speak again when he's ready. There – in perfect copperplate script.'

'Why is he waiting?' she murmured.

Stein grunted. 'He's made one statement which has rocked Rome – maybe he feels he should cool it for a while?'

Catherine turned to him. 'Or maybe they feel he should cool it.'

'It all comes down to politics in the end,' Stein agreed.

She reached for the heavy door knocker, swung it a couple of times hard, then saw a bell-push and pressed that too.

The crowd behind the police watched in silence. The TV crews looked up from their card game, momentarily interested, then knowing the form, lost interest.

One of these, a German, called out, 'No story! Go get drunk – get laid! No story from those bastards. Maybe he becomes a corpse again?'

This raised a few laughs – even from the policemen, who throughout the long day had been particularly humourless.

A pale face appeared behind a small barred grill in the

131

door. 'Father Pierre has nothing more to say at the moment,' the monk pleaded through the grill. 'He must recover from his ordeal. Please understand!'

Catherine reached into her bag and pulled out a small suede sack tied at the neck with cord. She held it up to the grill. 'Take this to him. I'll wait here.'

The monk smiled regretfully. 'Thank you, he will not accept gifts. Already he has refused –'

'It's not a gift,' she interrupted. 'He wore it once. Tell him it comes from the soldier and I'm returning it. Tell him that. Exactly those words.'

The pale face looked at her blankly, then at the bewildered Stein.

'Take it,' Catherine insisted. 'He'd want you to. It's important to him.'

The monk slipped his fingers through the grill for the bag.

'It comes from the soldier,' he repeated. 'You're returning it.'

'That's right. Tell him that.'

'And your name?'

'It doesn't matter. Just remember the words.'

A sliding partition blocked off the monk's face.

'You can't con these guys!' Stein exclaimed. 'They've had every trick in the book tried on them all day – and some new ones invented on the spot by these morons.' He pointed a thumb at the TV crews and a small group of reporters wending their way none too steadily toward the monastery from the direction of the Intercontinental.

'It isn't a trick,' she answered, very subdued.

Stein lit a cigarette and regarded her through the smoke, confounded by her extraordinary confidence. She said nothing as his cigarette burned to the tip, the minutes passing. The sound of an iron bar being drawn back seemed deafening, then the gates opened no more than a crack. Behind Stein, the others had heard the sound too. 'Opensesame,' Stein murmured, eyebrows raised.

A new face appeared in the crack, older and tougher. Shrewd eyes appraised them both. 'This lady only,' said the new monk. 'He will see only the lady.'

The TV crews had abandoned their card game and two men were already sprinting for the gate while others were switching on powerful spotlights. Further away, half-drunk reporters had quickened their weaving gait, sensing that something was happening.

Stein pushed Catherine through the gap in the gate. 'Go!' he urged.

'I might be a long time,' she said, turning, then the gate closed after her.

Pierre Labesse stood at the small window, just as he had done when he had uttered his first words upon returning from the unknown world of the dead. He looked down the slopes of the Mount of Olives towards the Jericho Road, which traverses the wilderness of Judah and the Mountains of Moab – the biblical burial place of Moses. His gaze settled on the town of Bethany, where Christ had come with his disciples on the first Palm Sunday – and where Jesus had raised Lazarus from the dead.

Behind Labesse, the white room had been cleared – at his own wish, though against the advice of the senior brothers of his order, who were themselves men of medicine – of all the life-support units which had kept him alive throughout his years in coma. All that was left in the cool room were the simple iron-framed bedstead he had lain on, two straight-backed chairs and a small prie-dieu upon which stood a mounted wooden crucifix.

By the altar stood the young monk who had been with Labesse at his moment of resurrection. Since then, the youth had refused to leave Labesse's side and the risen saint had gently but firmly dismissed the protests of his brothers and insisted he stayed.

Now, for the first time since the event, the youth spoke: 'Master? What do you see?'

Labesse did not turn – nor express any surprise. His astonishingly blue eyes moved upward to the gleaming points of stars which seemed to have appeared at that instant, for in that part of the world night falls like a blanket over the retreating orb of the sun.

'Why do you call me master?' he questioned, still not turning.

The youth was beside him now, on his knees. 'Are you my master?' he begged.

'Do you believe it so?' Labesse asked.

'I believe that my Lord ascended from this place to sit beside His Father and I believe He shall return here again in all His glory.'

Labesse pushed back the youth's cowl and laid his hand on his bared head. 'What are you called?'

'I am Matthew.'

Labesse smiled down at him. 'Matthew, you will find your answer – and many others besides – for which you can not find questions. Stay with me.'

'I shall not leave your side!'

'Then rise, Matthew, and open the door.' Labesse eased him to his feet and urged him to the locked door. 'Open it,' he repeated.

Catherine Weston stood outside, knuckles raised to strike the wood.

Labesse removed his right hand from his robe and held it out. In his outstretched palm lay the small suede bag. 'Come,' he said.

Catherine obeyed, and immediately the aura of peace inside the room permeated through her, filling her with tranquillity and stripping her of all her worldly anxieties. The world outside the room, its brashness, its cruelty, no longer existed for her. She looked directly into the eyes which faced her and she felt a greater love, a greater peace, than she had believed possible. Oh! Michael, she thought in sudden revelation, of course you did what you did! How could you not have saved him! She glanced down at the bag in his hand and saw the cord tied tight still, her knot undisturbed. 'You didn't open it!' she exclaimed. 'Yet you agreed to see me?'

'You told my brother that it was important. Important enough for you to treasure it over so many years. Important enough for you to bring it here from another land. These are reasons enough.'

'I didn't come here just to bring that. I came because I

am a journalist. I'm no different to any of those – out there. I'm here for your story.'

Labesse shook his head gently. 'You came to see me. That is the truth. You came to try and understand – and perhaps to heal a wound that still has not healed.'

Catherine clasped both her hands around his. 'Open it. Please open it!'

'Do you believe that I need to open it?'

She looked away but her eyes were drawn back to his, and for the first time his power of control over her caused the first tremble of fear. 'No,' she answered, her voice very small. Even as she spoke, her fear dissolved.

Labesse untied the knot and upended the suede bag, letting the long chain and its crucifix trail between his fingers. Catherine could see now the raw wounds at the centres of his palms.

He seemed to catch her thoughts even before they had formed. 'They have never really healed,' he said.

'But it's been years!'

'Yes,' he agreed, with the same gentle smile.

She reached out for the cold iron of the bedstead; her world seemed to be toppling – or changing – and she needed the support.

Labesse took her arm and placed her in one of the chairs.

'I'm confused,' she said, staring up at him. 'I don't understand.'

'You understand partially,' he answered. 'You know part. You know that this fell from the neck of one of my sisters and that it was tied to my body by those who wanted to destroy me. You know that I was saved. You know the man who saved me. The soldier.'

'Knew,' she murmured. 'He's gone. A long time ago. I don't know where.'

'You loved him – so he remains with you. How can you say he has gone?'

'He is not with me. He's gone from my life.'

'No one you truly love ever goes from your life.'

'How do you know about my life? I've told you nothing! Yet you seem to know everything about me?'

'Do you believe that I know everything about you?'

She lowered her face to her hands. 'Yes, oh God, yes!'

'Then, I know.'

'I don't understand, can't you see?' She lifted her head. 'Do you even know my name?'

Labesse smiled at her, as if she were a child. 'If I called you by your name, would that make all I have said more real? More the truth? Or if I called you by the wrong name, would that then make my words lies?'

'No.'

'Then how does your name matter?'

'It's Catherine,' she said. 'His name was Michael. The soldier.'

'Yes,' Labesse said. 'Michael.'

'Will you tell me your story?' Catherine urged. 'All of it? Everything!'

'I want you to tell my story. That is why you are here. Will you go with me wherever I go? Follow me in all I must do?'

'What must you do?'

'What you have asked. I must tell my story. In Rome. That is the chosen city.'

'Then why do you need me?'

'I need you to write what the crowd does not see – nor hear.'

Labesse took her hand and she was overwhelmed by the power which flowed from him. He said, 'The crowd sees only the spectacle. The truth of any man is not in what he does before others but what he does alone for others. It is important that this side of a man is shown also.'

'But my magazine controls – edits – everything I write. What they decide to publish may not be what you want written.'

'Christ once said, "Lay down your nets and follow me." And certain of His disciples, simple fishermen, obeyed. But He did not stop them being fishermen – they still fished, but they fished when they could as they travelled with Him. He even aided them. They were still fishermen but were not imprisoned by their work.'

Catherine frowned. 'You're asking me to give up being a journalist with a safe, secure job and become a writer –

136

your biographer – as we travel . . . wherever you decide to go?'

'Do you believe that no one would publish my story?'

'Of course they would! At this moment any publisher would. I could get whatever deal I asked for!'

'Is that why you would do it?'

'No.'

Labesse nodded, then smiled.

'When do you need me?' she asked.

'You are here.'

His hand still held her own, yet it was all of him, and more, that enveloped her; holding her safe from the disintegration of the life she had made for herself. She let it fall away and there were no doubts, no regrets, only freedom and ecstasy. I am here, she said inside, don't let me go, not now, not ever. And she knew he heard her.

'I'll have to resign,' Catherine said. 'I'll have to cable London.'

'Tell them what you are going to do. They will agree to let you leave them for as long as you need. They will also tell you that you may return whenever you wish.'

'When it's finished?' she asked, accepting his statement totally.

Labesse moved back to the window, watching once more, withdrawn. At last he answered. 'Go, do what you must do, then return here to me. There are things that, very soon, I shall need to say to those waiting out there.'

In London, Jonathan Barton ducked out of a taxi and into his favourite Italian restaurant in Soho. Inside, he allowed the manager to make a fuss of him while his sodden Burberry was removed.

'Your guest is already here,' explained the restaurateur. 'Waiting too long, I think – very many pink gins. A sailor perhaps?'

Barton let himself be trailed through the crowded restaurant, nodding cursorily to both sides as he was recognized by others also lunching.

'Sorry, James,' he apologized, sitting down at his table. 'This damn Labesse business. Just couldn't get away.'

James Auslaire was indeed a sailor, though dry-docked now at the Ministry of Defence in London. He was a rugged character with that type of wavy hair which looks as if it might have been crimped. Any blond colouring he might have had from his Swedish forebears had now turned a grizzled brown. Auslaire was one of Barton's famous 'unofficial but normally reliable sources within the Ministry of Defence' and he used him ruthlessly – but with discretion – in that role.

Auslaire raised the glass containing his fourth pink gin, his eyes twinkling. 'Heaven is here!' he toasted.

The table they shared was at the rear of the restaurant and enclosed in a booth. The manager had been warned to hold it for Barton. The newscaster ducked his head forward. 'Anything new on that downed Argentine Mirage?'

'Not us, chum. Not guilty. Take it from me. The Phantom crews have been thoroughly debriefed. Not too gently either, I'd wager. They stick to their story: collision. A jet aircraft. Not a big commercial airliner, not a small fighter. Midway. Could have been an executive jet.'

'Anyone screaming?' Barton inquired. 'Around that area? Brazil? Other South American states?'

'Just some poor insurance company somewhere. You know what one of those things cost?'

'That's an idea. I'll get onto my chap at Lloyds.'

Auslaire shook his head. 'Doubt if you'll get anywhere, chum. If no one's reported one down by now, they've got a bloody expensive reason. And it's a little late to start filling in claim forms.'

'Espionage? Soviets? The Argentinians themselves?'

'Hardly. Fortress Falklands is an open book, isn't it? Every time something new is done or sent there, we have a full-scale parliamentary debate. The whole ruddy world and its dog know what we've got on the islands.'

'So who the hell can afford to waive an insurance claim that large? How much? Half a million?'

'Double it. And not in dollars either.'

Barton lifted both eyebrows and sipped the drink which had arrived unordered at the booth. 'So what are the Argies doing about the loss of their aircraft? A Mirage doesn't cost pennies either – forgetting hurt national honour and all that crap.'

'Yelling. Strongly worded diplomatic notes are flying at ground-attack level between the FO and Buenos Aires.'

'And MOD reaction? Full alert on the islands? Invasion a possibility?'

'What do *you* think? This time we'll be ready for them.'

'Is that quotable?'

'Didn't say a word.'

'James, someone's bound to leak something soon. And I'd like to be the one to announce it first.'

Auslaire shrugged. 'The islands are always on a high-level alert – it's the nature of that particular game.'

'But this time you're expecting a strike?'

'Let's just say we're ready for anything.'

'That's an emotive statement? May I quote?'

'Won't rock the boat – it might even make the junta think again.'

'Thank you, James. You've just bought yourself lunch.'

Auslaire tilted his glass and Barton snapped his fingers, ordered another drink for his guest, then quickly decided on food.

Halfway through the meal, Auslaire said, 'So what about our chum Labesse? Still got his name plastered all over the front pages, I see. Had him for breakfast along with the kidneys and the scrambled eggs. He said anything new? "Next Garden of Eden going to be at Kew"?'

Barton placed his knife and fork together, then pushed the plate away. 'Nothing.'

'So what kept you? The lovely Mary Edgington?'

'She's sublimely happy building her career, and I'm just one of the bricks.'

'And you're miserable, dating hopeful starlets who stroke your ego – and a lot more besides. Tough life, chum.'

Barton grunted. 'Someone got in to see him. A girl. Magazine reporter. Damn annoying.'

'Labesse?'

139

Barton nodded.

'British magazine?'

'American, but she's from their London bureau. *Fact*. Know it?'

'Buy me a subscription for Christmas.'

'She's the only outsider who's got through the monastery gates. The rest of the press over there are hopping mad. Feel they've been cheated.'

'Cheque-book journalism with a perishing resurrected holy man? I say! Is nothing sacred?' Auslaire jibed, amused.

Barton shook his head. 'No money involved. *Fact* have denied that categorically. She was admitted after passing something through the gate to one of the monks. Later she came back out and – here's where the milk starts to curdle – ignored everyone, including the Reuters stringer who escorted her there, walked up to the Intercontinental and phoned her resignation through to *Fact*. Seemed to be half in a trance. God alone knows what Labesse said – or did – to her.'

Auslaire smirked. 'I bet God didn't get you that information.'

'Someone spiked the call. One of the Italian reporters. From one of their more conservative papers too. Not their style normally. Odd. He gave the information away afterwards to the rest of the press, bloody idiot. His paper will murder him.'

'He's a Vatican mole, matey, sticks out a mile.' Auslaire chuckled, between gulps of chianti. 'Spiked the call, eh! Charming. You fellows should fight our wars, we need a few dirty tricks on our side.'

'Name of the game, James.'

'Well, what's hers? Don't tell me she's been converted?'

Barton shrugged.

'Christ! If Labesse can turn a ruddy journalist around, what hope is there for us poor turtles without the armour-plated shell.'

'None whatsoever.'

Auslaire poured the last of the chianti for himself. 'So

140

what about the feller in Rome? Still out of order? Mainspring run down?'

'The Vatican have announced that it's the same virus infection which struck him down after the assassination attempt. He's in complete isolation.'

'Any truth in that old rumour that the Browning bullets which hit him were treated with some bug or other? The KGB scare?'

'Actually, we're running that as part of our lead story tonight. Seems a bit James Bondish to me, but it's horrifying enough to keep the viewers away from their phones over Labesse. We've had to employ temps to deal with the volume of calls whenever his name is mentioned! The KGB thing will be good emotive stuff but mainly we'll go for the "infected-blood" explanation. You do know that Italian blood-donors are paid?'

'Are they, by God? So maybe they're not too honest about what they've got swimming around in it? Grisly way of doing it.'

Barton crooked a finger at a waiter, received the bill and signed it, then stood up.

Auslaire stayed seated, nursing the last of the chianti. 'Going back to take the calls and keep Labesse's converts from chucking in their jobs? Doesn't the man realize we've got a massive unemployment problem already?'

'Saint,' said Barton.

'Oh, that's kosher now, is it? Message from heaven? Stone tablet arrived? "I hereby decree that my chum Labesse is no mere mortal like the rest of you, so treat him right or I'll blast you all to Hades." Or wherever?'

Barton draped his offered Burberry over his shoulders. 'In my business, James, when an official department refuses to deny a story, I take it to mean it's true. And the Vatican is as official as any department in anybody's bureaucracy. But the real point is that the reaction which Labesse is getting worldwide at this moment – even though he's said nothing more – makes the canonization issue and its official confirmation quite secondary, even irrelevant. People around the world – and not only Christians – have already accepted that he is something more than just a religious fanatic. Watch some of our man-in-the-street interviews, read the tabloids.'

'Of course they have!' Auslaire exclaimed, then belched. 'The poor devils need to believe that someone up there cares still. It's for sure that no one down here does any more. Take a look around you, chum: real people, not those you see inside a TV camera lens – they're disillusioned, given up hoping that something better exists! My view, let 'em have their risen saint, their Messiah – or whatever they believe he is. Great God! They haven't much else to pin their hopes on any more. I just hope that this time – if he's for real – they don't mess it up and nail the poor devil up like the last one.'

Barton gave a tight grin. 'They've done that to him already.'

'Don't mean a damn thing, chum. The human race is capable of repeating its mistakes until this world is blasted into atoms. And that isn't so unlikely either. I reckon Labesse is on a hiding to nothing. And you'll be there with your crowd, covering the event, when they hang him up again. He's making it easy, isn't he? Came in kit-form – holes ready made! Cheers.'

Barton walked out into the rain and his waiting taxi. He leaned back against the seat. Would we? he asked himself. Have we moved forward that slowly? Or are we too far gone? In the end, will we be so frightened – so unsettled – by what he says that we would, in some way, crucify him?

He heard the partition slide back and the cabbie speak. 'I'm sorry?' Barton apologized, missing the words.

'Heaven is here!' the cabbie shouted over his shoulder, indicating the crowd filling Cambridge Circus, chanting, while lifting their sodden banners against the weight of the rainwater which had soaked them through. The banners now were blurred but their message was still readable. HEAVEN IS HERE!

'It even rains in bleedin' heaven!' laughed the cabbie.

Barton shared the joke and felt better for it. 'ITN,' he said.

'That's right, guvnor,' called the cabbie.

* * *

142

Mary Edgington was waiting for Barton as he alighted from the taxi in Wells Street. By the state of her hair, she had obviously been standing in the rain. Now, she was behind the glass doors, wet and agitated.

Barton paid off the driver quickly and joined her. 'What's the flap?'

'Labesse. He's come out!'

They ran toward the newsroom, fast, Mary talking all the way. 'The girl – her name's Weston – went back in the early hours, stayed inside for the night, then appeared an hour ago and told the press boys Labesse would be coming out to make a statement and take a few questions.'

'What did she call him? St Pierre?'

'No.'

'What then?'

'The Master.'

'Jesus!'

'Quite,' Mary said, breathlessly.

'What did he say?'

'It's all on tape, watch it yourself.' She virtually hauled Barton into a video-editing studio. Inside, everything was set up.

'Run it,' Barton ordered.

Mary lit a cigarette and sat in a chair, her palm flat across her face as she inhaled deeply in short, quick breaths.

Pierre Labesse's face filled the screen.

'No!' Barton snapped. 'Run it from where he makes his exit through the gates.'

The video operator wound the tape back. 'We've got the girl,' he said. 'Do you want to see her?'

'Just him,' Barton said, quietly. 'Just Labesse.'

The tape stabilized and the figure of Labesse came into view as the heavy gates were opened. He was dressed in an oatmeal-coloured habit similar to those worn by the other monks who stood near him.

Flashbulbs exploded in concert like a perfectly timed artillery barrage and Labesse shielded his eyes against their blast. Israeli police moved in fast as impatient pressmen surged forward. The picture swung away abruptly from

143

Labesse onto the police cordon and the heaving crowd; microphones, miniature tape-recorders and cameras were thrust through the gaps so that the flashbulbs flared directly in front of the policemen's eyes, blinding them momentarily.

Barton edged forward on his seat. He could feel the anger of the Israeli police, the wild impatience of the press and the irresistible surge of the crowds. He had witnessed scenes like this before – the most frantic perhaps was that outside the hospital in Dallas after the assassinated President Kennedy had been admitted – but this surpassed even that. The crowds exuded an almost mad joy, enveloping even the hardened, cynical pressmen.

Then, quite suddenly, all was calm and the cameraman panned back to Labesse – much too speedily for comfortable viewing but he had made the right decision, for he just caught the moment when the storm was tamed as Labesse raised his arms.

'There's the girl.' Mary nudged Barton.

Catherine Weston stood near the risen saint. Not close, a shadow's length away, pale but radiant, nervous-looking yet serene. Not for one second did her eyes leave Labesse.

The crowd had stilled completely; not a word was spoken, no questions called; the only sound was the steady flashing from countless cameras. Barton felt his spine, then his scalp tingle. He wished more than anything else at that moment to be there.

Mary had placed her hand over Barton's arm but he was unaware of her. Only Labesse existed. He understood, at that instant, what had happened to the girl. Even miles away, after the event, the sensation that some powerful force was at work was overwhelming. Unconsciously he covered Mary's hand with his.

There were microphones set up on stands, an army of them, between Labesse and the crowd. He stepped forward to them and spoke:

'I have come, not to confuse, nor to tear down the doctrine of centuries. I have come to make clear what has been made unclear by those who have not understood the word of God. To interpret, in God's name, what has been

144

misinterpreted by man. I have come not to destroy faith but to strengthen it. Not to confound your beliefs nor to throw them into disorder – but to clarify and to strengthen them. Men have taken it upon themselves to decide for you what meaning lies behind the words of Christ. For this task, man is incapable. Man views a painting, sees the colours and the images they form – but only the artist knows the purity of the unblemished canvas beneath.'

Labesse pointed directly at the screen. 'Upon this you perceive the world. Yet, if an insect crawled across this screen, what perception would it have of the complete image? None. It sees only what is within the limits of its perception. Beyond those limits it is totally ignorant. Totally blind. The universe and the matter which comprises it is your screen and man is the insect.'

'Who are you?' a solitary voice called from somewhere.

Labesse replied, 'I am a man, born of woman, who has been with God.'

'Christ was born of a woman!' cried another voice. 'Do you claim to be divine also?'

Labesse smiled. 'By asking this, you question my earthly form. Yet I stand before you – a man!'

'But you died, returned to life, and claim to have been with God? If you are not divine, are you deluded?'

The clamour of questions was rising: 'Why were you brought to the Mount of Olives?'

'Do you claim to be the Messiah? Are you Christ returned, as some are saying?'

Labesse lifted his arms and shook his head sadly. 'Every question you have asked is about me. Yet the one question you should ask you have all ignored. It is not that I am here which is important! It is where I have been which should concern you. I say I have been with God but not one among you has asked me, "What is the nature of God?" A God that all people – in one form or another – believe in.'

'What is he like then?' someone called brashly.

Labesse seemed to chuckle and again shook his head as if amazed at such naiveté. 'He is not like anything!'

'Well, tell us what he looks like?'

145

'I have told you. He does not look like anything. He is! He has no counterpart, no object or being which He can be related to. If you were faced now with God, you would not see Him because you would not recognize what you were seeing.'

'Is God a force? Like electricity or nuclear power?'

Labesse's blue eyes seemed to twinkle. He selected the questioner, who stood in the front row with the pressmen. 'Do you understand these things?' he asked.

'The theory, yes.'

'So you would recognize the crackle and the shock from electricity? And the fireball of a nuclear explosion?'

'Of course!'

'Then God cannot be like either one.'

More questions flew but Labesse cut them off. 'I will tell you this much – and it is, perhaps, beyond your under-standing, for within it lies a mystery. The Son of God spoke these words: "They hated me without reason. But when your advocate has come, whom I will send to you from the Father, he will bear witness to me. When your advocate comes, he will confute the world and show where wrong and right and judgement lie. He will convince them of divine judgement by showing that the Prince of this World stands condemned." He also said, "There is still much that I could say to you but the burden would be too great for you now. But when he comes, who is the spirit of truth, he will guide you into all the truth. For he will not speak on his own authority but will tell you only what he hears, and he will make known to you the things that are coming. Everything that he makes known to you he will draw from what is mine." '

Labesse raised his arms again to forestall the barrage of questions demanding explanation of the words he had spoken. Instead, he said, 'Think on these words I have repeated. The explanation for these, and others besides, I shall give you very soon. I shall appear, once more, in Rome and there I shall lead you toward true under-standing. Think and wait for what is to follow. Meanwhile, beware of man's interpretation of the word of God, for it is written – and it is true – that the Prince of this World was given all influence by God over man.

'Your heaven *is here*. It always has been from the beginning, and it always will be, but you have allowed the keys to be laid in the hands of another.'

One angry voice called out, 'Are you attacking the true Church of God?'

Labesse considered for a moment, then answered, 'There are many churches and many men who interpret the word of God. There are even men who write it! There is but one true interpretation – one truth – and you shall hear it from God, through me.'

Labesse turned away, then stepped through the open gates of the monastery and disappeared from view, taking Catherine Weston and his accompanying brothers with him. The silence which followed his departure was broken as journalists ran for telephones and TV reporters faced their own camera crews.

ITN's Richard Bailey's haggard face appeared on the screen. He blinked and raised his voice against the babble of sound around him: 'Those astonishing words, the first spoken in public by the so-called risen saint Pierre Labesse, are certain to be viewed as heretical by the Vatican and will undoubtedly receive a hostile reaction. So, is this risen saint a charlatan or, as he has hinted, the prophesied advocate of God? Millions of people around the globe at this moment are making up their minds. In fact – according to polls taken in America and Europe, including Italy, the home of the Holy See – millions have accepted him as divine. Something Pierre Labesse has neither claimed nor denied, although – if we interpret his words spoken just now, correctly – it is something he purports to be. Richard Bailey, ITN, Jerusalem.'

The TV screen blanked out.

Jonathan Barton remained silent, Mary Edgington's hand still pressed to his arm, under his. The video operator stared at the dead screen.

Barton breathed in deeply. 'We'll need a counter-argument. Can we get Lovelace and O'Hara back tonight?'

'They're both on call.'

'Right. Have both of them watch the tape – but I don't want them spending too long with it. When we go on the air, I want them to still feel the impact. No deeply thought-out answers. We want their immediate reaction. From the gut. Emotive statements.'

'Lovelace is bound to scream heresy and O'Hara will probably proclaim the second coming,' said Mary.

'O'Hara may be right. Come on, let's get some wise heads together on this. This is once-in-a-lifetime stuff, so let's get it right!'

Mary lit a cigarette, still seated. 'If Labesse *is* what he's implying he is – God's advocate – are we ready for him?'

Barton gave a cynical smile. 'We put out world news. When has there been a time when the human race has not been more ready?'

'But what if he's the other thing entirely? The Bible warns of that too!

'Then we probably deserve it,' answered Barton without humour.

'The advocate of God?' asked Jonathan Barton directly into the camera immediately after the videotape of Labesse's controversial appearance had been transmitted nationally. He turned in his chair to a second camera. 'Tonight, we have with us, once again, in ITN's studio, Dr Harold Lovelace, Reader in Divinity at Cambridge University, and Father Timothy O'Hara, whose outspoken and sometimes radical views on the Roman Catholic Church and established Christianity are well known. Indeed his personal – not to say, astonishing – views on the so-called risen saint have caused a furore in religious circles. First we speak to Dr Lovelace. Doctor: Labesse as God's prophesied advocate? His "spirit of truth"?'

'Preposterous! The man is quite obviously suffering from delusions of grandeur and advanced religious mania. He is to be pitied – not exposed to public ridicule such as we've seen just now.' Lovelace almost shook in indignation.

'With respect, Doctor, I personally cannot see his appearance being, in any way, ridiculous. He seems in full

148

control of everything he says or does. There are certainly no visible signs of any mental aberration.'

'If that is the case, he is speaking utter heresy!'

'Yet there is a growing belief in what he says? You saw yourself, on our earlier report, some people are taking to the streets in Britain, Europe and the United States of America, hailing Labesse as a possible saviour of the world?'

'And *there* lies the danger!' Lovelace expostulated. 'The man may be deluded, but he is also terrifyingly dangerous.'

'So you still believe him to be an "ordinary" man?'

'I believe that, if he is not an ordinary man, then whatever power he may have most certainly does not come from God! Quite the opposite in fact.'

Barton interrupted swiftly: 'Then you are not entirely convinced that he is not without some extraordinary power? Supernatural power, perhaps?'

'Adolf Hitler had extraordinary power and we know that he was no saint! But your other term: supernatural? This is over-used these days. Horror films and videos, devil worship, sexual orgies, desecration of churches and grave-yards – the term supernatural has become synonymous with things ugly and depraved; it has become an entertainment medium. But real evil does not necessarily have an ugly or depraved image. Lucifer, Satan, call him what you will, was a fallen angel. In fact, he is described in the Bible as being a "being of infinite beauty and intelligence". In Ezekiel 28, God himself laments over Lucifer's fall from grace. He describes him thus: "You had the seal of perfection, full of wisdom and beauty." In this passage, God is describing the greatest being He had ever created. One who had unequalled power, wisdom and beauty. He named him "the Son of the Morning" and Lucifer, which literally means the "the Shining One". Hardly the horrifying, horned, winged and tailed demon which the entertainment business would have us believe. The real image of evil – like sin – is usually very attrative indeed! It is also disarming . . . as we have witnessed tonight.'

Barton asked, 'Labesse's reference to the Prince of this World – do you interpret that as meaning Lucifer?'

Lovelace's left eyelid had developed a flicker; he touched it to still the agitated nerve. 'Most people know the Bible warns us that God gave Lucifer this world as his domain after he had been thrown down from heaven – for a limited period of time. That period ends with the final conflict between good and evil. The prophesied Battle of Armageddon. At Armageddon, good will triumph and Lucifer will be destroyed for ever.'

'So the Prince of this World *is* Lucifer. Yet Labesse claims that he has come to destroy him? Hardly the words of someone in league with the devil?'

Lovelace seemed to gather himself, then spoke very clearly, measuring his words. 'They are exactly the words of someone in league with the devil. Another name given to Lucifer is that of the Arch-Deceiver, and there is no doubt in my mind at all that many people are being deceived.' Lovelace glanced at O'Hara. 'They should stop and think very deeply indeed on the events which are happening right now.'

Barton followed Lovelace's glance and turned to the black-robed Irish priest. 'Father Timothy. Labesse a cohort of the devil?'

O'Hara leaned forward in his seat, an intense expression on his round face. 'You know, good and evil are not two concepts separated by an impenetrable, divinely constructed barrier. It would be naive of us to think them so. Dr Lovelace gave the most pertinent example of this when he spoke of "perfect" Lucifer: a being who, in this modern age, might be described as one of the "beautiful people"; better looking than any earthly film star, intelligent, witty, charming – a person with undeniable charisma. He is also – undeniably – powerful! But who gave him all these attributes? God, of course, for God created Lucifer. Without any doubt, as we see from the Bible, Lucifer was a favourite – no, *the* favourite – son. If you wish to study this in chronological terms, Lucifer was created before Christ. But he was too perfect. He had no failings at all – until he developed what was later to become man's first and most dangerous sin – greed! He did not want to be a perfect second anything, he wanted to be first! And this he tried to be by attempting what we might now call a coup d'état. He failed and God cast him out. But God did not destroy him; instead, He gave him domain over our world – hence one of his titles, the Prince of this World. Why? Why do such a potentially dangerous thing? Because, and this is obvious, God did not win the battle entirely. He knew that even the best of His creations was corruptible, so He conducted a prolonged war of attrition with his Fallen Angel – a war that would be a test of power. We are the victims of that war, for if we fail to recognize the difference between God's will and the blandishments, the temptations of Lucifer, we will be damned for all eternity. Now the supreme mystery in all this – and heed that word because Labesse used it also – is that God, by His own definition, is the supreme indivisible being who is everything. He is part of all He created and we are equally part of Him because He created man.' O'Hara stopped and fixed his eyes on the camera. 'Therefore, Lucifer is also part of God, for only God could have created him. Who else is there? The most powerful description of God I will ever hear is His own statement: "I am the Alpha and the Omega, the Beginning and the End, the First and the Last." The meaning is perfectly clear. Everything, everyone, is an indivisible part of God. This is why I believe that you cannot separate good and evil. They run a parallel course, and sometimes they are totally indistinguishable from each other. I would venture to suggest that, at times, they even merge. So, God in His wisdom promised us an advocate – a counsellor – who will come at the time we need him most. I believe that now is that time and that our advocate is here to clarify God's truth for us – and believe me it certainly needs clarifying.'

'So you do believe that Labesse is the "advocate of God", Father Timothy?' Barton queried.

O'Hara gave a dry smile. 'I warned you to heed that word which Labesse has used so cleverly. "Mystery". Here is the mystery. God also tells us – warns us – of the appearance of a false prophet. A Jewish false prophet. A man who will appear at the height of Israel's turmoil – described in the Book of Revelations as a miracle-working

151

man who will masquerade as the Messiah. On a biblical timescale these two beings will appear very close to each other. Now, forgetting the higher issues, and on a more down-to-earth level, Pierre Labesse has neither performed miracles – unless one believes he arranged his own resurrection – nor is he Jewish. It is a recorded fact that he is an orphaned Frenchman raised by nuns in the French coastal town of St Malo. In other words, he is *not* Jewish as the Bible prophesies the false prophet must be. Perhaps Labesse is warning us to be prepared.'

Barton frowned, annoyed that the Irishman appeared to be procrastinating, yet was determined to nail him to some definite admission – either way.

Barton said, 'So he is not this biblical false prophet – he doesn't fit the prophecy – but do you believe he may be what he is implying he is? God's advocate?'

Lovelace interrupted instantly. 'May I say something before Father Timothy commits himself irrevocably on this. There is a precise warning in the Bible which says, "God will send the world a powerful delusion so that all who have not believed the truth may be comdemned." In other words, what we are deluded into believing as the truth will be lies. On this basis, if Labesse is a divine figure, we should take care in believing his words. He may not be – as I have said – a man deluded but he may have been returned here to create this delusion.'

'By God?' asked Barton, incredulously. 'Are you now saying, Dr Lovelace, that you accept that Labesse is, as you just put it, a divine figure? Despite your earlier dismissal of him as such?'

Lovelace grimaced and hesitated. 'I . . . did say, *if* he is a divine figure.'

'Father Timothy?' said Barton turning.

'What Dr Lovelace says is perfectly true. There is the warning of a delusion. It will be our greatest test.'

'But whatever Labesse's purpose – going back to my original question Father – do you believe him to be what he is implying he is? That is, God's advocate, a divine figure sent to guide us?'

'I believe, Mr Barton, exactly what Labesse has stated

himself. Which is, he has been with God during the nine-hour period of his death. It is a known fact that people who to all intents and purposes have died have had experiences – some call them dreams, but I do not – which are beyond what we would call normal. I believe that these people have experienced a glimpse of what lies beyond. Pierre Labesse had far more than a glimpse; he saw God in His glory and heard His word. I have not the slightest doubt that we *must* listen to what he has to say. I pray that we do not make the mistake of ignoring him or – even worse – make the mistake of Calvary again.'

'Dr Lovelace?' queried Barton. 'One last comment, briefly?'

Lovelace shifted uncomfortably. 'I can only repeat my earlier warning – the Bible's warning – of the possibility here of a delusion. If Labesse is not mad, he is certainly dangerous and he could well be utterly evil. Great evil is spreading around the world in this time, we can all feel it and see its manifestations reported in detail daily on this very programme. Let us all pray, Barton, that we are not, at this time, witnessing its strongest hour.'

Father Timothy O'Hara saw the long black car, waiting, further down Wells Street and walked towards it, his face set and troubled. He reached it and stepped inside.

The English cardinal gave a thin smile, then rapped on the glass division.

'You saw it, Eminence?' the Irishman asked.

The cardinal nodded.

O'Hara fell silent, watching London's night-life flow past through the window. He thought: I wonder what it is like not to care. Not to believe in anything beyond the certainty of a wage packet at the end of the week.

The cardinal spoke. 'I think you overstepped your brief this evening.'

O'Hara turned, faced his superior, then looked away. 'We weren't given much time between seeing the recording of Labesse and the interview. He raised points which needed answering and my instructions were not relevant. I had to think on my feet.'

The cardinal smiled drily. 'That is exactly how Rome will see it. You thought with your feet instead of your brain. However, *I* do not believe that. I believe, Father, your answers came – in part – from your heart. I believe you are beginning to doubt Rome's judgement. Could I be right in this?'

O'Hara faced him. 'There is a certain feeling inside me which tells me – no, warns me – that we may be making a mistake here, Eminence.'

'Father, a direct answer, please, to an equally direct question: Do you believe Labesse is sent to us from God?'

'He is not sent to us from man, Eminence.'

'From God, Father. That is my question.'

'From beyond man. From beyond our understanding. Yes.'

The cardinal studied his hands for a long moment, O'Hara watching him, seeing for the first time the confusion, even torture, on the thin ascetic face. Finally, and in no more than a whisper, he uttered, 'I too.'

'Then.tell Rome! Have them stop this . . . game.'

'Strategy,' the cardinal corrected. 'They will not. I cannot! Not even for the sake of my conscience. To make any public statement would begin an internecine struggle at the uppermost level of Church power and that we dare not allow – nor contemplate. Besides, though we both agree that Labesse is sent from . . . somewhere beyond our understanding . . . this does not necessarily make his purpose *good*. There are forces at work here which display signs of being horrendously destructive in regard to the faith – *wherever* this force emanates from.'

'Even if that force is God Himself?'

'Even if it is God Himself, yes. The Roman Catholic Church has been built – stabilized – on certain solid foundations which some might term pure dogma, but, without our total obedience to these tenets, and complete belief in their authority, we are in deadly danger of tearing down the temple. My greatest fear at this moment, Father, is that we may be drawn by Labesse into a situation whereby

154

the protection of our established dogma – our doctrine of centuries – becomes so compulsive that we will develop what one might call the "Samson complex". We would tear down the temple ourselves rather than see it destroyed – or altered.'

'Eminence! Seek an audience with the Holy Father – tell him what you fear. He, more than any man alive, would understand.'

'That is impossible.'

'Surely, Eminence, no matter how ill he is, he would be able to listen?'

'I said, it is impossible.'

'Then what is left to do?'

The cardinal sighed. 'What we have always done, Father. Obey.'

'Mary?' Barton called, entering the reception area at ITN after the transmission was over. 'I thought you'd gone.'

She shook her head.

'Something wrong?'

'I've just seen who was in the car O'Hara drove away in.'

'Who?'

'A certain Englishman you'd address as "Your Eminence". The one who matters.'

Barton raised one eyebrow. 'Was he now. So? More ammunition for your theory of Rome muddying Labesse's pool? All right, I'll give you that O'Hara is one priest they'd rather not have and the Catholic hierarchy normally avoid him like the plague, but really! Maybe they don't approve of the interviews? Disciplining him? Jesus! They couldn't wait, could they, if that's the case?'

'No,' she said emphatically. 'If it had been that, the chuaffeur would have parked the car directly in front, wouldn't he? Why wait down the road?'

'You saw that?'

'I'd some notes on cassette in my car – I'd gone for those. I saw O'Hara walk directly to the car. A black saloon, a Daimler, I think. With the division. I couldn't miss it.'

'And you actually saw him?'

'He welcomed O'Hara into the car. I know they're trying to discredit Labesse.'

'Mary, if *you* stop being objective, it affects us all!'

'I know.'

'Go home and forget it.'

'Another thing,' she added hastily. 'Guess where O'Hara is staying in London?'

'Not with him, surely?'

'Brown's Hotel.'

Again Barton's eyebrow lifted. 'A bit upmarket for O'Hara. Are you sure?'

'Yes. He had to leave a number with us. Brown's.'

'Oh, come on, O'Hara isn't going to trade his radical views for a suite at Brown's. I can't buy that. Sorry, darling.'

'How old do you think he is, Jonty?'

'Fiftyish . . . maybe more?'

'And ageing. There'll be no red hat for Father Timothy O'Hara, and he knows it. Blew that long ago. He knows where he'll end up too. Some Catholic Siberia. Somewhere with no public platform to spout his radicalism – and precious little comfort for old bones. If they've bought him, that's how they've done it – promised him something better.'

'All right,' Barton conceded, carefully. 'So? So O'Hara's been bought. He's gone on the tube to really blow up Labesse's balloon, which they know is bound to burst. They know that any media event can only take so much hype and exposure before it collapses. What do you plan to do about it?'

'Nothing. You know we couldn't prove anything. The Vatican is virtually impregnable – harder than the Kremlin, according to those who know about these things. Remember the Banco Amrosiano affair?'

'So, no story. Why bother about it? Throw it over your left shoulder and let Rome play its dirty tricks. Everyone's doing it. Who cares?'

156

'I'll tell you why. Because I have this unshakable feeling about Labesse. The man in convincing. He's convinced me, Jonty, and I'm the toughest bird in this building. And I think O'Hara is having doubts. I believe Labesse is reaching him too.'

'He was different tonight. Lovelace too – he virtually backward-somersaulted on himself.'

'I heard,' Mary said, digging for a cigarette in her bag. Barton lit it for her.

'How about a drink and some coffee?' he offered. 'They'd let us in at that Greek place around the corner.'

She shook her head. 'I have this extraordinary feeling that everything is changing. It's a good feeling – and I don't want it to stop. I believe that Labesse is terribly important for us.'

'Mankind?'

'Damn mankind. I mean us ... people ... you, me, those closest to us. I can't feel it in wider terms. It's just ... well ... personal. Can you understand?'

'Perhaps. Labesse is certainly mesmeric. I admit that I felt that. He's blessed with power, wherever – or whoever – it originates from.'

'Jonty, I don't want to drive home tonight – I don't want to be alone. I feel too alive, too full!'

'So stay at my place. Bags of room and we can chat half the night.'

'As a friend?'

'What else? Get your coat.'

'Jon, listen! What do you think they'll do to him? Labesse?'

'They?'

'They ... the Vatican ... people ... us!'

Barton sighed. 'Jimmy Auslaire said we'll probably crucify him.'

Mary shuddered. 'We wouldn't destroy him. Would we?'

Barton took her arm, then turned her to him. 'You, more than most people, know the world we live in. You answer the question.'

'I don't want to. I don't dare.'

'Then forget what he makes you feel. It's not our place

157

to be involved. We're the ones who stand on the side and report the news; we don't make it. Pierre Labesse says he's going to Rome. If he does, we'll cover it. If he doesn't get there, we'll cover that too. There is nothing more we can do.'

Mary linked her arm in his. 'We've told his story,' she said. 'At least we've done that.'

'It isn't over yet,' said Jonathan Barton. 'It's only been three days.' He held her close to him and led her out into Wells Street. It was almost a new morning.

6

Cardinal Secretary of State Giorgio Cinalli faced the new day from a window on the third floor of the Apostolic Palace, his self-assurance rocked by the appearance of Pierre Labesse on television the night before, his rest afterwards disturbed. Every word Labesse had uttered had exerted more pressure on his already troubled spirit, but one statement more than any other tolled liked a warning bell in his mind: Labesse was coming to Rome. Cinalli's jaw hardened, then he turned away from the window. 'So be it!' he murmured.

Upon his antique desk his correspondence was arranged in such a manner that he could see instantly what needed immediate attention, which matters were troublesome, and which were formal, requiring no more than the approval of his office. The expert hand of his Sostituto was evident throughout. Benito Marco's organization of Cinalli's power was faultless – and sometimes this worried the Secretary of State very much indeed, for he knew that any man too well organized by another is perilously close to being controlled. Cinalli made a mental note to curtail Marco's influence – after the problem of Labesse had been dealt with.

There was a knock on the great carved doors and the Sostituto entered. 'They are here, Eminence,' Marco announced.

Cinalli nodded.

Father Phillipe Recamier entered the large chamber, supporting the aged nun from the orphanage in St Malo. He placed his lips to Cinalli's ring, and the nun, though weakened to the point of collapse, followed suit.

Cinalli frowned as he lowered himself into his own chair

behind the desk. 'Perhaps it would be wise to have a doctor see to Sister Theresa before we begin?'

Marco's quick eyes settled warningly on the Cardinal Secretary's face. 'Eminence, I have already arranged for a doctor. This matter is of some urgency and must be dealt with immediately. Sister Theresa will receive the very best attention as soon as she has divulged her information.'

'If you are sure she is able . . .?' Cinalli questioned, still concerned.

The aged nun answered for herself, her voice pathetically weak. 'I have sinned, Eminence. I beg you to hear my confession.'

Cinalli stood up. 'Wait outside,' he commanded the two men.

Together, the Sostituto and Recamier walked outside to the antechamber. They waited in silence, hearing only a muted, hollow drone as the ritual of confession was conducted in the high-ceilinged chamber beyond the great double doors.

The Sostituto took a cigarette from a silver box on the table between them, offering one to Recamier. Lighting them both, Marco asked, 'These facts are verifiable?'

Recamier's face was drawn, his naturally prominent facial bones jutting out more than usual so that the hollows of his eyes and cheeks were accentuated, making his face cadaverous. The Sostituto had noticed this change but had put it down to travelling and lack of sleep.

'Sostituto?'

Marco made a gesture of impatience. 'Concentrate please, Father. If news of what you have discovered is leaked – to certain newspapers or press agencies, for example – would the facts stand up to investigation?'

'I have brought you the truth. Any investigation will uncover the very same facts. The only unverifiable fact is of Labesse's Jewish origin. There is no way the press can discover this – unless it is your intention to have Sister Theresa make a public confession?'

Marco's shrewd eyes lifted. 'The Cardinal Secretary's intention, Father. Not mine. I have not the power to make such a decision.'

160

'Of course,' Recamier said, meeting Marco's eyes.

'I sincerely hope, Father, that your loyalty to the Church has not weakened. You do still appreciate the necessity of its actions here?'

'I understand why. But I confess to a fear for my soul.'

'Your soul is not endangered,' Marco said coolly. 'You have discovered the truth, have you not? You have not fabricated these facts?'

'No.'

'Where then is your fear?'

Recamier's expression turned inward. 'It follows me like a spectre, unseen but evident.'

'Name it.'

'I dare not.'

Marco relaxed in his chair. 'A psychiatrist could name it instantly. Anxiety, or guilt. The fear of breaking the rules of right conduct inbred in you. At present you are experiencing a phobic reaction brought on by guilt.'

A hard, grim smile touched Recamier's mouth. 'You are a man with a highly developed intellect, while I have a mind susceptible to instinct. I feel when something is wrong – you deduce and subsequently offer explanations. What I feel in this instance is a terrible fear – worse, an evil presence. Not guilt.'

'Superstition? I find that difficult to believe in a man who is trained to gather facts. Leave superstition where it belongs, Father: in the Middle Ages, along with the Inquisition.'

'The Inquisition still exists, Sostituto. Are we not practising it now? Is not Pierre Labesse its victim? The rack, the hot-irons, the torture may be gone, but the purpose and the outcome remain. You intend to destroy another human being who will not accept your doctrine.'

'The doctrine of the Church,' Marco corrected. 'But if you must believe in this presence of evil you feel, then look no further for its source than Pierre Labesse. *He* is evil. It is his spectre which follows you.'

Recamier wrapped his arms across his lean body as if protecting himself. 'I pray to God that you are correct, for if it is not Labesse, the source of this evil lies here.'

161

'Father,' Marco warned. 'Be very careful. You endanger yourself.'

The doors parted. Cinalli stood between them, supporting the weeping nun. 'Have her treated,' he ordered. 'Afterwards we will discuss further arrangements.'

Marco led the nun away, giving Recamier a withering look.

'Father?' said the Cardinal Secretary.

Recamier entered the chamber.

After Phillipe Recamier had recounted all he had learned in St Malo, Cardinal Cinalli sat facing him and Benito Marco across his desk. He raised his eyes to the frescoed ceiling, his expression perplexed. Finally, after the extended silence had become almost unbearable, he addressed both men: 'Who know of these things?'

Marco answered. 'We three, Eminence. No other.'

'Then let it remain so.'

'Eminence!' Marco protested. 'To make use of these facts of Labesse's life necessitates our leaking the information.'

Cinalli lowered his eyes. 'Benito, sometimes the cleverest of men can be astonishingly stupid.'

'Eminence?'

Cinalli shook his head slowly. 'Consider what Father Recamier has learned. First, Labesse is a Jew. Next, according to this woman who runs the bordello in St Malo, he mixed freely with prostitutes and degenerates – not adopting or following their vices or lifestyles, but studiously discussing matters of the spirit, even teaching them of a better life outside their dubious and sinful environment. These people scorned our Lord and His teaching yet they listened to Labesse. Labesse at that time was not ordained as a priest but, according to this woman Simone, he spoke in such a manner that he might have been! She informed Father Recamier that some of her . . . women . . . gave up their sinful lives – '

'Eminence,' Marco interrupted. 'Forgive me. It is a fact that Labesse was later called to God – so, if he had the Spirit within him, it would come out under such circumstances. But this is unimportant for our purposes. The type of newspaper which will receive this information is not interested in printing stories which involve God. They exist – they profit – from the disclosure of filth. The story they will print will involve Labesse's name in a sexual scandal – even though he "taught" the prostitutes some home-spun "gospel of the spirit".'

Cinalli raised his eyebrows. 'And that is all they will print? You truly are blind, Marco. Already we have attempted – for our own purposes – to elevate Labesse to a station which people will find unacceptable. You conceived this scheme to alienate true believers from Labesse. Very well. So I ask you to think for one moment about Father Recamier's discoveries. Whose life was also condemned for His involvement with prostitutes and degenerates? Who also had the power to heal by faith? – which, according to what Recamier has heard, Labesse had a certain gift for. Who, also, was a Jew!'

Marco stared at the Cardinal Secretary of State. 'No!' he snapped. 'I will not say it.'

Cinalli nodded. 'You may not – but the newspapers will. Within seconds of receiving this information, they will realize that a parallel exists between the life of a rebellious, radically minded Jew from Nazareth whom we venerate as the Son of God and an obscure French monk who has risen from the dead whom we canonized. We tread here on dangerous ground. Too dangerous. I intend that not even my fellow cardinals shall hear this information. Father Recamier, everything you have learned you will forget. Do you understand?'

'I understand, Eminence.'

'And you will obey this direction?'

Recamier's haggard face appeared to fill and brighten as though the darkness which had touched him had cleared. 'Eminence, I shall obey, gladly.'

Cinalli leaned forward, his eyes still on Recamier. 'Then you shall obey this also. Go with Sister Theresa into retreat until this is over. I shall make all arrangements personally. For now, please wait outside.'

Recamier stood and placed his lips to Cinalli's

outstretched hand, then left, his shoulders straightened, the weight taken from them.

With Recamier gone, Cinalli's anxieties flooded out. 'Benito, I am seriously disturbed by what our people must be thinking – how they are viewing our vacillation over Labesse's canonization. The monks in Jerusalem know it to be true! How long can we go on keeping silent?'

'I fear that we cannot, Eminence. The canonization decree was in the papal apartments – I have taken the prudent step of having it brought here.'

Cinalli glared at his Sostituto. 'You move above your station. Take care.'

'Eminence, I accept your rebuke, but I acted in your best interests. At present the Sacred College of Cardinals – as a complete body – are still unaware of the situation regarding the Holy Father. Only those cardinals you have chosen to advise are aware. Soon you will be under pressure from the rest to authenticate the Holy Father's decree – or deny it.'

'Deny it? How can I do this?'

'I agree it would be impossible. But I have a suggestion which could be a solution to your problem.'

Cinalli noted the pronoun but gestured nevertheless for his Sostituto to continue.

'Eminence, I am sure you recall the first name given to what we now call the Sacred Congregation for the Doctrine of the Faith?'

'Certainly. The Congregation for the Holy Inquisition of Heretical Error. Created in the year 1542.'

'Heretical Error,' Marco repeated. 'A crime Pierre Labesse confessed from his own mouth last night to the entire world. If this were 1542, he would be damned instantly.'

'If this were 1542,' Cinalli said, slowly, 'he would be doomed.'

Marco nodded, carefully. 'But this is not 1542, Eminence. Our methods now are more civilized! However, the charge against Labesse is the same now as it was then. It demands that he be present for the examination and, if necessary, correction of his new teachings. He should be judged for his crime against the faith. His utterances appear to be heretical – but he should be given the opportunity to defend himself and his views . . . before the decree of canonization is confirmed.'

Cinalli protested. 'Why should he obey us? Why come here to . . .' He halted.

Marco gave a thin smile.

'He is coming to Rome,' Cinalli breathed.

'At our summons,' said Marco. 'At least that is what we shall tell the world. The statement he made last night was his answer to our summons. He is prepared to be examined by Rome.'

'And if he chooses to deny this? Or does not enter the Vatican? What do we say then?'

'He cannot deny that he is coming to Rome – he has already stated he is coming. The procedures of the Sacred Congregation are secret; if he denies that he has agreed to appear for examination, we shall answer simply that all procedures are secret – implying, but not stating, that this is his reason for a public denial. As far as his actually entering the Vatican . . .' Marco strugged. 'Who will contradict us if we say he entered here in secret?'

The Cardinal Secretary arose, and from a side table poured two glasses of claret. He handed one across his desk to his Sostituto. 'And what will this deception gain for us?'

'Time, Eminence. Unless we delay the confirmation of the papal decree of canonization, we are in his hands. Once we have proclaimed him as St Pierre to the world it is *we* who are doomed.'

'St Pierre,' Cinalli repeated softly. 'Dear God. Peter!'

'*St* Peter, Eminence.'

Cinalli looked away from his Sostituto, his eyes coming to rest on a near life-size bronze of Christ in agony on the cross. 'How far must we go!' he whispered. 'What is God's will?'

Marco stood up, took the hand of the Cardinal Secretary of State and lowered his lips to his ring of office. 'God's will is to protect Holy Mother Church.'

'At any price?'

'Even the terrible price Christ paid Himself for the sake

of our mortal souls. Eminence, Christ ordered those who believed in Him to seek out and destroy the Anti-Christ. We need not seek him – he is coming to us.' The Sostituto's hard, clever eyes fixed on Cinalli's face for a brief moment, then he bowed and walked from the chamber.

Alone again, Giorgio Cinalli sat hunched over his desk, his large hands clasped around the goblet of wine, the awesome, and growing, responsibility of his burden crushing him. He pushed himself upright and through his mind ran a stanza of a poem he thought he had long ago forgotten. An English work he had learned as a young student – and even then, had felt the telling weight of the words. They had been written about his Saviour, Jesus Christ.

> I fled Him down the nights and down the days;
> I fled Him down the arches of the years;
> I fled Him down the labyrinthine ways
> Of my own mind; and in the midst of tears
> I hid from Him, and under running laughter.

Now, as he remembered them in his moment of torment, the words seemed equally to have been written for Pierre Labesse. And, as with Christ, there was no escape from him.

The monastery in Jerusalem had a garden set at its centre, surrounded by gently curving arches through which were its cells, its chapel and its refectory, where the monks gathered for their silent mealtimes.

The garden fed the monks as well as assuring them of a pleasant open space under God's heaven where they could meditate or discuss in their usual hushed tones the nature of God Himself and His plan for the world. In the garden were orange tress and date palms heavy with fruit, and vines clustered with grapes from which they pressed their wine. There, too, was a fountain fed by clear spring water which also served to irrigate the soil.

Mortared to this fountain, around its circumference, was a stone bench upon which sat the tall robed figure whom

Rome saw as its deadliest enemy on earth. Before him, on the coarse grass, sat the woman who had fallen under his enchantment and who, in direct contrast to Rome, believed utterly that he was God's messenger – and sometimes, when he spoke, even more.

Pierre Labesse lifted his fine, sensitive features to the sun, allowing the rays to tint the skin which for so many years had not felt its blessed warmth.

'What shall I do in Rome?' Catherine Weston asked, in response to his previous instruction.

'Prepare the way,' answered Labesse, his face still tilted upward to the sun.

'But your brothers are making all the arrangements. What more can I do? You told me to stay by you, to listen and to write. Why are you sending me away?'

Labesse reached down and took her hands in his, holding her in his startling gaze. 'My brothers prepare the way for my present. You must prepare the way for my future.'

Catherine shook her head, her hair made lighter now by the sun, though only four days had passed since her arrival in Israel. 'I don't understand,' she said.

Labesse smiled and it caused a tremor through her body. She glanced away, feeling foolish. He grasped her hands tighter. 'There will come a time when you will know. And that knowledge will be your strength.'

'Will I need strength?'

'More than you have.'

'Then I shall break.'

The skin around Labesse's eyes crinkled, tightening the scars there and on his forehead. 'You will not break. Your love will allow you to bend beneath any weight placed on you.'

'My love for you, Master?'

'Your love *of* me.'

'I feel afraid.'

'Why?'

'Because you know already what might be done to you – and I may not have the courage to stand beside you.'

Labesse pulled her to him and embraced her. 'You will,' he told her.

'Like Michael?' she whispered.

'Like my soldier.' Labesse replied, and lifted his face once more to the sun.

PART THREE

The Hound of Heaven

1

The small boy saw the body, first, as a hump in the rolling swell. And dark, even against the gunmetal grey of the bitter ocean. He sat and watched it because there was little else to do in that part of the world and too much time to ponder. Mostly, he thought about food, for he never had enough to fill even his meagre stomach, but also, he thought of warmth, for he was perpetually cold. He supposed these two things were linked together in some way, as he could never separate them in his mind. But as he watched the dark hump steadily approaching the beach, his thoughts were focused – in grave concentration – on the latter.

The boy had seen bodies before – many, after the great battleship named after a famous hero had been sunk – so they held no fear for him: even bodies which had spent much time in the ocean and therefore had little or no resemblance to any human creature. Why should he fear bodies? Bodies wore clothes, sometimes, and clothes gave warmth. This was a basic fact of existence and he understood it well.

He remembered that some of the older children had been lucky enough to find bodies from the battleship upon which the clothes had not been blown-off or burned away; and some of these had not even been rotted too much by the salt water or torn by the teeth of whatever fed off them in the icy ocean. The father had caught them stripping the corpses and had admonished them severely, but, because he was both compassionate and strong, he had let them keep the sodden, ripped flannel material which once had been uniforms. Then he had gathered up the pile, salt water dripping onto his tough but broken boots, damaging them even more, and after drying the clothes by the fire

171

had walked the two miles to the village to discuss the matter with the women who were expert with needle and thread.

The boy had gone with him and listened as the father had cajoled the women into converting the ruined mass into clothes for his small but growing flock of orphans. He had succeeded and the boy was impressed – but then it took very little to impress the boy when it came to the matter of the priest.

However, in the matter of the contents of the clothing, things had taken quite a different turn. The priest had been firm – even angry. These, he told the children, as with the neck chains and rings found on the corpses, had to be returned to the authorities. He warned the village women also, in case they found items sewn into the material. One of the women foolishly had demanded to know why the priest did not keep the money for himself and his ragged flock, and the priest had looked at her as if she were an insect he could crush with his boot. She had murmured for a moment, then sewed faster than any of the others.

On the long walk back, the small boy had asked who would receive the money from each wallet and the priest had stopped, still holding the tiny hand in his own, then lowered himself to his haunches and answered, 'The children of the dead ones and their mothers.' Then the boy had cried for his own lost mother and the priest had gathered him up and carried him the rest of the way.

The very next day the children, and the entire village, had watched the priest board the creaking old bus, the precious items locked in his stout leather grip, and set off on the long uncomfortable journey south, where the men who flew the roaring silver aircraft and sailed the great ships were based. Only there, the priest had announced to all assembled before he had boarded the bus, could the items be dealt with lawfully.

The journey, naturally, was costly – what journey was not? the villagers agreed. But the priest believed that the authorities would repay his expenses. Ah! But the priest was a foreigner, and therefore it was to be expected that

172

he was a little crazy. Crazy enough, said some – after the bus had disappeared into the distance – to appoint himself the guardian of, and provider for, children whom nobody wanted in a land which God had long since abandoned.

The boy had frowned at this insult, and with the braver ones in the small band had kicked hard at the ankles of those who dared to say such things of their protector. Their padre and their adopted father.

The villagers had chased them away – which was not an unusual occurrence – agreeing afterwards that the priest had no right to bring the brats, orphans of total strangers, to that area. Then they had raised, once again, the rumours that the priest had connections with terrorists in the cities up north, and that the orphans were none other than the spawn of the *desaparacedos*, the disappeared ones. Naturally they whispered this, for it was dangerous to voice such stories out loud, and they dared not imagine what repercussions might follow were they overheard. Had they not, after all, allowed the priest to settle outside the village in the small abandoned church and rebuild it with his own hands? Had they not supplied materials for this task and, later, also for the erection of a smaller building for the children? Perhaps the authorities might misinterpret their lack of opposition? *Undoubtedly* they would! they all agreed, trembling over more wine. Also, the priest bought food from them, did he not? To feed his many tiny mouths. Worse still, they had attended his church! Let the matter rest, advised the wiser ones. No more dangerous talk or we'll have both the authorities and terrorists to fear; time solved all things and the one thing they were not short of was time.

Also, they were afraid of the priest.

The black hump was now on the crest of the wave which would dump it onto the shore. The small boy leaped up from his squat and, anticipating the wave, clung to the body with all his strength before it could be dragged back by the undertow.

The black covering over the body was carbon, and most of it had once been skin. There were no shoes on the body

– nor legs below the waist – but the torso and arms were intact. The head could have been anything. Except a head.

The boy stood up, making a clicking sound with his tongue to show his displeasure and his disgust. He was disappointed. No clothes; no warmth. He bent over again to roll the body back into the waves, then he saw the glint of gold embedded in the webbed black claw. He dragged the body higher onto the shore as far as he could, then squatted beside it, peeling the blackness away carefully until the ring was exposed.

Many thoughts scuttled through his mind as he studied this unexpected gift thrown up by the sea, almost all of him wanting to wrest it from the black claw and run. Run far away, where food and clothing were considered normal and not matters of everyday survival. Almost all of him. The one part that remained unaffected by this urge was deep inside, where his love and respect for the priest, his father, remained isolated.

He examined the ring closely. It looked like a ring a priest should wear. He knew that never again in his life – however long there remained of it – could he offer such a gift to someone he loved. Hesitantly, he lifted the claw, then, squeezing his eyes shut, he tugged. When he opened his eyes, the ring was heavy in his little hand and one charred finger lay on the sand, alone.

The boy glanced around, fearful that his act might have been witnessed, but there was no other soul in sight. Working swiftly now, he rubbed the ring clean on his dark flannel jacket – once part of the clothing of some other victim of the sea – then tucked it away safely.

The body was another problem entirely. After the priest had received the gift of the ring, he would guess immediately where it came from, for it was certain that neither he, his children nor the villagers could own a ring of such weight in gold. It was also certain that the priest would be angry and demand to be taken to the spot where the body lay.

The boy studied the cold waves. He knew that, put back into the sea, the body would return to the shore. There remained only one course of action to take – it had to be buried. But could he do it?

He found the strength, half out of fear of the priest's anger, and the rest out of a desperation to offer his love, in gold, to the man who had become his father.

First he dragged at the body, then pushed, but to no avail. Then, like the waves which had delivered it, he rolled it with agonizing slowness up to where they could not reclaim it again. Here, in the sand, he set to work with his bare hands, digging out a shallow grave, which he finally topped with pebbles. Satisfied with his work, and by now exhausted, he took out the ring once more and polished it hard on his sleeve until the gold cross at its centre gleamed like the sun.

Unable to contain himself any longer, he ran wildly to offer his present to the man whom he loved more than any other human being in the entire world.

The priest was in the chapel when the little boy found him, kneeling at the poor altar, deep in prayer. Seeing this, the boy sat on one of the rough wood forms which the priest had fashioned with his own hands and waited. He would have liked best of all to have surprised the priest by placing the ring on the altar, to await his usual appearance for evening prayer. That would have given the boy untold pleasure, for then there would have been something precious on the altar as in other, less poor, churches – and not just wood and coarse metal worked by the blacksmith. But it was not to be. The ring was in his jacket and the priest was already there.

After an age, the priest arose, backed away from the altar, genuflected, then turned. He smiled, and the boy was glad. It was not often he saw a smile on that beloved face.

'Little Eduardo?' the priest inquired. 'Why are you sitting alone? You are welcome to pray with me.'

'Father, I did not wish to pray. I was waiting.'

'Waiting? For whom are you waiting?'

'For you, Father. Waiting for you to finish praying.'

The boy pushed his hand into his pocket to draw out the ring, but as he did so the words he had practised for the moment of giving vanished from his head. They were gone. All the important things he wanted to say. His gratitude, and that of the others too. His admiration. His respect. All this, and much more, had gone, like the wisps of smoke from the candles which even now fought the draughts in the small chapel.

Instead he said quietly, 'Father, I love you,' and held out his hand with the ring.

The priest blinked, then his face turned pale. So pale that to the boy he looked like the bearded corpse of the blacksmith's father whom the priest had recently buried. Slowly the colour drained back into his face and the boy silently thanked the Virgin that she had not called Father Thomas to her side.

The priest sank slowly to his haunches and faced the boy. Carefully, and with a tremor the boy had never heard in his voice before, he said, 'Little Eduardo. I do not care how many times you have told small lies in the past; I do not even care if you tell lies tomorrow – but tell me no lies now! Where did you find this ring?'

'It is for you, Father. For you to wear. It is a fine ring for a priest. Perhaps there is no other like it in all the world!'

The priest nodded. 'Yes. It is all those things, and I accept it from you and your love with it. I treasure them both with all of my heart. But, Eduardo, I must know where you found it.'

'Will you keep the ring? It is my gift. Keep it for the church. We have no gold.'

Again the priest nodded, a hint of white cutting through his dark beard, but, although his eyes were soft, the smile did not reach them. 'I shall keep it for the church. Where, Little Eduardo?'

The boy pointed at the altar.

The priest shook his head. 'No. Where did you find it?'

The boy shrugged his narrow, bony shoulders inside the flannel jacket, which was made large so that he could grow into it. 'Where you find rings. On a hand. I think another great battleship has been sunk. Perhaps there will be more clothes for us?'

All of this he spoke in breathless bursts because the priest had already lifted him over his shoulder and was sprinting hard for the beach.

'Father!' the boy screamed. 'I buried him! Was that not right?'

The priest patted the boy as he ran, and then the ocean was there before them and the sky was already darkening as the evening descended.

'There!' the boy yelled. 'There! Where the stones make a mound.'

The priest put the boy down and charged forward to the spot. Feverishly, he dug with his hands. The boy came up beside him with a large flat stone for a shovel but the thinly covered corpse was already visible.

'Oh, dear God!' the priest cried, for the first time speaking in English. In despair, he dropped his head and wept silently to the astonishment of the boy.

'Father! You know this man?'

The priest turned to him, his eyes blurred with tears. 'As I am your father, so he is mine. Was mine.'

'That is how you knew the ring!' the boy exclaimed shrilly. 'Your eyes told me you knew it!'

The priest tried to lift the body but realized immediately that it was useless. It was too far gone. He grasped the boy. 'Little Eduardo, do this for me. Get all the other children and find wood. Dry wood. Bring it here. And bring the tin of gasoline I keep for making the small engine work. Then go to the church and bring the holy things I used the day we buried the father of the blacksmith. You remember where I keep them?'

'Yes, Father. In the small cupboard by the altar. Do you want your Bible also?'

The priest nodded, still overcome.

'Won't you come with me, Father?' the boy pleaded. 'Perhaps the others will not listen to me?'

'Tell them all that I am waiting here – on the beach – for them. I will not leave here until they come.'

177

'You will wait with your papa – like the son of the blacksmith?'

'Yes, Little Eduardo, I will wait with my papa. Go now – and hurry!'

The children gathered in the dark of night, silently, as if sharing a great secret, and kneeling like the priest as he cremated the charred remains, completing the incineration process which the blast and flame had, marginally, failed to do.

They watched him from under lowered eyelids, his strong face now a a mask set in stone, his grief burning beneath like molten rock. He took great care with his task and, to his children, he seemed to have exchanged his grief for discipline, for undoubtedly it was a ceremony of greater solemnity and dedication than that which he had conducted for the dead father of the blacksmith, they concluded later. Indeed, had it not been for this dedicated performance, they would certainly have doubted the worth of spending so much time in the cold – there was, after all, very little left of the body. And if God had got the rest – practically half – surely the ceremony should be halved? Nevertheless, they put up with the discomfort because it was their father's papa; the ring which he held throughout the long ceremony with such devotion – but never, *ever*, placed on his own finger, though as a son he had the right – was proof enough of that!

After it was done, and he had gathered up every last piece of remaining bone, he placed the ashes in an earthenware jar, sealing the lid with wire he had bought when he had repaired the little church, then wrapped the bones in the tarred paper he had used for the roof to keep out the rain and wired this too. Both packages he carried to the church with the children following, and there, to the accompaniment of a few sighs and many stifled yawns – mostly from the girls, who tired sooner – he conducted another ceremony. For this, the ring was at last on the altar, shining amazingly between the candles. Little

Eduardo was radiant. Surely no other church in the world had such a decoration?

Then, when the children were exhausted enough to sleep where they knelt (they had pinched each other to stay awake for the sake of their father), came the terrible blow.

Father Thomas turned to them, with a face as barren as the Patagonian desert on the fringes of which they existed, and told them that he must leave them.

There was a moment's silence as the dreadful news was absorbed by small tired minds, then the girls began wailing and the younger boys, caught up in the terror of another abandonment, followed suit. It took the older children and the hopeless expression on their father's face to calm them.

'Not for ever,' Father Thomas comforted them. 'For a while, yes, but not for ever. I shall return. You are all my charges and I could not abandon you.'

He selected Big Eduardo, who was the eldest boy, and Maria Rosa, the most sensible and motherly of the girls, then instructed them in all that had to be done: the upkeep of the church and their living quarters, the daily schooling (which was to be a general revision of all he had already taught them) and, of course, prayers. This last was not to be neglected under any circumstances. They must pray each day for the soul of his papa, and for his own safe journey and return.

Where? This was the question they all longed to ask yet were afraid to in case his destination was so far away that their desolation would be made worse. Perhaps he sensed their fear, for he offered no information.

Finally, he gave Big Eduardo money for food and any emergency which might arise, and this act, instead of giving them a sense of security, alarmed them so much that the weeping began all over again. Sternly, he chastised them, accusing them of having little faith in both himself and God. This stopped the wailing, for they needed a father's harsh – but loving – discipline at that moment.

With order and confidence restored, he oversaw the putting to bed of all of them and blessed each in turn. He appeared to shed no tears, but one of the girls – the youngest, with fearful burns on her tiny face from the petrol bomb which had destroyed her home and family – swore later that when he kissed her it left her face wet and salty. She insisted later that, if they had been tears, then he had cried for all of them and not her alone, although secretly she believed – with reason – that she was his favourite.

He sat watching over them through what was left of the night, then, very early next morning after breakfast, with all of them trailing behind, strode to the blacksmith's forge and purchased from him a small iron box with a strong hasp and lock. Inside this he placed the relics of his papa's body, tugging at the lock many times to ensure it held, as the blacksmith, like most of the village, tended to be lazy when it came to work.

For the long walk to the village, Big Eduardo had carried his leather grip – to Little Eduardo's fury, though of course he could not have managed it himself – and this, after the visit to the blacksmith, was handed over at the place where the bus would stop.

By this time, the villagers had begun to gather, seeking answers as they always did, but Father Thomas offered none, except to say that good friends of his from the big cities in the north would be interested in how well they treated his charges. Or, he added ominously, how badly.

When at last the bus arrived and the children, bravely, under Big Eduardo's eye, had made thier goodbyes – each in turn without tears but with much dry sobbing and whimpering behind Maria Rosa – Father Thomas mounted the rickety steps. There he turned and stared once at the gathered villagers with that cold look they feared – a definite warning, they agreed afterwards – then entered the old bus and sat alone, away from the other passengers, stone-faced again. He turned once as the bus chugged away, to raise his hand and make the sign of blessing over his children.

With the bus over the crest of the rise, the children began weeping uncontrollably and the villagers moved in to console them, though whether through honest sympathy for God's unwanted ones or fear of the priest's unspoken threat was uncertain.

One thing *was* certain. They were marginally less afraid

of the wrath of God than of the dark, brooding priest whom they had named, for his sternness and his straight-backed bearing, *El Soldado de Deus*. The Soldier of God.

The Fuerza Aerea Argentina base at Rio Gallegos was guarded as if it were the last redoubt at the Battle of Armageddon. Everywhere, anti-aircraft guns and missile batteries were angled in readiness for any attack at the grey, but empty, sky. Around the perimeter of the base, sandbagged defensive positions were humped at close intervals, like bulky sleepers on a dead landscape.

If there was a distinct air of readiness, there was also, beneath this, a vibration of fear which seemed to increase whenever a flight of Mirage 111A fighter-bombers shrieked away or one of the Dassault-Brecquet Super-Etendard fighters, a deadly Exocet missile tucked under its starboard wing, wound up its engines in its waiting-bay.

On the control tower, observers scanned the sky with high-powered binoculars while radar scanners performed the identical task electronically and more effectively at greater distances.

But the tangible aura of fear was not caused by the probability of an air strike by the Royal Air Force. That, every man and officer was confident they could contend with – and probably repulse. The fear had its root in a legend. A legend which was all too real. The legend had a name and a spectre. The spectre was death garbed in black, its name the Special Air Service. The invisible devils of the SAS – they were not viewed as ordinary men – could appear from anywhere at any moment like black wraiths, killing indiscriminately and expertly in a thousand different ways. The aircraft might be their ultimate target but the men on the ground were defending them, and therefore they too would be destroyed. Nobody, the legend propounded, ever saw an SAS trooper and lived. Men died where they stood, silently, and even the medics had to be ordered to approach a victim. Not for fear of booby-traps, though these might well have been set, but quite simply

181

out of a deep, near-superstitious terror of making contact with one who had died at their hands.

And when they arrive, the men were warned, beware, because some will surely come in disguise. This is their way. Distrust everyone or you might die without knowing it.

For this reason, the priest, when he was first spotted striding out with his grip and iron box by the outer-perimeter guards, was brought to an abrupt and near-fatal halt by a raking burst of machine-gun fire. The soldiers' suspicions seemed to be confirmed by what he did next – or, more exactly by what he did as the first of the fifty or more bullets hit the ground before him. He vanished. He was there, in the open, as fingers squeezed on triggers, then in one astonishing flurry of movement he was settled behind the lowest rise imaginable in what should have been a flat area cleared of any cover.

If he had not shouted out, they would never have known where he lay hidden.

Naturally they did not believe his claim to be a priest, so they laid down another burst of fire to encourage the truth. But he was no longer there, and the dust their bullets had thrown up clouded their line of fire so that, in panic, they were now spraying every inch of ground in sight. Except, that is, behind them. Which was where the priest was. Directly behind them, in the sandbagged dug-out.

Because the machine-gun was a heavy M-60 and virtually fixed in position by sandbags, the two men could not swing it around when he spoke. But they could move and did so, fast – even as the priest reiterated his claim. One of the soldiers actually had his bayonet out of his sheath and on the way to the priest's throat, while the second had both hands within an inch of his carbine. For that brief moment, they believed that they were already heroes and that their names would be sung by all in Argentina. Their dream was brief and it soon dissolved into abject terror.

The priest reacted so fast that their retinas still retained the image of him crouched before them even after he had struck. One of his hands, stiffened like a blade, flew at the throat of the man who held the bayonet, the other sweeping upward in a blurred scything motion, causing the bayonet point to pass within an inch of his beard as the soldier's arm reached its limit of movement and was dislocated from his shoulder with a crack. At the same time, the priest kicked sideways, his worn but stout leather boot connecting with the ribs of the soldier who had reached for the carbine – but low, so as to wind and incapacitate, and not rupture the heart. The soldiers lay on their backs, unsure of where or how they had been struck, but they knew they were dead. As the priest reached down for one of them, the man fouled himself and the stench filled the dug-out. He squealed and continued squealing even after the priest was struck brutally from behind and lost consciousness on top of him.

None of the soldiers would touch the iron box or the grip which they found behind the spot the priest had used for cover, so they slapped him until he regained consciousness, then made him carry both, staggering ten yards ahead of all of them, as they marched the half-mile or more to the base itself. When he fell, they ran at him and kicked out, then darted back immediately out of reach, for they believed he could still kill them if they got too close. They hurt him because that was part of the reaction from fear.

The base commandant apologized immediately, recognizing Father Thomas from his previous visit of mercy with the ID tags and personal items which had belonged to the drowned sailors from the *General Belgrano*. Of course he remembered! Even though some years had passed. Any man who makes such a long journey, and in such a cause – he enthused while phoning the medical officer – could not be forgotten. The guards? New conscripts. Young boys fresh from school. Stupid, terrorstruck adolescents. To such children, a stranger in a black cassock was certain to be one of the 'black devils' in disguise. Forgive them, Father, I beg you.

The doctor was delayed, but finally arrived and glanced levelly at Father Thomas. 'For a priest you have hard hands,' he remarked. 'One of the men you hit has two fractured ribs. The other will not talk for a while.'

Father Thomas studied his hands and said, 'I am a

builder and a farmer as well as a priest. Soft hands soon become hard under such labour.'

The doctor grunted, then probed at the wound caused by the rifle butt at the rear of his patient's head. 'You'll have a headache,' he observed.

'I have already,' admitted the priest.

'Take these,' advised the doctor, placing capsules in his hand.' He swabbed blood away and grimaced. 'You'll need stitches.' Without waiting for comment, he proceeded.

Father Thomas remained stoic throughout the minor surgery, not flinching as the needle pierced his scalp. The doctor patted his shoulder. 'All done,' he said. 'I wish my other patients would sit as still.'

'Boys,' the commander interjected. 'Give them time.'

The doctor packed his bag to leave, then stopped at the door. 'Those "boys" you hit believed they'd killed you. They still don't understand how you're alive.'

'They almost did,' Thomas replied. 'I had no option. Please tell them I'm sorry for causing them injury.'

'Since when has the Jesuits' Superior General included unarmed combat in the curriculum of the Society of Jesus?'

'Not during my training, doctor.' Thomas smiled. 'At college – before I was called to God – I enjoyed the Eastern disciplines better than our Western predilection for ball games.'

'Then you remember very well, Father, if I may say so.'

'What may I do for you, Father?' asked the commandant after the doctor had departed, eyeing the iron box on the priest's knees. 'Surely not more items belonging to our sailors?'

Thomas shook his head, and for the first time winced in pain. 'May I ask a question of you, sir?'

'*Please*, anything!' replied the commandant expansively.

'Where my parish is, there is no communication with the outside world. My people are peasants; they have no radio, no telegraph – '

'Communications,' the commandant interrupted, frowning, 'are difficult at this time. I would like to offer you our facilities but you must understand our situation at present. We are observing strict radio silence in case the British

184

make use of our signals for intelligence purposes. This is a strike base, Father.'

'I understand. Perhaps, then, you can advise me of any news of the outside world? Any ... announcement ... from Rome?'

'From *Rome*?' The commandant shrugged. 'If there were an announcement from *Washington* or *London*, I would not know it.' He smiled. 'Father, we are ruled by a military junta. A hard-line group who consider that any news from outside – in our present situation – will be damaging for morale. No doubt in Buenos Aires some civilians will pick up the BBC World Service or the Voice of America on radio, but our own broadcasts are heavily censored. If I play to you now something from the capital you will hear military music and much propaganda. Also, and forgive me for saying so, Father, but the Church is not the best loved of institutions by our leaders. Too many priests – of course, I do not include yourself – are deeply involved with left-wing revolutionary elements. You have proved yourself a patriot by your kind act, but your colleagues ...? I'm sorry to have to tell you that many Catholic priests have been arrested for aiding revolutionaries. The Church should not involve itself in politics. Rome must understand that freedom must be protected – and sometimes by means she might consider ... unacceptable.'

Father Thomas explored the injury to his head with his fingers, then said, 'I am not a political man, but surely freedom cannot be protected? By definition, it must be free to be attacked. The choice to defend it is what must be protected.'

The commandant smiled. 'For a non-political man, you make surprisingly political statements.'

'Could I beg a cigarette from you?' asked Father Thomas.

'Please! In the box before you. British. I am afraid I still smoke our adversary's brands. Take as many as you wish.' He reached over his desk and flicked his lighter. 'So?' he inquired, this done. 'Is there any other facility I may offer you?'

Thomas drew deep on the cigarette, his eyes on his host.

'Transport. By air. To Buenos Aires – or at least to your next base northwards.'

The commandant stood up and walked to the window, obviously embarrassed. 'We are at our highest point of readiness; an instant-reaction alert,' he explained. 'There has been an incident between the British and ourselves. We lost one aircraft. A Mirage – the same as you see out there. We might have lost two more had our pilots been less experienced; they escaped the enemy through the very worst weather conditions. I suppose God is on our side,' he added, inspecting his command with steady eyes.

He could see the priest in the window, in reflection. The man intrigued him. Virile, perhaps close to forty, but obviously he kept himself fit. Why choose chastity? Why God and all the impossible things He demanded? A man like this should be enjoying himself. Women for him would never be a problem. But he had decided, long before, that one should never delve deeply into the life of any priest. Who could tell, or understand, what drove a man into stripping away everything that promised pleasure in the pursuance of an ideal? Of course, he was a Catholic himself and believed firmly in God, the Virgin and the Lord Jesus – but there were limits! Praise God there were other men better suited to a vocation. But this priest appeared more shaped than suited. The word was not exact but it was close. A hard, strong individual – not muscular, not physically intimidating, but, yes, hard. Silently hard. Sealed almost – and honed, like a razor stropped to perfection then locked, unused, in its case.

The priest, the commandant was certain, had witnessed violent death, but the question that lay unasked in his mind was whether he had been witness – or participant. Called, he decided. He had been called, and after the calling came the shaping. Yet is seemed that, even after the shaping was completed, there still remained – if perhaps only in part – a ferocity, pinioned down by self-discipline, which was infinitely more dangerous than blind, unchecked violence. As evidence, the condition of the two perimeter guards.

The commandant turned to face the dark, bearded figure

186

who was sitting very still, clutching the iron box. 'I saw a transport aircraft outside, an F27,' Thomas said.

The commandant sat down and lifted his eyebrows. 'Ah, you are familiar with aircraft? They are my passion. All types, from the biplane to the B52. You have flown yourself, in the past?'

'No, but like most men of my age I have done my period of military duty.'

'You enjoyed it?'

'Sir, the F27?' Thomas insisted, ignoring the question.

The commandant lifted his pen and drew a creditable impression of the Fokker Friendship on his desk blotter. 'It is a question of priorities. How can I explain to my superiors that I let a simple priest – forgive me, Father – persuade me to deplete my force? Yes, I know the F27 has no strike capability, but you follow my reasoning? Father, please, I am grateful for the service you have performed already for us – the families of the bereaved also are grateful, but . . .'

'You are a Catholic?' Father Thomas inquired.

The commandant smiled weakly, embarrassed and uncomfortable now that this final pressure was placed upon him. He sighed. 'Naturally. Who is not? Everyone is Catholic,' he quipped lightly, but noticed that the priest's eyes had hardened. An unmistakable expression of determination filled them. He began to rise, his hand at the same time reaching for the intercom to his aide.

Thomas leaned forward and restrained him. 'You leave me no choice but to tell you something that I do not wish to. If you will not help me, then I must place my burden on your shoulders.'

'Father, please – !'

'A burden which you must not share, not even with your highest superiors.'

'I'm sorry, Father, perhaps your injury – ?'

'What I have to tell you may directly concern all that is going on here now – and probably the wider issue of possible war itself. First, I want your vow that you will not reveal to anyone what I say until I reach my destination.'

The commandant stared at the priest, almost totally

convinced that he was dealing with a lunatic, yet held by the intensity of his statements. 'But I have a responsibility . . .?'

'There is a greater responsibility. I promise that, when I reach my destination with your aid, you may reveal what I must tell you.'

'Where is your destination?'

'Rome. The Vatican itself.'

'Why come here? To me? You can travel by train to the capital, then – '

'Too long. I have to fly. Now!'

The commandant's eyes dropped to the iron box. 'You hold that box as if you guard your life. Is that why you go to the Vatican? What is inside that they must have it so urgently?'

'Your vow, Commander?'

'I cannot make such an undertaking. Tell me if you must, but I cannot vow.'

Thomas paused, then his rigid shoulders sagged. 'Very well,' he breathed. He reached inside his muddied black cassock and placed the heavy gold ring on the blotter. 'Please – do not touch it,' he said.

The commandant stared at it, wanting to touch the partially melted precious metal.

'Do you recognize this ring?' Thomas asked, leaning forward still, his question so quiet that it might have only been in his dark eyes.

'I . . . do not know? The cross . . . It seems like a priest's ring?'

'More than a priest. It is Peter's ring. The ring fashioned for the Holy Father on his election – to be removed only on his death and broken with silver shears.'

'Impossible!'

'No. It is the Fisherman's ring. It was removed from the hand that wore it by a child too young to be involved in a conspiracy. I saw the body . . . what was left of the Holy Father . . . myself, last night. It was burned beyond human recognition but that ring came from its hand.'

'Burned . . . then perhaps –?'

'It was he. I know that ring. I have kissed it, here in

Argentina when he toured South America. There is no doubt, Commander. The burned body which wore that ring was the Holy Father. He died in an explosion, a violent explosion. I have seen blast victims before and he was one. From my experience, I would guess at an explosion involving highly inflammable fuel. Jet-aircraft fuel.'

Quite suddenly, the commandant's face had become as white as the desk blotter upon which the ring lay. 'Mother of God!' he whispered. 'Our lost Mirage ... The British delivered a communiqué to us stating that our fighter was in collision with an unidentified aircraft. We did not believe them. Our pilots who returned swore that a British missile hit the Mirage.'

'They're lying,' said Thomas.

Though the colour was returning to the commandant's face, he had not moved. He sat still, barely breathing. Then he dropped his head into his hands, murmuring hoarsely. Thomas fell silent and closed his eyes as the officer prayed.

After some moments Thomas reached out and laid his hand on the lowered head. The commandant looked up, slowly. 'This constant state of alert – we are all pushed to the edge ... those pilots, they were pushed too far.'

'It is done. Nothing will change what has happened.'

'But we were told nothing of a papal visit! Why was he flying in such an area without prior notice? It was complete madness!'

'Perhaps because he wanted to stop the madness. If you knew nothing, and the collision occurred in the airspace you cover, then it is likely that neither Buenos Aires nor London knew either. Would you have launched an air strike on the Malvinas if you thought he might be on them?'

'Never. The junta would not dare. Not if his aircraft landed and he radioed his presence there.'

'Then it is probable that this is what he tried to achieve. In secret.'

'And one of my pilots killed him! Dear God!'

'It is God's will. Will you help me now?'

'Of course!' the commandant said, then fixed his eyes on the iron box.

189

'His remains,' Father Thomas affirmed, answering the question he knew would come.

The commandant shook his head in bewilderment. 'If he is truly dead, then how is it possible that the whole world does not cry out?' He leaned over and flicked a tab on a control panel which immediately fed martial music into the room. Angrily he turned it off. 'Why are they still playing this? Don't they realize? Perhaps you are wrong, Father?'

Thomas shook his head firmly. 'I believe they do not know. I even believe it is possible that the whole world does not know. If it was a secret peace mission, then only very few in the Vatican will have been advised of it. They may not choose to make any announcement until they are given firm proof that he *is* dead. That is why I must fly to Rome without any delay.'

'And why,' added the commandant, 'I should not make explanations to Buenos Aires. Leave this to me, Father.' Through the intercom he gave rapid orders to his aide regarding the readying of the F27 transport and details for its flight plan to the Argentine capital. This completed, he released the tab and withdrew a pad from his desk. While writing, he spoke: 'Father, the purpose of your journey is this. The box you carry contains the remains of a man in my command. We had a death recently through an accident with heavy machinery in our main hangar. The serviceman is actually buried here in Rio Gallegos but that is of no matter. I am writing here an order giving you the right to the official use of military transport, and with it I shall include a copy of the death certificate. I will mention in this order – which I shall sign personally – that the airman wished for his remains to be taken to Rome as he was a devout Catholic. You, at my request, will be the bearer of these remains. If you are pressed for further explanation, you must simply say that you were travelling to Rome in any case, and offered to undertake this task out of kindness. Do not get drawn into giving details – the military mind reacts more promptly if it has only to deal with a direct order, and this you will have.' He tapped the pad, then, using the intercom again, gave instructions for a copy to be made of the death certificate of one Jose Lucero, airman-mechanic, and have it readied imediately. He addressed Thomas again:

'You will be flown to VII Brigada Aerea base at Moron, Buenos Aires; there, you will request military transport to the civil airport and an escort through emigration and security controls – believe me, Father, you will need this assistance carrying a sealed container at such a time as this. All these things are covered in my written order; simply show the documents and you will have no problems. Do you have any questions? Perhaps you need money? Let me give you enough at least for the air fare to Europe. No, no protests, I shall recoup the amount without too much difficulty in my accounting.'

'I have some American dollars for emergencies –' Thomas began, but was immediately cut off.

'Then save them for your other expenses. I give you enough in local currency for a return ticket. You are returning I hope?'

'Of course.'

'Then please return here and tell me all. Now we must set you on your way.'

Thomas stood up. 'I am sorry to have placed this responsibility on you. But there was little else I could do.'

The commandant waved away his apology, urging him to the door while thrusting the signed and officially stamped order plus an envelope filled with money into his hand, dismissing the priest's thanks with a sharp, impatient grunt. In the outer office he bawled for the copy of Lucero's death certificate, which he received instantly; this too he pressed on Thomas.

Outside, in the chill air, he turned with concern. 'Are you sure you are able to fly? Your head injury?'

'Just get me onto the aircraft,' replied Thomas, following him out to the runway apron.

The twin-engined Fokker F27 was parked separately from the fighters, three hundred metres away.

'Let me carry the box,' offered the commandant as they hurried forward in its direction.

Thomas shook his head firmly. 'A Jesuit's fourth vow is

a promise of special obedience to the Pope and the under-taking of any mission asked by him. Through his body coming to me, I am bound as much to him in his death as in his life. I cannot relinquish this responsibility. This is my burden, Commander. You already have yours.'

The twin turbo-props were already spinning when they reached the plane, the crew already aboard. At the steps, the commandant shouted, 'Bless me Father!' then, as Thomas raised his hand for the blessing, pressed his lips to the cold iron box. For the first time since he had learned the truth, his control deserted him and tears rushed to his eyes, only to be whipped away by the backwash from the propellers.

As the aircraft taxied away, then made its take-off run and lifted, the commandant stayed on the edge of the runway, watching until it was swallowed by the clouds. He lowered his tear-streaked face. 'May God help you carry your burden, Father,' he murmured, then walked slowly back, past the long lines of warplanes.

2

The chaos at Ezeiza international airport outside Buenos Aires resembled the decks of a great ocean liner about to take its final plunge. Nobody was coming aboard and all the passengers were frantically jumping ship, leaving an angry crew who only half believed they might survive.

Immigration control was bedlam and all documents were given the hard eye by the beleaguered officials. British passports were dealt with at a special desk and their owners subjected to harassment, abuse and occasional outbreaks of violence. One of these lay on the littered floor as its owner crouched over it, blood from his split fingers smearing the pages as he gathered it up, the pain in his kidney region – caused by the same truncheon which had struck his hands – preventing him from straightening up. Shaken, he observed a pair of scuffed toecaps come into his low line of sight, peeping from under black material. Then a strong arm lifted him to as near an upright position as he could manage at that moment. The tall, heavily built Englishman wrapped his fingers in a handkerchief.

'Grateful thanks, Padre,' said Hames-Ambury, then placed the flat of his large hand to his back and worked at the bruised muscles. 'Wars don't start on the battlefield,' he grumbled, face contorted. 'They bloody begin at the airports, when poor sods like me – who're old and wise enough to know they should vamoose sooner – run for the exits. Christ! they can hit hard – apologies to your cloth and your calling, Padre, no offence intended. I say, you do speak English, don't you? Not yattering to myself like an idiot?'

'Can I help you to your flight?' Father Thomas offered.

'If you've ever wondered what happened to the Hitler Youth, ponder no more – they're all over here. Except they're big boys now. Oh dear, you're with the opposition. Sorry I spoke.'

Thomas turned slightly to the uniformed airman who had driven him from Moron, Brigada Aerea base. 'He speaks virtually no English. Just an escort. Where's your baggage?'

'Oh, that's been sent through to be picked clean. No doubt they'll leave something of the carcass. What's in the steel hatbox, the triple crown?'

'Which flight are you on?' Thomas inquired, ignoring the Englishman's banter and keen to get on now. The airman had begun to shift uncomfortably, obviously not wishing to be involved with a man who had fallen foul of the authorities.

'Stop before you, I should think. This the new method of dealing with rogue RC priests? Escort out of town? Driving dangerously on the *left*, Padre?'

'I have to go, I'm sorry.'

'Don't we all, old boy. Come on. I can just about heave the body onto the bus.'

The Argentine airman spoke rapidly in Spanish as they marched quickly toward the departure gate and Thomas replied in the same language soothingly.

'Bothered, is he?' asked Hames-Ambury.

'It's a difficult time,' Thomas replied.

'Hey, I do the understatement, Padre. British preserve, that.'

At the final check-in point before boarding the aircraft, Thomas thanked the airman and was forced into performing a rapid blessing over the young man.

'Thinks he's for it?' asked the Englishman as they pushed their way down one aisle of the 747.

'He believes a British nuclear submarine has been ordered to take out his base outside Buenos Aires.'

'If that's what they believe, no wonder I got a thrashing,' Hames-Ambury muttered gloomily. He sat down next to Thomas in a seat not allocated to him. A sweating Dutchman remonstrated with him until a steward fought through to them, looking exhausted before the long flight had even left the ground. 'Dicky heart,' lied Hames-

Ambury, easily. 'The padre here is riding shotgun on me in case I keel over and need the password past old whatshisname. Give him my seat, old love, makes no difference worth a damn.'

The steward led the cursing Dutchman away and Hames-Ambury strapped himself in with a sigh. 'Fancy a noggin, Padre?' he asked, dragging a dented silver hip-flask from his dishevelled suit.

Thomas shook his head and closed his eyes. The engines whined miserably as the electronic starters fed in power, then rumbled as they caught, vibrating the great airliner as both decibels and octaves rose higher.

Hames-Ambury peered down at the slumped figure beside him, leaned over and clipped the seatbelt closed. 'Argies give you a rough time, chummy?' he murmured and tried to ease the iron box off Thomas's lap, but even in exhausted sleep the priest's fingers were clamped to the metal. Thomas stirred. 'All right, Padre, wanted to make you comfortable, that's all. Not a mid-air mugging.'

But Thomas merely muttered something in Spanish and was asleep again, even though the engines roared as the captain held the 747 on the brakes. With a shudder, the aircraft thundered down the long runway and heaved itself into the sky.

Father Thomas awoke with a sudden twist of his head to his left, ricking his neck and momentarily disorientated.

'All right, Padre,' said Hames-Ambury. 'We're still flying. The grim reaper hasn't got us yet.'

Thomas rubbed his neck and winced. His fingers strayed to the back of his head.

'Belted you too, eh?' said the Englishman. 'Here, drink, do you good, stoke the old fire up. Five hours and a bit, if that's your next question. Time flies!'

Thomas leaned back into his seat and blinked his eyes at the porthole and the darkness beyond. He reached into his cassock and found the painkillers the doctor at the airbase in Rio Gallegos had given him. He swallowed one, refusing the flask offered by his fellow passenger.

'Best get acquainted,' said the Englishman. 'Hames-Ambury, Bertrand – as in Russell, not the circus feller. That's me done. You're . . .?'

'Thomas.'

'Which bit?'

'Just Thomas. Father Thomas.'

'Right-ho, who needs more than one name anyhow, though I've got a sackful. Parents wanted a large family but hadn't the stamina. Gave me the lot. Broadside. I say, which bunch gave you the thump on the head?'

'It doesn't matter,' said Thomas wearily.

'Not to you, Padre. Does to me.' Hames-Ambury thrust a bent card at him. It gave the Englishman's name and the information that he was a correspondent for a well-known British newspaper.

'I'm sorry,' Thomas breathed and rubbed his neck again. 'I've no information to give you.'

'Pity. Doesn't hurt to let the populace know what kind of thugs we're fighting.'

The Jesuit nodded, then turned. 'Why do you travel to Italy, Mr Amsbury? Are you reporting a story?'

The Englishman's eyes shifted to his hip-flask. He unscrewed the cap. 'You sure?' he asked, then shrugged and swallowed briefly. 'Wild-goose chase,' he said. 'Been chucked out by the Argies, so I thought I'd follow it up. Colleague based on Rio bought a bit of information from an airport hand. Lockheed Jetstar made a refuelling stop there last Saturday, private job, all the executive trimmings, registered Milan, Italy. Long-range wing-tanks, the works. Crew stayed on board, main cabin lights stayed off, passengers slept through the fill-up. But the guy with the nozzle had to get up on the wing at one point and got a glimpse inside. Curtains were drawn over all the portholes but there was a gap in one – or maybe someone inside peeped out. Anyway, according to the fuelling hand, the feller he saw inside was your boss. Now that's a bit odd y'see, because as you know he's not made one appearance since Saturday and the Vatican is happily putting it abroad that he's severely under the weather.'

'I didn't know,' Thomas said evenly. 'My parish is far south in Patagonia. News is hard to come by there.'

'Hard to come by anywhere in Argentina right now, Padre – and for the last two weeks. The whole bloody shooting match is about to begin again if I'm not far wrong.'

Thomas tugged cigarettes from his pocket and offered them, his eyes steady on Hames-Ambury's florid face. He lit both, inhaling deeply. 'I see no reason for Rome to fabricate a story about the Holy Father's health.'

'How about if he was doing a bit of the old peace-shuttle business? Crept into BA to do a little plea-bargaining for God and sanity? Not that the junta would listen, mind you. Worse than Chile, this new bunch, I can tell you. Been through both lots, and these work harder at it.'

'So what do you plan to do?' Thomas inquired, his eyes still on the Englishman.

Hames-Ambury pulled again at his flask. 'Do a stopover in Milan, check out the Jetstar's owner, beard him in his villa, and try to win the Pulitzer prize.'

Thomas nodded and stubbed out his cigarette.

'Heard about your "risen saint"?' Hames-Ambury asked cheerily.

'I'm sorry?'

'Monk. Claims he's a saint. Beatified, canonized, been to heaven, chatted up the Almighty, then popped back with the interview. Exclusive.'

'I don't follow?' Thomas said, bewildered.

Hames-Ambury raised his big shoulders, then dropped them, air exploding from puffed-out cheeks. 'Booze has got me. Sorry. Altitude. Does it every time.'

'What about this monk?'

'Saint,' the Englishman corrected, pulling a twisted grin. 'Unofficial. Passed away, then changed his mind. Doctors got it wrong, my opinion. Happens all the time, check the hospitals. Mind you, he's got the whole bit, I'll grant him that. Stigmata, message from God – verbatim – "Heaven is here", don't worry folks everything's going to be all right.' He turned, suddenly and unexpectedly very angry. 'Balls, the lot! Nothing's going to be all right. *You've* seen it, Padre, been through it, yours truly too! Religion? Sorry, but I think you'd be better off selling vacuum cleaners – hoover up some sins, do just as much good.'

'I'm sorry you feel that way,' said Thomas. 'We do the best we can – probably that's not enough.'

The journalist settled heavily in his seat, the whisky crippling him.

'Where is this monk?' Thomas asked, guessing he'd been drinking heavily earlier.

'Which one?' Hames-Ambury muttered.

'You just mentioned him.'

'Him? Jerusalem, where else. Told you he'd stage-managed it. Best place in the world if you plan to rise from the dead. He's planning on going to Rome. You'll run into him.' He closed his eyes. 'Tell him, cheers. Thinks the Vatican will cheer too, grant him his sainthood, official, rubber-stamped. Not bloody likely, they've done a Pilate on him, washed their hands, shut up shop, sorry, use the tradesman's entrance. No hawkers, no unordered saints, thank you! Going to have a bit of shut-eye, Padre, wake me in Milano – or if they dish out any free booze.'

'Similar things have happened before,' said Thomas. 'The Franciscan, Padre Pio, his hands bore the wounds of Christ and he was credited with second sight, yet his predictions were treated as apocryphal – having no authority whatsoever. There is no reason why the Vatican should treat this monk's claims any more seriously. Would your paper accept a report from you if there were no facts to back it up? I should not think so. You cannot blame Rome for their refusal to accept – or comment – on this man's predictions; that would devalue everything the Catholic Church stands for.'

'Anything you say, Padre,' Hames-Ambury murmured, then was asleep.

The flight seemed to go on interminably and Father Thomas himself slept until he was woken for food. He ate in silence while his fellow passenger blearily ate beside him, ordering more whisky, which he consumed in extraordinary amounts. After this he only opened his eyes again as they refuelled at Dakar.

198

At last the huge jumbo jet thumped down onto the concrete at Milan, and Thomas, feeling wretched by now – almost twenty-four hours had passed since he had boarded the 747 at Buenos Aires – wished the hungover journalist luck as he departed, though certainly not meaning it, then settled in again for the short hop to Fiumicino international airport.

The changing note of the four enormous engines caused his private thoughts to disintegrate and he leaned forward to see through the porthole the Eternal City, bathed in drab autumn sunlight. Below him the autostradas stretched into Italy while the highways spread outward from the city centre, passing ancient monuments and structures which had somehow managed to survive mankind's continual attempts to destroy them and himself.

Thomas adjusted his watch to Rome time, discovering it was past four in the afternoon and, within minutes, the airliner touched down at Fiumicino. He unstrapped himself, retrieved his leather grip from the overhead locker, and moved slowly forward with the exhausted mass of people until, finally, and blessedly, his scuffed boots rested on the hard ground of Rome.

It had been many years since he had been back and, had the iron box not been clutched to his chest, he might have rejoiced. But he had returned in sorrow and soon the city and the world beyond would share his grief.

He strode forward feeling utterly alone, and missing his children desperately.

As Father Thomas was entering a Fiat taxi-cab at the rank outside the main airport building, Catherine Weston was exiting from customs and immigration after arriving on the El Al flight from Tel Aviv. Had she not paused to change a small amount of sterling into lire to cover her taxi fare, she might have seen the priest being driven away.

As it turned out, she hired a taxi only three down the line from Father Thomas and instructed the driver to take her first to a hotel she named and to wait there while she registered. She managed this quickly, then, without checking her room, freshened up swiftly in the Ladies' and re-entered her cab. She gave further instructions to the cabbie involving visits to various newspaper offices in Rome and also the local bureau of the world's leading news wire-service. Having completed her business on behalf of the man who, in a few short days, had both changed and renewed her life so unexpectedly, she ordered her cabbie to drive up the Via Della Conciliazione to St Peter's Square. Here she alighted from the taxi and for ten minutes studied the area, which was in fact not a square but rounded, with a wide oblong forecourt at its westward end overlooked by St Peter's Basilica. From above, the square might have resembled a squat bottle or vase of the type made by potters for centuries.

Whilst her driver waited patiently, smiling over the growing fare the beautiful signorina was due to pay, Catherine walked along Bernini's colonnades to the south of the rounded area, then, moving to the centre once again, paused by the towering Obelisk of Caligula, which pointed like an accusing stone finger at God. Only once, as she stepped back into the cab, did she glance at the Vatican walls. Goliath, she thought, half amused, and I'm preparing the ground for David.

'Papa sick,' said the cabbie, pointing at the crowd gathered beneath the windows of the papal apartments. 'They wait. When he becomes better, all here full. Maybe half-million people come. Too many people.'

Maybe before, Catherine thought, and directed the cabbie back to her hotel. She turned to look at the retreating square through the rear window and felt a sudden and quite terrible contraction in her heart. She closed her eyes. Master, I have prepared your way, she said in her mind, directing her silent words toward Jerusalem.

Earlier – and, unlike Catherine Weston, not checking into a hotel – Father Thomas had ridden directly to the Vatican. At the little street of the Via del Belvedere, he paid off his driver in dollars, having no Italian currency, and approached the Swiss Guard, who wore non-ceremonial uniform of blue and black – for this entrance to the Vatican through the Porta Sant'Anna is considered very much secondary to the Bronze Doors of the Apostolic Palace and the Arch of the Bells. To the Guard's alarm he asked for an escort to the offices of the Secretary of State by one of the men from the Vatican Central Office of Vigilance, the Vatican's anti-terrorist unit. The Swiss Guard glanced at the sealed iron box and immediately made for a telephone, keeping hold of the dishevelled, rather wild-looking, bearded man, purporting to be a Jesuit, in his guard post throughout the call.

Father Thomas had chosen this back entrance purposely, for he knew that using either of the others would have caused him to be tied up in red tape, as under no circumstances was he prepared to reveal his purpose to any minor cleric. There was only one man he wanted to see, and to accomplish that swiftly he had no choice but to create some degree of alarm. To have used the same method at the busy Bronze Doors or the Arch of the Bells would also have brought too much attention upon himself publicly – destroying the secrecy which he believed to be paramount.

His request was granted. In triplicate. Three hard-faced men clad in drab blue uniforms came up at the trot and positioned themselves around him without overtly giving away their role to bystanders as his captors. Thomas knew that he was dealing with tough professionals who, if the need arose, would kill him, so without hesitation he handed over both his grip and the sealed box, then his passport, identification papers and his return air-ticket to the the Argentine capital.

The Vigilance unit were uncompromising in their attitude, for it was not inconceivable that the man before them was either a terrorist with a bomb enclosed in the padlocked iron box or a genuine priest involved in the growing Christians for Socialism movement – the so-called 'Critical Christians', whose liberation theology borrows freely from Marxism, and who work constantly for the creation of a radical new Catholic doctrine for the poor in Latin America. Such priests, they knew, were trained in the use of firearms and fought alongside left-wing guerrillas, killing in the name of God. Such a one could be a problem if let loose freely among the staunch conservatives of the Vatican establishment for whom they had less than Christian love. Vigilance units took no chances whatsoever.

One of the three, obviously the senior officer among them, checked each document thoroughly while the other two hovered tensely, deep mistrust evident on their faces. Beneath their jackets, the outlines of pistols encased in shoulder holsters were clear. The senior man looked the Jesuit over, comparing Thomas's face with his passport photograph. What the man saw he did not like at all. A figure above medium-height, dressed in a dusty black cassock, which in places was ripped, and a grubby clerical collar. The face on the passport photograph was younger, perhaps by five years, with a beard far less mature, but there was no mistaking that the photograph and the reality were the same man. The eyes gave that fact away instantly: dark eyes, brooding on some secret injustice, with little compassion displayed for the camera. Concealing eyes, thought the man, as hard and as reflective as crystal, yet at the same time flat and expressionless. Disciplined, yet slightly wild. Feverish. Too many contradictions. Quickly, he glanced out onto the street. Dusk was falling and few people were about, but some tourists with cameras were showing an interest in the proceedings.

'We'll strip-search him when we get him off the street,' said the security officer. 'We don't want to give those gawpers something to film. You! Father, if that's what you really are, no fuss otherwise we get rough. Understood?'

Thomas nodded, quite cool, and that worried the Vigilance unit. They knew just how intimidating their presence could be to a suspect, but this one seemed undisturbed. He appeared to have everything worked out, anticipating their actions in advance.

'Let's go,' ordered one of the men.

'Wait!' snapped their leader. 'That box. I'm not planning to open it until it's been checked out by a bomb squad. For the present it had better remain in here. We'll have to clear the tourists back.' He cursed.

Thomas spoke. 'If you involve any outsiders – even the

police or the army – I can promise you that all of you won't have jobs tomorrow. Around my neck is the key to open the lock; the key will be used only by the Cardinal Secretary of State; the contents of the box are for his eyes only. I strongly suggest you telephone his Sostituto and inform him of this.'

The senior man nodded his head and half smiled. 'Sure. Only the Cardinal Secretary. So we take it to him and suddenly he's spread all over several priceless Michaelangelos. And for not allowing this to happen we lose our jobs? Father, you're so amusing you'd make my wife laugh. But thank you anyway. You've confirmed that what you've got in that box isn't friendly. We call in the bomb squad, they can destroy it somewhere safe. You, my friend, are in trouble.' He reached out for a telephone.

Thomas looked at him steadily, then he made a statement: 'I have told you the truth. If you choose not to believe me, I cannot change your minds. What I am able to do is this. The moment you are connected to any outside authority, I shall kill you. Even if both your men hold me under their guns, I shall kill you. Also, I shall probably kill one of them before the other finishes me.'

'But you're a priest, Father!' the leader laughed, mockingly. 'You must obey the sixth commandment.'

'He's a crazy,' said one of the others.

'Possibly,' Thomas said tiredly. 'But I've come too far and this is too important.'

The Vigilance officer's hand touched the telephone, his eyes resting on the Jesuit, and whatever he saw in them stopped him lifting it. 'What is in the box?' he demanded, cautiously.

'Only the Cardinal Secretary may know that.'

'You're not leaving me any option.'

Thomas hesitated, then said, 'Call the Sostituto. Tell him you have a Jesuit here and say I said this for the Cardinal Secretary's ear alone: "I am obeying the fourth vow of the Society of Jesus even beyond death." Do it. Believe me, you will be glad you did.'

The man, still hesitant, studied Thomas. He nodded, lifted the telephone, asked for the Sostituto, and when

203

Marco came to the phone repeated what he had been told. He also gave the information that Thomas had travelled from Argentina and was undoubtedly dangerous. For some time there was silence on the phone, then Marco's voice snapped back rapidly. The security man nodded, his forehead creasing. After a pause he said, 'Monsignor, he has a package he refused to open and says it may only be opened by the Cardinal Secretary. A metal box, Monsignor, locked. It could easily be a bomb.' He listened further, then handed the receiver to Thomas. 'He wishes to speak to you.'

Thomas pressed the phone to his ear. 'What is in the box, Father?' Marco demanded. 'Proof,' Thomas replied simply. Marco said, 'Hand me back to the Vigilance officer.'

The man took back the receiver and listened attentively. Finally he replaced it on its cradle. 'Right, we go up,' he said, slightly shaken, but still unwilling to let his professional instincts be cast aside. 'But before we do, we stop and put that thing in another container filled with sand.'

'Very well,' agreed Thomas, 'but I carry the box.'

The Vigilance officer cast a professional eye over it carefully, feeling with his fingertips for anything that might be a detonator on the outside, then rechecked all Thomas's pockets himself. Half satisfied, he stood back and looked the Jesuit over. Then he reached forward and unclipped the Jesuit's steel watchstrap. 'Can't be too careful,' he said. 'Remote-control detonators can fit into most anything these days. OK, you can carry the box with pleasure. Let's go see what Monsignor Sostituto has to say. You do anything I don't like, Father, and we'll cripple you, fair enough. He wants to talk, so we'll shoot below the waist so you won't lose your voice. I'm not making a joke, all right?'

They walked out of the guard post in a tight group, watched by the tourists, and proceeded into the subway leading up into the the Cortile del Belvedere; they crossed the courtyard and entered the Apostolic Palace. Here they stopped while two of the unit fetched sand-filled fire buckets and placed the box in one, upturning the second on top without losing too much sand.

'You reckon you can carry that, Father? Or you want some help?' laughed one of the men.

Thomas glanced at him, then dropped onto his haunches, clamped both arms around the lower bucket and straightened. There was no bravado in the act.

'All right,' said the senior man. 'Third floor. Monsignor Marco said he'll be waiting.'

As they entered the lift, all three had their Beretta automatics out of their holsters and in their hands. 'Up here,' murmured the Vigilance officer close to Thomas's ear, 'the level of our responsibility becomes critical. Up here, we don't cripple. We kill. Even if there is the possibility of a mistake. If whatever is in there seems threatening, we'll shoot to kill. All of us. You'll never get past us to the top floor. Nobody will get the Papa ever again.'

Thomas could feel the man's eyes boring into him at his side as they both leaned against the back wall of the lift, but he continued staring ahead at the other two facing him, arms outstretched and rigid, guns held double-handed, one aimed at his head, the other slightly lower at his upper chest, just above the top bucket. As the lift jolted to a standstill, a cold pressure formed behind his left ear; he heard the oiled clunk of the hammer being drawn back as if it had occurred inside his head.

'Walk slowly and smoothly,' warned the officer. 'Now, go forward.'

Sostituto Benito Marco was waiting outside the lift, but well back. 'Has he been thoroughly searched?' he inquired.

'Not to the skin, Monsignor. We had no time.'

'Father, please bring the package into my office,' Marco requested and led the way. Inside, Thomas, still under the threatening, ready guns, lowered his heavy burden to the carpet. Sand began to spill out from between the two buckets.

Marco cast the officer a congratulatory smile. 'A wise precaution,' he said. 'Now, please stand guard outside the door.'

The Vigilance officer shook his head firmly.

Marco smiled. 'If he's here to kill anyone it can only be the Holy Father, and to do that he has to get through that door and past all of you. I wish to talk to this man alone. If he is an assassin, he'll kill me but he will not get past you. That is what is important. Outside, if you please.'

The three-man team filed out with heavy reluctance. At the door their leader took out the key. 'Monsignor, I'm sorry, but I shall have to lock this from the outside. I must warn you that, if he takes you as a hostage in an attempt to reach the top floor, we'll shoot to kill him even if it is through your body.'

Marco gave this grisly warning a perfunctory nod and waited for the key to turn in the lock. He raised his eyes to Thomas. 'A Jesuit's fourth vow is of special obedience to the Pope and the undertaking of any mission ordered by him. You relayed the words that you were obeying beyond death. As you are alive yourself, though certainly you look half dead, it cannot be that you are obeying the vow beyond your own death. Therefore we are talking of something – someone – of far greater importance than yourself. Excuse my brutal but accurate logic, Father. You mentioned proof?'

'I wish to see the Cardinal Secretary,' Thomas stated.

Marco's gaze hardened. 'You've got this far and you'll get no farther until I am convinced there is a need. Please, the proof?'

Thomas remained still, then sighed as if the fight had left him and withdrew the iron box from the sand-filled buckets. He felt under his collar, tugged fiercely and snapped the string which held the key around his neck, worked it into the padlock and withdrew the papal ring. He placed it in Marco's outstretched palm.

The Sostituto switched on a desk lamp, held the ring under the bulb and lowered his head to it. After a few moments, he straightened, his eyes falling to the box. 'And the rest?' he asked, his voice flat.

'His relics.'

Marco crossed himself quickly and lowered his head, murmuring in prayer. Thomas joined him.

The Sostituto looked up. 'Who else knows?' he asked.

'One Argentinian, the base commander at Rio Gallegos. I had no choice but to tell him. I needed air transport or

I'd still be sitting on a train right now. He won't say a word. He's of the faith.'

'You're certain.'

'I am.'

'So only him?'

'May I sit down please?' Thomas asked, momentarily swaying.

Marco came closer as he crouched over in a chair, head bent between his legs.

'You've had an accident?' the Sostituto asked, looking down at the stitched scalp. 'Do you need a physician?'

Thomas looked up, his face grey. 'Argentina is on full alert; the guards at the air base thought I was British.'

'It's probable you have slight concussion. You were lucky to get here without collapsing on the journey.'

'I had to make it,' Thomas said, his eyes moving to the iron box then back to Marco. 'On the plane, a man, British, works as a journalist, his card is in the pages of my passport, he's following a tip-off that the Holy Father was seen in a private jet in Rio de Janeiro. While it was being refuelled, he said.'

'He's here?' Marco asked, carefully. 'In Rome?'

'Milan. The jet carried Italian registration, he traced its owner to Milan.'

The sharp sound as Marco sucked air between his teeth made Thomas look up again. 'He's right, isn't he?' said Thomas.

Marco nodded.

'Why?' Thomas blurted. 'Why haven't you made any announcement?'

Marco laid a hand on his shoulder, then walked toward a cabinet and poured some brandy into a glass. 'Drink a little of this, Father. Then I'll have a physician look you over.'

Thomas took the offered drink and swallowed it all. '*Why?*' he repeated. 'I have a right to know, I've brought him to you.'

'You have no right whatsoever,' Marco said sternly. 'What you have accomplished does not give you the right to knowledge of high policy. It is sufficient to say that the

Holy Father was conducting a mission he did not wish publicized. The aircraft carrying him was involved in some kind of accident – we presume – and his body, providentially, was discovered by you.'

'By one of my children,' Thomas interjected. 'I run a small orphanage.'

'Did the child – or perhaps the other children – understand who had been found?'

'No. The body was terribly burned. Unrecognizable. They had no idea.'

'You have done well, Father. Your devotion to Holy Mother Church shall not go unrewarded.'

'I don't want rewards.'

Marco moved toward the door. Thomas said, 'How long do you think you can keep this secret?'

The Sostituto stopped. 'I'm not prepared to discuss this further. The matter is well above you. But common sense should tell you that the state of the world at the moment is very grave and the loss of the most popular, most loved and trusted religious leader for decades would be a disaster at this time.' Marco swung away and rapped on the door. 'Open please,' he called. 'Everything is well.'

The Vigilance officer unlocked the door with caution and surveyed the room with quick eyes. He relaxed. The priest was slumped in a chair and the Sostituto stood at his desk, locking a drawer. The iron box had obviously been opened, for its lock lay in the sand, though the lid was closed. He waited while the Sostituto studied the priest's papers.

Marco said, 'Father Thomas needs medical attention. Arrange this. For the present you will place him in my own resting room in the Cardinal Secretary's apartments. I want a guard on the door until I tell you otherwise. Under no circumstances is Father Thomas to speak to anyone. Not even the guard. Is that clear?'

'Monsignor,' the officer nodded.

Marco turned to Thomas. 'You understand, Father, that it is necessary for these precautions to be taken?'

Thomas got to his feet unsteadily. 'Yes,' he answered.

'He threatened to kill us,' said the officer, not entirely

convinced that all was well. He had a nose for such things and he knew something was just not right.

'He has concussion. I doubt if he knew what he was saying. Have him attended to.'

'He knew, all right,' remarked the officer under his breath, then helped Thomas from the room.

'You'd better get someone in here to clear up this sand,' Marco said, turning the pages of Thomas's Argentine passport. He waited for the door to close, then immediately lifted his telephone and spoke to a nun on duty in the Vatican telephone exchange. He ordered an international call to be placed to Buenos Aires, Argentina, and gave the name of the Cardinal Archbishop responsible for the largest Catholic diocese in the world – almost nine million people. All Marco wanted was information on one of them. The nun checked her lists for the number and advised that she would call back.

The Sostituto went back to the passport again. The man who had brought the remains of the Pope to Rome had an English name. Leslie James Barrett. Thomas was registered as his chosen name for the purposes of his vocation. Marco found nothing surprising in this information for, just as forty per cent of Argentinians are of Italian descent, so are many others originally of British stock. Yet Benito Marco was not the kind of man who immediately accepted, or trusted, facts which appeared conveniently to fit a particular circumstance.

While he waited, one of the Vigilance guards came in with a nun and together they swept the carpet of the damp sand, leaving an ugly patch which Marco frowned at, hands pressed to his temples, after they had left. He knew he should call the Cardinal Secretary of State but delayed, waiting for the call to come through first. At last the phone pinged and he snatched at it.

'Benito!' exclaimed the accented voice at the other end of the line, then repeated itself in echo. 'How are you? How is the Papa? I hear he is unwell. This is not bad news, I hope?'

Marco switched to Spanish, as the Cardinal Archbishop's Italian was terrible. 'Absolutely not! I merely need some information if you would be so kind, Eminence. Yes, the Holy Father is unwell, but nothing serious, I assure you. How are things with you? I hear there are troubled times coming in Argentina.'

'Not coming, Benito, they are here already. This nationalist fever in the Argentine blood is a curse. But I must not say too much, Benito. You follow me?'

'Of course!' Marco said, half shouting as the line disintegrated with static. He paused, the receiver away from his ear, as the noise continued. He knew the line was almost certainly tapped by the junta. 'Eminence!' he began again. 'There is a Jesuit Father whom the Cardinal Secretary wishes to steal from you. An excellent man who will do well in Rome. To tell the truth, he is in Rome at present for a short visit. Cardinal Cinalli would like very much to keep him here – and the man is willing to do this.'

'Another Jesuit?' cried the Argentinian, who was himself not of the Society of Jesus. 'Keep him, Benito!' he laughed. 'Let Rome be taken over by you Jesuits. There's too many in Latin America as it is. What do you wish to know?'

'Everything about him, Eminence!'

'What's happened? Has the Superior General lost his records?' Again came the laughter. 'So you want a reference? It shall be done.' A cautious note crept into the Cardinal Archbishop's voice. 'He has not been involved in any sphere of activities outside the Church, has he, Benito? No question of a political problem?'

'None at all, he is a good priest uninvolved with politics. I understand he runs an orphanage for the children of the needy. In Patagonia.'

'Poor fellow, life is desperately hard down there. No wonder he wants to stay in Rome. I hope, if he stays, some provision has been made for the children?'

'I shall personally appoint someone, Eminence – after I have cleared it with yourself, naturally. The children shall not suffer.'

'Very good. Please give me details on this Jesuit.'

'He has an English name –'

'So do most of our banks!' cried the Argentinian happily. Marco chuckled with him but his eyes showed no humour, only concentration. He proceeded to read out all the information he had from Thomas's documents, knowing that if the priest was involved politically he could be in serious trouble on his return because now that attention had been drawn to him – and undoubtedly the conversation was being recorded – he would be checked out thoroughly by the Argentine secret police. Marco shrugged mentally; Thomas was an expendable pawn in a powerful game: an unexpected piece which had to be considered carefully.

'I'll have my people look into the matter,' the Cardinal Archbishop bellowed. 'You'll have the details within a few days – but I warn you the mails are terrible just now.'

'No!' Marco said quickly. 'That would take too long. I would prefer if you or your assistant calls me by phone with the information. Father Thomas is scheduled to leave tomorrow evening and I need to act without delay. At least to give him a definite decision while he is here with us.'

The Argentinian hesitated, then said, 'Very well, I'll see to it. Now, you are certain there is no danger with the Papa's health?'

'None!' called Marco, the line fading again. 'Please call me as soon as possible.' The line crackled and died. Marco replaced the receiver. He made himself a drink, then sat again at his desk and lifted his internal phone and dialled a number. 'Eminence,' he said, 'I must see you immediately. Something urgent has arisen.' He replaced the telephone, finished his drink, then unlocked a desk drawer and removed the Fisherman's ring. The iron box was on his desk. He opened the lid and placed the ring inside. Then he gathered Thomas's documents, put these inside as well and closed the lid. The business card belonging to the English journalist which he had removed from the passport he left on his desk.

3

Cardinal Secretary of State Giorgio Cinalli sat slumped in his big winged leather chair, Father Thomas's iron box containing the remains of the Pope before him on a low onyx table. He had believed himself prepared for this moment – and that he would still be firm in his resolve to go on with the deception. Yet now, faced with the evidence, he found himself shaken, winded as if by a body blow. And his determination to continue had drained from him, so that his heavy flesh felt loose and flaccid under his robes. He recalled his hard words at the secret meeting and pictured himself, bull-like and powerful. It might have been a different man. The temptation to give up was overwhelming. Why was God not at his side, strengthening him?

Standing in front of him, his Sostituto could see his superior weakening, something he had half expected, never fully convinced that Cinalli could handle total power. Now it was up to him. 'Eminence,' Marco said. 'Consider, please, before you make any decision. Nothing has changed –'

'Nothing has changed!' cried Cinalli. 'Here are the remains of your Pope, incinerated, and lying in this crude box and you dare say nothing has changed?'

'Eminence, I implore you, listen to me. The Holy Father's remains and his ring are proof of his death – but they only confirm what has already been accepted by yourself and the other cardinals. Now you know he is dead. But I still say to you that nothing has changed. Labesse is not dead and he still threatens the Church. The Church which you now know you control. He is preparing at this moment to attack Rome. By Sunday he will be here.'

'Sunday? Are you certain?'

'I received firm information from our contacts in the press before I came to you. Labesse has sent a woman to Rome to arrange coverage of his appearance. The day after tomorrow. She has contacted every major newspaper, television and radio station, and the international agencies as well. Labesse plans to further his heresy by speaking in public on Sunday night. The woman is a professional and is making sure that he receives full coverage. She declares that he plans to reveal "the true word of God". Eminence, this "revelation" is to be made in St Peter's Square.'

'He dare not!' Cinalli exploded.

'Labesse is a Catholic monk. He has the right to speak there – or even in the Basilica itself.'

'We'll excommunicate him first!' Cinalli cried in fury.

'That would need the sanction of the Holy Father, eminence, and you think, perhaps, that we should announce his death?' Marco paused. 'He died while in the Vatican, yet over the South Atlantic. Will the contents of this box lie in state?'

Cinalli fell back in his chair. 'We are trapped by our own deceit.'

The Sostituto sat down facing Cinalli. 'We have almost two entire days in which to find a solution – we must not throw away that time. Recall your own words: "Whatever we do is in the name of God." You need now, more than ever, to have faith in the course He has set you. He has chosen you to protect His Church. You dare not fail Him. I understand that grief has weakened you – I too feel grief – but now is not the moment to grieve. Satan is almost at our walls, and he intends to breach them. If you accept defeat now, you will be betraying Our Lord.'

'What more can I do?'

The Sostituto rested easily in the chair, his eyes on Thomas's box, thoughtfully.

'What more can I do?' Cinalli repeated desperately.

Marco reached forward and placed his hands on the iron box. 'Eminence, grant me time. Let this weight you carry fall on me. I will answer to God for my actions. I alone.'

Cinalli stared deep into his Sostituto's eyes, then turned

away and faced the burning coals of the fire, their flames flickering over his face.

Marco arose and quietly left him. He needed no answer.

On the Sostituto's instructions, Father Thomas had been moved while under sedation to a small cramped room at the top of a narrow, winding flight of stairs in the east wing of the Apostolic Palace. The nun who had nursed Thomas in Marco's rooms had objected vehemently, but the Vigilance officer ignored her, pleased that the Sostituto had finally seen sense. As far as he was concerned, the bearded stranger, priest or no, was dangerous, if not unbalanced.

The room was a perfect cell, circular, resembling a turret, with two slit windows with fixed, thick panes. Below them – if a very thin man smashed the old thick glass and squeezed his body through – was a sheer drop into a tiny cobbled courtyard, rarely used except by the palace domestics. There was one stout door at the top of the winding stairs and this was the only entrance or exit. A Vigilance guard, armed, was positioned on the cold stone steps outside.

The turret room had no sinister origin, being merely a forgotten place in the vast rambling palace which served for storage. The lumber was removed and in its place was a folding canvas bed, and a commode, basin and water for toilet needs.

While this was being arranged, Marco spoke to the nun in his office, informing her that the unfortunate Jesuit had suffered at the hands of state torturers in Argentina and was, as a result, partially deranged by the ordeal. For the present, he must be kept heavily sedated and 'supervised' until suitable arrangements could be made. Hearing this, the nun had argued respectfully that, if this were the case, the poor father should be taken instantly to a hospital with adequate psychiatric facilities, but Marco had stated that this was out of the question. He hinted broadly that Father Thomas had information of crucial importance to the Vatican regarding the Argentine junta and their dealings with a high Catholic personage in Latin America. In hospital he might easily, in delirium, reveal secrets the Vatican did not want known by the ever-ready-to-criticize left-wing press. The sister, Marco was sure, was intelligent enough to be aware that certain difficulties had arisen recently in that part of the world as a result of the un-Christian activities of a few radical priests. No, sadly, Father Thomas must be kept away from the outside world, and, yes, though he agreed the conditions were spartan, their very austerity served to keep him from doing himself injury if he became violent. Sudden violence, as the good sister knew, was always a danger with a disturbed mind. Yet, murmured the nun, might he be made a little more comfortable? At this, Marco had frowned reprovingly, reminding her that the poor – even in Rome – had to bear far worse conditions. After the nun left, Marco smiled, certain that by morning the rumour would sweep through the Vatican that a half-demented priest, who might be hero or villain, was being held under guard in the Apostolic Palace. A rumour bound to leak beyond Vatican walls. He was not displeased at this thought, for such a rumour might serve his purpose admirably.

That night, he slept in the palace, but only after he had lain awake on the comfortable bed in what he called his resting room – but which was, in reality, a small, well-equipped apartment – his thoughts centred on the man he considered to be a deadly threat to the life of the Catholic Church and his own career: Pierre Labesse. He also considered, at length, the priest whose obvious devotion to Holy Mother Church had caused him to accept brutality in Her name; to travel halfway across the world although in no condition to attempt this; and to threaten to kill Her own servants if they attempted to call in outside resources – resources who would undoubtedly demand explanations which would reveal the secret he believed, correctly, the Vatican was concealing. And he had done all this without knowing the motive behind the silence of his rulers.

Such a man as this was a potent weapon indeed and he had come at a time when the Catholic Church needed him most. It was almost as if God Himself had sent him. All

215

that had to be done, Marco concluded, just before he switched off his bedside light, was to find the way to convince Father Thomas that he was God's instrument. How, he would work out the following morning.

His answer came early, in the first hour of the morning. His telephone bleeped insistently until it reached his subconscious brain. He awoke and lifted the receiver, pulling the light-cord and checking his watch at the same time. It was a few minutes after one o'clock.

In Buenos Aires it was eight in the evening.

A hollow, young voice, speaking perfect Roman Italian, asked for confirmation that he was speaking to Monsignor Benito Marco, Sostituto to His Eminence Cardinal Secretary of State Giorgio Cinalli. Marco affirmed that he indeed was. Upon this information, the young man introduced himself as the personal assistant to His Eminence Cardinal Archbishop Juan Carlos Mendoza and said that he was phoning from Argentina with certain information requested by the monsignor.

Marco lit a cigarette while these formalities were completed, wondering if the young priest had any idea how much the call was costing. At last Mendoza's assistant began giving details. Marco reached for pencil and pad and, using swift shorthand, took down every word. After seventeen minutes had passed he thanked the young man, congratulated him on his thoroughness and obvious efficiency, promised to remember his name, and replaced the receiver.

For a while he lay smoking, then crushed out the butt, got out of bed, poured a glass of ice-cold hock from a misted bottle in the refrigerator, lit another cigarette and sat at a small writing desk with a low lamp focused directly on the signs he had written. Using a small portable typewriter he translated all the symbols into words, then read through the completed typescript carefully.

This done, he returned to the bed, took the telephone over to the writing desk and had the nun working the late shift on the switchboard call the ex-directory home telephone number of one Chief Superintendent Charles Harrison of the British Thames Valley Police, Special

216

Branch. Yes, he assured the nun, he was perfectly aware what the time was in England.

Marco received his call within minutes. He put down his half-finished glass of chilled hock and heard the deep, surprisingly wide-awake voice at the end of the line.

'Monsignor?' said Harrison, his tone serious, knowing that the man he was speaking to did not make social telephone calls even at respectable hours. 'You need my assistance? Nothing wrong, I hope?'

Marco began without preamble. 'I have a name and a number from a British passport issued in London in the year 1970. I need to know, urgently, whether this document is genuine or fake, and if it proves to be a forgery, anything you can find out about its bearer. Also, there must be on record a duplicate photograph of the man the passport was issued to. Please find this, have a copy made and take it yourself – no subordinates please – to a Catholic church situated in central London which I shall name in a moment. If the priest there now was in charge of the parish in 1970, he might remember the face in the photograph – if he is no longer there, trace him. I have his name, which will make your task easier. Of course I can trace the priest myself from our own records but that will still entail con- tacting Britain, and as you are going to the church yourself you are likely to trace his present whereabouts before I can. I need all this information at the latest by tomorrow night or very early Sunday morning. This is an internal matter and I would prefer it to remain confidential – at least for two more days. If you can hold back putting in an official report on this inquiry until Monday, it would be appreciated. Are you willing to assist me? I assure you this is of utmost importance to the Church.'

There was no response from Harrison but Marco could hear the crackle of paper and waited while the police officer wrote down all he had requested.

Then Harrison said, 'I'll call you back as soon as I have information. First with news on the passport and then with the follow-up on this priest. I'll need everything you have: all passport details, the priest's full names, and the name and address of the church.'

The Sostituto read out the relevant information from his meticulous typescript.

Harrison copied swiftly but carefully, then said,'Monsignor, the passport could be one of four things: a genuine travel document applied for and granted to its legitimate owner; a genuine document as before but stolen from its legitimate owner and now in the thief's possession or sold by him to a third party; a genuine document but applied for illegally; or, a complete forgery. Is the passport in your possession?'

'No. All I have are the details I gave you.'

'But they are accurate and you are certain that the document exists?'

'It did once. Now I cannot guarantee that. But the information is totally accurate; it was copied down from the original.'

'Very good. Well, the first three things I mentioned I can check without having the document available for tests, but the last – forgery – will be impossible to prove without it. That is to say, we won't be able to prove it to be a forgery without the presentation of it for evidence. All we can do is to say that this particular passport has never been issued by Her Majesty's government, therefore it must be a forgery.'

'That is irrelevant as far as I'm concerned,' said Marco. 'My request is merely for confirmation of authenticity – or falsification.'

'Then I'll start my inquiries immediately,' answered Harrison. 'I can hold back any official report until Monday . . . possibly Tuesday. After that, if the passport is a dud, the wheels will already be in motion and I won't be able to remain silent. You'll hear from me.'

The Sostituto replaced his own receiver, finished his wine – which by now had lost its chill – and topped up his glass once more. He sat back in the chair, putting his thoughts together.

Father Thomas, alias Leslie James Barrett, had taken a circuitous route to enter the Roman Catholic priesthood – even, it might be concluded, a devious one. Why? An Englishman, bearing a British passport and a letter of

218

introduction from an obscure Catholic priest running some backwater parish in London, heads for Argentina and promptly applies for entry – successfully – into the Jesuit seminary in Buenos Aires. Why? Years later, he manages to gain Argentine citizenship and, with this, the Argentine passport Marco now had before him. Why Latin America? Why not North America? For that matter, why not Britain or Europe? Why not Rome? It was clear that Father Thomas had excellent command of Italian – and obviously Spanish and English also. A man such as he could do well in the Vatican itself! *Why?*

Marco sipped more wine and lit yet another cigarette. The answer seemed obvious. Thomas alias Barrett, and perhaps alias someone else entirely, had a secret in his past which he had hidden successfully for well over a decade. Very well, Marco decided, uncover the secret and you have a lever. If Father Thomas, the devoted and dedicated servant of God, could not be convinced that he was the instrument of His wrath, then other means of persuasion could be brought into play. God willing, Charles Harrison would uncover the secret – and soon.

Marco looked down at his desk, saw the business card announcing Mr Bertram Hames-Ambury which he had retrieved from his office earlier, and fingered it thoughtfully. His hand reached to the telephone once again, hesitated, then lifted the instrument. The number he wanted was within Italy so he dialled direct. The voice that answered him, in contrast to that of Harrison, was gruff and still almost completely asleep.

'Angelo,' Marco said. 'Benito Marco. Wake yourself up.'

'Moment, please. Give me a moment or two.' There was the sound of a heavy clunk as the receiver hit something, then rustling. The voice came back on the line. 'Sorry, I was sleeping deeply. Pills, I'm afraid. I need them unfortunately. Do you know it's the middle of the night!'

'Morning,' Marco corrected. 'Listen carefully to what I have to say. I shall not be too precise, so concentrate. The matter of your aircraft which is in need of some serious repairs?'

'I understand,' said the voice, still bleary though clearing rapidly now.

'An Englishman will try to see you regarding the aircraft. He is very concerned regarding someone he knows whom he has been told might have flown in the plane.'

'He has been here already. He came straight away to see me . . . I assumed, from his . . . er . . . company in London. He seems a heavy drinker. I intended to call you about him.'

'I see,' said Marco steadily. 'And you convinced him that his friend had not flown on the aircraft?'

'I think so. But he insisted on seeing the aircraft. I told him that it was being repaired – abroad. He told me his . . . friend . . . had been seen on the jet in Rio. Of course I told him that no one he knew was on the plane – only two of my own company executives. I suggested that one of these looked somewhat like his friend.'

Marco fell silent.

'Hello?' called the voice.

'Did you tell him where the plane flew to after Rio?'

'Certainly. It did no harm. Buenos Aires. That was down on the flight plan anyway; it seemed the best thing to say.'

'The worst,' Marco said icily. 'He had just travelled from Buenos Aires – not London, as you assumed.'

Silence fell at the other end of the line. Then the voice spoke hoarsely: 'What shall I do?'

Marco looked at his fingernails. One had snapped clean across; he could not remember when it had happened. 'Convince him not to repeat his story to others. At least until Monday.'

'How?'

'That is up to you.' Marco hung up. He picked at his fingernail until the broken part lay on the leather desk-top. He stared at it, then with a gesture of impatience swept it away with his hand. He poured a final glass of wine and drank, grimacing at the tepid, now slightly bitter taste, then stood up and stretched out on his bed.

Marco admired the works of William Shakespeare – indeed, he was considered an authority on the bard within the Vatican – and the work he most admired was *Macbeth*.

Now, for the very first time, he felt, not simply understood, the relentless warning inherent in that tragedy. Once a terrible deed is done it cannot be undone; it can only be made worse.

He switched off the light and closed his eyes. But he did not sleep.

Father Thomas slept fitfully, the sedative almost negated by the turbulence in his mind. In brief moments of wakening, he saw dull, flat moonlight piercing the slit windows and settling like a sickly vapour on the grey, tiled, stone floor. He could not comprehend where he was or how he had arrived in this strange cold room. Twice he vomited into the commode, when the banging in his head became too much, but blessedly he fell into an exhausted sleep before the moonlight retreated and the first heatless rays of the morning sun replaced it.

He slept even while a nun cleaned him up and changed the commode – nor did he stir as a further sedative was injected into his arm by the troubled nursing sister under the fixed stare of Sostituto Benito Marco's small bruised eyes.

4

In London, that same Saturday morning, Jonathan Barton received two telephone calls, early. The first was from Mary Edgington, informing him that virtually every flight to Rome over the weekend was booked solid following the previous night's announcement on ITN News that Pierre Labesse, the risen saint, would speak in St Peter's Square on Sunday evening and that the crew they were sending over to cover the event had no choice but to fly charter.

Barton grunted sleepily, without surprise; he had expected as much. He muttered grumpily – for he always surfaced badly – that at least 'Heaven was here for the airlines', then asked if any other world-shaking news had occurred overnight. Yes, declared Mary, B. Hames-Ambury, journalist with *that* newspaper, notorious anti-temperance protestor and bottom-gooser, had managed to get himself kidnapped from his hotel room in Milan. At this, Barton guffawed loudly and bet her five pounds that he was simply missing presumed drunk, then kissed her down the receiver and flopped back on his pillows. The red-head beside him, all of eighteen years old, rolled over on to her back, inviting Barton to continue the previous night's passionate battle. The ringing telephone ensured his defeat.

James Auslaire's voice cheerily announced, 'Leave the poor bitch be and take a ride on the Circle Line,' then the phone clicked dead.

Barton leaped up, the girl forgotten, flipped the switch on the coffee percolator, shaved quickly, dressed in casual but warm clothes after glancing at the miserable weather, poured coffee while munching Swedish crispbread smeared with sugar-free marmalade, drank while scribbling a note for the girl whose name he could not remember, then grabbed his Burberry and tweed hat and charged down to the street for a cab.

Circle Line, in the agreed terminology between Auslaire and Barton, meant a crash meeting at which urgent information would be imparted. The cryptic direction was also literal, with the meeting point being Baker Street underground on the bridge over the tracks.

The Ministry of Defence officer was already in place by the time Barton arrived, studiously concentrating with a bewildered frown on a small fold-out map of the subway system. He let Barton pass, then followed him down to the platform just as a train thundered in. They entered separate carriages, allowing several stations on the circular route to pass by before Auslaire worked his way down the train at two further stops. At the third, he sat down beside the hatted TV newsreader.

Barton closed the newspaper he had purchased and said, 'How's your pension? Still intact?'

'You'll look after me, chum.' Auslaire smiled.

It being a Saturday morning, the compartment was sparsely occupied.

Barton raised his eyebrows in question.

Auslaire took the newspaper off Barton's knee and tapped an item on the bottom of page one. 'Word has it that your fellow journalist has a secondary employer – some say, primary.'

'Century House?' queried Barton, mentioning the name of the building housing the British Secret Intelligence Service. 'You surprise me. I thought Ambury was as leaky as a night-watchman's nose.'

Auslaire grinned. 'You and not a few others. But he's well placed. Any journalist with a couple of pints of blue blood in his veins gets his feet in the doors which remain closed to you mere plebeians.'

'Is he what this is about?'

'Surely is, Jonny.'

'The kidnap? Commercial or political?'

'Not announced, but the spooks say political and they've got real sources. But right-wing, not the other way.'

223

'Well, that's not too bad. His daily rag will stand him in good stead with them. Same side of the political fence.'

'Not so, in this case.'

Barton waited, then said, 'What's he been involved in?'

'He'd just exited from BA in a hurry. Had some coming-home goodies for mother.'

'And SIS think the Argentines made the snatch? But what the hell was he doing making a stopover in Milan? Surely they weren't going to debrief him there?'

Auslaire shook his head, dislodging a lock of wavy hair. He pushed it back. 'Here's the story and you can use it, exclusive, just as long as you hold off until you get the nod – through me. Depending on circumstances, that should be soon. Deal?'

'Deal. If it's good.'

'You'll love it. SIS station head in Rio bought information that our presently sick friend in Rome was seen, hale and hearty, inside an executive jet refuelling at Rio international. Last Saturday. Remember our conversation?'

Barton looked at him, the roar of the train buffeting his eardrums – loud enough, almost, to be the rolling thunder of the mid-air collision he saw in his mind. He sat rigid in his seat, swaying stiffly with the motion of the train.

'Saturday,' Barton said, at last, his mouth dry. 'The time factor . . . ?'

'Works,' stated Auslaire. 'If the exec jet was pushing hard, it works.'

'Holy shit!'

'Accurate description,' agreed Auslaire.

'And the jet was Milan-registered of course,' Barton snapped. 'Hames-Ambury got hold of the story through an SIS contact and decided to play newsman even though the information was bought and probably duff. He stopped over in Milan to check out the owner.'

'Angelo Segretti, aristocrat, industrialist, multi-million-aire – not in Italian lire only – and prominent member of Opus Dei. That's a – '

'I know what Opus Dei is,' Barton cut in. 'Right-wing, elitist, semi-secret society founded in Spain 1928 by a Catholic priest with journalistic training. Jose Maria

Escriva de Balaguer y Albas. Wields enormous background power in the Roman Catholic Church. To get into its highest rank – the Numeraries – you have to be single, have high academic degrees or social position, and be prepared to devote plenty of time to the organization. There are lower ranks consisting of co-operators; they are exempted from meetings, don't have to go to the annual retreat the top boys have to make and don't even have to be Christians! Special permission by the Holy See. The name, translated, means: God's work.'

'You just saved me a lot of breath,' said Auslaire. 'And wasted the hour I spent swatting.'

'And Opus Dei is supposed to be behind this kidnapping?'

Auslaire nodded. 'So say the whispers.'

'On the basis that Segretti is a member?'

'In the stratosphere. Air's thin up there; maybe his brain cells ran out of oxygen.'

'You do realize what you're telling me? If Opus Dei is involved, then almost certainly the Vatican is also.'

'Reads that way, chum. It's a cover-up, Roman style. Watergate II, with pasta.'

Barton shook his head, his expression displaying disappointment. He said, 'I can't use it, James, not without real collateral to back it up.' His eyes rested easily on Auslaire's face, half closed, as if he were still sleepy, but his mind was at that moment wide awake and razor sharp. 'It's a set-up, isn't it? The story's good. Even possible. But it's garbage! They're trying to use us. Century House. Hames-Ambury has got something they want and they want him back – whole, not in pieces.'

Auslaire looked out of the window at the filthy tunnel flashing by. 'Sorry. Orders. Warned them you'd see through it. They swear blind they actually bought the Rio story though.'

'What has Ambury got?'

'*I* don't know! I don't think the fool knows himself.'

'So he's a courier and he made a collection from a drop – probably routine – and went gallivanting instead of coming straight home like a good boy. All right, let's assume, for

225

argument's sake, that the Rio information might be genuine. So now the SIS can't work out whether he's been snatched for what he's carrying or for making embarrassing inquiries about the Pope. Opus Dei is right-wing enough to support the new Argentine junta – there's plenty of Italian blood in Argentina – and powerful enough to silence someone who may have stumbled on a colossal Vatican cover-up. A nice fat dilemma, James, and at a guess I'd say they want to use ITN to step up the pressure. They get Ambury back intact, plus package secreted in which-ever orifice he prefers, or ITN tells the world that the Vatican, with the aid of, quote, "a secret, right-wing society of committed Catholics" is involved in a conspiracy to hide the fact that the Pope is dead. If I wrote it like that, do you think I might be close?'

'On the back of an envelope, yes,' agreed Auslaire.

'Our legal department would adore me to use the story. Why the hell don't SIS go to the BBC, they're supposed to be the bloody official voice, after all!'

'Too many principles in that house, chum. You heard the current in-joke? Moscow would rather have one sleeper in the BBC than two active agents in the cabinet.'

'Well, sorry,' Barton said, firmly. 'Tell your friends that the BBC could stand being sued until doomsday but we've got shareholders and a bottom to our pocket.'

'I'll relay your message.'

'They'll work out another deal to spring Ambury – or they'll use muscle.'

'Sure,' Auslaire grunted.

'So do you believe the Pope was on the jet, or is SIS creating fiction to fit possible fact?'

'You mean, do I think he's saying Hail Marys to the fishes in the South Atlantic? God alone knows. My view, the whole ruddy world has gone bonkers. Risen saints. Chaos. A third of the world fighting each other. Roll on Armageddon, I'm going home to study the Book of Revelation!'

'Jim,' Barton said, serious now. 'I'm sorry. But I can't ask the board to take on the Vatican.' He laughed. 'We might have Opus Dei members on it for all I know!'

'Right! You don't know *who* you're dealing with these days. Incidentally, you're likely to find a billet-doux has been delivered to your happy organization just for your blue eyes. It'll warn you that whatever you heard on this train ride to nowhere is subject to the Official Secrets Act and the penalties therein. So watch yourself.'

'Charming!' Barton exclaimed.

'That's life, chum. Never know who your friends are.'

'It's funny,' said Barton. 'The lovely Mary is firmly convinced that the Vatican is up to something – but she figures their deviousness is all directed towards Pierre Labesse. You know what I think I'll do, Jim? I'll suggest that we run a story that the Vatican may be pulling a stunt like the Kremlin did with Andropov. Giving out disinformation while the power struggle for succession goes on behind the walls. Might get them to confirm whether the Pope is alive or dead?'

'If it makes you feel good,' said Auslaire, with a tight grin. 'My stop! Mind how you go, chum. Don't step on the cracks.'

'I'll walk straight and true, no problem!' called Barton as the Ministry of Defence man drifted into the crowd on the platform.

Barton stayed on the train for a few more stations, wondering if the man who was so beloved all over the world was indeed at the bottom of the South Atlantic or simply lying ill but alive behind the walls of his city in Rome. And, if he were dead, then who in the Catholic hierarchy could hope to match him. He decided there was nobody – and for that reason, he preferred to believe, until it was disproved, that the Pope was still alive. He could not know, at that time, just how close he had been to the truth.

Chief Inspector Charles Harrison of Special Branch returned Sostituto Benito Marco's call from his desk at Thames Valley police headquarters in Kidlington, Oxford, at five mintues to ten, Saturday morning – almost exactly at the moment that Jonathan Barton of ITN was stepping off the Circle Line train at Baker Street station. Harrison, too, had seen the story in a newspaper reporting, with sparse detail, the kidnapping of a British journalist in Milan, Italy, but apart from vague professional interest, the item meant nothing to him. His mind at that precise moment was centred only on Marco's request – which, as it had turned out, had suddenly become something of a problem.

Harrison was fifty-two, separated – which he blamed directly on his occupation, although he still held the view that marriage was for life despite its difficulties – and, as a devout Catholic, would not consider divorce no matter what his estranged spouse thought about it. Since his separation, brought about by the presence of another – now sacked – officer in his marital bed, he had given all of himself to God and his duty. But strictly in that order.

He had known Benito Marco for years, meeting him first in Rome during a pilgrimage he had made to his spiritual home one blinding Italian summer. He admired the man instantly and this had manifested itself when he had invited the Sostituto to speak at an annual dinner of the Police Catholic Association. Marco had accepted for his own Machiavellian reasons and Harrison, though shrewdly realizing this, was pleased and proud. The following year, the policeman was voted unanimously into the vice-chairmanship of the association, and Benito Marco had recruited another useful ally.

Harrison had to wait, holding the phone patiently, while he sucked at a mild throat-sweet which he had found helped since he gave up smoking. He was thankful that it was possible to call the Vatican with direct dialling, for he did not wish his conversation to pass through any manned switchboard. He held the view that a conversation linked through a manned switchboard might just as well be broadcast over a tannoy.

In his ear, a thin, flat voice said, 'Marco. Do you have what I need?'

Harrison coughed and threw the sticky throat-sweet into his wastepaper basket. 'Concerning the first request, yes, but I'm afraid that a complication has arisen.'

'Yes?'

'The document in question is in neither of the first three categories I mentioned, but nor is it completely in the latter.'

'By this you mean, forgery?' asked the Sostituto. 'Surely it is forged or it is not?'

'Agreed. But the question has arisen: forged by whom? You see, some forgeries can be sanctioned by HMG, although of course still considered deniable – if circumstances warrant denial.'

'Understood. Government departments, for example.'

'Not necessarily our own. A foreign government – should we say, with a special relationship – might ... er ... not be taken to task for producing such a document for its own uses. As long as such usage benefited HMG in the long or short term.'

'So this passport was "produced" and issued to one of their people. A person employed perhaps by one of their security agencies?'

'Exactly. This particular document was one of a batch, now defunct.'

'And the name of the man it was issued to?'

'This is the problem. I cannot get that information without making this inquiry official and pushing it to a much higher level. It will probably leave my hands entirely – even my service – and pass to another. Obviously I cannot control it if I go deeper. And there is no guarantee that, in the end, the identity of the subject will be divulged. Indeed, I can almost guarantee that it will not. I have a contact who works in a sensitive department in their London embassy and he became very withdrawn after I requested him to check the document in question. In fact, he ended up asking me questions, but of course I had no answers. It's highly probable they'll demand some explanation – even though I asked for the matter to remain unofficial.'

'But that will take them time. If it proves essential, I shall provide some background which will halt any problems for yourself. For the moment leave it the way it is.'

'That might help.'

'What of the second matter?'

Harrison popped another throat-sweet into his mouth unconsciously. 'I'm leaving shortly to deal with that. The priest is still there, I checked that out through our own records but mentioned that my interest was purely personal. As soon as I've seen him, I'll call you – from my home. Incidentally, no photograph. There isn't one on record – not surprisingly. Of course his former employers will have one but there's no earthly use asking for a copy. Do you have any idea what he might look like?'

Marco hesitated, and just when Harrison thought he might be lied to, the Sostituto said, 'I know the man.'

'I see,' the policeman said warily.

'You don't,' Marco replied. 'All you should understand is that this inquiry is crucial to the existence of the Church as we know it.'

Harrison frowned and shifted uneasily in his chair. 'I will find it hard to break the law, Monsignor. Even for my faith.' He did not relish being put to the test.

'You are not expected to, Chief Inspector. Not at any time.'

The policeman breathed gently, with relief, disguising his growing misgivings from the calculating mind at the far end of the line. He spoke, injecting confidence into his voice. 'Then you can supply me with an accurate description of the subject. That will make things very easy.'

'A man changes a great deal in fifteen years and I suspect this one has changed more than most. He has the look of one who has suffered much. I shall give you a detailed description of his appearance at present but I would not rely on this as far as the priest is concerned. He too will have aged and is certain to be confused by my description. Base your inquiry on this fact: the priest wrote a letter, in his own hand, not typescript, for a man aged perhaps twenty-five or twenty-six. This age I have worked out from the forged passport, so it might well be false also. The letter was an introduction addressed to whomever it may concern declaring the bearer worthy of entry into the Roman Catholic priesthood. It can hardly be termed a character reference, for this priest's words give away the fact that he barely knew the man he had written it for. Nevertheless, it contains a powerful plea to have this man considered for the priesthood. Undoubtedly, he was deeply impressed, even moved, by this man; he felt he had much to offer the Church. He was right. This man has more to offer the Church than any I have known.'

Harrison continued writing down all that Marco had said, then asked, 'Can I assume that the letter was also written in 1970?'

'It is dated 2nd October of that year. I have no reason to believe that this is not accurate.'

'Could the letter also be a forgery?'

'I can see no motive for that. We are not exactly overburdened with candidates for the priesthood. No. On its own merits, it seems a genuine, sincere document.'

Harrison paused and Marco, sensing he was perhaps holding back some opinion, asked carefully, 'Is there some view you wish to put forward?'

Harrison scratched at his greying moustache. 'More of a warning, I'd say.'

'Go on.'

'I mentioned that this particular batch of passports is now defunct – and my information is that some might have been issued as blanks. The kind of men who are issued with blanks are well trained in several devious arts. They could – and do – when it is necessary fill in the document themselves. They are issued with a kit specifically for this purpose. The correct ink, indenting stamp, precise instructions, and also a selection of perfect visa and border-crossing stamps. What I'm getting at is this, Monsignor. The man you say you know – if he is the person who originally was issued with the blank – may now be a priest of the Roman Catholic Church, but believe me he was once something else entirely. I want you to be aware of that. I'd guess he was probably, all those years ago, a highly trained assassin.'

Marco considered this astonishing statement for a few seconds, then said, 'I must not make any prejudgements, but I thank you for mentioning this. It will of course be

231

something which will be put to this person – at the appropriate time.'

At this, Harrison felt considerably easier. Reading between Marco's words, he made the assumption that a priest was the subject of Vatican disciplinary action and, unwittingly, fed himself the same fabrication which Marco had given to the nun of a leftist priest mixing in Third World politics. Something he was strongly against.

'I'd better finish now and go to see the priest,' said Harrison.

'Call me as soon as you have accomplished this,' Marco reminded.

'Monsignor, how is the Holy Father? The news one hears over here is very vague.'

'The Cardinal Secretary assures me that all that can be done is being done. I have not seen the Papa myself but, like all of us, his life is in God's hands,' Marco said solemnly, covering his own back.

Harrison muttered a few words of concern, then sorrowfully replaced the receiver.

Charles Harrison drove his Rover steadily through the rain, making good time on the journey despite a frustrating series of traffic jams, which always blocked the main streets in the suburbs on Saturdays as shoppers converged haphazardly on their stores. When he could, he swung the car into side roads and drove between rows of dreary, identical houses, in which, he thanked his God, he did not have to dwell. Harrison's own home in Henley-on-Thames stood in its own modest gounds, detached and alone, like himself. He liked it best that way, he told himself often. A policeman doesn't have neighbours, he had long ago decided, only patronizing or wary cohabiters of the same stretch of land.

He reached Euston, then headed toward Kings Cross and Pentonville Road. Along this, on a cut-off to the right, he found the church. Ignoring the line in the gutter forbidding him to park, he switched off the Rover's engine, locked the car securely, and had to force the partially rusted railinged gate, which gave finally with a hideous shriek as it ground on stone. The church door was closed and locked. Sign of our times, he thought angrily, as he made his way around the side of the grubby building. He found the vestry and, in it, the priest.

He was, as Marco had predicted, an old man. Too old to be responsible for any parish – especially this one, which could never reward a clergyman with anything more than heartbreak. The area, the church and the eyes of the man who tended them were all bleak. For the first, hope had receded, replaced by rebellion and the graffiti which proclaimed its coming. For the church and the man, there remained only faith – and that had been sorely tried.

But Harrison was made welcome with a show of greeting that only the lonely or the shallow can achieve.

'Father D'Arcy?' Harrison inquired, homburg in his hands despite the drizzle.

'You've come! Good, good. You're wet, come inside. It's dry if not much warmer. Don't get many police officers inside, I'm sad to say. Too busy, I suppose, with the problems without!' He was thin, with dry skin that creased like crushed paper. His cassock was frayed at the sleeves and hem, with neatly sewn patches at the elbows in the same black material. But the visible part of his clerical collar was virgin white and crisp. In his hands he held a jamjar containing cloudy yellow liquid and a dripping paintbrush tainted by the same colour.

Father D'Arcy put these down carefully on a newspaper-covered table. 'They use these spray cans of paint,' he explained. 'One day it's the railings, the next the walls – or even the door. The words! You wouldn't believe me if I told you.'

'Yes, I would,' Harrison answered with feeling.

'Ah! I suppose you would. Deal with it all the time, don't you. Why? I ask myself. What have we done to them? At my age I'm allowed to say that sometimes I feel that God looks the other way. It has all become too much for Him.'

'They do it because they were promised a dream which didn't come true.'

'Do you think that?' D'Arcy asked, his eyebrows raised high over his bent spectacles. 'Is that it? There's no worthwhile dream in this world, I'm afraid. It's all to come. Is that old-fashioned of me?'

Harrison shook his head. He removed his mackintosh and let the old priest take it from him.

D'Arcy hung it carefully on a row of hooks, shaking it fiercely first. He indicated a chair, then lowered himself into another opposite Harrison. 'Now! How can I assist you in your inquiries?' he chuckled.

Harrison smiled too, then took a notebook from inside his jacket. 'As I indicated on the phone when I asked how long you had been here, I am interested in an incident which occurred many years ago. You met someone, a man, in October 1970. He would have been in his mid-twenties. He may have been disturbed in some way . . . I get that impression because he approached a parish priest, yourself, for an introduction into the priesthood – '

'You're being polite, Inspector. What you really mean is that he must have been disturbed to have come to this half-derelict church instead of going to one which at least looked like a going concern.'

Harrison gave a tight, embarrassed smile.

'Of course I'm correct,' smiled D'Arcy. 'However, you too are correct. He was disturbed. Well . . . lost is perhaps more the word to describe his predicament.'

'You do remember him then.'

'Certainly. He stepped right off the street. It was raining, like today – only more so. Evening. It was dark. I'd lit the candles.'

'Can you give me some information about him? His name, for example?'

'Oh, the first time I saw him he would not give his name. Mind you, I didn't press him for it either. People who walk off the street into a church they do not normally attend – if they attend any church at all – are usually less than open with information about themselves.'

'So you saw him more than once.'

'Three times, to be exact. Each time his appearance

234

worsened. He looked haunted – I mean, literally. I feared for his health as well as his soul.'

'Did you discover what his problem was?'

D'Arcy crossed his legs, then reached down and picked at the frayed hem of his cassock. 'You understand, I am sure, that I cannot tell you that.'

Harrison nodded slowly. 'Then he was a Catholic. He made his confession to you?'

'He was a Roman Catholic, yes. Beyond that I can say no more. You are also?'

'Yes.'

'Then you are fully aware of my position.'

'Would it make any difference if I told you that this inquiry has not been instituted by the police but by . . . an important personage . . . in the Vatican.'

D'Arcy digested this information gravely. Then said, 'In a matter of this sort, even if this "important personage" from Rome was sitting where you are now and requested – even ordered – me to divulge such information, I am afraid that I would not.'

'Even if you were told that this information, and I quote' – Harrison consulted his notebook – 'is "crucial to the existence of the Church as we know it"?'

D'Arcy sighed, uncrossed his legs and smoothed the skirts of his cassock. 'A young man came to me out of the rain, a complete stranger, tortured by . . . whatever he had on his mind . . . to seek my help. He placed the responsibility for his mortal soul in my hands. His confession shook me. I thought I'd heard the very worst of men's deeds before – but this was a litany of horror. And I, in God's holy name, absolved him and gave him both guidance and a penance to perform. I accepted the responsibility for absolving his sins, knowing full well that I could not share it. But I am saying too much. My answer to your question is that the Church has made her laws and she must obey them herself. If she flouts her own edicts for her own sake, then her existence is truly threatened.'

'I would agree with your view.' Harrison paused. 'I was given to understand that you supplied him with a letter – a form of introduction, in case he really wanted to enter the priesthood. May I ask you if he actually came to see you with this idea in mind or' – he shrugged – 'if it came later, after he had spoken with you?'

'You really are very much a policeman, Chief Inspector. What you're trying to have me say is that perhaps I suggested to the young man that devoting his life to Christ might be a suitable penance. Dear me, no! He was three quarters of the way to Christ already.' D'Arcy mused for a moment. 'Or perhaps, in retrospect, he had already found Him but hadn't realized it. Sometimes, you know, Christ gives us a sharp tug in His direction and we just don't know it. I suppose what I did was push a little while He was already pulling.'

Harrison nodded in understanding.

'Tell me,' said D'Arcy. 'Your powerful friend in Rome? Does he consider this man to be a threat? A personal threat?'

'I had considered the possibility. In fact, I have already gathered some circumstantial evidence which tends to be borne out by what you . . . haven't . . . told me. I've warned him that he might be dealing with someone with, shall we say, a violent past.'

D'Arcy nodded, sagely. 'He would do well to heed your warning.'

Harrison stood up to leave.

'Oh! Must you really?' cried the old priest. 'Stay, do, share some tea with me?'

'I'd enjoy that, but unfortunately I have my duty to perform.'

'To Rome, or to the police?' asked D'Arcy with eyebrows lifted.

Harrison smiled. 'I'll drop in and see you from time to time,' he promised. 'And try and have the local boys show their faces around here a little more. Save you some work with the paint remover.'

D'Arcy opened the door on the foul weather. 'I don't mind really. In a way it shows they still fear God. Just angry, disillusioned children who want their Father to smite them and prove He's still around . . . somewhere.'

Harrison took out his wallet and thrust a large note in

the old priest's hand. 'I'd like to help toward the upkeep,' he said, half turning. 'In its own way it's still a beautiful church.'

D'Arcy crumpled the note and thrust it into a pocket. 'Thank you,' he said, with a small, grateful smile. 'Thank you.' He looked up at the blackened stone. 'Yes, in its way, it is beautiful.'

Harrison left him and walked back to the Rover. As he drove away, D'Arcy was still standing by the open door, watching, like a solitary sentinel guarding a forgotten fortress.

As soon as he had put the telephone down on Charles Harrison, Sostituto Benito Marco's plans for the day began to go awry.

First he received a telephone call from an anxious confidential secretary employed by Angelo Segretti informing him that the industrialist had already left for Rome in one of his private aircraft and asking whether Monsignor Marco would meet him at the L'Eau Vive restaurant in the Via Monterone. Signor Segretti had ordered her to ensure that a private table in the back room of the restaurant was reserved for their luncheon and to request that the monsignor was there by twelve thirty. She had already reserved the table by telephone before calling the monsignor and she hoped, in pleading tones, that he would cancel any clashing appointments. Signor Segretti had urgent matters to discuss, which could not, under any circumstances, be discussed on the telephone.

Marco had consulted his appointments diary and agreed to cancel a routine meeting at the IOR, the Istituto per le Opere Religiose or Institute for Religious Works: a deceptive title for what is essentially the Vatican's bank. Very well, he assented, though disquieted; Marco did not like crises and this sounded like one. Fifteen minutes later, when he got his first glimpse of that day's newspapers, his disquiet turned to alarm. Hames-Ambury's disappearance had made the front page, though not the lead story, of all the major Italian dailies and was mentioned in both *The*

Times and *Herald Tribune* as well. The lead story in every one of the Italian papers covered, as he had expected, Pierre Labesse's intentions to fly to Rome on the following day and to speak in St Peter's Square. London and New York also gave Labesse front-page space, but in their publications the so-called risen saint had to share the leader with coverage of the renewed, and growing, Falklands crisis, and United States military losses in Nicaragua. The Pope's illness was relegated to page two in all but the *Catholic Times*.

Marco slammed the papers down on his desk. He felt hemmed in and needed to strike out at the pressures that were steadily closing in on him.

He calmed himself, then ordered coffee and a light breakfast to be brought to him. He needed something in his stomach to fuel his brain.

After he had eaten, he returned to the problem of Segretti and his overreaction in the business of the British journalist. He knew that the abduction was made at Segretti's instigation, for who else was aware of the situation? Perhaps it was not so bad, thought Marco. What else could have been done, short of the unthinkable? Bribery? No. An abortive attempt to have bought the man off might only have made him dig deeper. Besides, the Italian police had a poor record in rescuing kidnap victims. Kidnapping was so prevalent in Italy at that time that it had almost become more of an institution than a crime. Perhaps Segretti had been clever rather than foolish – and if he'd bought off the investigating police as well . . .! Marco felt considerably better. Things were still under control. And the panicky lunch appointment? Segretti had realized that the papers would cover the story – sensationalizing it as usual – and he'd want to reassure Marco in person that all was going smoothly. So, until twelve thirty came around, Marco decided to put the matter out of his mind.

He moved his thoughts on to Pierre Labesse, his classically trained brain searching for a solution. The most effective method of disposing of an enemy, he considered, was by bringing him into your own camp and making him your ally. Another, more drastic, solution invited possible martyrdom – and in Labesse's case this was not only possible, it was a certainty. But how, when the enemy was marching on your gates with the declared intention of attacking your citadel – and with the burgeoning support of the populace – do you invite him inside without seeming to capitulate? With Labesse, this seemed impossible. But somehow he must find a way, or he would be left with only one final solution. He did not shrink from this, for he considered Labesse to be deadly, and in the Roman Church's history there had been precedents enough – but these were enlightened times and, just as it was said that all roads lead to Rome, so might, in this event, all blame. Yet, whichever way he ultimately decided upon, he had no other recourse but to act. No retreat was possible; the enemy was coming and the citadel could not be abandoned. And time was fast running out.

His internal telephone rang and the Cardinal Secretary's voice told him to come immediately. He set aside his worries, but did not abandon them.

Marco arrived outside Cinalli's office in time to see a short figure clad in a thick oatmeal-coloured habit close the tall double-doors then turn and walk past him, bowing respectfully as he did so. Marco was shaken, instantly recognizing the monk's face from the television coverage of the events in Jerusalem. Without any doubt at all, he knew that the monk was the Father Superior of Labesse's order. He knocked once on the carved wooden doors and entered immediately into the presence of his superior, who was – for the moment – the most powerful man in the Roman Catholic Church. He wondered, as he did so, if that power had just been wielded to arrive at some accommodation with the Church's enemy.

Cinalli waved him to a chair. 'Do you know who that was?' he asked.

Marco nodded curtly, surveying the heavy figure before him. In harsh daylight, the Cardinal Secretary looked worse than the night before. His normally critical eyes were empty and red, as if he had wept throughout the long night, the thin tissue around them bruised and sore. He was wearing his rimless spectacles – something he normally avoided in the presence of others through vanity, though now he seemed not to care. His complexion was sickly, with two high spots of colour on his cheeks, as if he had contracted a fever. But his lips, though dry, bore a smile.

Marco's insides twisted and he felt sudden irrepressible anger. He sensed weakness, even capitulation, in the room and wanted no part of it.

Cinalli raised a letter from his desk and held it forward, offering it almost meekly to his deputy. But Marco would not take it. He would not touch it.

'It comes from Father Labesse,' Cinalli said, still holding it out.

Marco swallowed, but still did not move.

Cinalli lowered the letter and laid it down on the desk, his hands pressed flat on its edges, smoothing it. 'He has written to me in the words of Paul: "Why dost thou judge thy brother? Why dost thou set at nought thy brother? For we all stand before the judgement seat of Christ. Let us not therefore judge one another any more: but judge this rather, that no man put a stumbling block or any occasion to fall in his brother's way. I shall speak only of those things which God has imparted to me for I do not wish to build on another man's foundation. It is written in the Scriptures: To whom He was not spoken of, they shall see: and they that have not heard shall understand." ' Cinalli took his hands from the letter and looked up at his Sostituto.

Marco's face barely hid his fury. 'He dares to parody the words of such as Paul?'

Cinalli turned his face to the tall windows. 'Those who have been closest to him accede that he has the right. That he may be . . . above Paul.'

'Then they have been duped by evil. He is a saint by our word alone, not by any declaration of God.'

Cinalli turned sharply. 'We create saints in God's holy name. He has empowered us through His Church to do this for Him.'

'Understand fully what he has written, Eminence. He is asking you – ordering you – to step aside and let him destroy the basis of the faith. He says, clearly: I do not

240

wish to build on another man's foundations. Our foundations. Of course he does not wish to build on our foundations! Every word he has spoken until now shatters all we stand on. Are you ready to stay inside as the Church crumbles under you? For that is what he intends for you. It is plain enough. His brothers are diseased by his evil – and now you too have been touched by it.'

'It is not so!' Cinalli roared.

'Then cast him aside as Christ did when tempted by Satan!' Marco was on his feet now, standing over the desk, his fury greater than his respect for the office of the man who ruled him. He stabbed the letter with one slender finger. 'He is offering you peace – except it is not peace but surrender. "Accept me," he is saying. "Forget the pain of harsh decisions; sit back and do nothing – and let me destroy you." ' Marco snatched up the letter and thrust it forward, almost into Cinalli's face. 'Get thee behind me, Satan!' he uttered, icily.

The Cardinal Secretary stared at the letter, edging away as it neared his face. Without looking up at his Sostituto, he grasped it and ripped it in pieces. Marco took them from him, as if leaving even the pieces in the room could contaminate Cinalli again.

'You see,' said Marco. 'He has failed. Now we shall destroy him.' He turned away, leaving behind the husk of the once strong man he had known. He knew, from that moment, that the awesome power of the Church rested in his hands.

The restaurant L'Eau Vive is probably unique among the haute cuisine establishments of the world. It is run by a female missionary order and is almost entirely patronized by the highest-ranking Roman Catholic clergy. The sisters who act as waitresses do not dress in their vocational clothing but in elegant dresses, and are usually both young and beautiful. The only way an outsider might guess that these desirable young women are betrothed to Christ is by the gold crosses they wear on chains around their necks.

The L'Eau Vive is located well off the normal tourist

241

track in an incongruous back street close to the temple built by Agrippa in 27 BC, the Pantheon, and it was here that Angelo Segretti waited, in trepidation, for Benito Marco to arrive.

Segretti was well known in the L'Eau Vive and had no difficulty with his reservation in the rear room of the restaurant where prelates of the Catholic Church usually dined. Although it was barely twenty minutes past midday, the place was already beginning to fill. Segretti sipped distractedly at his aperitif, unaware of what he was drinking. For the first time in his life he was terrified. He could see, in horrifying detail, his sumptuous lifestyle being slashed down by the law, leaving him nothing, not even his freedom. He glanced down at his wafer-slim platignum wristwatch then, as the silver sliver touched the half-hour, looked up to see Marco approaching his corner table.

The hostess, also a sister, came over to welcome the Cardinal Secretary of State's deputy, inquired what his pre-lunch drinking pleasure was that day, and discreetly moved away. She knew when privacy was required by her clientele.

Marco pulled his chair in closer. 'You look sick,' he said, quietly. 'Pull yourself together. It is done. We live with it for a couple of days.'

'No,' moaned Segretti. 'You don't comprehend.'

Marco's eyes flicked sharply to Segretti's face and saw the agony – and the fear. 'I won't believe it!' he snapped, his voice a whisper.

'It was nobody's fault! I swear it!'

'Take control of yourself. Drink something. Now tell me.'

Marco's aperitif arrived and he moved his gaze to the lovely girl, smiling his thanks. He sipped, then leaned forward once more. 'Why did you have to choose this place!'

Segretti moved his head from side to side in anguish. 'I couldn't think. It just came into my mind. I thought you wouldn't want me to meet you in the Vatican.'

'Correct,' said Marco, fiercely. 'How?'

'He was bound – security – they had to restrain him. You must see that?'

'Yes?'

'He was very drunk – in the hotel they could hardly move him. Even when they got him out into the country, he was still unconscious. Also he was – unwell. He had a bruise over his kidneys, large, I have seen his body . . .'

'The men hit him?'

'They swore they did not.'

'So? For God's sake! How did he die?'

'He must have vomited some time when the men did not notice – maybe they were sleeping.'

'And he choked to death. What are your men? Imbeciles?'

Segretti again began the motion with his head.

'Stop that!' Marco spat. 'We will now order and then we shall eat. We will appear to enjoy our meal. Do you hear me? Now listen. You will deal with this the same way as you deal with any business crisis – efficiently. Work out what must be done to save yourself and then do it. You are too powerful to pay any penalty – and you're wealthy enough to pay some unfortunate to take the punishment if the body is found. Find such a man and buy him – but pay him well, because you will also be buying his silence. If he has family, arrange that they will be well supported also. Pay as much as you have to and more. Only then will you come out of this with a clean name. Have you heard me?'

Segretti looked up from his drink, then raised the menu as he slipped on gold-framed spectacles. 'Everything,' he answered. 'I will do everything you say. What about the body?' The menu shook in his trembling hands.

Marco glanced at him, as if surprised. 'What body? You know of no body. The man you buy will know about it. You are Angelo Segretti.'

'The Englishman? He came to see me.'

'And you saw him, did you not. He talked, asked questions about you – as journalists often do – had a few drinks and left your house. Isn't that what happened?'

'Exactly as it was,' Segretti answered, his gaze locked onto Marco.

'Then that is the end of it. Now we must order.'

'Yes,' answered the industrialist. 'Of course. Whatever you wish.'

The Sostituto raised his glass and glanced around at the other prelates also lunching. Seeing two cardinals, he dipped his head in respect, then half turned towards Segretti: 'To Rome,' he toasted. 'And Holy Mother Church.'

Around the room other glasses were raised for his toast.

5

In the end, she decided she would do the tour, the whole tourist bit. Why not, I'm here! But not like a sheep, herded and prodded through selected pastures. Alone. Without the shepherd. So she entered the citadel.

She had hoped to find God inside but all she had found was man. Did God need magnificent edifices of stone and marble, or gold, or idols, or heart-stopping works of art which gave you neckache when you looked at them? They were all transferences, heaven to earth – or at least how they imagine heaven to be. How wrong they were. She knew this to be so. He had told her, shown her with word-pictures that heaven existed, unseen but here, all around. You walk through heaven each day, he had said, and you don't know it. Sometimes he was a scientist who worked in a realm beyond present or even future understanding; sometimes a geneticist who took the strands of life and, as if she were an infant, taught her their alphabet, knowing that their words, their grammar, would always be beyond her. But, always he was part of God, the essence of Him. It shone incandescently from all of him, leaving her in no doubt that he was an ethereal being. Now, if not before. God had touched him, held him, endowed him with part of Himself. Called him, and then sent him back, His messenger. That was what he was: God's beloved chosen messenger. And she called him master, as his brothers did. But, just as he was beloved of God, she too was chosen and beloved – by him. And this made her glow, and walk with assurance through the mansions of the citadel, although she sensed the enmity towards her in these inanimate objects of stone, marble and gold. Everything, he had taught her, speaking as superfuture scientist, geneticist and omniscient emissary, feels. Everything has life because, through atom to universe, all is part of the whole and each part is the whole. The superstructure of creation is at the same time finite and infinite. He had thrown her a small rock and asked her its composition. She had refused to answer because she knew that, to him, her answer would have been fatuous. It is you, he had said, after her silence. And me. And God.

I am Catherine Weston, she told herself, and I am stone and I am God. And I am still blind. But each day brings. a glimmer of light.

Michael, why didn't you wait for the bandages to come off?

Father Thomas stood at the narrow window of the turret room, sickly and drained and perhaps half mad, as they believed him to be. Below was the patch of cobbled courtyard, slick and tinged green by damp from the pipes which descended into it, expelling their waste into small grilled gutters. Above was the sky, flat and grey, with streaks of white cloud, like a child's slate worked on at random with the side of the chalk. Also about half a million starlings, wheeling and diving, now in now out of his sight. Straight ahead were rooftops and monuments: the humble to the magnificent. Behind was the door, stout and locked from the outside. Also, a guard.

He supposed that they were still suspicious, and accepted that this was not surprising under the circumstances: so, in turn, he accepted their treatment of him, sure that his obvious loyalty, his proven determination to serve, would make them realize he was no threat.

The guard had opened the door three times during that day to peer at him woodenly before locking it again. And a nun had visited him twice to read his temperature and, for all he knew, his mind as well – for the drugs she injected made his tongue heavy and his mind light, skipping from question to question; but the questions always unasked.

Now it was nearing evening, and the nun had not come a third time, so the drugs were rapidly losing their effect – as drugs did, if you knew how to deal with them once they were over their peak. Nor would she return – at least not to sedate him. He knew that part was over. He had been left alone for his mind to clear, and without food, so that it would be sharp and receptive, like a man after fasting.

Soon the Sostituto would come, the man he had christened, in his drugged ramblings, the raven, because of his glossed hair and chiselled features.

And although he had told him he had no right to know, still he would tell him, why.

In Jerusalem, night had already fallen, and outside the old monastery on the Mount of Olives the media had withdrawn, expecting nothing more from the risen saint until his announced departure for Rome. A small cadre of Israeli policemen continued to mount guard on the building, more at ease now, chatting with huddled groups of pilgrims but avoiding the remaining die-hard pressmen who refused to give up no matter what the monks told them.

At the north-east wall of the monastery, where the garden lay, a low arched door pierced the masonry. Outside this stood a solitary policeman, thankful for this duty, for it gave him the opportunity to smoke unobserved. As he heard the rattle of the iron door-handle in the dry wood, he quickly crushed his cigarette under his heel and stood back. Two figures emerged through the door, the first slight and, even in the darkness, obviously no more than a boy. The second was tall and had to stoop under the arch. Both were monks dressed in habits, their cowls raised.

The policeman made to turn away after a brief nod of greeting, but something held him. An aura. The tall monk gazed at him, and later the policeman would relate repeatedly to anyone who would listen – and there were many – that the monk's face shone as if a suffused light glowed behind his eyes.

'Come,' said Pierre Labesse. 'Walk with us.' And the policeman followed.

They ascended the Mount of Olives until they reached the mosque at the summit and, within its grounds, the small circular Church of the Ascension.

The policeman felt strangely disturbed, part of him wanting to leave, part longing to stay close to the tall cowled figure. As a trained professional at his particular job, he abhorred indecision in others, yet now he was vacillating himself and uncomfortable in the feeling that another person was controlling him.

Labesse stopped and lowered his cowl, turning toward the man as they stood in the compound strewn with Roman pillars and pedestals. Behind his head were the black depths of space with the stars seeming to have exploded around his head. Or from inside his head. Heaven, at that moment, seemed as close as the marvellous face.

'David stood here,' announced Labesse. 'And the Son of Man. Here stood the prophet of Islam. From here God took His only Son back from man. From here the Messiah will descend. The truth is evident in all these things and all are indivisible.'

At first the policeman believed that the words were addressed to him alone, but then he saw the others: dark figures, heavily bearded, their hair worn long and curled – his own religious leaders; two Islamic mullahs, sombre and watchful; and another thickly bearded figure, broad and strong, but grey, a patriarch of the Greek Orthodox Church. There were others too – the Catholic priest from the Church of the Ascension, a Coptic priest who tended the Church of the Holy Sepulchre, a Syrian and an Armenian. The policeman wondered how they had suddenly appeared, then realized that they had been there the whole time, waiting. He had not noticed them. All he had been able to see was the tall monk who seemed to wear the stars as a crown.

Labesse was speaking again. No one asked any question of him. And when he had finished, each knelt and pressed their lips to his hand before he left them to descend the Mount of Olives to the monastery.

The policeman walked beside him and he was afraid. But it was a fear of life and no longer of death.

After all had departed, the Catholic priest stood alone on the summit facing the Old City, his mind in turmoil. He remembered every word Labesse had uttered – it was impossible to forget them – but one word tore at him repeatedly, like a lie from one truly loved. *Indivisible*. It could not be so. Islam, Judaism, Christianity. Islam saw Christ as a prophet. The Jews had caused His crucifixion. Here stood David and Christ. Here Mohammed. From here, the Ascension. From here also the Messiah shall descend. The omega point of all beliefs. But *indivisible*? It was blasphemy spoken with an angel's voice – but it was still blasphemy.

In an agony of indecision, the priest gazed at the stars. One other stood here also, he remembered. Judas Iscariot. Poor, wretched, tortured man. I feel for you now, and I understand. Betrayal is to take the responsibility for love; to love more than others and, though knowing your actions will be misunderstood, sacrifice all for that love.

He made his decision. Rome must know what would be said at its walls.

6

Sostituto Benito Marco returned to the Vatican in time to receive the promised second telephone call from Chief Inspector Charles Harrison.

'Negative,' said Harrison. 'He won't talk. Everything he was told he considers should remain in the confessional. He's old and he's stubborn, and not even a direct order from the Pope would shake him. And I agree with him. But one fact seems certain,' Harrison continued forcefully, his news delivered like blunt, chopping blows, 'your man has a past. One that shouldn't be toyed with. Look, you haven't offered precise information and I haven't asked it, but I must ask you this: have you received a tip-off that Barrett – or whoever he is – could be a threat to the Holy Father's life? It struck me, in the car, after I'd seen Father D'Arcy, that this might be the motivation for your inquiry.'

'Positively not,' replied Marco firmly.

'Good. Because if he were, I would advise you to review Vatican security.'

'So you're convinced that he was previously . . . an assassin.'

'From all the evidence – circumstantial and hearsay though it may be – yes. The worst kind. Official.'

'Did Father D'Arcy tell you anything which gave you the feel of the man?'

'Disturbed. Cracking up more each time he saw him. Which was three in all. Seeking absolution as a last resort. Hence the priesthood. I'll tell you, from experience, when these types crack, it happens fast – faster than they know it themselves. But a word of warning, there's no such thing as a reformed professional killer. Only a changed one. He may have learned about Our Lord – even accepted Him now – but Satan was his first teacher. Remember that in

250

whatever dealings you have with him. Are you sure you don't want to tell me more? I can help you. I too am a professional.'

'Thank you, but it isn't necessary.'

'As you wish,' said Harrison doubtfully. 'The offer's there.' The policeman rang off.

Marco replaced his receiver, then pressed his palms together as if praying and rested his chin on them. So it is up to me, he thought. But Giorgio Cinalli, Cardinal, and Secretary of State to the Holy See, you cannot escape your part.

He lifted his telephone and called a number in Paris, France.

Marco decided to inform the Cardinal Secretary immediately of his solution, because of the time factor. There was, of course, the danger that the longer Cinalli had to agonize over it the greater the chance of his resolve slipping again. But Marco believed he could handle that. Once a man is already deeply involved in a conspiracy, making the decision to turn back, although the urge may be strong, is difficult. Sometimes it is easier to abdicate and allow himself to be drawn forward.

He found Cinalli in his apartments, apparently asleep, but in reality just lying on his bed with his eyes closed. The Cardinal Secretary opened his eyes at his deputy's knock, mumbled words of admittance, then allowed himself to be helped from the bed and into his drawing room.

Marco had decided to play it gently, but resolutely, not allowing Cinalli any opportunity for retreat – or refusal. For this he had weapons, deterrents, which he was fully prepared to use, for even broken men can prove extraordinarily defiant just before the axe falls.

'I have been praying for guidance,' announced Cinalli, from his great armchair. 'Also thinking.'

'You are unwell, Eminence. You must not tax yourself,' advised Marco.

'Would you care for wine?' asked Cinalli distractedly.

251

'For the moment, no. Thank you, Eminence. For yourself perhaps?'

Cinalli shook his large head slowly, as if weary of its weight.

'I would like to talk seriously with you, Eminence,' Marco confided.

'Do we ever talk otherwise – these days?' Cinalli replied.

'This is more serious than any conversation we have ever shared.'

Cinalli appeared not to hear him. 'You were right to chastise me. I was seeking an easy way. Labesse, to his Father Superior, is a man above all other men. I was almost convinced of this myself after speaking with the good father.'

'If Labesse is a man above all other men, then he is doubly dangerous,' Marco remarked.

'Please . . .?' invited Cinalli, hand extended. 'You came to speak. Continue.'

Marco inclined his head, respectfully, then began: 'I have placed the relics of the Holy Father in a secure place –'

'Where?' Cinalli demanded, the sudden mention of the physical evidence of the conspiracy he was mentally blocking out shaking him, so that his reaction verged on anger – against himself.

Marco hesitated fractionally. 'In the Borgia chapel.'

'There!' Cinalli exclaimed. 'Why?'

'Because the chapel is in the Secret Archives; because these are owned by the Pope; and because no one may enter them without his personal concession. Thus, under the circumstances, there could not be anywhere more secure.'

'But in that . . . profligate's private place of worship!'

'It is a chapel. Its previous connections are irrelevant.' Marco failed to mention that one connection with the Borgias was decidedly relevant, but this he would raise later.

Cinalli spread his hands resignedly, then dropped them into his lap.

Marco continued: 'Certain developments have occurred

during the day which I have not brought to your attention, Eminence – I have been concerned regarding your health. But it has become imperative, now, that you hear of them.'

At this, Cinalli passed a hand over his face, dreading his Sostituto's next words, yet knowing he had no alternative but to listen. Unless of course he resigned his office, and even that act was unlikely to save him. The web of conspiracy had him trapped beyond redemption. He motioned Marco on.

'Two matters. The first concerns the death of the Holy Father and your decision, in conjunction with the selected cardinals, to keep this fact secret. The second concerns the man whose . . . "resurrection" caused that unavoidable decision to be made.' Marco paused, then asked, 'Have you read your newspapers today, Eminence?'

'Briefly,' muttered Cinalli.

'You noticed, perhaps, an item regarding the abduction of a British journalist in Milano?'

Cinalli shrugged, then nodded.

'This abduction was carried out on the orders of a member of Opus Dei.' Marco overrode Cinallis's startled interruption. 'There was no alternative. It was you the movement was protecting. The journalist had uncovered information that the Papa had been seen on board a private aircraft at Rio de Janeiro. How he got hold of the information is unimportant. What is important is that action was taken to stop him verifying his information with hard facts. If he had succeeded in getting these, the story would be in the newspapers now. He was very close to the truth. His informant in Rio had passed on the number of the aircraft, and the journalist traced this registration to Angelo Segretti. He actually met with Segretti, and Segretti called to warn us.'

'Segretti should have denied it!' snapped Cinalli.

'He did, but sensed the man did not believe him. The plane *had* landed in Rio, that he could not deny because of the logging of the registration number there. Also, as far as Rio, the aircraft's flight plan was declared in advance – as you were aware. The change of course to the Falkland Islands – instead of flying onward to Buenos Aires, which the captain declared as his next destination due to a fictional change of plan by his employer – was to have taken place under the guise of a malfunction of the aircraft's navigational equipment. This, as was agreed with the Holy Father, was the only way of keeping the peace mission a total secret until he arrived in the Falklands. Tragically, it was not the Lord's will that he should do so.' Nothing could save Cinalli from the horror of Marco's next statement. 'The journalist is dead.'

Cinalli seemed not to comprehend, for he did not react overtly, but simply stared forward.

Marco repeated himself. 'The journalist is dead. He had been drinking heavily. I have a few facts . . . it appears he vomited while in a stupor and choked to death. He was bound, so it is possible that he could not move.'

Cinalli murmured a few words to the Holy Virgin, inaudibly but the plea in them was clear. 'Segretti?' he asked blankly, after a while.

'Safe. Protecting you still – by remaining silent.'

'He is a loyal servant of the Church,' Cinalli responded, as if no crisis existed.

'The body might be found,' warned Marco. 'Segretti is seeing to it that you are in no way linked with the abduction . . . or the tragic death.'

'The Church must be protected at all costs,' said Cinalli in a dull monotone.

Marco knew that he had retreated inside himself almost totally, and that he must be drawn out again if he were to be any use at all. 'Eminence, you must listen carefully to what I tell you. It is imperative that you understand. Please!'

Cinalli heaved a deep sigh, raised his hands from the arms of the chair, then let them flop back as though his energy had been drained. 'Very well,' he murmured.

Marco's eyes were hard, and fixed resolutely on his superior. 'I have had fresh word from Jerusalem. The father from the Church of the Ascension called to speak with His Holiness. Naturally I intercepted the call. Labesse had his brothers arrange a gathering of representatives from a number of religious sects in the Holy City. He spoke with

254

them on the summit of the Mount of Olives. He revealed to them part of what he will preach when he comes to Rome.'

Cinalli's dull gaze quickened. 'Proceed,' he said, cautiously.

'He made a number of statements – but it is the first which you must hear immediately and pass judgement upon. He made this claim. All the religions of the world are indivisible. The Islamic prophet Mohammed and Christ are indivisible – the same holy being in differing forms. That God has sent His son in many guises and on numerous occasions – Jesus Christ Our Lord being only one. We have been tested, time and time again, and each time we have failed Him by either not recognizing our "saviour" or destroying Him, as the Jews did Jesus. There is no one true Church of Christ – all claims are of equal merit. We must recognize the claims of all. We must recognize that Christianity and Islam and Judaism are *indivisible*. His heresy grows by the hour. This man *must* be stopped! Eminence, I know how we must deal with him.'

Cinalli lowered his heavy face to his hands. 'He is our Saul of Tarsus,' he whispered, then looked directly at his Sostituto, his eyes searching. 'He destroys us!' Fear filled Cinalli's eyes, though still he sought hope. 'But God's hand touched Saul . . .'

'It is not *God's* hand which has touched Pierre Labesse, Eminence.'

The telephone rang. Cinalli glanced toward it, but Marco sat motionless as though he could not hear the insistent ringing. The Cardinal Secretary seemed to sense that his deputy was not going to answer it, so he pushed himself out of his chair and lifted the receiver to his ear. The earpiece made several clicking noises, then the line cleared. A French-accented voice spoke Cinalli's name and the Cardinal Secretary confirmed that he was speaking.

The French cardinal, calling from Paris, enunciated his next words carefully, made aware of Cinalli's state of mind by Marco's personal call to him earlier. He said, 'Giorgio. Remember the things we spoke of when last I saw you. I said to you: God has entrusted His Church into our hands. We are its guardians. Do you believe this?'

Cinalli nodded his head as if the Frenchman were before him, then murmured, 'I remember.'

'Can you remember why I said this, Giorgio? Do you recall it was because there was a fear among us, the guardians of His Church, that we might not be able to do enough to stop Labesse?'

'I remember,' Cinalli repeated.

'Labesse comes to Rome tomorrow,' said the Frenchman.

'I know.'

'Giorgio, recall please the last words you said to me – when we were alone.'

Cinalli stood, swaying slightly, his mind refusing to work, then, as if by silent prompting, the same lines came back to him which had sprung to his mind when he had first heard Labesse was coming to Rome. Lines from a poem. And with the lines came the title. With the title, recall.

He said, 'Satan has awakened his Hound of Hell. We must find our Hound of Heaven.'

'Those were your words,' affirmed the French cardinal. 'What did you mean by them?'

Cinalli put his hand flat on the exquisite Louis XIV table upon which the telephone rested, settling his weight forward. 'I was speaking of our last resort. Of his destruction.'

'Of Labesse's destruction?' asked the Frenchman, determined to have Cinalli speak the name aloud.

'Labesse, yes.'

'Cardinal Secretary,' said the Frenchman, reverting to cold formality. 'Your Sostituto has found our Hound of Heaven.'

Cinalli turned to face Benito Marco, and in his mind it seemed as if the cold voice on the telephone and the hard, fixed eyes before him belonged to the same man. If not that, he thought, then the same conspiracy, luring him even further to his destruction. But even sensing this, he relented – silently, though Marco could see it in his eyes.

256

'Listen to what he will tell you,' said the Frenchman. 'And do what must be done. There is no retreat possible.'

Nor any escape, thought Cinalli, as the line clicked dead. He wondered why he had been so weak when he was known as 'the strong man'? Sham. My hands sweat, my stomach is water, I flounder when I should be striking for the shore. What have I lost that I had before? What allowed me to speak deadly words and mean them? Was it God? And now He has deserted me – so that I am, like Samson, shorn, weak and pitiful? Lord, return my strength. Send me forward. Let me do what must me done. *Thy* will be done.

He waited, perhaps for an answer, or a sign, but none came. Finally, as he knew he must, he said, 'What must I do?'

Marco told him.

At the Sostituto's orders, the nun had taken Father Thomas a complete change of clothing. And bathe him, Marco had said, but do not take him from the room.

He was sleeping again when she entered, a young sister behind her with a large copper bowl filled with hot water and towels over her arms. These delivered, the nun sent the young one away, for she knew the girl to be a virgin and would suffer a virgin's shame on seeing a man's body. The nun herself was no virgin; she had known men before Christ claimed her, so the anatomy of men held no secrets.

The odour in the turret room was stale because the windows did not open, so she had the Vigilance guard wedge the door open for five minutes while she arranged the things she would need. When this was done she closed the door herself and knelt beside the narrow canvas bed for a few moments, offering her prayers for him. He stirred, opened his eyes and saw her, but did not move.

Her devotions over, she raised her eyes to him.

He smiled through his matted beard and she noted his fine teeth with pleasure though, for long afterwards, it was his dark gaze that would remain with her – level and penetrating, laying her open but not discarding her; at the same time compassionate and dangerous.

She lowered her eyes and her hands reached for his clothes. He neither resisted nor helped her, submitting as if this were a necessary preparation he must endure.

The fact of his nakedness could not shock her, but his scars did. Old scars too cruel to have been caused by accident. Dead, white star-shapes on his back and on his front deep indentations closed-up and puckered, running evenly spaced from shoulder to groin. He said nothing, offered no explanation, even as she gasped.

After she had bathed him and towelled him dry, she offered her hand and he grasped it, pulling himself upright with his own strength, yet using hers as his guide. She handed him fresh linen, and watched him dress, his powerful torso brushed with dark hair from his pectoral muscles to his rigid abdomen. Younger, he would have been slimmer, lithe and beautiful like a hard-muscled girl, but as a man he was broad and solid, yet sculptured.

He brushed his own beard but let her brush his thick black hair, while he sat like a statue immobile, unresisting, as she fought the tangles. In the new black cassock Marco had provided, he stood tall and strong, turned slightly to the narrow window, watchful like a sentry. A true Jesuit, thought the nun, transferring for a brief moment her love for Christ. His soldier.

She left him, still watchful; waiting.

Benito Marco decided that Thomas should meet Cinalli in more austere surroundings than the Cardinal Secretary's opulent private apartments, as in these, allowing for the extreme poverty he knew Thomas had left behind him in Patagonia, the priest might be halfway to being an enemy. Also, the spiritual presence of God was essential to his purpose; Thomas had responded to Him with complete disregard for his own well-being, even abandoning his orphans, which made him an unequalled weapon of persuasion.

The bearded, freshly clothed priest seemed to be

expecting Marco as the Sostituto dismissed the Vigilance guard and entered the small turret room.

'Follow me,' ordered Marco from the doorway, then led the way past the still-lingering guard towards the building which bears no identifying nameplate but which all in the Vatican know as L'Archivio Segreto Vaticano: the Secret Archives of the Vatican.

It was late evening and the building was empty apart from a custodian who sat before a large plain table in a bare wood-panelled room, one hand resting on an open visitors' book, a pen poised in the other expectantly. They approached him, their shoes ringing on the marble floor, then stopped momentarily while Marco signed the book which allowed them to progress further. Softly, the custodian informed the Sostituto that the Cardinal Secretary was awaiting their arrival, beyond.

They walked on, moving deeper into the heart of the building, through caverns whose sides were wooden shelves packed tight with ancient parchment tinted violet by a fungus which even the best efforts of modern science had failed to eradicate. All around them were secrets – some too controversial and dangerous to be viewed except by each successive pope, and then never passed on to any other man. Somewhere, perhaps, lay the date, divinely prophesied, for the end of the world and the method of its passing; they might have passed it by, but neither man thought of it nor coveted its knowledge. They had come to meet a man, not their Maker.

Cardinal Giorgio Cinalli knelt in the small Borgia chapel off one of the shelved corridors, his large head capped in scarlet bowed deep into his robes. The chapel was illuminated by dim electric lighting and although candles stood on the altar they remained unlit for the calamity of fire in that building was too terrible to contemplate. He completed his devotions and turned to the two figures waiting in the doorway.

Cinalli's face still bore the scars of exhaustion and inner torment but he held himself straight, calling on his last reserves, blocking out his conscience. His eyes seemed filled with a newly found strength brought on by the passing of his agony of indecision. The road before him appeared straight and shadowless with the light of God beckoning him onward. In self-delusion, even the thin, ascetic figure of his deputy, who had become in the past days a spectre of doom, was transfigured so that he was his companion and fellow-traveller – even guide – down the road to restitution. God had made his decision for him. God would forgive him.

His gaze shifted and rested on the strong figure sent to him by the Lord.

Yes, he thought. This is he.

Not an angel, glowing in glory, but a man, dark and intense and committed to Him. With a force, held in check, which was intimidating, like a half-tamed animal, chained and secured – but choosing to remain so. Yet a watchful silence was also evident, like a threat. I am obedient to my Master, said the eyes, but to obey Him, I must recognize Him; approach me in His robes at your peril.

The Hound of Heaven, thought Cinalli. And only I may slip your leash.

Cinalli extended his hand and Thomas moved forward, lowered himself and pressed his lips to the cardinal's ring.

Above him, Cinalli laid his hand on the dark, grey-flecked head. He let Thomas rise, then indicated that he should kneel beside him before the altar upon which rested the remains of the Pope, still in the simple iron box. Marco knelt beside them and responded with Thomas as Cinalli said prayers for the dead.

When this was done, they remained on their knees in silence, until Cinalli arose, bowed before the altar, and moved away. Marco and Thomas followed him.

There were four ornately carved chairs, tall-backed and cushioned in faded velvet. The Cardinal Secretary indicated that Thomas should sit in one. Behind them, Marco slipped away.

Cinalli said, 'You have performed a great duty in God's name, Father.'

Thomas answered, 'I am His servant.'

Cinalli turned and rested one hand on the iron box. 'You

heard His voice and answered His call. He speaks again to you now, through me.'

'If He seeks me, I shall hear Him,' Thomas responded, his voice sure.

Cinalli looked away towards a Vasari fresco, his gaze remaining on it as if in appreciation though, in fact, he did not see it. All he was aware of was his divine purpose and the priest God had sent him in such extraordinary circumstances.

Without looking away from the fresco, he said, 'God sees inside your soul, Father. He knows your sins – and your secrets. He knows all that you are, you were, and shall be. Your sins are His pain, your deeds in His holy name, His joy. Confess now, before Him, the sins you concealed when you entered His Church. Confess them to me and I shall judge you in His name.'

The Cardinal Secretary turned back and looked directly into Thomas's eyes, seeing a quick anger glaze in them, then fade, as though a battle he had fought long and hard had suddenly been lost in one flaring moment. He seemed to lack the strength even to measure his loss.

'I needed Him,' Thomas uttered hoarsely, through the storm.

'And He found you, my son. He sought only the truth from you, yet you lied to Him?'

Thomas shook his head, and with it most of his body, violently, as if he had had been struck with force; first one side, then the other. The movement was both denial and rejection. Also, agony.

'He knew my sins! Yet He brought me to His Church. He knew!'

Cinalli's voice hardened. 'His demand when you come to Him as His servant is that you confess all your sins. Instead, you kept secrets from those who brought you into His house.'

'Then He will punish me,' murmured Thomas, head low.

'Has He not already, my son?' asked Cinalli, his tone softer, his hand reaching forward to Thomas's shoulder. He could feel the trembling beneath his fingers.

261

'A thousand times, Eminence.'

Cinalli nodded his head in understanding. 'And until you confess, He will punish you a thousand times more.'

'I have confessed,' said Thomas but with little protest.

'Before you came to Him. Before you became part of Him and His Church. But to remain inside His house you must confess again. Now, before me.'

Thomas raised his tormented face, his eyes beseeching. 'I exist only for Him. If you cast me out from His Church, you would cast me into hell.'

'My son, you are, even now, in hell, though you serve His Church. Confess.'

Thomas's head dropped, his words barely audible. 'My sins would damn me.'

'Confess!' Cinalli cried.

Thomas collapsed to his knees, as if felled by the loud exhortation.

Cinalli bent over the distraught priest. 'Confess!' he whispered, sharply.

After an age, and then slowly, the broken words came from the kneeling figure and, like Father D'Arcy years before in London, the Cardinal Secretary listened with growing horror, for it was a confession of human savagery: of killing, in which the victims were so numerous that numbers had lost meaning; of torture, conducted with impersonal coldness and without conscience or regret; of barbarity, meted out with modern sophisticated methods which made the brutality of the past pale in comparison. A confession of death in which none were spared; not men, not women. Not even children.

When it was over, Cinalli turned away, unable to remain near the kneeling figure. Instead, he knelt himself before the altar, in silent prayer. He had asked for the light of God to come to him, His hope, His warrior, but instead had come a cohort of Lucifer.

Behind him he heard a deep sob, then Thomas fell prostrate beside him, his body rigid as if in agony or in death. In compassion, Cinalli reached out and laid both hands on the stricken priest.

'Do you seek God's forgiveness for these mortal sins?' he asked, his words forced.

Thomas moved his head.

'You must ask it!' Cinalli ordered.

'Dear God, I do!' Thomas uttered. 'I *beg* His forgiveness.'

'May your penance be as cruel as your sins,' said Cinalli.

'Let it be so!' Thomas whispered. 'Let it be so.'

Cinalli grasped the prone figure and using all his strength hauled him to his feet. Still holding Thomas's shoulders, he searched his eyes for truth, then released him and took up the iron box, thrusting it at him. Thomas held it, swaying slightly, his arms locked tight.

'Were you prepared to kill to protect this secret?' Cinalli demanded.

Thomas stared at him. 'I said I would.'

'And you meant your words?'

Thomas tried to avert his face but Cinalli clutched at him and turned him back.

'At that moment . . . yes.'

'And if he were alive now, would you kill to protect him?'

'I would lay down my life for him.'

'Would you kill to save his life?'

Thomas could find no refuge from the figure in scarlet before him.

'Answer!' Cinalli almost shouted.

'Yes,' Thomas answered hopelessly, believing that the truth had destroyed him.

'And would you kill to save the life of Holy Mother Church?'

'I would fight for Her life with mine.'

'And kill for Her?' Cinalli went on relentlessly.

'If it were God's will.'

'Do you accept me as the highest representative of the Church now that the Holy Father is dead?'

'Yes.'

'That I am the instrument of God's will?'

'Yes!'

Waiting and ready, Benito Marco re-entered the chapel, bearing a flat silver case worked exquisitely in gold. He stopped beside Thomas and opened the case. Inside, nestling on purple velvet, lay a large solid-silver crucifix, the Christ figure perfect in detail even to each thorn in the crown, except that the central thorn on the slumped head was longer than any other and needle-pointed.

'The Borgia cross, Eminence,' the Sostituto said.

Thomas's eyes were fixed to the beautiful crucifix but Cinalli did not look at it. Still gripping Thomas's arms, he shook the priest roughly. 'Listen to me!' he ordered.

Thomas turned back, trapped between the two powerful men – and the glittering Borgia cross. Cinalli's heavy face came nearer: 'The Church is without its Vicar of Christ. She is being torn asunder without the guidance of Her spiritual father to save Her. Her very life is in my hands. And yours. Aid Her.'

Thomas did not respond, a stillness settling over him. A tightening. Control.

'I remind you of your lies before God. I remind you of your answers to my questions. I remind you of your acceptance of a penance as cruel as your sins.'

'What do you want of me?' asked Thomas.

'It is what God wants of you, my son.'

Thomas remained silent, waiting for the moment of truth he had known would come.

Cinalli spoke, his voice tremulous but his eyes bright with conviction. 'You have murdered wantonly and without remorse in the name of Satan. I ask you to kill, once more, in the holy name of God.'

Thomas stared at Cinalli with shrouded eyes, still silent, as though time were measureless to him. Finally, he asked, 'This is my penance?'

'It is His will. He sent you to us for this purpose.'

'For this? In defiance of His commandment?'

'Because of His commandments! It is not for you to understand. You are the instrument of His will. You will act with His blessing and with the blessing of Holy Mother Church.'

Thomas shifted his gaze to Marco, then back again to the Cardinal Secretary. 'In His holy name,' he said. 'Swear it! "In His holy name"!'

264

'I swear it. In His holy name, I swear it,' Cinalli answered.

Thomas turned again to Marco. 'You have heard?'

Marco nodded. 'I have heard.'

'And you agree?'

'I agree.'

'Do you agree to what has been asked of me!'

Marco's eyes shifted momentarily, then returned to Thomas's set face. 'I agree,' he said, tightly.

Thomas faced the altar, standing perfectly still, his eyes open, as though waiting. Then, slowly, he moved forward and laid the iron box on the altar, genuflected, crossed himself and stood back.

Cinalli touched him. 'There is little time left, my son,' he said.

Thomas turned to the Sostituto. 'And this?' he asked, touching the gleaming silver of the Borgia cross.

'The weapon of the Lord,' Marco answered.

Thomas's fingers traced the lines of the figurine upward, from the nails piercing the feet to the thorns crowning the slumped head. Deliberately, he pressed one finger against the longer central silver thorn, drawing blood instantly.

'Who?' Thomas said.

'We will show him to you. Tomorrow,' Cinalli replied.

'Where?'

'Rome. He comes to us.'

Thomas lifted the heavy crucifix and laid it face down on the velvet, his eyes drawn to the single raised ruby set at the joining of the cross-members.

'Who has condemned this man?' he asked.

'He has condemned himself,' Cinalli answered. 'By his own words he stands condemned.'

Thomas turned the crucifix face upward again, then pressed the silver and gold case closed. 'As Christ did,' he said.

'God condemns him,' Marco said, coldly. 'Through His Church.'

Thomas glanced at him. 'Then I pray that His Church will not stand condemned also when it is done.'

He took the Borgia cross from Marco.

* * *

265

In Milan, northern Italy, later that same evening, two men, obviously British by their style of dress, mounted the steps to the city morgue and after announcing themselves to the duty clerk were directed to a drab cold room furnished only with a battered bench and a Madonna affixed to the wall askew.

They sat side by side on the bench but apart, not speaking. One of the men arose and tried to straighten the Madonna but it was fixed firmly; he gave up, sighed and sat down again. 'Typical,' he breathed.

The other simply raised his eyebrows.

A third man entered the room, fair and pale; and very Roman. His green surgical gown was stained; some of the stains were blood. He looked down at his hands apologetically, not offering one for shaking. 'Rossi,' he said. 'Come.'

The Englishmen followed him down a corridor, then preceded him through a door which he held open graciously. The small chamber had a curved roof, like a tunnel, and the brickwork of its walls and ceiling was painted with a thick cream gloss. At the base of both side walls were open channels which served as gutters. The place stank of formaldehyde and opened bodies. The chilled air sharpened the smell.

A wooden table filled the centre of the chamber and on this lay the flabby naked corpse of a man, the shroud which had covered him pulled down below his genitals. One of the Englishmen held a handkerchief over his nose but the second seemed unaffected by the stench of death. The man with the handkerchief nodded his head. 'Yes,' affirmed the other.

The pathologist took a card from a pocket in his gown. 'Bertram Hames-Ambury,' he read with perfect pronunciation. 'Very good. As you can see, gentlemen, I have had to open the body. My work is not performed with delicacy, I'm afraid. He died by inhaling his own vomit. Drowned in it, to be accurate. The lungs were blocked. Not a pleasant death, but then he would have been unconscious. His liver is a museum exhibit, incidentally. His alcohol consumption must have been prodigious. Quite the worst I have examined.'

'Can we get out of here?' asked the man behind the handkerchief.

'If you are satisfied?' Rossi inquired.

'Please!'

The second man nodded.

'Very good,' said Rossi, and pulled the sheet over Hames-Ambury's corpse.

'But there is someone who wishes to meet with you before you go.'

'Who?' asked the stronger man.

'He's outside, in my office,' Rossi said ambiguously.

The pathologist led the way again, but this time stayed outside as he opened the door to his office.

The man seated inside behind an untidy desk arose and offered his hand. The man with the handkerchief ignored it and sat in a vacant chair, his head lowered between his knees. The other shook the extended hand and said, 'Carlisle, British consulate. This is Manton. He's ill.'

'Some are affected,' said the swarthy Italian behind the desk, but without sympathy. He offered no name.

'You wanted to see us?' said the one who might have been called Carlisle.

The Italian nodded and sat down. He flipped something small and hard onto the desk. 'Dottore Rossi found this during his examination.' He looked first at the small cylindrical object which resembled a steel bullet rounded at both ends, then at both men.

'Who are you?' asked the one called Manton, recovering his composure.

'Liaison,' smiled the Italian.

'That's not good enough!' snapped Manton.

The Italian frowned in mock-disapproval, then smiled quickly. 'We all have our masters,' he said.

'Where was that found?' asked Carlisle.

The smile had not left the Italian's face. 'In a most uncomfortable place.'

'Has it been opened?' Carlisle asked, his eyes hard.

The Italian drew a thin thread of exposed microfilm from a side pocket and held it out. 'An accident. The capsule opened in the sterilizer.'

267

'Then you have no idea what was on it?'

'Sadly, no. Though we would like to very much. If it concerns us, that is.'

'It does not!' snapped Manton. 'That was the personal property of a British subject.'

'I hope so,' retorted the Italian, no longer smiling. 'That is all, gentlemen. I don't want to keep you from your . . . consular activities. And be so good, please, as to inform your masters that we do not appreciate having foreign intelligence operations being run on our territory.'

'I told you,' Carlisle said. 'It is nothing to do with you.'

'Of course,' replied the Italian.

Manton snatched the exposed film away while Carlisle pocketed the anal capsule. They turned to the door.

'One thing more,' said the Italian. 'Signor Angelo Segretti hung himself one hour ago. Or that is how it seems at present. Let us hope that this is truly the case.'

'Segretti is nothing to us,' Carlisle said carefully.

'Yet your man went to see him the evening he was kidnapped.'

'He was a journalist. Perhaps he wanted an interview.'

'Upon what subject would a British journalist wish to interview an Italian millionaire? His wealth perhaps? Or his power?'

'We've no idea. Contact his newspaper.'

'No need,' smiled the Italian. 'The man we caught trying to bury the body sang the complete libretto of this particular opera, a special performance, just for our ears. We have all the men involved now.'

'Which leaves you where?' asked Carlisle.

'It leaves us with certain suspicions, the proof of which died at the end of a suicide's rope.'

'Then your case is closed.'

'Oh, I think it would have been closed anyway,' the Italian remarked drily. 'Sometimes priorities come before justice – as I'm sure you gentlemen know.'

'Goodbye,' said Carlisle.

'It's strange,' said the Italian with a detached air. 'Signor Segretti's two personal pilots have also disappeared. Also one of his aircraft. You don't think perhaps that they were involved?'

'That's your problem,' said Carlisle, blandly.

'I want to leave – *now!*' Manton snapped.

'You feel unwell again?' asked the Italian.

'Goodbye,' Carlisle repeated.

'*Arrivederci*,' said the Italian, broadening his smile.

Outside, in the fresh air, Manton breathed deeply as they crossed under the yellow street-lights. 'The wretched man knows,' hissed Manton as they entered their car.

'Knows what?' asked Carlisle sarcastically, starting the engine but not moving off.

Manton exploded. 'You people! Why can't you leave things alone!'

'You're a diplomat, Manton,' said Carlisle, turning fast. 'You're front-of-house; smooth, starched and groomed for the "people who matter". OK, so stay out front, but always remember it's people like me who supply you with the information to keep you there. Without us you couldn't bargain, you couldn't wheedle your way in and out of deals, you wouldn't be worth shit!'

'There's no need to be abusive.'

'Oh, there's a need all right. So we may have discovered a cover-up inside the Vatican. So you're embarrassed. Tough. If the Pope *is* dead, that's tough too but that is not what's important, is it? Is it!'

'It is to us. Our planes may have been involved. The whole position is extremely delicate.'

'Delicate! Jesus. Listen to me, Manton. Hames-Ambury had a suppository up his arse, right! Our agent in Buenos Aires who took that bloody sterilized film is now as dead as Ambury is. And they'd have cut him open while he was still alive! God knows what he told them. God knows what was on that film! We don't have anyone as well placed as he was. We're blind and deaf at that level now. They're up to something – that we know – and nobody will listen when we say it's going to be more than just a straight invasion. They won't go that route again. They've tried it and they lost – hopelessly. They daren't lose again, you know that! The situation is fucking dangerous, Manton.

And I don't give a damn what the Vatican is doing. I don't care if the Pope *is* dead. I care about the Falkland Islands and the Antarctic continent, and you should too, because that's the area which is going to give people like you real bargaining power for the next fifty years! Do you really believe that we've built a billion-pound fortress in the South Atlantic to protect a few sheep-herders? For Christ's sake, Manton, this is the real world.' Carlisle slammed the car into gear angrily and let out the clutch with a thump.

'You're going too fast,' Manton commented.

Carlisle slowed a little.

'So what happens now?' asked Manton.

'Nothing. The Italians will shove their heads right into the ground. Opus Dei aren't mafiosi they can lock up or deport – they're the bloody government.'

'The Vatican will be told that we know.'

'So just lie – as usual – deny it on gold-edged engraved board.'

'We'll have to.'

Carlisle glanced away from the road quickly. 'Shall I tell you what I think? I think that only the very top men in the Vatican know what's happened. I think they're involved in an internecine power-struggle right now and they daren't announce the death of the Pope until they sort it out. This is big-time politics. Real power. You're a Catholic – you tell me who they've got who can replace this particular Pontiff?'

'I don't know. But that is what conclave is for – to settle the matter of succession.'

Carlisle gave a thin ironical smile. 'What does conclave entail, Manton? No, don't tell me – I'll tell you. Conclave is like the Americans losing both President and Vice-President in mid-term, and the entire government shutting itself away for an indefinite period until they decide on a new leader. And they announce to the entire world that they are doing this. Now, outside this conclave, no one has any power. The defence systems are useless because the only people who can give orders are locked away, sealed up, must not be interrupted. And if the Soviets make a preemptive strike – tough shit! That, in real terms, is what conclave entails.'

'That is a ridiculous comparison,' Manton protested. 'The Vatican is a unique institution. You cannot compare it with anything else.'

'Why not?'

'Because it is more than a political base – it is the guardian of a worldwide faith.'

'And you think that the Roman Catholic faith can't be threatened?'

'Threatened, yes, but not wiped out as you are implying. It has no enemy which is that powerful. Not communism, not Islam. None.'

'Which proves why you're a diplomat and I'm a spy. You look outwards for your enemies, I face in.' Carlisle paused. 'Manton, what's unusual about Milan tonight?'

'Unusual?'

'Look around you.'

'It's . . . it's just Milan.'

'A very quiet Milan. A late Saturday night and we're not stuck in a traffic jam?'

Manton shrugged. 'Perhaps there's a football international being played?'

'They've gone to Rome, Manton, and not for a football match.' Carlisle switched on the radio. 'News time,' he announced, listened briefly, then jabbed the station-selector buttons, pausing as each came through. He turned the radio off. 'So what's the lead story?' he asked, accelerating hard into a bend.

'Pierre Labesse. He's news at the moment. The Italians love a saint. Slow down.'

'A risen saint.'

'I don't subscribe to that theory.'

'You may not but it looks like half of Milan does. They've gone to Rome to see him. He arrives tomorrow.'

'Don't exaggerate. A section of the population might have gone.'

'Multiply that "section of the population" with those of other cities – and other countries – and you've got a large

271

chunk of Catholics going to see and hear a man who has openly denounced their faith. Your faith.'

'Labesse is nothing more than a nine-day wonder,' Manton snapped.

Carlisle swung the car into the driveway of the British consulate and switched off the engine and the lights. They sat for a few moments in the darkness, then Carlisle said, 'I fancy those same words – or their Latin equivalent – have been heard before in Rome. A very long time ago.'

Manton turned to him. 'I wouldn't have seen you as a believing sort.'

'I'm not. But I recognize raw power when I see it – and I can smell conspiracy even upwind at a thousand yards. And so should you.' He pushed his door open, impatiently. 'Come on, let's go in and save what's left of the empire. Rome can look after itself.'

7

It was Sunday, a bright, glorious day of hope, and the sun blazed resplendent: a king's welcome, in gold. The people too were bright, and sure, like lost travellers who had at last found the true path home. There were flowers everywhere, as though the ancient city had become a garden overnight. Those who could not find flowers carried small branches full with leaves which they held above their heads to the sky, dancing and laughing, yet always orderly. The police stood by, amazedly, having nothing to do but watch – but they too smiled, for it was a day and a time like no other they remembered. It was as if all had come in rapture to heaven's gate.

The square was almost full by midday and the obelisk of Caligula was the hub around which the crowds wheeled. Below the balcony of the papal apartments a section of the crowd chanted, 'Papa! Papa!' but were rewarded with silence and closed shutters. Here and there owners of transistor radios who had them tuned to Vatican Radio heard messages that the Pope was still unwell and could not appear – also vain pleas for quiet in St Peter's Square. But not once was the name Pierre Labesse heard from the broadcasting station in Santa Maria di Galeria.

Whenever an airliner was spotted in the astonishingly clear blue sky, cries went up from the crowds – chanting the same name in differing languages. 'Pietro! Pierre! Peter!' and with the cries, up went the branches and the flowers, creating, as if magically, a waving carpet of blooms and greenery.

The big closed vans for television outside-broadcast coverage were already in position in a barricaded area at the south of the square in front of Bernini's colonnades, manned by crews from Italy's RAI TV network and transmitting pictures via the Eurovision link to other countries as well as Italy itself. Behind the railinged barriers, reporters moved along the lines of people nearest to them, seeking out interesting items and listening for voices in their national language, then thrusting their microphones into the crowd when they heard one. At any one time a dozen different languages could be heard and they were all ecstatic.

It was a gala day, a day of light and a new beginning.

Above the square, behind the shutters of two corner windows on the top floor of the Apostolic Palace, there was no joy. Sister Luciana smoothed the coverlet of the empty bed in the small bedroom, though it was as perfect today as it had been the whole week. Quietly she moved around the room, searching vainly for things to do while her beloved Papa was away – she knew not where – hissing angrily, and a little jealously, at the noise of the crowds below. Such adulation was a Pope's due, she thought fiercely, and should not be given to a usurper to his throne – for this was how she viewed Pierre Labesse. Risen saint or no, he had chosen his moment with devious cunning. Yes, she hissed, come now! while the Papa cannot be here to confound you. But he will return – after his secret, critically important business has been done (for this was the story given to her by Cinalli after he had extracted a vow of secrecy from her), and then he will surely confound this spawn of Satan. Yes!

She crept to the shutters, touching the prie-dieu affectionately on the way, and very carefully opened up a tiny crack. She watched the growing crowds with a glower. Deluded, she thought. Led by Lucifer, who has your noses tight in his claws. Dancing! Singing! A bacchanalian orgy outside this holy place. Yes! Who else but Satan could be at work here? Just wait until the Papa returns! She returned to the bed and smoothed the cover yet again, shutting out the noise with her mind because, surfacing through her anger and her jealousy, was the beginning of fear. Fear that the world she had known for so long – her only world – this great city of God and Christ Jesus – was being shaken and might crumble.

274

She heard voices in the study and rushed out towards the sounds, heart leaping. But it was only the Cardinal Secretary and with him the one she did not trust, the thin, clever one who always appeared at the times of greatest importance but otherwise shut himself away on the third floor. And another. A tall stranger, his bearded face strained, as though he had travelled hard or slept badly. Yet strong, despite this fatigue, and reserved; his dark eyes taking in his surroundings but not awed by them as any other simple priest might be. He stored details without expression, Luciana noted, yet when his eyes rested on her, they smiled – though his face remained set. The Papa would like you, dark priest, she thought, appraising Thomas. He would like you very much. You have seen suffering as he has done; experienced it as he had experienced it; felt the blows but stood hard against them, undefeated. The eyes said it all.

'Is your work done, Sister?' Cinalli asked in his deep voice.

Luciana bowed. 'There is little to do, Eminence,' she answered, flicking her eyes to Benito Marco, who had switched on the large colour television set as she did so. A picture of the crowds filled the screen, without sound. How clever you are, she thought: I steal a glance through a crack in the shutters and you see it all with a touch of your finger. And how impudent. Leave that alone! It's not yours and never will be.

'Then leave us,' ordered Cinalli.

'Eminence,' Luciana murmured and moved to the door. There, she stopped.

'Sister?' the Sostituto inquired.

Luciana ignored him, addressing herself to the Cardinal Secretary. 'Eminence, when will the Holy Father return?'

'You will be informed in good time,' said Cinalli.

'There are preparations I must make –'

'In good time!' Cinalli snapped, too quickly, and Luciana sensed the nervousness in him.

You are as frightened as I, she thought, shaken. And I think you lie to me. Papa! Please return. Holy Mary, Mother of God, keep him safe.

'Go now,' ordered Cinalli, impatiently.

Luciana waited outside the closed doors, listening, but heard no sound. She saw the handle begin to turn and moved away quickly to her own bed-sitting room opposite the lift, feeling the Sostituto's eyes on her back at each step.

Benito Marco closed the door and turned the key. 'She's gone,' he said.

Cinalli nodded with a frown. 'These old women,' he muttered.

Marco moved to the central of the three windows in the study; he unlocked it and parted the shutters slightly. The noise exploded into the room, adding sound to the television picture. He beckoned Thomas over.

'Our sources have informed us that he will speak from the east, facing the Basilica.'

'There is no platform?' Thomas queried. 'No sound system?'

'They have been arranged. Note the barriers forming an avenue where the Via Della Conciliazione enters the square. Before he arrives three trucks will be backed up the clearway; two are flatbed trucks which will park side by side, forming a square platform-base. Each will carry one half of the raised platform which will have open railings on all sides with a gap to the north where steps will be positioned for him to ascend. The third truck carries a powerful generator and the complete sound-amplification system. This will be positioned further away, at the exit of the Via Della Conciliazione. The television people will also have microphones on the platform and they too will have public-address speakers, directed from the south of the square.'

'He's well organized,' Thomas observed.

Marco shook his head. 'He has no organization. The television and radio networks have supplied everything, without any charge. We have been told, reliably, that the expected viewing and listening figures will be unprecedented. Greater by far than the coronation of the Pope.'

Thomas pulled the shutters together and closed the window. 'Which is why you don't want him to speak.'

'Why we dare not allow him to speak,' Marco corrected.

'What does he intend to say?'

'Only he knows. But it is certain that he will compound the damage already done.'

'More heresy!' Cinalli exclaimed. 'And blasphemy. The destruction of all accepted Christian belief – that is his intention.'

'One man?' said Thomas. 'One man can do that?'

Both Cinalli and Marco fell silent.

'Who is this man that causes so much fear?' asked Thomas, perplexed.

'That does not concern you,' Marco answered flatly.

'It is better you do not know,' Cinalli added. 'The deed you must do is enough for your conscience to bear, my son.'

'Is he the monk from Jerusalem? The one who claims to be a saint?'

'What do you know of him?' Marco inquired carefully.

'Nothing. The journalist I spoke with on the aircraft mentioned a monk from Jerusalem who claims sainthood – he said he intended to come to Rome. He was reported to have died, then was resuscitated. The journalist was very drunk and made little sense. Except for the story regarding the Holy Father.'

Cinalli gave Marco a startled glance but the Sostituto remained stoically expressionless. Thomas misread the Cardinal Secretary's involuntary reaction, taking it to mean he had hit on the identity of the man he had to kill, unaware of Cinalli's lack of knowledge regarding Hames-Ambury's presence on the flight from Buenos Aires – a fact which Marco had deliberately not mentioned to Cinalli at the time because of the Cardinal Secretary's mental state.

'He is the man,' Marco agreed. 'He claims that during the period of his so-called "death" he sat at the hand of God and received a "revelation" which he must tell the world.'

'Heaven is here?' Thomas quoted.

'You have heard him?' Marco asked sharply.

'Those are the words the journalist used.'

'Those words are the basis of the monk's "revelation",' Marco said.

'But they could mean anything – or nothing? The Church has radical priests right now who are making statements which are clearly heretical. Rome disciplines them. Why kill this man?'

Marco studied Thomas for a moment, then said, 'The very ambiguity of those three words is what makes them dangerous. Father, you are unaware of what has been happening. What do you hear of the outside world in Patagonia?'

'Very little. Sometimes nothing. And in Buenos Aires at the moment there is heavy censorship of all news.'

'Precisely. The monk's name is Pierre Labesse. He is a Frenchman by birth. By an accident of fate he has a legitimate right to canonization. The Holy Father misguidedly – but then how could he know what would happen – made the decision to begin the beatification process when Labesse was still alive but in coma. The Holy Father believed, quite genuinely, that he was following the will of God. He knew that Labesse might be in a coma for the rest of his life – or what is life by modern scientific medicine. The monk was kept alive by artificial means for an extended period – until so-called brain death occurred. When this happened the Holy Father gave orders that all life-support aids should be withdrawn and Labesse should be allowed to die. This was done at one minute past midnight last Saturday.'

'But he didn't die.'

'He died – or appeared to die – but, as you have said, he was resuscitated.'

'After how long?'

'Nine hours.'

'They attempted to resuscitate a man after nine hours!'

Marco shrugged. 'We are not sure what happened,' he lied easily. 'It is probable that the physician made a mistake. I agree, nine hours is too long.'

'He'd be a vegetable. The brain damage would be irreparable!'

'Exactly. So he could not have truly died, could he? But

the withdrawal of life-support brought him out of coma – I understand that this has happened before.'

'But you think he is deranged – now?'

'Dangerously deranged. He has called himself "God's advocate" and declares the Church's doctrine to be wrong. Only he knows the true word of God – that is his claim and he comes here to Rome today to proclaim it.'

Thomas looked at the picture of the teeming crowds on the television screen for a moment, then said, 'And they believe him?'

'Father, the Holy Father canonized him at the moment of his "death". His "death" was certified by an Israeli physician who refused to refute his diagnosis. Yes, they believe that he has been resurrected and that he is a saint – and that every word he speaks comes directly from God Himself.'

Thomas stared at the screen, then at both men. 'Have you thought what you are doing, Eminence?' he asked Cinalli.

'Long and hard, my son. There is no other way.'

Thomas shook his head. 'When this monk dies they will make him a martyr. His words will have more power than they have now.'

Marco cut in. 'We have realized this danger – and accounted for it. Eminent doctors will diagnose the cause of death to be caused by a brain tumour. They will also affirm that substantial cell damage occurred in the brain due to oxygen starvation during the period of his "death". His words – his "revelation" – will be regarded as the product of a damaged mind. Then those misguided unfortunates outside will turn back to the Church, afraid for their souls.'

Cinalli added, 'When we announce the death of the Holy Father, Pierre Labesse will not matter to the people. Their grief will be absolute, overshadowing any other.'

'When will you announce it, Eminence?'

Marco answered. 'After it is done and you are out of Italy.'

'Will I get out?' Thomas asked carefully.

279

'Of course. There will be nothing to connect you with his death.'

Thomas glanced at the television set. 'They're moving the trucks in,' he said.

Cinalli had already noticed and was facing the set. He had turned pale, as a condemned man might at his first sight of the scaffold. He crossed himself.

Marco moved forward quickly and switched off the set. 'His Eminence needs rest,' said Marco, firmly.

And escape, thought Thomas. He brings me this far in the name of God, filled with resolution, yet when the time approaches, he is as hollow as an empty church with his doubts lingering on the air like pungent incense. I'll walk away, he told himself. When they lead me to the open gates, I'll walk away and keep on walking. Through the crowds. Ignoring them and the man who will stand alone, believing in his madness that God had called him. But he knew he would not. He would do as Marco had instructed. He would make the long journey through the crowd, forcing his way through them until he stood below the platform. And he would wait, with the Borgia cross, ready to offer Christ to an Anti-Christ; everlasting life, and death, in one secret movement that had more treachery in it than an assassin's raised arm holding a blade behind his victim's back. And why? The answer was simple. If he did not obey them, he would cease to believe in them – and that was a barren road he would not travel again. The Church had filled him when he was lost and empty; taken his hand when he stumbled blindly through a Stygian night of his own making. He was not prepared to lose his way again. Do this one thing then be gone. Back to his children, who were his reward and God's blessing on him. One man must die so that my faith can live, he thought finally, and it was both statement and question. And only by waiting, ready, at the foot of the platform, would he know which held the greater truth.

'Are you ready, Father?' Marco asked.

If not now, then when? Thomas asked himself silently, but to Marco he said, 'I am.'

* * *

At Fiumicino airport as the afternoon sun began its descent, the crowds awaiting the arrival of Pierre Labesse were beginning to swell in numbers as those who could not get into St Peter's Square made their way there.

In the VIP lounge, Catherine Weston relaxed in an overstuffed armchair, drinking coffee and smoking, one eye on the screen of a suspended television set, while an ITN ENG-crew set up lighting and sound equipment around her. She wished she was still in the square as she had been earlier that day, sharing the joy of the crowds. There was still an hour to go before the El Al flight from Jerusalem would land on Italian soil.

'We'll be ready in a couple of minutes,' said Richard Bailey, ITN's reporter who had flown in himself from Jerusalem the previous day after covering the whole 'Labesse circus' as the ENG-crew had christened their assignment.

Bailey had seen Catherine before, in Jerusalem, when she reappeared with Pierre Labesse after being the only journalist, or outsider – apart from the Dr Levin, who had certified the monk's death – to gain admittance to the monastery and the 'risen saint' himself. The reporter had discovered, later, that she had left Jerusalem for Rome; he had been determined to find her when he arrived there himself and interview her. His hunch had been right – she would be waiting to greet Labesse in the obvious place, under the circumstances: the VIP lounge at Fiumicino.

At first she had been reluctant, even slightly rude, when he put forward his request for an interview, pointing out, firmly, that only 'the master' had any answers of importance. But Bailey had been persistent and eventually she had agreed to a short interview.

'Ready, Miss Weston,' Bailey said. 'Any time you want to begin.'

Catherine crushed out her cigarette. 'Fine,' she murmured, as he sat beside her.

Bailey turned toward the camera and made his preliminary introduction, then faced her. 'Miss Weston, you are the only person that we know of who has spoken alone with the man the media and now the world have named the risen saint: Father Pierre Labesse. What has he said to you?'

'He asked me to follow him.'

'Which you have done. In fact you have preceded him here, to Rome. Why was that?'

'To arrange media coverage for his appearance here.'

'Miss Weston, I have personally interviewed many evangelists and Christian reformers in the past and they have had a . . . businesslike . . . attitude to their public appearances – but it seems to me that in the case of Pierre Labesse this is not the case?'

Catherine smiled broadly, almost laughing. 'You mean why aren't we selling tickets?'

Bailey returned her smile. 'So, to be blunt, money – or donations, if you prefer – is not important.'

'Money has not even been considered.'

'Yet,' Bailey continued cautiously, 'isn't it a fact that money has been pouring into the monastery in Jerusalem which houses the brotherhood of which Pierre Labesse is a member? We have reliable information that the amounts received could total close to half a million pounds.'

Catherine nodded. 'People from all over the world have been sending money. Large amounts and small. I have no idea what the total is.'

'Certainly half a million, possibly more,' said Bailey.

Catherine gave a small shrug. 'However much it is, it will go to the Church.'

'To the Roman Catholic Church?' Bailey asked incredulously.

'The brotherhood is a Roman Catholic order. Yes, of course.'

'But is it not true that the Vatican have ignored Father Labesse – even rejected him. They have refused to confirm his canonization – though the Father Superior of his order has stated clearly that this is a fact.'

'Officials of the Catholic Church have rejected him – not the Church itself.'

'By that you mean the Vatican.'

'I mean some in the Vatican. But they will change.'

'Change? Change their attitude toward Father Labesse?'

'Completely. They will welcome him. Recognize him.'

'Recognize him as what?'

'As what he is.'

'What do you believe he is, Miss Weston? You appear to have given your life over to him – you must have very definite views on this.'

'Certainly, but it's better if others make up their own minds.'

Bailey paused. 'Miss Weston, it is impossible not to make the comparison between the scenes we are witnessing in Rome today and an occurrence recorded in the New Testament. A similar tumultuous popular welcome – coincidentally on a Sunday. I mean, of course, Palm Sunday. Would you care to comment on this?'

'You are making the comparison, not I,' Catherine said, her attention drawn back to the television screen which showed scenes, recorded earlier, of Labesse boarding the El Al flight in Israel, applauded by a huge crowd. It might easily have been Rome. She turned back. 'I suppose you could say that the people at that time were reacting with their hearts – just as they are now.'

Bailey leaned forward, pressing her now. 'If you allow that the comparison is legitimate – even uncanny – then hasn't it crossed your mind that a short while after Palm Sunday another, quite terrible, event took place – at Calvary.'

For a split second her composure slipped. Then she gave a half-smile. 'I think the world has grown up since then, Mr Bailey. Don't you?'

Bailey chose not to answer but instead thanked her and, turning to the camera, ended the interview. The stark lighting was extinguished and the crew moved back, then began breaking down their equipment, ready for their next location.

Bailey remained seated, touching his lighter flame to Catherine's cigarette. 'You do realize that a lot of people across the world see him as some sort of Messiah? You're a journalist, you must be aware of it.'

Catherine inhaled, deeply. 'The media have made him seem that way. You – we – are image-makers, we can

283

build the smallest event into something of world-shaking importance within days – if not hours. We don't report news any more – we create it.'

'The media didn't create the Labesse phenomenon,' Bailey objected. 'He began that himself – by returning from the dead. The Vatican, whatever they may feel about it now, created the "risen saint" image. Labesse was the instigator of the "I've been with God" story. Labesse said he was coming to Rome to make his "revelation". All the media have done is build on the image already evident.'

A cool sexy female voice came through the public-address system announcing the arrival of a Pan-Am flight, in Americanized English.

'Precisely,' said Catherine when it was over. 'They built on the image. But not just on the image. They built on the facts which were evident. They made comparisons – then sensationalized them. Crucifixion. Resurrection – '

'And location,' Bailey interrupted. 'Jerusalem, the Mount of Olives. Come on, it was a natural from the beginning! Christians are crying out for the return of the Messiah. Islam has become a mad dog. Anarchy reigns supreme. They want to believe that the Son of God is here.'

'And you've given them what they want. Whatever the consequences. Pierre Labesse has never said that he is the Son of God.'

Bailey pondered for a moment, staring at his tanned hands. 'You know, when it began, back there in Jerusalem, the first time I saw him and heard him speak I honestly believed that he just might be . . . the Messiah.' He turned to Catherine and smiled wanly. 'Really.'

'So what changed your mind?' she asked.

Bailey shrugged. 'I suppose . . . well, I've had time to think, to evaluate . . . to be realistic about it. I was jet-lagged, exhausted. I wasn't thinking logically.'

'And you haven't seen him again – since,' added Catherine.

'Nobody has from the outside – except you. Do you believe he may be the Messiah? It sounds ridiculous in this age, I know, but thousands believe just that.'

'Mr Bailey, I believe that he is something – someone –

so important to this crazy world, which seems to have run amok, that by building him up or portraying him as something he may not be might destroy his credibility as . . . what he is.'

'And what is he?'

'I don't know.'

'Why do you call him "master"?'

'Because he is above us. He is a teacher who knows what we long to know and at present are incapable of understanding.'

'A guru?'

Catherine smiled. 'Oh, far more than that!'

Bailey moved closer to her. 'You said, just now: "portraying him as something he may not be"? Does that mean you think he might be something more than what you perceive him to be now?'

Catherine met his eyes. 'I don't think about it. I'm frightened by the thought. I'm very close to him. I know him as a man, yet more than a man and to think of him in . . . higher terms . . . might drive me mad. I'm not prepared, not ready for that. Can you understand?'

'To be faced with God? Yes, I can understand. None of us is prepared for that. Do you remember he said, "You would not recognize God even if you saw him"?'

'Yes. In Jerusalem.'

'I've thought about that statement a lot since then and I have a theory about what he meant. Would you recognize a stranger, another human being, if you didn't know him?'

'No, of course not.'

'Why?'

'Because I wouldn't know him. Because he was a stranger.'

'But how would you know he was a stranger?'

'Because I wouldn't recognize him – this sounds like a riddle.' Catherine laughed.

'It is,' Bailey agreed. 'The unsolvable riddle. You wouldn't recognize him because we are all different. We are all human beings, arms, legs, torsos, heads, yet we are different. A stranger is someone you don't recognize even though he or she is another human being.'

'What are you saying?' Catherine asked, intrigued.

'I don't really know. Except one thing seems very clear: If I met God walking down a deserted road and He was a man – a stranger – and I walked right past Him, I wouldn't recognize Him as being God. Who did you see when you first saw Pierre Labesse?'

'A stranger.'

'You didn't know him, yet he agreed to see you.'

'He knew I was coming. He seemed to know me.'

'How?'

'He just did.'

'Christians believe that Christ knows and recognizes each of us.'

'No!' Catherine snapped, suddenly angry. 'Leave him be!'

'I think the media have the right to question just who Pierre Labesse may be, Miss Weston. He belongs to the world now – even though we might have made it so.'

The sexy voice announced, 'El Al flight 451 from Jerusalem arriving . . .' and Bailey was up and moving, the ENG-crew already through the doors.

But Catherine did not move, for Labesse was already there – inside her. She felt his strength controlling her clamouring fears. *Master, I feel afraid. I may not have the courage to stand beside you. You will*, he told her.

He descended from the huge silver aircraft in glory, still in his simple woollen robes, which shone white under the arc-lights and the shellburst of flashbulbs, but were not humbled by them. The cowl of his habit was raised, covering his head, perhaps against the growing chill of evening. Once, for the cameras, he lowered it, revealing his marvellous face, which was no longer a pale mask of half-death but tanned, setting off the penetrating azure blue of his eyes; vigorously alive, strong, yet sensitive and fine. The smile which played continuously on his lips was gentle when it finally broke, and as beckoning as the stars.

He spoke not a word into the prepared battery of microphones, but stopped before them and let his eyes and his smile be his voice. And perhaps he was wise, for the chanting of his name would have obliterated whatever he said. He moved away, a line of his brothers identically dressed behind him, and allowed himself to be led to a waiting coach.

Catherine stood before it and when he saw her he embraced her for many moments; she clinging to him as if he were her lover – or a father she had believed dead.

The roads too were lined with those who bade him welcome; mile after mile of chanting crowds who tossed flowers and greenery in profusion onto the coach and the motorcade of police, press and television crews which accompanied it. And in the wake of the motorcade came a cavalry of motor scooters and cars, headlights flashing and horns blaring in the steadily darkening evening.

The noise from the gigantic crowd which packed St Peter's Square could be heard many miles before they neared the area. Even in the closed, silent coach the massed voices were audible. Hearing them, Labesse nodded contentedly, and Catherine, seated beside him, gave a shy smile as if they were a gift she had prepared for him.

'Now,' Labesse said – the only word he had spoken until that moment and the only word he was to speak until he ascended the platform.

Catherine looked away from his face for the first time since she had seen him descend the aircraft gangway and saw, over his robe, the chained crucifix she had taken to him in the monastery in Jerusalem. Labesse saw sorrow touch her eyes and reached for her hand and held it.

'Michael,' she said, her eyes brimming, both in the emotion of the moment and in memory. 'Your soldier.'

His hand increased pressure over hers and he smiled to comfort her but offered no words. For Catherine, the gesture was enough.

They were in the streets of the city now and flower petals fell past the windows like scented snow. The noise was deafening – not a storm raging, but a song sung by a choir of hundreds of thousands, powerful and beautiful. His name, over and over again.

Catherine shuddered. It was exhilarating and uplifting.

287

And it terrified her. He squeezed her hand to calm her and suddenly there was the rearing Obelisk of Caligula marking the spot where St Peter had been crucified and, silhouetted behind it, the great golden dome of his Basilica. And three hundred thousand candles. The universe had fallen outside the gates of the Vatican.

8

The noticeboard outside the blackened London church had been cleaned and repainted, its new lettering gold on a gleaming varnished wood background, declaring the name St Thomas's Roman Catholic Church and giving details of services few would ever attend. Chief Inspector Charles Harrison spied it immediately on locking his parked Rover, and grinned, knowing where the twenty pounds he had given the old priest had gone. He pocketed his keys and stepped through the already opened gate.

Father D'Arcy stood at the open church doors bidding goodnight to his straggling flock. He saw Harrison and raised a hand, then quickened his farewells, almost urging the people home. With the last gone, he took the police officer's arm and led him into the church. 'Thank God I could get hold of you,' he said breathlessly.

'The sign looks well,' Harrison said.

'Oh! Yes, thanks to you. Yes indeed. Very generous.' D'Arcy's manner was courteous – but impatient.

'I came as soon as I received your message,' said Harrison, sensing his urgency.

D'Arcy pointed at a pew and, leading Harrison by the arm, sat down beside him on it. 'Of course you are aware of what is occurring in Rome tonight,' he said, lowering his voice.

'I've been listening on the car radio. It sounds like chaos – though the crowds seem well controlled,' Harrison answered, equally softly.

D'Arcy gave an impatient wave of his hand. 'The matter we discussed – during the week – there is something I feel you should be told. Possibly I am just being an old man – fearing shadows in the dark which move quicker than I can – but I have to voice my fears.'

'Go on,' Harrison urged.

'It's Labesse. Or rather, it concerns Labesse.'

Harrison nodded.

'Your inquiry – on behalf of Rome – it should have struck me sooner, but that's age for you.'

'What about my inquiry?'

D'Arcy sighed. 'The word, I think, is concommitance – an accompanying factor or circumstance.'

'Father!' Harrison whispered. 'You'll have to be clearer. I have no idea what you're trying to tell me.'

'Forgive me. Listen,' D'Arcy had gripped Harrison's arm at the elbow; his strength was surprising. 'Your "important personage" in Rome. You have to get hold of him. Tell him he's chosen the wrong man. I think I know what – he, they, Rome – intend to do. I'm not judging – I'm not qualified to judge their actions – but you have to tell them – they're *using the wrong man!*'

Harrison shook his head in bewilderment.

D'Arcy glanced at the altar at the far end of the nave as though for guidance. Finally, with a heavy sigh, he said, 'I have no choice but to tell you everything. May God forgive me.'

Father Thomas knelt, alone, in the small turret room, beneath the narrow window. He tried to pray, to reach his God, but his mind was blank, as though his skull contained only a hollow cavity. The words he forced through his lips seemed meaningless, even alien; a language once known and loved but now forgotten. I'm going back, he thought. In the end, nothing changes. He recalled, vividly, a memory from a past which seemed not to be his, yet was. A younger man, slim and dark and callow, listening with the intensity of a poet to a lecturer on a podium quoting Virgil. And hearing, and memorizing, but without the experience of life to understand.

Facilis descensus Averno.

The descent to hell is easy.

Thomas raised himself up from his knees, the sound of the crowds a hammer to his brain.

Let it be so! His words, his acceptance. His tragedy.

Benito Marco entered the turret room carrying Thomas's grip. 'It is time,' he said. 'Soon he will be in the square.'

'Do I wear these clothes?' asked Thomas, indicating his cassock.

'Yes. They will serve our purpose. I shall escort you part of the way – to show you how to avoid the main mass of the crowd. Your bag will be taken to the guard post at the Porta Sant'Anna and left there. Collect it when it is done.'

'My passport? Air ticket?'

'Inside. Also, some money. Swiss francs. If you have difficulties you may need them. This is important: do not under any circumstances re-enter the Vatican. Go to the guard post, take your bag and leave the country as soon as possible.'

Thomas gave a smile of deep irony.

'Why do you smile?' the Sostituto inquired testily.

Thomas shook his head but the smile still touched his mouth.

'Come with me,' said Marco, at the door. 'Where is the Borgia crucifix?'

Thomas patted the heavy weight beneath his cassock. Marco handed him a velvet bag. 'Put it in that – afterwards. The guard on the gate will bring it to me.'

They were walking now, with haste, the Sostituto a little ahead, as though he wanted to distance himself from Thomas now that the moment was here.

They travelled first along the rambling passageways of the vast fifteenth-century palace then downward, bypassing the lifts and instead using narrowing curving staircases until they reached the cellars. Here their progress was once again on the horizontal, through chamber after underground chamber; a journey which seemed to take on – in the madness of their purpose – a nightmarish air of fantasy, like some unending subterranean odyssey.

At some point, they passed from under the Apostolic Palace into the crypts and grottoes of the Basilica itself, moving past religious relics as old as the faith itself. Then they descended again, the air becoming even colder, the passages narrower, the floors uneven and the brickwork

Roman. They had marched through history and through time: from the present back to the medieval and now to the very beginnings of Christianity as they walked within feet of where the bones of the Apostle Peter were found.

Then, quite suddenly, the soundwaves rolled down to them as if somewhere lay a vast cavern and an underground sea. But no sea existed – except that of massed humanity in the square. It was a trick of acoustics. Sound brought to them down the massive pillars and foundations of Bernini's colonnades.

Marco stopped. 'I leave you here,' he stated. 'Go up the steps you will find one hundred metres on. They will lead you to the surface. From there follow the curve of the colonnades at the rear; this will lead you to the Via della Conciliazione – remember I showed you where the barriers were placed for the passage of the trucks?'

'I remember,' Thomas said, very cold now, his flesh numb.

'The barriers are still there, keeping the way clear for the coach bringing him from the airport. When you reach the barriers, hold the Borgia cross openly to your chest – higher if the crowd is too thick – so the police will notice you and allow you through to the platform.'

'You've arranged this?'

'I've arranged nothing!' Marco snapped. 'They are simple policemen on duty outside the Vatican. The Vatican is a sovereign state with a priest as its ruler. You also are a priest – why should they stop you?'

Thomas put his hands to his mouth and blew on them. His breath clouded in the beam of his torch, his face jagged and filled with hollows in the upward shining light as he clutched the torch against his chest.

'Do what must be done,' said the Sostituto and turned on his heel, walking quickly away down the passage, the beam of his own torch moving ahead of his quiet footsteps.

'Goodbye,' Thomas murmured, but no one heard him, least of all Benito Marco. He moved on alone, the noise swelling with each chill step.

* * *

The telephone was already ringing in the Sostituto's private apartment in the Apostolic Palace as he unlocked the door. He snatched at it and acknowledged Charles Harrison's voice with surprise. He listened, not uttering another word for two minutes, his already pallid complexion paling further. Finally, he spoke. 'The priest must be senile,' he said. 'Or insane. The Church does not murder its enemies any more – these aren't the Middle Ages, Chief Inspector. However, thank you for calling me.' Marco replaced the receiver. 'Too late,' he added, to the walls.

'A priest!' Catherine Weston exclaimed as the coach proceeded slowly between the barriers at the end of the Via della Conciliazione. She looked down at the striding, beared figure, turning as the coach passed him. He seemed almost in a trance, his gaze fixed forward as though unaware of the heaving, jubilant crowds behind the barriers or the coach which brushed against his cassock as he walked.

Labesse had his head lowered, under the cowl of his habit, as if in prayer, but he turned slightly to her and nodded.

'I'd have thought they'd have banned them from attending,' Catherine remarked. 'Instant excommunication.'

Labesse smiled, then looked away as the coach halted, facing the cabs of the two huge trucks.

Catherine saw the priest pass again, moving faster now. Then he was swallowed up by the closing throng, his progress through them marked by occasional flashes of silver at his shoulder as the floodlights caught the large crucifix he was grasping.

Labesse arose and stepped down from the coach into a fusillade of camera flashes which seemed to come from everywhere at once: a starshell bursting directly over the heads of the crowd. He threw up his arm protectively in front of his cowled face then walked, police on either side in strict escort, to where a set of steps had been positioned under a gap in the rails arranged around the platform.

Mounting these, he began moving slowly along the rails, bending over to touch hands raised in appeal to him.

Thomas stood at the front, his body pinned by the crush against the point where the bodies of the two trucks joined under the carpeted platform. Using his elbows and considerable strength, he gained room for himself despite protests behind and to the side of him. He felt a searing heat on his neck and clapped his hand to the scalding candlewax which had spattered on him. Again he was forced forward as Labesse neared, the hard silver of the Borgia cross threatening to crack his ribs.

Marco's voice: *He must not speak!* In his mind but clear and real as if it came from behind his crushed body.

Then Cinalli: *Satan has him. He has the power. The power to lead the world astray. The Anti-Christ as foretold.*

Then Thomas's own fervent, silent plea: *Dear Lord, help me, Your servant. Aid me at this hour.*

But Labesse was coming closer and even God had not the power to release his hard-pressed soldier. Or chose not to use it.

Then Labesse halted and stood back, straight and still, surveying the massed crowds. He turned to the battery of microphones and lowered his hood, then raised one arm to the stars, the other down at the crowd, one finger extended, slowly sweeping over them.

'*Paradiso è qua!*' he cried. Heaven is here.

The square erupted, the people going wild beyond any human restraint. They screamed his words back at him, deafeningly. '*Paradiso è qua! Paradiso è qua!*' Then the statement was picked up in other languages and these too joined in the great cry. Here in English, there in Portugese, French and German and Spanish – all at once, as though the Tower of Babel had disgorged its inhabitants into the square.

Thomas pushed backward, trying to get leverage from the edge of the platform, but his strength was ebbing and he felt that some force beyond his understanding had him pinioned, crushing out his life.

Labesse raised both arms and the chanting faded, then died.

Thomas felt the pressure ease and gulped air into his lungs, retching with the effort. He looked upward again, searching for Labesse's face behind the cage of microphones. He glimpsed his long fair hair, then saw, on the wide tanned forehead, white scar tissue which ran into the hairline.

Cinalli's voice came again, tellingly: *He has taken the words from the Bible and twisted them for his own evil purpose. Read the Revelation of John and see the truth – the warning of his coming.*

And Thomas had read, and now he remembered:

'Then out of the sea I saw a beast rising . . . and the dragon who is Satan conferred upon it his power and rule and great authority . . . and the whole world went after the beast in wondering admiration. *And upon its head it appeared to have received a death-blow; but the mortal wound was healed.*'

The crowds had fallen into absolute and eerie silence.

Marco again: *We dare not allow him to speak!*

And, apart from the urgent voices in his head, Thomas could hear a sound that was familiar. Too familiar, but from another lifetime, and he felt his mind slipping fast. A distant, steady, whipping beat.

The descent to hell is easy.

Dear Lord save my children.

Save the children!

He threw up his arm, the Borgia cross extended, the floodlights hitting the silver and reflecting off it, casting mirrored fragments over the crowd – flitting over them as his arm trembled.

'The body of Christ!' he shouted with all his strength. His voice, in the dead silence, was picked up and amplified across the square through the speakers.

Pierre Labesse stood back from the microphones, then moved around them to stand over Thomas. He reached up and took the chained crucifix from around his shoulders, then bent over and placed it over the priest's head.

By the steps, Catherine Weston stood rigid with shock, her sight now a handicap: she ached for her lost blindness and the acuteness of her other senses as they had once been – so that she would know. 'Michael,' she whispered.

Labesse touched the priest's head. 'The Lord's faithful soldier,' he said.

The whipping beat Thomas had heard seemed to have grown but perhaps it was only in his mind. He looked at the face above him but saw only blood. A mask of deep crimson. And, behind it, startling blue eyes. Peaceful eyes, filled with compassion. With the power of forgiveness. Forgiving even now. Forgiving even *this*.

I am in another place and another time. Centuries ago. The centurion at the foot of that other cross, bound by the orders I must follow. I cannot stop this.

Labesse had dropped to one knee, his arms stretched down to the priest's shoulders. There was a growing rustle from the crowd; scattered words, like leaves in the wind.

'It is the hour,' said Labesse, lowering his face.

The Borgia crucifix was between them, grasped in the priest's trembling hands. 'No!' he pleaded.

Labesse released his shoulders and gripped his hands instead, then with awesome strength drew the silver crucifix upward to his face. 'Do what you must do. Do it quickly. Do it now!' He pressed his lips to the head of the crucified Christ-figure, his eyes steady on the stricken face below him. From his eyes came an order.

For Cardin the roar of the monsoon rain hammering onto the green roof of the jungle faded to a distant hiss through which he could hear his own breathing. His feeling of unreality was growing now and he wondered if the fever strains which tainted his blood had taken over completely. Why have I been placed here? he demanded. I don't believe. Not in God. Not in love. Not in peace. I'm a paid killer with a loaded gun and when I die I'll die screaming. Then Gaillard, the Creole, was there, pressed up beside him – when he should have been lying at the base of the tree, bleeding out his life. 'Get him down,' said Gaillard. 'I can't do it alone,' Michael told him. 'You have to!' Gaillard snapped through his terrible pain. And somewhere San Li was dying too. And Rent was already dead. 'What's going on?' Rent demanded, suddenly alive. 'No!' he whispered, but it could have been a roar of anger. 'Not a chance!' 'I have to try,' Cardin said softly. He could hardly believe he had spoken the words. Then Rent was gone, down somewhere in the crowd. Gaillard said, 'He turned his gun on us.' Gaillard's eyes were fixed on the clearing. On the crucified figure. And on the face above Cardin. Cardin stared at him. 'Why?' Gaillard said, 'Some things don't have a reason. You just know.' He looked again at the face above him. 'Remember me,' he said. 'You will be with me for ever,' Labesse promised.

'I saved you!' Michael cried.

'Now you save more than me,' said Labesse. 'This is not an end. It is a beginning.'

As if by its own volition, Michael's finger touched the ruby on the back of the cross and pressed.

Unseen, a tiny needle flashed outward from the largest thorn in the silver crown then instantly retracted. A spot of blood welled up on Labesse's lip, the poison delivered.

His blue eyes were stricken first – as if unimaginable horror had suddenly passed before them. Then he threw his hands to his head, pressing it on both sides as though it were exploding from within and he could hold in the force of it. Then his mouth opened and there seemed to be blood in it.

Some said later that he cried out with the pain – others that he called God's name – but no one could be certain, for the crowd had become a roaring beast, obliterating any sound which might have come from him. To the east, behind the platform, they surged forward against the barriers which formed the clearway, then ran headlong in a mass for the two trucks. Everywhere people were falling from sight, not rising again.

Already, the police sirens were wailing in agony as the trapped patrol cars tried to extricate themselves from their swamped positions. Progressively, their swirling blue lights were extinguished – as if the cars themselves had been crushed underfoot.

Throughout the chaos and pandemonium, the television crews continued transmitting, though all sound from the platform and remote microphones around the square was lost as cables were ripped from junction boxes.

Michael Cardin fell as the first wave of the huge surge began. He collapsed to his hands and knees as those who had stood beside him were crushed to death. With tears still falling from his face, he crawled under the trucks, making for the steps. He made it to them and climbed onto the safety of the platform, the railings rocking but still, amazingly, in position.

Labesse was down, on his back, his arms thrown sideways, and Michael saw a girl kneeling over him, her face over his as though kissing him. The noise was unbelievable and the entire platform seemed to shake with it. One of Labesse's brothers tried to mount the platform but fell back, his habit covering heads until it was ripped away and he disappeared. Michael ran to Labesse's side.

The girl looked up at him, her tears worse than Michael's own. '*Michael!*' she cried out, and it was a scream.

For half a heartbeat he did not know her but then he fell beside her. He stared at her incredulously, his already reeling mind stunned now, leaving his body immobile.

She shook him hard. 'It's me!' she screamed. '*Me! Catherine!*'

He glanced at Labesse, his hand moving to his heart. The beat was still there. Fast. Too fast. Racing. But still he could do nothing. The world was falling but nothing touched him. The wreckage passed by him, leaving him unscathed but already dead.

Somehow he found words. 'He's alive,' he said, lifelessly.

Catherine hit him. 'Come back!' she screamed again. 'Help him!'

But the jungle had him again, pulling him back, and the sound that went with it. But man sounds, not animal. The heavy whipping beat.

A helicopter leaped high over the dome of the Basilica, then circled the square, its lights flashing as if in warning. It closed in, hovering high over the platform, caught in the glare of lights hastily elevated by the television lighting crews. As it descended, its downdraught and engine noise added to the chaos, causing the microphone stands to vibrate and rattle before toppling into the heaving crowds. The machine was white, and emblazoned on its side it bore the papal crest. It dropped lower, swaying in the hover.

Cardin could hear, as if in the distance, a voice shouting over and over. He turned to the helicopter. A helmeted figure was screaming insanely at him as the spinning barrel of the machine-gun beside

298

him blasted flame. 'Come on, you crazy bastard! They've gone! Leave them!'

He lifted the limp form and carried it to the aircraft, feeling the machine lift slightly. 'Damn you, wait!' he bawled and turned back for Gaillard's body.

But it was Catherine who was kneeling at his feet. He stared down at her.

'Help him,' she repeated. He looked for Labesse and found him in his arms.

'Please!' she pleaded.

He turned away to the helicopter and saw inside a white-robed nun, waiting to receive the still form. Also, two Vigilance guards. He hesitated, then his vision seemed to focus and his eyes hardened. 'The Porta Sant'Anna,' he yelled at Catherine. 'The Gate of St Anne! Go there! Wait for me!'

Without waiting for her reply, he lifted Labesse's body into the helicopter, then climbed onto the nearest landing skid, gripping the horizontal safety handrail set above the open sliding-door with his left hand. One of the Vigilance guards lunged at him, ready to push him off the rocking aircraft. Michael caught the outstretched arm in a fierce grip with his free hand, jerked the man towards him, then broke the arm over the lip of the metal floor, at full stretch. He hit him once with force behind the ear, middle knuckle extended for the sharp downward blow. The man's screaming ended, though his agonized cry was only one of thousands around the platform.

The pilot had swung around in his seat, unsure of what was happening, causing the helicopter to tilt crazily only a few feet off the platform. The second guard had unholstered his gun but was clinging desperately to the back of his fixed seat as the aircraft lurched, the deadly blades whipping dangerously close to the toppling crowds. Michael snapped one foot out at the guard's head, felling him, swooped for the Beretta, snatched it up from beside the terrified nun, then lost his footing on the landing skid as the pilot heaved the aircraft upward. He hung by one arm, the automatic falling from the other as he fought against the downblast from the whirling rotors.

He looked down, feeling the sickening effects of vertigo as the helicopter rose vertically at speed, his fingers locked vice-like around the safety rail, gravity dragging at his hanging body and threatening at any second to rip his arm away. Below, the square was a heaving mass of movement; black insects panicked by a boot which had crushed the life from hundreds of them. With a final effort, Michael hooked one dangling leg around the skid, feeling it bang against the back of his knee. He raised his lower leg, clamping the skid tight between calf and thigh, then let go with his tortured hand. He swung outward into space, and heard the nun shriek.

Hanging upside down, the madness of the square now above him, he felt no panic, though cold terror held him rigid, unable to move, his body swinging from one tightly clamped leg which was already beginning to cramp. Far away he could hear the strident blare of sirens and saw blue flashes on adjoining roads leading into the square. He guessed that they were ambulances. He saw one long beam of light pierce the darkness around him then flash past as the pilot flew the aircraft forward once more. He supposed the light had come from one of the TV crews.

He pulled up his head and saw the stark white face of the nun frozen in the open doorway. Hopelessly he threw one arm upward and found the skid just as the great dome of the Basilica passed below him. Now, he urged himself, and dragged himself up with more strength than he imagined possible from his wracked body.

His face was level with the floor of the helicopter. He could see Labesse, prone on the floor, his face still a contorted mask. *They knew!* Michael thought. *They must have known.* Yet they made me do this to the man whose life I had saved. A man who had shown me life. Brought me back from my own hell. His grip now was sure, his arms locked tight on the skid support, his legs curled along the skid firmly. He felt his weakness ebbing – and his anger growing. They chose a killer, he told himself, but they never intended to kill. They did not dare kill this man. Dead he would be a martyr – his own words to Marco. But alive – a vegetable – incurably brain-damaged, he was a threat to no one. His revelation would be regarded as the product of a damaged mind – Marco's words. And all the time they must have known what this man meant to me. They chose a killer. Now they have one.

He felt the helicopter descend as it approached Vatican Hill at the extreme west of the city state and somewhere, before the pilot landed on the heliport atop the rising hill, Michael Cardin dropped off and rolled into green cover. A killer once again in his element.

He heard the voice of Benito Marco shout, 'Find him!' and darted silently towards it, spotting the group of figures illuminated by the flashing lights of the chopper. He saw the prone body carried from the aircraft on a stretcher by two Vigilance guards, the nun running alongside, aiding the guard with the broken arm. From the comatose Labesse there was no sound. Then the rest of the group broke away, moving down the hill cautiously, guns drawn, flashlights picking at the surrounding greenery. Two of these came too near him as he tracked the stretcher party and Marco. He crippled one and half killed the other, soundlessly. They were no match for him. Not singly or together. He was a master of the night, and of stealth. A silent killer; with no weapon except his own body.

He saw now the truth of it all, as the part of him which was still a priest fought to stay alive. Yes, he still believed – but he no longer believed that he had found the way to God that he had sought so earnestly after the experience in the jungle. The Church had taken him in – succoured him – but it was not what was meant for him. The crucified man. It was always him. From the moment he had drawn the nails from the tree – until now. *This*, now, was always going to be the end of it. Or a new beginning. He believed implicitly that he was part of some greater purpose which he might never understand. They had chosen a killer and God too had chosen him – as His instrument. He knew what he had to do. Right or wrong, it had to be done. And coldly, as he shed his cassock, he dismissed all arguments of morality from his mind. This was his purpose. Good or evil, it had to be. And Labesse's voice was clear in his mind. *Michael, the Lord's chosen soldier.* Not priest. *Soldier.*

The leash had truly been slipped on the Hound of Heaven.

They skirted the Wall of Leo IV and then walked onward until the single track of the little-used Vatican railway was ahead of them, the small antiquated station looking absurd and anachronistic when compared with the nearby white office block which housed the headquarters of the Pontifical Commission, the civil government, under the Pope, of the Vatican city state.

Upon the platform of the station stood two men, apart, like strangers awaiting the same train; one tall and cadaverous, half lit by the meagre lighting and dressed in priestly garb; the other shorter by far, and paunchy, carrying a leather bag which he switched nervously from hand to hand as if already late for an important appointment and agitated by the delayed departure of the stationary, grumbling train.

The train also appeared absurd. One engine, diesel, its motor rumbling, and behind this, two carriages: the first ornate, for human occupation; the second a freight-car, loaded already with wooden crates containing goods from the Vatican's mosaic factory. Other crates lay on the platform, in haphazard piles, awaiting loading – but on some other night.

The shorter man moved to one of the crates, placed his bag upon it, then unbuttoned his costly overcoat and withdrew a dull-gold fob-watch from his waistcoat and frowned. His suit had a fine stripe, set against a conservative blue, the cut indisputably English and hand-made. His face was dark-jowled but above the jawline his skin had the pink, pampered smoothness of the very rich. He could have been Greek and a shipping magnate – but he was Italian, and a physician. He was also a member of Opus Dei.

Further along the platform, Father Phillipe Recamier, the French Jesuit, narrowed his deep-set eyes and, hunching his shoulders, moved nearer the edge of the platform and saw the stretcher-bearing group of figures emerging from the gloom, the white habit of the nun appearing first, flowing like a wraith beside the still form on the stretcher. Recamier wished himself away from the small ghost-like station. Away from the Vatican itself. But mostly, away from the conspiracy. He wished himself back in the cold monastery outside Rome where the Cardinal Secretary had sent him with the aged nun he had brought from St Malo. He ached for its peace and its solitude – and its simple way of life. Go with Sister Theresa into retreat until this is over, Cinalli had ordered, and he had obeyed. But after retreat comes the final battle – and Sostituto Benito Marco, rather than Cardinal Secretary of State Giorgio Cinalli, was the real general for this treacherous campaign. Marco had called – and Recamier had come. And what choice had I? he asked himself bitterly. The first step in any conspiracy is the hardest – the last is inevitable.

'They're coming, dottore,' Recamier called down the platform and began advancing towards the paunchy figure. The physician hurriedly opened his bag and withdrew instruments, ready before time, as though eager to heal – though that was not his task. Not this night.

The group were heading up the platform now, coming under the dim lighting, and moving swiftly. Even before they approached the lights, Recamier had recognized the Sostituto's quick, stilted strides, the paces small and almost feminine. But also, as a trained observer of men and events, Recamier recognized that a change had occurred in the man. The smooth self-assurance had cracked, evidenced by a quickness of eye and a turning of head.

And Recamier saw the still figure of Labesse on the stretcher, his hands over his chest but not in repose. Clawed, as though frozen in convulsion. He recalled the bar in St Malo and the French whore, Simone, who loved the man he had helped to destroy. He recalled the parakeets, silent on their perches: 'They don't speak, m'sieu; they've given up.' The birds had been chained – he realized this for the first time. Silver chains, but nevertheless strong. Elegant restraints but still chains. He feared for the ageing Sister Theresa; seeing the child she had raised in this state now might kill her. But at least she would be dead while he would have to live on with the knowledge of what had been done. Worse, he would be faced, daily, with the evidence of the deed. He knew that Marco would see to it that his days with Vatican Radio were over for as long as Labesse lived – if it could be termed living – and probably for as long as he lived, also. A man who holds secret, dangerous knowledge is unlikely to be placed in a position to broadcast it.

Recamier saw that one of the Vigilance guards was half dead with pain, his swarthy skin a sick yellow and flooded with sweat, one arm hanging loose inside his blue uniform but angled backwards, against the joint. Marco paid him no attention but immediately directed the physician to the stretcher.

The doctor made a speedy examination, nodded without comment, and directed the guards bearing the stretcher into the ornate carriage. Meanwhile the injured man had slumped against the wall and had vomited. Recamier glanced at him in concern and, at that moment, saw – or imagined he saw – a dark, fleeting shadow slip across the short siding leading to the loading-bay, then duck beneath the train. But the light was appalling and his senses were dulled by the time he had spent in enforced seclusion and the horror of what was being done. What he was a part of.

The nun tugged at the Sostituto's arm, indicating the injured man, but Marco shrugged her off impatiently and urged the doctor onto the train. He turned to Recamier. 'Is everything arranged?' he snapped, his eyes flicking past the French Jesuit into the gloom beyond the light.

'As you directed,' Recamier confirmed.

'Stay with him constantly,' Marco ordered. 'The doctor will remain at the monastery until his condition stabilizes.'

'A brain haemorrhage,' said Recamier.

'Causing irreversible damage,' Marco added. 'The result of the withdrawal of the life-support machines. If you are forced to answer questions – that is all you will say.'

Recamier nodded.

'I shall handle the press release from the Vatican,' Marco said. 'Only if I have no choice – under media pressure – to confirm where he is being cared for will you become further involved. Until then, your part is to stay with him, and *listen*. I must know *instantly* if he shows any signs of lucidity – although the doctor pronounces that impossible. Nevertheless – even a word or an intelligible phrase, and you contact me. You understand what I am saying, Father?'

A grim smile formed on Recamier's cadaverous face. 'If he shows any sign of intelligence he becomes again a danger. I understand very well, Monsignor.'

'Father,' Marco said, with steely eyes. 'Always remember this: the preservation of power which is benevolent sometimes requires measures which may seem to be evil. The Vatican and the Church have survived intrigue, conspiracy, treachery – even murder – because of one ideal, one word. Faith. That man shook centuries of faith in a few days. He almost destroyed it. Would you have me stand aside and let that happen? Would I be judged a better Christian if I had failed?'

Recamier turned aside and boarded the carriage. He looked down at Marco through the lowered window. 'And if he were from God?'

'Then I am from the devil,' Marco replied, unsmiling. He stepped back, glancing at the engine, then walked the few steps towards it. Recamier drew his head back inside.

The Sostituto approached the engine and slapped the door of the driver's cab. He repeated the movement impatiently, then climbed on the step, his head in line with the closed, sliding window. The glass shot past his eyes and his scream died in his chest as an iron-hard ring clamped around his throat, blocking any sound. Marco saw another hand reach forward, resting momentarily on the right side of his face, the base of the palm in line with his jaw. He never felt the sharp movement which snapped his vertebrae, nor did he see the face of his executioner. But he knew him nevertheless.

Father Recamier walked the length of the corridor to the last of the four compartments. In the third, he saw the two Vigilance guards seated by the window, opposite each other; both were dozing. In the fourth, the nun was seated, feet up and legs outstretched on the luxurious couch, her head lowered on her chest. The physician also sat on the couch, at her feet, and in that frozen second before realization, Recamier thought it outrageous that his hand was resting on the nun's stockinged ankles. He noted also that the nun's habit was rising and falling shallowly over her breasts while the doctor's elegant waistcoat under his undone jacket was utterly still. He glanced once at Labesse, seeing instantly the tightened chain of a crucifix at his exposed throat – then ran for the guards.

Both were unconscious and he could not revive them. Somehow he could not bring himself to search for their injuries. He backed out of the compartment, then stepped down onto the platform, the only sound being the low growling of the engine. He felt exposed and vulnerable. And terrified. It was as if a spirit had struck, and he recalled the black chill which had stalked him in St Malo.

He found the driver in his cab – like the guards and the nun, unconscious. Marco was on the track, he could see him through the cab's forward windows, and he lay as if he had been thrown from them. Splayed and broken; discarded rather than killed, though undoubtedly he was dead.

The Jesuit stepped down from the engine and every part of his body was trembling. He stopped once, leaning against the vibrating train, drawing in breath deeply to steady himself and trying to find his voice, which had deserted him. He moved on, climbing back into the ornate carriage and back to Labesse. He was drawn to the strangled body, and within him there was an irresistible urge to fall beside it. Die there if necessary. Better there than on the platform. Better there than anywhere.

He stood shaking in the doorway, leaning against the gleaming varnished wood, then fell to his knees.

Recamier would never know how long he knelt there, nor if he consciously prayed or simply reached out to his God without word or thought. The period was timeless, a few seconds or perhaps hours. All he would remember, later, was the electrifying touch of the hand on his head,

306

and when he looked up, the blue forgiving eyes which seemed to be waiting for him.

'*Qui êtes-vous?*' Recamier whispered, in wonder.

'*Je suis Pierre*,' answered the risen saint. I am Peter.

8

Catherine waited by the Porta Sant'Anna, long after the wailing of the ambulances and the grieving had faded to the hushed silence which follows loss.

She did not think, dared not, for her world was upended and she clung by her fingertips to the only spar of hope available. *Come*, she pleaded, sometimes in her mind, sometimes aloud, in a small tight voice which she stifled with her hands. *Don't desert me. Not again. I'm blind again. And lost.*

At first she had waited in the open, standing alone, her golden hair strewn across her face and wet, though it had not rained. The Swiss Guard had watched her disapprovingly, for a woman out alone at night in Rome, even outside the hallowed walls of the Vatican, must expect to have her intentions questioned. Then a taxi had passed, a hyena who had circled the square in the hope of picking something from the carnage. But there had been nothing left. The quick had walked away, the dead were carried off. And those who grieved for the man who had been the light in their darkness waited outside the Arch of the Bells or the Bronze Doors of the Apostolic Palace. The Gate of Sant'Anna was a back entrance reserved for tradesmen. And lost lovers.

She had flagged down the taxi and told him, *wait*, in her hard professional voice which was another lifeline in her distress. *Wait, mister coachman, for ever if necessary*. The driver had agreed, keeping the meter clicking, half turned in the front seat appraising her with lustful eyes, even attempting at first to flirt and worse besides. A priest's whore, he decided, for he did not believe that any priest practised celibacy. They eat, so they make love. And there were certain types of women whom only a priest could satisfy.

But in the end he gave up and slept, the meter ticking in the silence, like a time bomb no one had set.

She saw him first in the glow from the guard box and for a moment pretended it wasn't him because that would ease her disappointment. But of course it was. His face was still a stranger's but her fingertips, even over thirty feet, and her blind memory, told her: *yes!*

She could feel him sit beside her, everything black, a million non-light years before. *Your headband's slipped. It's temporary.* Stay. Don't go away! *Right now I've got nowhere to go so we may as well sit it out together.* Oh, but you *had* somewhere to go, Michael. To *him.* Or what you *thought* was him. *Michael, I'm frightened, frightened for you.* And, dear God, for me, too. *Will you love me, Michael? Not now, not bed.* I mean *love* me? *I'll try, I want to. I could love you easily, Catherine. Michael, I'm blind. Please don't push me aside.* Not again. *Michael, blind or sighted, I'll never give you the chance to leave me again. He* knew you would come to me. He told me and I never heard him. He's given me his soldier. Which means he's dead. He's done what he had to do. I can't feel sad because he's still with me – just as he said. *No one you truly love ever goes from your life.*

Michael had stepped away from the guard post, carrying a grip. the same one, she thought, with the false bottom that you thought I didn't know about. Blind people have great touch, Michael Who. He wore a shirt, grey and short-sleeved, giving his arms a powerful look. *What do you do, break rocks?* You kill people. The shirt had no collar, giving his neck a naked, exposed look, somehow fresh under his ruffled hair, as though he'd scrubbed himself then towelled and it wasn't the middle of the night, but morning, he was stepping into. He seemed not to notice the night-cold.

He came straight to her, no hesitation, no glancing around, straight to the taxi, opened the door, sat beside her, gripping her. 'They used me to silence him. To destroy his mind,' he said. 'There was nothing left. So I killed him. That's all I'll say about it – ever. If you want me – you have me. I'm here. But you'll have to come with me. I can't go with you. I can no longer be a priest but there is still work to do.'

She reached her hands to his and closed her eyes. 'I'm blind,' she said.

Then he held her, tightly, and they might never have been apart.

Epilogue

The children had never been so happy. Their father had returned as he had promised. And with him he had brought them a mother. She was beautiful and they loved her instantly, and she them, more perhaps than if she had borne them herself inside her body. The girls touched her hair for hours, as she sat with them, never ceasing to wonder at the fine gold of it. A more precious gold then even the ring which had belonged to their father's papa. The boys stood shyly by at first, loving, yet afraid to show their love. But after a while she broke down their reserve and healed their past hurt with her eyes and they too came to her. Little Eduardo last, because his hurt had been the greatest and his mother's memory was still fresh in him. But in time, his new golden mother became both the memory and the reality.

There was no sadness any more in the children, though there was, for a time, a bewilderment, which, because they did not dare damage their new-found bliss, they refused to acknowledge. Their father no longer wore his patched black cassock, or the white collar at his throat. And the church was not a place he spent time in any more – although sometimes he would seem to be lost, and on these rare occasions would go inside and stare at the new silver cross he had returned with on the altar. But he did not kneel. He stared. And once, when the youngest girl, whom he loved dearly, followed him and lay her burn-scarred face against his strong legs, clutching his hard hand, he had lifted her to his breast, still staring at the silver crucifix, and tears had fallen from his eyes, though his face had not convulsed with emotion but remained unmoved; rock-hard and strong.

Also, he carried a gun. Under his winter jacket. Old,

but well oiled, and wrapped at its handle with white tape, like a bandage, so that his children thought that once it had fallen and had been hurt. The boys loved the gun and, when the half-soldiers came, usually at night with other children, they would creep from their beds early, as dawn arose, to watch as their father stood beside them, shooting at fearful cardboard figures. They noted with pride that their father always hit exactly where he pointed the bandaged gun, the barrel becoming his own finger, but black. And always, the half-soldiers, many of whom were little older than Big Eduardo, would stand around him, their eyes alight, as he taught them, with a serious face, how to make their gun barrels become a pointed finger. The children remembered that this was the look he used to wear when he had taught them about God and Jesus and Mary.

But that was before his papa had swum half across the world, through fire, to die on the beach at his feet. Now, he was different, but it did not matter because he seemed to love them more; and they returned this greater love. For had he not brought them their new golden mother?

The newly elected Pope walked from the sacristy of the anteroom before the balcony of St Peter's Basilica, his pure white cassock a perfect fit and over it the red velvet mozzetta.

Cardinal Giorgio Cinalli knelt before him as he entered and pressed his lips to the new papal ring. His heart swelled inside his breast, his whole being glowing, sure in the knowledge that God's hand had guided him to this moment. He clutched the hand, refusing to release it. He had been God's chosen instrument to achieve this result. He who, divinely inspired, had stood up in conclave and loudly proclaimed the name of the man destined to take up the staff of Peter. He who had thrilled as the packed ranks of cardinals had, in chorus, shouted the word '*Eligo!*' in agreement. Reaching down, the Pope raised him, then clasped him close, holding him, seemingly oblivious to the clamouring thousands in the square below.

Standing aside, behind a group of cardinals, a tall figure

suddenly stooped to the large television set which, until that moment, had been transmitting pictures of the massed faithful who had travelled from around the tension-torn globe to pay homage to their new Vicar of Christ. He turned up the sound, ignoring the protests and disapproving looks from the cardinals as he did so.

The Pope released Giorgio Cinalli and raised a hand for silence, then gave the tall priest a small nod, indicating that the set should be turned up further to make the RIA newsflash more audible.

The Italian newsreader said, '. . . The junta have announced that the weapon used was a neutron bomb, a thermonuclear fusion weapon which produces increased lethal radiation while the destructive blast and fallout are significantly less than an equivalent nuclear-fission weapon. A neutron bomb kills all organic life, while sparing property except within a small radius. In 1978 President Carter of the United States of America stopped production of this controversial weapon, and the Argentinians have not revealed where they obtained the device. There is no information available yet as to the casualties on the Falkland Islands but expert opinion is that few could have survived the attack. Until now there has been no reaction from the British government, but heavy retaliation is expected . . .'

The picture changed, showing the packed square once more, and the tall priest lowered the sound, then approached the Pope, through the murmuring and gesturing cardinals.

Outside, it was a glorious day and the Pope had turned to the open windows and the balcony beyond, where within moments he would step out to receive the adulation of his flock.

Phillipe Recamier asked, 'What is it you see, Holy Father?'

The Pope answered while still turned away, his blue eyes seeming to pierce the sky: 'Lucifer rising.'

His eyes are like blazing fire,
and on his head are many crowns.
He has a name written on him
that no one but he himself knows.

REVELATION 19:12